"We are living in an age of liberati[...] age [...] fear. No sooner do stereotypes and false myths about homosexuality begin to disappear in one place than they reappear in a more virulent form somewhere else. Gay fiction can invent new languages to undermine these lies by speaking the truth about gay life . . . It can question all decisions about what art is and what it is not, what can be represented and what cannot, what is private and what is not."
—George Stambolian, from the Introduction

ACCLAIM FOR *MEN ON MEN* AND *MEN ON MEN 2*

"A SUPERB SELECTION . . . ALTOGETHER, THE BEST GAY FICTION AROUND."
—*Kirkus Reviews* on *MEN ON MEN*

"STRONG, UNPREDICTABLE, ENTERTAINING . . . even better than the original *MEN ON MEN* . . . a very good book."   —*Christopher Street* on *MEN ON MEN 2*

"SOME OF THE HOTTEST (IN OTHER WORDS COOLEST) STORIES I'VE READ ANYWHERE . . . a rich late-eighties mix of love and death."
—Brad Gooch, author of *Scary Kisses*, on *MEN ON MEN 2*

GEORGE STAMBOLIAN is Professor of French Literature and Gay Studies at Wellesley College. In addition to editing the two previous volumes of *Men on Men*, he is also the author of *Marcel Proust and the Creative Encounter*, *Male Fantasies/Gay Realities: Interviews with Ten Men*, and the editor of *Twentieth Century French Fiction*, and *Homosexualities and French Literature*. He contributes to *Christopher Street*, *The Advocate*, and the *New York Native*.

MEN · ON · MEN

3

· BEST · NEW · GAY · FICTION ·

EDITED AND WITH AN INTRODUCTION BY

GEORGE STAMBOLIAN

A PLUME BOOK

PLUME
Published by the Penguin Group
Penguin Books USA Inc., 375 Hudson Street, New York, New York 10014, U.S.A.
Penguin Books Ltd, 27 Wrights Lane, London W8 5TZ, England
Penguin Books Australia Ltd, Ringwood, Victoria, Australia
Penguin Books Canada Ltd, 2801 John Street, Markham, Ontario, Canada L3R 1B4
Penguin Books (N.Z.) Ltd, 182-190 Wairau Road, Auckland 10, New Zealand

Penguin Books Ltd, Registered Offices: Harmondsworth, Middlesex, England

First published by Plume, an imprint of Penguin Books USA Inc.
Published simultaneously in Canada by Fitzhenry & Whiteside Limited.

First Printing, October, 1990
10 9 8 7 6 5

A hardcover edition of *Men on Men 3* has been published simultaneously by E.P. Dutton and in Canada by Fitzhenry & Whiteside Limited.

ACKNOWLEDGMENTS

"A Happy Automaton" by Bruce Benderson. First published in *Pretending To Say No*. Copyright © 1990 by Bruce Benderson. Reprinted by permission of New American Library.

"Meeting Imelda Marcos" by Christopher Bram. Copyright © 1990 by Christopher Bram. Published by permission of the author.

"The Ride Home" by Peter Cashorali. Copyright © 1989 by Peter Cashorali. Published by permission of the author.

"English as a Second Language" by Bernard Cooper. Copyright © 1989 by Bernard Cooper. Published by permission of the author.

The poem "This Is Just to Say" by William Carlos Williams from *William Carlos Williams: Collected Poems, Volume I, 1909–1939*, copyright © 1938 by New Directions Publishing Corporation, appears in the story "English as a Second Language" by Bernard Cooper. Reprinted by permission of New Directions Publishing Corporation. All rights reserved.

"Enrollment" by Philip Gambone. Copyright © 1989 by Philip Gambone. Published by permission of the author.

"Blond Dog" by Robert Haule. Copyright © 1989 by Robert Haule. Published by permission of the author.

Excerpts from the lyric of "What'll I Do?" by Irving Berlin, copyright © 1924 by Irving Berlin, copyright renewed 1951 by Irving Berlin, appear in the story "Blond Dog" by Robert Haule. Reprinted by permission of Irving Berlin Music Corporation. International copyright secured. All rights reserved.

"Myths" by William Haywood Henderson. Copyright © 1990 by William Haywood Henderson. Published by permission of the author.

"Lights in the Valley" by Andrew Holleran. Copyright © 1990 by Andrew Holleran. Published by permission of the author.

"My Face in a Mirror" by Alex Jeffers. Copyright © 1990 by Alex Jeffers. Published by permission of the author.

"Great Lengths" by Joe Keenan. Copyright © 1988 by Joe Keenan. Published by permission of the author.

"Willie" by Michael Lassell. Copyright © 1990 by Michael Lassell. Published by permission of the author.

"Popular Mechanics" by Craig Lee. Copyright © 1989 by Craig Lee. Published by permission of the author.

The following page constitutes an extension of this copyright page.

Ⓟ REGISTERED TRADEMARK—MARCA REGISTRADA

Printed in the United States of America
Set in Janson
Designed by Leonard Telesca

PUBLISHER'S NOTE

CONTENTS

INTRODUCTION

THE FIRST PART of this collection of new gay fiction presents stories by writers who have not appeared in the earlier *Men on Men* anthologies published in 1986 and 1988. A few of them such as Christopher Bram and Paul Monette are already well known to the reading public. Others are seeing their fiction in print for the first time. They come from New York, San Francisco, Boston, Alaska, and Wyoming, with a large contingent from Los Angeles, a city not previously represented in these anthologies, where interest in gay writing has grown in recent years thanks in part to the excellent series of readings organized by James Carroll Pickett at A Different Light Bookstore and the various literary events sponsored by the Words Project for AIDS, directed by Eric Latzky. Fourteen of these seventeen stories have not been published before.

The second part is offered as a special tribute to Robert Ferro, Michael Grumley, and George Whitmore, three writers who died recently of illnesses related to AIDS, and to whom the entire collection is dedicated. Without the support of Robert and Michael I doubt if I would have accepted the task of editing the first *Men on Men* anthology, and I greatly regret that George was unable to complete the story I had invited him to write for this third collection. Certainly, many others have died, including Sam D'Allesandro whose work appeared in that first volume, but since Ferro, Grumley, and Whitmore all belonged to the early workshop for gay writers,—the Violet Quill,—I thought it appropriate to include stories by those members of the group who are still actively writing fiction—Andrew Holleran, Felice Picano, and Edmund White. Their stories honor their friends but also stand, added here, for all the stories we have lost.

Despite these losses, gay fiction in America continues to prosper. Here are a few of the dozens of novels published over the past year: Steve Abbott's *Holy Terror*, Christopher Bram's *In Memory of Angel Clare*, Dennis Cooper's *Closer*, Eric Gabriel's *Water Boys*, Gary Indiana's *Horse Crazy*, Joe Keenan's *Blue Heaven*, Randall Kenan's *A Visitation of Spirits*, Kevin Killian's *Shy*, David Leavitt's *Equal Affections*, Armistead Maupin's *Sure of You*, Felice Picano's *Men Who Loved Me*, and John Weir's *The Irreversible Decline of Eddie Socket*. New journals have appeared— *The Pyramid Periodical* for gay people of color, and *Tribe: An American Gay Journal*—as well as a new gay press, Amethyst, directed by Stan Leventhal.

The year 1989 also saw new awards for lesbian and gay literature: The Lambda Literary Awards sponsored by the *Lambda Rising Book Report* and offered in a variety of categories for works of lesbian and gay fiction, nonfiction, and poetry; awards presented by the Words Project for AIDS for books encouraging a greater understanding of the AIDS epidemic; and the Bill Whitehead Award for an individual who has made a significant contribution to the development of lesbian and gay writing—an award created by The Publishing Triangle, a new organization formed to promote awareness of, and ensure access to lesbian and gay literature. In 1990 this list will also include two awards for outstanding works of lesbian and gay fiction offered by the recently established Ferro-Grumley Foundation.

These awards celebrate the achievements of lesbian and gay fiction, but also point to the obstacles that remain. Many book-stores in America still resist stocking lesbian and gay titles. Several mainstream periodicals continue to reject stories be-cause of their lesbian or gay content. Even lesbian and gay literary scholars have, with few exceptions, largely ignored the works of contemporary writers. Although this "neglect" reflects the traditional historical orientation of academic scholarship, and although most writers have welcomed this freedom from excessive scrutiny, the time has come to reduce the distance between those who make literature and those who study it. The institutions are in place: the Division of Gay Studies of the Modern Language Association, the centers for lesbian and gay studies at the City University of New York and Yale University, and of particular importance at a time when we are losing writers to the epidemic, the literary and historical archives being established at the Lesbian and Gay Community Center in New York City and the Beinecke Library at Yale. The task for future scholars is clear: to incorporate contemporary gay fiction into the long tradition of homosexual literature and culture while recognizing the distinct contributions of today's writers and their place within a rapidly evolving lesbian and gay community.

This community has supported the growth of gay fiction while expressing concern about its future development. Some have urged writers to seek a larger audience in order to counter the danger of creating a literature that is overly introspective or ghettoized in its vision. Others have voiced the fear that efforts to reach a broader readership will be corrupted by the desire for commercial success, which may force writers to sacrifice the particularity of their experience and its power to contest social myths. This position was forcefully stated by Jewelle Gomez: "As the work we do as gay and lesbian writers begins to take on value in the larger society, we run the risk of forgetting how vital our willingness to be outsiders, to be tough, has been to our ability to express ourselves."

The debate over the purpose and future of gay fiction is, of course, an extension of a larger debate within the gay community between those who advocate assimilation and those who wish to affirm a distinctly gay identity, between those want to play the game of our dominant culture and those who want to change the game in order to give greater freedom to so-called cultural minorities. In political terms there is a struggle, as Virginia Apuzzo has said, between legitimacy and liberation—a struggle that is likely to continue for some time.

The new lesbian and gay culture that has emerged over the past three decades is so rich and diverse that it is easy to view it as a fascinating world unto itself, as intriguing as any other culture would be to those who are part of it. At the same time this new consciousness of a gay world has obliged its members to rethink their relations with American culture in general. This double perspective, at once inward and outward, also defines gay fiction. After receiving the Bill Whitehead Award for 1989, Edmund White remarked that "what gay fiction does best is to describe our differences, pinpoint our individualities, express our conflicts and desires, no matter how ill-sorted they may be." White went on to say that gay writing can be a powerful cultural instrument because its questioning of sexual conventions probes many of the essential moral and psychological issues of our time. He suggested that by penetrating deeply enough into our own world we can also reach the larger world with its own conflicts and differences.

This volume of stories is a collection of differences—in style, from comedy to lyric romanticism and fierce realism, and in setting, from the drug-dealing streets of Manhattan to the parched Indian lands of Wyoming. Differences too in the way each writer describes gay life and explores the desires, ambitions, and fears that shape our existence today. These writers share, however, a keen sense of history and an acute awareness of the social realities that in turn influence our thoughts and emotions: the transformation of the family, political oppression, racism and homophobia, drug abuse and AIDS. The epidemic is, unquestionably, the most insistent of these realities. It challenges and tests our beliefs, makes time directly perceptible to our hearts and minds. "AIDS creates such a magnitude of *loss*," Robert Glück has written, "that now death is where gay men experience life most keenly as a group. It's where we learn about love, where we discover new values and qualities in ourselves."

Although most of the stories in this collection are not about AIDS, all are about relationships that dramatize our encounters with reality by describing our successes or failures as lovers, our friendships, our chance meetings with strangers, our conflicts with parents and siblings. A relationship is yet another place where our triumphs and losses are magnified, where we "learn about love" and how to invent our identities in the face of all who would question our right to do so. There are so many different kinds of relationships presented in this collection, such a spectrum of conflicts and couplings, that when I reread the stories I had selected, their characters seemed to move about each other as in a dance with variations.

Joe Keenan's comic account of a madly elaborate seduction in

"Great Lengths" is matched by Christopher Bram's psychologically dramatic story of a seduction accomplished for more troubled motives in "Meeting Imelda Marcos." Matias Viegener's "Twilight of the Gods" adds a surprising twist by describing a triangular seduction in which Roy Cohn, Rock Hudson, and Michel Foucault discuss death and movie stars while receiving injections in a Paris hospital.

The focus of Bernard Cooper's "English as a Second Language" is less seduction than a man's tentative movement toward a love affair that is delightfully shaped by his discoveries about words and their meanings. Edmund White's protagonist in "Skinned Alive" has two successive affairs that reflect on each other like panels of a diptych and expose a hidden pattern of desires and fears. Another pattern emerges in Peter Cashorali's "The Ride Home": two couples, each composed of an Anglo and a Hispanic, react in disturbingly different ways to the specter of AIDS and the problems of mutual dependency. In Robert Haule's haunting story "Blond Dog," on the other hand, sickness overcomes obstacles and brings together two trios: child, mother, and father; man, lover, and friend. White's retelling of the myth of Marsyas, Cashorali's fascinating use of *Santeria*, and Haule's creation of a wonderous dreamscape point to the interest shared by many gay writers in imagining alternative worlds that, like homosexuality itself, provide new ways of looking at life and exploring the mysteries of death.

Still other stories explore worlds that have been neglected or pushed to the margins of our society. Michael Lassell offers an uncompromising portrait of racism and homophobia in "Willie," which describes an interracial love affair set in the period of the Vietnam War and the Black Power movement. Bruce Benderson's "A Happy Automaton" plunges into the murky rooms of crack addicts in New York whose violent lives are governed by their own sexual and moral laws, whereas Felice Picano's "Why I Do It" reinvents the old story of master and slave by presenting the extraordinary symbiotic relationship of two men who panhandle in the subways of Manhattan. Finally, William Haywood Henderson describes cultural change in "Myths," the story of an Indian boy and his uncle who attempt to live the traditions of the berdache in a society that has no place for alternative cultures.

Like the principal characters in the preceding group of stories, Craig Lee's protagonist in "Popular Mechanics" is an outsider, a boy who finds no place among the social and ethnic groups of his California high school and whose final initiation is also a comic and violent coming-out. The gay and mentally disturbed boy in Noel Ryan's "Big Sky" suffers a double alienation from his schoolmates in Montana and from the members of his own family, with the exception of his distant, dying father with whom he shares one saving memory.

The family as it appears in many stories in this collection is a place of enduring memories, although not always pleasant ones, a storehouse of old angers and frustrating silences, a battleground where parents and children test the limits of their humanity and their compassion. My story, "In My Father's Car," contrasts a son's memories with his father's and then plays both against shared memories of historic violence and loss. In Alex Jeffers's "My Face in a Mirror" a man afflicted with AIDS finds new strength in his lover's son, a boy who is rapidly losing his innocence to the harsh realities of a hostile world.

Three other stories describe the conflicts of siblings. In Bil Wright's "When Marquita Gets Home" a father's death leads to painful changes in a gay man's relationship with his sister, whereas Martin Palmer's "Journey" probes the growing moral distance separating a man from a sister who no longer seems capable of understanding him. In Paul Monette's "Halfway Home," conversely, the distance between a dying man and his brother suddenly shrinks, bringing back bitter memories together with unexpected revelations of need.

Finally, two stories about endings and beginnings. Andrew Holleran's "Lights in the Valley" describes the pervasiveness of loss—from AIDS that carries off our friends to old age that strikes our parents—but the narrator tells his story with such strength of feeling that his own voice seems to affirm the continuity of life. This affirmation is also expressed in Philip Gambone's "Enrollment," a story that celebrates birth and simultaneously presents the initiation of a little girl into the traditions of her family and the initiation of a newfound friend into the family of his gay brothers.

*   *   *

Dorothy Allison has remarked that the coming-out story is "the essential homosexual theme, as persistent as the romantic love story and the coming-of-age novel." Although coming-out stories in the strict sense are found less frequently today, every work of gay fiction is a coming-out story in that it expresses truths about ourselves that many still wish we would keep hidden. Curiously, this "new openness" has been criticized by some within the gay literary community itself who regret the passing of a time when the need to describe homosexuality by indirect means forced writers to invent an allusive language. They believe that by destroying the old homosexual culture based on secrecy and guilt, liberation also reduced the need for discipline and restraint and has thereby lowered the quality of a literature that once produced such masters as Gide, Proust, Wilde, and Thomas Mann.

There are many ways to dispute these views: The great writers of the past were not always allusive or indirect in their presentations of homosexuality. Gay fiction today has not become merely an unrestrained display of erotic fantasies as some rashly predicted it would be. Gay writers, like all writers, must still make disciplined choices about what to say and not to say. More important, writers today do not write like Proust because this is not the time of Proust, any more than it is the time of Dickens or Conrad. Every writer may not be a genius, but each is in history and must write from within the particular social, political, and cultural context of his historical moment.

We are living in an age of liberation, but also in an age of fear. No sooner do stereotypes and false myths about homosexuality begin to disappear in one place than they reappear in a more virulent form somewhere else. Gay fiction can invent new languages and generate new meanings to undermine these lies so often built on willful ignorance. It can challenge by its very existence the oppressive assumption that heterosexual experience is somehow natural, generic, outside of history. And it can question all decisions about what art is and what it is not, what can be represented and what cannot, what is private and what is not. These are ultimately moral questions, and as surprising as it may seem to some, gay fiction today is a moral art.

George Stambolian
November 1989

PART ONE

HALFWAY HOME

• PAUL MONETTE •

MY BROTHER USED to tell me I was the Devil. This would be while he was torturing me—not beating me up exactly, since he didn't want to hurt his knuckles and maybe miss a game. But he'd pounce and drag me to the floor and pin my shoulders with his knees. Then he'd snap his fingers against my nose, or drool spit in my face while I bucked and jerked my head, or singe my hair with matches. He was ten, I was seven. Already he had enormous strength. I never thought of Brian as a kid. He'd loom above me with that flame-red Irish hair, his blue eyes dancing wickedly, and he was brute and cruel as any man. There are boys in Ireland now throwing pipe bombs and torching cars. That was Brian, a terrorist before his time. And I was his mortal enemy.

"Is Tommy gonna cry now?" he'd taunt me, rubbing those knuckles across my scalp. "You big fuckin' baby."

And I would, I'd cry, not from pain but sorrow. I'd blubber and bite my lip till Brian would release me in disgust, full of immense disdain because I couldn't take it. He'd lumber away and grab his glove, off to find one of his buddies from Saint Augustine's, tough like him. I'd stare in the mirror above the dresser in the room we shared, still gasping the sobs away, hating my sallow skin and my blue-black crewcut.

That's why I was so diabolical to him, because I didn't look anything like Brian or Dad, both of them fair and freckled, lobster-red in the summer sun, big in the shoulders like stevedores. I got all the Italian blood instead from Mom's side, so that I was the only Sicilian in a mick neighborhood. Hell, it seemed the whole county was Irish, from Hartford all the way to New Haven. And the Irish hated everybody, but especially wops. So I never stood a chance, lean and olive and alien as I was. But the reason I cried had nothing to do with my differences, not then. It was because I wasn't good enough to play with my big brother. This boy who never ceased to make me suffer, beating me down and plucking my wings like a hapless fly, and all I ever seemed to feel was that I'd failed him.

I haven't thought about any of that in twenty years. Well, nine anyway: since the day my father was buried in the blue-collar graveyard behind Saint Augustine's. Brian and I had our last words then, raw and rabid, finishing one another off. He was twenty-eight, I was twenty-five, though in fact we hadn't really spoken for a least ten years before that. As soon as Brian understood I was queer—and I swear he knew it before I did—he iced me out for good. No more roughhouse, no more nugies and body checks. I didn't exist anymore. By then of course Brian had become a delirious high-school hero, the darling of the Brothers as he glided from season to effortless season, football and hockey and baseball. Me, I was so screwed up I missed being tormented by him. I played no games myself.

It doesn't matter anymore. I sit out here on this terrace, three thousand miles from the past, and stare down the bluff to the weed-choked ocean, and the last thing I think of is Chester, Connecticut. Once a day, toward sunset, I walk down the blasted wooden stairs jerry-built into the fold of the cliff, eighty steps to the beach below. At the bottom I sit at the lip of the shallow cave that opens behind the steps, the winter tide churning before me, the foam almost reaching my toes.

I brood about all the missed chances, the failures of nerve, but I never go back as far as being a kid. I put all that behind me when I came out, Brian and Dad and their conspiracy of silence. I never look in the mirror if I can help it. My real life stretches from coming out to here, fifteen years. *That*'s what I'm greedy for more of. Sometimes out of nowhere perfect strangers will ask: "You got any brothers and sisters?" No, I say, I was an only child. I never had any time for that family porn, even when I had all the time in the world.

Which I don't have now. I know it as clear as anything when I turn and climb the eighty steps up. I take it very slow, gripping the rotting banister as I puff my way. This is my daily encounter with what I've lost in stamina. The neuropathy in my left leg throbs with every step. I wheeze and gulp for air. But I also love the challenge, climbing the mountain because it's there, proving every day that the nightmare hasn't won yet.

The cliff cascades with ice plant, a blanket of gaudy crimson that nearly blinds in the setting sun. The gray terns wheel above me, cheering me on. I feel like I'm claiming a desert island, the first man ever to scale this height. As I reach the top, where a row of century cactus guards the bluff with a hundred swords, I can look back and see a quarter mile down Trancas Beach, empty and all mine, the rotting sandstone cliffs clean as the end of the world.

Not that the Baldwins own all of it. But the beach house on the bluff sits in the middle of five acres, shaded by old trees, shaggy eucalyptus and sycamores eight feet thick, which makes it feel like it's been there forever, no neighbors in sight on either side. To the north is a pop singer's compound, a great white whale of a house that's visible from the coast road, all its new-planted trees still puny and struggling for purchase. To the south an aerospace mogul has gussied himself a Norman pile complete with drawbridge and watchtower, which the surfers in the Trancas Wash call Camelot.

The Baldwin place is like none of these—a lazy overgrown bungalow with red-tile roof, balconies off the bedrooms and a drizzling Moorish fountain in the courtyard. Built in 1912, when the Baldwins *did* own as far as the eye can see, twenty-two miles of coastline all the way south through Malibu to the edge of Santa Monica. Till the thirties this was the only house on the water, with a bare dirt road that snaked up into the mountains where the big ranch house stood, seat of the vast Spanish land grant. Gray remembers his Baldwin aunts saying the only way to the beach house was half a day's ride on horseback from the ranch.

That's how it feels to me still after two months here, remote and inaccessible. I've only had to leave twice, to go see my doctor in Hollywood, about an hour away—who had the gall to tell me I was fine, without a trace if irony. "He's right," insisted Gray, who drove me there and back, "you look ter-rific." I'll say this much: considering I'm on Medi-Cal, living on six hundred bucks a month disability, I'm doing very well to be in a house in a eucalyptus grove, with a view that seems to go all the way to Hawaii. No hit record, no Pentagon kickbacks, and I live like a fucking rock star. You get very used to being lord of all you survey.

But even here reality intrudes. Yesterday was full of portents, now I see that. I didn't go down to the beach till almost five, because I woke up late from my nap. The sun was already dancing on the ocean when I started, and gone below by the time I reached the sand. Immediately it's colder, even with the gold and purple rockets trailing in the afterglow. I saw right away there was junk in the mouth of the cave, beer cans and an empty bag of chips. I was furious. I snatched up the litter, grumbling at the trespass. The property line goes to mid-tide. In theory nobody ought to walk on my three hundred yards of beach at all.

I started back up the stairs sour as a Republican. No one had ever violated my grotto before. Maybe a sign was in order: No Loitering. This Means You. Then, at about step 60 I got this terrible stab in my heart—doubled me over. I dropped the trash and sagged against the crimson ice. Oh shit, I was going to die of a heart attack. Even in that bone-zero panic I could feel a sort of black laughter welling up inside. Leave it to Tom Shaheen not to die of AIDS, after all the drama and street theater.

It passed as quick as it came but left me heaving, clammy with cold sweat. For a minute I was scared to breathe too deep, and kept kneading my chest in some fruitless amateur version of CPR. But no, the pain was gone. If anything there was a queer feeling of utter emptiness at the center of the chest, the way you feel when someone walks out on you.

I took the last twenty steps most gingerly. It was folly to think my little coronary event wasn't AIDS-related. I was probably heading for a massive stroke, the virus in my spinal column swirling like eels in a sunken ship, and I'd end up mute and paralyzed. Generally I don't waste a minute, especially out here in Trancas, figuring how short my time is. I've been at this thing for a year and a half, three if you count all the fevers and rashes. I operate on the casual assumption that I've still got a couple of years, give or take a galloping lymphoma. Day to day I'm not a dying man, honestly.

But I reached the top pretty winded and shaken, gazing down the bluff with a melancholy dread that things could change any minute. I've given up everything else but this, I thought, don't let me lose this too, my desert island. I couldn't have said exactly whom I was addressing, some local god of the bluff. Not big-G God. I've been on His hit list now for a long time. If He's really out there, I'm douched.

Then I saw Mona. She lay on one of the white chaises, her back to me and the view, smoking a cigarette. From the top of the beach stairs it's maybe twenty paces across the lawn to the terrace. I flinched and tried to think if I could sneak around her, but no way. Mona's like my sister, she doesn't have to call first. But after my *crise de cocur* I wanted to collapse. And Mona doesn't indulge me like Gray. She wants me *up*. For a renegade dyke committed to anarchy, in fact, she is remarkably Donna Reed in her dealings with me, cutting the crusts off sandwiches.

I started across the lawn, emitting a tentative whimper. Mona turned in startled delight. "Pumpkin! I've just come from the workshop!" She leaped off the chaise and darted toward me. Her tortoise-rim glasses covered half her face, her platinum hair beveled and moussed. "They were appalling, all of them," she said, reaching a hand with black-painted nails and scratching the hair on my chest. "Dumb little standup routines, clubfoot dances, thrift-shop chic. The usual. But oh, there was this girl from Torrance, squeaky clean— "

She stopped and peered more closely at my face. "*Cara mia*, are you all right? You're looking more than usual like the French leftenant's woman."

"I just had a heart attack."

"Come on, I'll make you hot chocolate." See? Very Mom-is-it-lunch-yet. "I brought you a tin of shortbread. Twenty-two bucks at Nieman's. Now this *girl*. Rosy as a cheerleader, practically carrying pompoms. I was wet all day."

She steered me across the terra-cotta terrace, through the peeling colonnade and into the musty cool of the house. I tried on a pouting scowl, but Mona was off, full of raptures about her little bimbette from Torrance. In the kitchen I sat at the zinc-top table, a palimpsest of dents and scratches, while Mona free-floated about, putting the milk to boil.

The workshop she speaks of is Introduction to Performance,

a grab-bag of mime and movement and "auto-exploration," thirty dollars for three Saturday sessions, a veritable magnet for the egregiously untalented, who will probably never perform beyond their bathroom mirrors. But it keeps the wolf from the door of AGORA—our feisty open space in Venice that we reclaimed from a ballpoint pen factory, famous throughout the netherworld of Performance, with its own FBI file to boot. Except "our" is not exactly right. It's Mona's. I am no longer an impresario.

"Someone was looking for you today," says Mona, mixing the cocoa.

"A rabid fan, perhaps."

"Some guy. Looked like he sold insurance. He came by during the break—said nobody'd seen you around your apartment since Christmas."

"Probably sent to cancel my disability. I've been getting these 'Aren't you dead yet' letters from Sacramento."

We took the tray of chocolate and biscuits into the parlor. Through the arched gallery windows the sunset had turned to dusty rose. Mona went to the woodbox, knelt and laid a fire, more butch than I. I cozied up in an afghan as old as the shedding velvet that covered the swayback sofa. No one has bothered to upgrade anything at the beach house, not for decades. When Gray dies this last piece of the Baldwin vastness will be disposed of, and then some starlet can swath it in white upholstery, so it looks like everyone else's house. Meanwhile the tattiness and furred edges are just my cup of tea.

Once the fire is crackling, Mona snuggles in under the afghan with me. "You know," she says conspiratorially, "we don't have anything set for tomorrow night. Queen Isabella canceled— the piece isn't ready. If you just did forty-five minutes, you'd save our ass." I begin to shake my head slowly, as if I have a slight crick in my neck. "Oh, Tommy, why not," says Mona, more pettish now. "It'd do you good. You're stronger than you realize."

I turn and give her a withering look. Mona is of the persuasion, diametrically opposed to the *Aren't you dead yet* theory, that I am not really *sick* sick, and thus should push my limits. "My life on the stage is like a dream to me now," I reply in a dusky Garbo voice. "I have put away childish things."

"People still call and ask, 'When are you having Miss Jesus?' I swear, we could fill the place three months running."

Mona sighs. She knows I am not convinceable. Not that I'm unsympathetic. I understand the longing for a break-through gig that sets the whole town buzzing. In the first two years of AGORA, before I retired, Miss Jesus was a sensation whenever I did it. Bomb threats would pour in, and church groups from Pacoima would picket back and forth in the parking lot, practically speaking in tongues. Mona and I were devastated to only have ninety-nine seats, with ten standees additional permitted by the fire laws, because at the height of the outrage we could have packed two-fifty in.

I lay my head on her shoulder and offer her the plate of shortbread. She shakes her head no thanks. We sit there slumped against each other, watching the fire, not needing to talk. I love the smoky elusiveness of Mona's perfume, a scent she swears is the very same Dietrich wears, a beauty tip passed in whispers through the shadowy dyke underground. She seems more pensive than I today, unusual for her, an action girl. I think she's about to ask me something about my illness, like how do I stand it, but then she says, "Do you ever think about your brother?"

I shoot her the most baleful look I can summon. "In a word, no."

"But don't you ever wonder? He's prob'ly got kids—" She waves her hands in a circular motion, flailing with possibilities. "I mean he could be *dead*, and you wouldn't even know."

If anything I grow more icily impassive. "I believe I'm the one who's passing away around here."

"Don't be defensive. I just wondered."

"Mona, how is it you are the only person in the world who knows this person exists, and yet you forget the punchline. He *loathes* me. I make his skin crawl. I have not imagined these things. He said them, over and over for years, knuckles white with passion. Get it?"

She pulls her head slightly in under the afghan, rather like a blond turtle. Cautiously she observes, "People change."

I scramble out of my side of the blanket. Kneeling almost on top of her, I push my face close and hiss. "Girl, what's your problem today? I did not request an Ann Landers consultation.

I *hope* he's dead, frankly, may he rot in hell. And I hope his orphan children are begging with bowls in the street—"

"Sorry I brought it up."

"Well, it's a little late for that now, isn't it?"

I'm actually feeling rather juiced, more energy than I've had in days. Mona knows I'm not going to actually pummel her. I'm a total wimp, abuse-wise. She may even think it's good for me to blow off steam. I am speechless though as I pant with rage, my head reeling with images of Brian. Midfield, running for daylight. Serving Mass with Father Donegan. Riding away laughing in his first new car, surrounded by his mick buddies, leaving me in the driveway eating their exhaust. Not even the really painful stuff, the punishment and the hatred, and still I want to let out a primal scream, as if I know I have to die before all of this is really put to rest.

Then we hear a knocking on the screen door in the kitchen. And the really strange thing is this: suddenly Mona looks terrified. She blanched a bit as I railed at her, wincing as I rose above her in high dudgeon. But now when I clamber off the sofa to go and answer, her face is ashen, the hand on my arm beseeching, as if I am about to let a monster in. I *know* who it is, and zap Mona with a perplexed frown—what's *she* on—as I amble into the kitchen. "Coming!"

Gray stands resolutely on the back stoop, a bag of groceries in either arm, which was why he couldn't let himself in. The beach house is never locked, unlike the compounds on either side, which have laser rays and aerial surveillance. "Did I say I needed anything?" I ask as I bang the door wide.

"Just a few staples," he says, trooping by me to set the bags on the zinc table, then turns and searches my face. "How you feeling?"

Earnest Gray, in drab and rumpled Brooks Brothers mufti, his wispy vanishing hair making him look much older than fifty-one. But then WASPs on the high end age in an absent-minded fashion, like the old shoes they never throw away. In addition Gray has been effectively retired his whole life. He is also the least vain man I have ever known.

"I had heart failure coming up from the beach, but otherwise I'm dandy. How much was all this?" I grab my jacket from behind the door to pull out my wallet, but Gray, who is already unloading muffins and ginger ale, waves vaguely, as if money is something vulgar that gentlemen don't discuss. "Come *on*, Gray, you can't keep buying me groceries."

And I wave twenty dollars by his shoulder, but he has that maddening WASP habit of pretending things aren't happening. "I thought I'd barbecue tonight," he says with boyish enthusiasm, and I lay the twenty on the table, in no-man's-land.

The irony is, Gray doesn't have a lot to spare, despite being the last of one of the nine families that owned California. There's a trust of course, and coupons to clip, and the beach house is his for life, as well as the gardener's cottage on the ranch where he's lived for twenty-five years. But none of this amounts to very much actual cash, because the old man poured almost everything into his wacko foundation. With all those connections no one ever expected Gray to grow up to be a loser, unable to make his own harvest in the fields of money. In fact, he's spent most of his life giving away his share, as a sort of patron saint of the avant-garde.

"That one he injected looks smaller to me," observes Gray, slapping a couple of steaks on the counter. He's talking about the eggplant-purple lesion on my right cheek, the size of a nickel. This is the only visible sign of my leprous state, and on my last visit the doctor gave it a direct hit of chemo. It doesn't look any different to me. Gray is the only one who ever mentions my lesion. Everyone else steps around it, like a turd on the carpet. "And look, we'll make some guacamole," he says, triumphantly producing three dented avocados.

Then Mona is standing in the doorway, giving a hopeless impersonation of demure. Gray spots her and instantly wilts. "Oh, I'm sorry," he murmurs fretfully, unable to meet our eyes, gazing with dismay at all the groceries he's unpacked, as if he's come to the wrong place.

"Listen, I was just leaving, you guys go ahead," declares Mona magnanimously.

"Don't be silly, there's plenty," I say, perversely enjoying their twin discomfort. They don't exactly dislike each other, but they're like in-laws from different marriages, unrelated except by bad shit. "*You* make the margaritas," I command Mona with a bony finger. And because I am the sick boy, what can they do? Guilt has gotten more dinners on the table than hunger ever dreamed of. Mona goes right to the liquor cabinet, and Gray is already peeling the avocados. Like a veritable matchmaker I decide to give them some time alone and run up to my room for a sweater.

First thing I do, I check my cheek in the mirror. Maybe he's right, one edge is somewhat lighter, but nothing to write home about. It's not like I could cruise a boy at the Malibu Safeway. I move to shut the balcony doors, catching a glimpse of the gibbous moon as it flings its pearls on the water. Then I grab my red-checked crewneck from the dresser and shrug it on.

Even though I only brought a single duffel bag with me here when I came just after New Year's, right away this place felt more like home than my own place ever did. My bleak one-bedroom in West Hollywood, with a view out over four dumpsters, looks like a garage sale driven indoors by rain. Nothing nice or comfortable, not a nesting person's space by any stretch. Whereas here I have a lovely overstuffed chaise across from the bed, swathed in a faded Arcadian chintz, and a blue-painted wicker table by the window with shelves underneath for books. The ancient curtains are swagged and fringed and look like they would crumble at the touch. If it sounds a bit Miss Havisham, don't forget the sea breeze blowing through clean as sunlight every day.

Above the mahogany bed is a poster of Miss Jesus. The cross is propped against the wall at AGORA, and I'm leaning against it in full drag, pulling up my caftan to show a little leg. The expression on my face can only be called abandoned. My crown of thorns is cocked at a rakish angle. In the lower right-hand corner, in Gothic script, it says "Oh Mary!"

This is only the third time I've managed to put Mona and Gray together, and I find myself excited by the prospect of spending an evening, just us three. The two of them have come to be my most immediate family, somewhat by elimination, my friends all having died, but I couldn't have chosen better. I realize I want them to know each other as well as I know them, for when it gets bad. When I'm curled in a ball and can't play anymore, sucking on the respirator, and then of course when it's over. They'll be good for each other, so opposite in every way.

I've forgiven Mona already for bringing up Brian. It clearly won't happen again, she's not *that* dumb. The memory overload has passed, and once again my brother has faded into the septic murk of the past. What surprises me is this: as I trot down the spiral stair and hear my two friends laughing in the kitchen, I am so happy that some part of my heart kicks in and takes back the curse. *I hope you're not dead and your kids are great.* That's all. Goodbye. Fini.

Gray is regaling Mona with the tale of his three Baldwin aunts—Cora, Nonny and Foo. Mona is riveted. These three estimable ladies, maiden sisters of Gray's grandfather, the old rancher tycoon himself, had the beach house built for themselves and resided here every summer for sixty years. I who have heard this all before never tire of the least detail.

We bear the steaks and our margaritas out the kitchen door to the side terrace, where Gray lights the gas barbecue. At the other end of the arbor we can hear the fountain playing. The moon is all the light we need. It's too cold to actually eat outside, but for now there's something delicious being together around the fire, knocking down tequila and imagining the aunts.

"They used to put on plays and musicales, right here," says Gray, gesturing down the arbor, then to the gentle slope of lawn beside it. "We'd all sit out there. I don't remember the plays, except Foo wrote them. They were very peculiar."

"And none of these women ever married?" Mona stares over the rim of her drink into the shadows of the arbor, willfully trying to conjure them. "Were they ugly?"

"Oh, no, they were all very striking. Wonderful masses of hair, even when they were old ladies. And they wore these flowing gowns like Greek statues."

"They sound like Isadora Duncan," I say.

"They sound like dykes," Mona declares emphatically, then turns to Gray. "Weren't they?"

I feel this sudden protective urge toward Gray, as he lays the steaks sizzling on the grill. He has barely ever admitted to me that he's gay himself. There's not a whole lot to admit, I gather. He seems to carry on his rounded shoulders centuries of repression. But now he shrugs easily as he slathers on the barbecue sauce. "You'd have to ask them," he declares. "I never really gave it a thought. Something tells me they never really did either."

Mona is very quiet, but the answer seems to satisfy her. I have a bit of a brood myself, thinking how much the history of my tribe lies behind veils of ambiguity. Ever since I've been at the beach I've had this romantic longing, wishing I'd lived here during the aunts' heyday. But now I wonder, were they happy? Or were they trapped, making the best of it, away from the rigid straightness of the ranch? They seem more real to me tonight than half the people I know in L.A., who can't take my illness and talk to me funny, as if I'm a ghost.

"Isn't it curious, Tom," Mona says softly. "They ran a little art space, just like us."

Gray laughs. "Not quite. You guys are much more over the edge." He says this proudly. "Their stuff was more like a *school* play. Historical pageants, that kind of thing."

He bends and studies the meat, poking it with a finger. And yet, amateur though the aunts may have been, they were obviously the core influence on this, their oddball nephew. Gray Baldwin was subsidizing beat poets and jazz players in Venice—hundred here, hundred there, covering rents and bad habits—when he was still in high school. If you were way out enough, dancing barefoot on broken glass, painting the sand by Venice pier, Gray was your biggest fan. All the while, of course, he was having a sort of extended breakdown, growing more and more dysfunctional, estranged from the Baldwin throne. And no one pretends that Gray put his money on names that lasted or broke through to greatness. Marginal they stayed, like Gray himself.

"Still," Mona says puckishly, "I wish *I'd* had women like that around. In my house the drift was very home ec."

"I don't want to overcook it," Gray murmurs gravely, "but I can't really see."

"I'll go get the flashlight," pipes in Mona, darting for the kitchen.

"And I'll set the table." I hurry in after her. We are both laughing, at nothing really. Not drunk at all, just glad to be here together. Mona doesn't have to say she finally gets Gray Baldwin; I know it already. She grabs the flashlight from the shelf above the stove, while I fetch plates and three not-too-bent forks. We will have to share the steak knife. Minimal, everything's minimal here, that's the way the beach house works. Mona is lurching toward the screen door, I am making for the dining room, when suddenly she turns. "I love you, Tom," she says, blinking behind her tortoise rims, half blushing at the overdose of sentiment.

"Yeah," I reply laconically, but she knows what I mean.

In the dining room I set us up at the big round pedestal table, the base of which is thick as the mast of a schooner. In the center of the table is a bowl of white-flecked red camellias, three full blooms floating in water. These I picked days ago from the bushes behind the garage. They last a week in water, which is why I like them. Most cut flowers are dead by morning, just like all my friends. I move to the sideboard and pull a drawer. Laid inside are heaps of mismatched napkins, from damask to burlap. I take out three that are vaguely the same shade of green, and caper around the table, setting them under the forks.

Through the window from the courtyard Gray and Mona call in unison: "It's ready!"

"Great!" I bellow back at them, tucking the last napkin, and then I look up—

And Brian is there.

For a second I think I've died. He's standing in the archway into the parlor, the dwindling firelight flickering over him. He can't be real, and for the moment neither am I. But he is more stunned than I am. He gapes at me, and his mouth quivers speechless. He wears a dark suit and tie as if he's going to a funeral. Still it's more like a dream—I want it to be a dream. Somehow I've summoned him up by too much invoking his name.

Then he says, "Tommy, I should've called. But I didn't know how."

The beach house has no phone. Brian is apologizing. I'm very slow, like I'm still dreaming. Finally I say, "Mom died?"

"No, she's the same."

But then why has he come, and how? Nobody knows I'm here. Merrily through the kitchen the others come parading in, Gray with the steaks on a platter, Mona bearing the salad. They stop laughing as soon as they see the pair of us standing frozen. I turn helplessly to make the introductions, and suddenly I understand. Gray is completely bewildered, but Mona gives a brief shy nod in Brian's direction. It's Mona who's betrayed me! All that bullshit about the stranger at the theater, the *faux*-innocent speculations about my long-lost brother. Without being tortured even a little she gave out full particulars of my whereabouts.

"Gray Baldwin, this is my brother Brian," I say with chill formality. And as Gray steps forward to shake his hand I add with acid tongue, not looking at Mona, "I gather you know Ms. Aronson."

"I was out on business, Tommy," Brian says. His face is thicker and slightly doughy, the dazzle gone. "I just decided to wing it and come say hello. But then I couldn't find you, and then—" He makes a fruitless gesture, vaguely in Mona's direction. "—I couldn't leave till I saw you."

I am so unbelievably calm, considering. "Well, you've seen me," I retort, giving no quarter.

Gray's super WASP manners can't stand it. "We're just about to eat. Will you join us?"

"No no, I ate already, you go ahead."

There's a general fluster of embarrassment, everyone clucking apologetically. Gray and Mona hurry to take their seats. Gray beckons insistently to Brian, indicating that he should sit, even if he's not eating. I stand stonily, and Brian makes no move. Gray and Mona are serving the dinner so fast it's like Keystone Kops, a blur of slapstick. Finally, because even I don't have it in me to just say get out, I relent and nod curtly to Brian, and he follows my lead and sits. Instantly a plate of sliced steak and salad is plunked in front of me. Gray and Mona are already eating, as fast as they can, smiling gelidly at my brother.

I stare across at Brian. "So. What've *you* been doing the last nine years?"

He doesn't know if the question is real, or just a caustic put-down. Neither do I. "Oh, same old grind," he replies, studying his hands. His hair is still like fire. "I got married," he adds almost sheepishly.

I say nothing. Mona, downing the dregs of her margarita, gives it another go. "And he has a son. Seven, right?" She beams encouragement.

"Right, Daniel," Brian responds, and then shifts the weight

of his big shoulders forward, almost yearning across the table toward me. "What about you, huh? She showed me around the theater. That's great."

"I've got AIDS."

Brian looks down. "Yeah, she said."

I turn to Mona. "I don't know why we're bothering. I believe you've covered the major points."

"Tom, give it a break." It's Gray, who never makes the slightest ripple of protest, so it must be bad. "Eat," he says.

And so I do. Anything to stop this racing panic of rage. I cut my meat into little pieces, tasting the char on my tongue like the ashes of all I've lost. I listen with genuine curiosity to the surreal conversation they have without me. As it's Brian's first trip to L.A., they speak of the weather, the smog, how it all looks like a movie set. I am already looking anxiously at Gray's and Mona's plates, realizing they are nearly done, and they aren't about to stick around for ice cream.

Brian is telling about his own house, on a marshy shore in Connecticut, 1710 and picture-perfect. Again I hear the old chatter from Gray, the aunts and the ranch and the musicales, twenty-two miles of ocean free as Eden. But now it isn't charming anymore. I feel threatened and helpless, not wanting Brian to know so much. It's as if my desert island is being stolen, right in front of my nose.

But the story fascinates Brian, who explains that he works for a builder, same job he's had for fifteen years. "Tommy knows him," he says, glancing a small remark in my direction, but nobody really looks at me. We are all just getting through this. Nevertheless, the last thing I will do is acknowledge Jerry Curran, the pigfuck who rode shotgun through my brother's arrogant youth.

Mona lays her fork and knife side by side on her empty plate. I give her a pleading look as she announces she has to leave for the theater. When Gray takes the cue, siding the dishes, drawling that he'll be heading back to the ranch, Brian looks as desperate as I do. Either of them might have stayed, I realize, if I hadn't been acting so truculent and glacial. Clearly I have bought this meeting one on one with Brian with my own special horde of bitter pennies.

I have no choice but to follow Mona and Gray through the

kitchen and out to the yard, chattering as if nothing's wrong. What's so unusual, after all? A guy's brother drops by to surprise him. It's the most natural thing in the world that they'd want to be alone. I lean my elbows on the windowsill of Mona's Toyota as she starts the car. She turns and plants a kiss on my nose. "God, he must've been beautiful," she sighs. "Now take it easy, okay? Fratricide is very hard to clean up."

"Don't worry, this is going to be short and sweet."

"And remember, I need forty-five minutes tomorrow night."

I laugh heartily, pulling back as she swings the car around. I haven't performed in fifteen months, since the week the first lesion appeared on my arm. I move to the pickup as it pulls out of the garage. I shove my hands in my pockets and grin at Gray in the truck. We never touch goodbye or any other time. "Thanks for dinner."

"I'll be down Monday to fix that screen," he says. "Remind me to check the fuses." Endlessly polite, Gray wouldn't dream of saying too much about my brother. Family is something you talk about from three generations back.

"I thought I'd run away far enough that no one would ever find me."

Gray chuckles. "Foo always said we never should've let 'em build that coast road."

"I'm with Foo," I declare, waving as he drives away, crunching over the gravel. At the end of the drive he doesn't turn and follow Mona down the infamous Highway 1, but shoots across all three lanes and heads straight up the mountain road through the moonlit chaparral. I turn and head back to the torments of Chester, Connecticut.

Brian is standing in the parlor by the fire. He's taken off his jacket and loosened his tie, and he's paging through an old scrapbook, yellowing photos of picnics out on the bluff, aunts in costume, miles of open space. "This is quite a place," he says cheerfully. "You rent it by the month?"

"It's free," I reply flatly. "Was there something specific you wanted?"

He closes the album and sets it down, wearily shaking his head. Just in that second, sullen and heavy, he reminds me of my father. "Tommy, we shouldn't be strangers. We never should've let all this time go by."

"Really? I was for giving it a couple of milennia—you know, like they do for toxic waste." He turns to me full-face, his arms beginning to reach toward me, and I have this flash that he's going to drag me down. I scuttle back a pace and hurl my next volley. "I believe where we left it was that I caused Dad's stroke because I was queer. Jerry Curran and Father whatsis were holding you back, remember? So you wouldn't kill the little fag. Am I forgetting the nice part?"

I can see the zing of pain across his furrowed brow. It excites me that I've made my brother wince—a first. "So I was wrong," says Brian, weirdly meek and powerless. He also seems to have a set speech he needs to get through. "I treated you terrible. I hated my own brother, just because he was gay. I don't want it to be that way anymore."

If it's meant to disarm me, it succeeds. Suddenly I feel drained and almost weepy, but not for Brian's sake. I step past him and slump down heavily on the sofa, the afghan curling instinctively over my legs. The whole drama of coming out— the wrongheaded yammer, the hard acceptance—seems quaint and irrelevant now. Perhaps I prefer my brother to stay a pig, because it's simpler. And even though he's not the Greek god he used to be, fleshier now and slightly ruined, I feel *more* sick and frail in his presence. Not just because of AIDS, but like I'm the nerd from before too. "You can't understand," I say, almost a whisper. "All my friends have died."

There is a long long silence before he speaks again. He sits on the arm of a battered easy chair, and I feel how uncomfortable he is in this room. The dowdiness unnerves him. Our sainted mother kept her house tidy enough for brain surgery. But it's more than that: he can't stand not being on his own turf. He's always been a neighborhood tough, the same as Jerry Curran, their territory staked, pissing the borders like a dog.

"I didn't have any idea," says Brian, "that all this was happening. I'd read about it and push it out of my mind. Nobody we know—" He stops, thinking he's said the wrong thing. But I don't care. His ignorance is oddly comforting, proving I don't have to like him. "It just hasn't touched our world. Is there anything I can do?"

"Sure," I say. "Find a cure. And then we'll sprinkle it all over Bob Manihan's grave, and Ronnie's and Bruce's and Tim's, and we'll all be as good as new."

Protracted silence again. This could go on all night, at this rate. I see him stealing little looks at me, fixed no doubt on the purple on my cheek. I wonder how sick I look otherwise, compared to a decade ago. In between I had some years when I felt pretty sexy. Pumped my tits regular, rode my bike with my shirt off, and connected up with a run of men as dazzling as any on Brian's team. Now I feel pained, almost cheated, that he can't know what I was like, that I had it all for a while. Not that I was so beautiful, or anybody's hero, but a man after my own kind.

Then I hate myself for caring what he thinks. The whole idea of talking about myself seems like a kind of special pleading. "So tell me, what're they like? Daniel and—I don't even know her name."

"Susan." Visibly he relaxes. Home turf. "Oh, they're terrific. Best thing could've happened to me."

And he's off on a staggering round of clichés, as if none of the rest of this lurching conversation had ever happened. Susan teaches special ed, and Daniel plays peewee hockey. A pair of golden retrievers and a summer place in the Berkshires. Somewhere in there the crusts are cut off the bread. Brian is hypnotized by the sound of his own voice, pouring it out like an aria, morning in America. He makes it all sound like the fifties, a decade I only caught the tail end of, but even at three years old I wanted to poop all over it.

"We go see her on Sundays," Brian says, and I realize he's talking about my mother. "She's pretty bad. Barely knows who I am. But she seems to like seeing Daniel."

Within a year of Dad's death she was in a fog, and two years later she'd shrill into the phone: "Who? I don't have a son. I don't have any children at all." Somehow she remembered only her miscarriages, before Brian and me. I never called again.

"At least she's still in her own house," declares Brian with passionate Irish pride. This is the kicker, that our zombie mother gets to wander through her lace-curtain rooms, frail as a Belleek cup, instead of being a veggie in a nursing home. Nothing in Brian's voice betrays that he's bitter about having to shoulder this burden himself, or pay for the daily nurse/companion.

Then he segues into a peroration about his business, and here

I really tune out. I remember the great drama that erupted when Brian graduated Fordham, deciding not to go after the glittering prizes of Wall Street, opting instead to throw in his lot with Jerry Curran. The only time I ever recall my father faltering in his worship of Brian, who had to woo the old man shamelessly to convince him Curran Construction would make him rich. Which it did, but more than anything else it let him stay on his own turf, so he and Jerry could strut and raise hell, till life and high school were one and the same.

"I don't know, maybe we got too big too fast," observes my brother with a labored sigh. And I realize things aren't perfect at Curran Construction, but haven't been following what he's said, so I haven't a clue what's wrong. Last I heard they were pouring an interstate and building twin towers in Hartford. Brian stares at the blue-red coals in the fireplace, lost in a troubled reverie. This alone is startling enough. In the twenty-five years I knew him before the breach, I never saw him stop to think. He was always in motion, always grinning, as wave after wave of cheering greeted his every turn.

"The stress must be pretty intense," I remark, lame as a radio shrink. "Sounds like you need a break."

"Yeah, I need somethin'." The brooding is still in his voice, but I can hear him shutting down. It's not that he won't discuss it any further with me, but that he doesn't want anymore commerce with his feelings. This is a peculiar phenomenon of straight males—the shutdown valve—which I used to think was the exclusive province of the Irish. Now I know it crosses all cultures, instinctive as the need to carry weapons. Brian turns back to me with a smile, as if he's never felt anything at all, and reaches over and slaps my knee. This is his idea of a kiss.

"You still a good Catholic?"

He laughs easily. "Sure, I guess so. We go to Mass on Sunday. Don't ask me when I made my last confession."

There's a Bing Crosby twinkle in his eye. I feel the old urge to desecrate, to flash my dick in church. "According to them I'm evil, you know. That's the latest doctrine, from God's mouth to the Pope's ear. 'Intrinsic evil.' " I spit this last phrase out like it's poison.

Brian writhes slightly on the chair arm. He wedges his hands between his thighs, clamping his knees together. "That dosen't mean gay *people*," he retorts. "That's just about . . . acts."

A regular moral theologian, my brother. "Oh, fabulous. You can be gay, but you can't have a dick. Pardon me while I piss out my asshole."

"Tommy, you know what the church is about. Sex is for making babies." He grimaces and rolls his eyes, as if to bond us against the folly and the hypocrisy. "Nobody takes that seriously. Including half the priests."

"Excuse me," I hiss back at him, scrambling out of the afghan. "Maybe you guys get to wink at the priest while you fuck your brains out." He doesn't like my language, not one bit. "But they're still beating up fags in Chester, because Her Holiness says it's cool."

"Hey, ease up. It's not *my* doctrine."

"And sixty percent of the priests are fags anyway!" I'm wild. I have no idea where that statistic came from. It's like I've been waiting for a little doctrinal debate for years. "They *hate* us for being out. They liked it the old way, where you get to be special friends with the altar boys, and maybe you cop a feel off little Jimmy Murphy after Mass—"

"For someone who doesn't believe, you sure get yourself worked up."

"Don't give me that smug shit." I can feel his coldness, the backing off, though he doesn't move from the arm of the chair. "I bet you get all kinds of points for coming to visit a dead man. Corporal act of mercy—you should get a big fuckin' discount in Purgatory."

I'm pacing in front of him, panting with fury, and he sits there and takes it. But there's no satisfaction. I feel impotent and ridiculous—feel as if Brian has *won*. All I can do is wound him and push him away. I stagger against the mantel, my forehead pressed to the great splintered slab of wood that's anchored in the stone.

"Dad went to Mass every Sunday too," I declare with a wither of irony. "And you know what? He was still a scumbag drunk who hit me for nothing at all. He used to hit me for *reading*. And when I finally told him I was gay, he told me I made him want to puke." Then a very small pause. "Isn't that where you learned it?" Nothing, no answer. He's still as a rock.

"So you'll forgive me if I keep my distance from all good Catholics."

Brian stands and reaches for his jacket, thrown over the back of the sofa. "I thought we could heal it up between us. I was wrong. I don't want to upset you like this. You've got enough to deal with." He shrugs into the jacket and turns to me. There is oddly no shyness between us, and nobody looks away. Perhaps this is the proof we are brothers. "Look, if there's anything . . ."

He lets it hang, and I shake my head. "You can't help me."

He nods, and we move together. Through the dining room and kitchen, then out to the yard, shoulder to shoulder across the grass. The silence between us doesn't feel strained, and is even rather soothing. We are ending it before it comes to blows. This is so sensible, we are practically acting like WASPs. The faint spoor of a skunk feathers the night air, and the moon is still bright, casting ice shadows across the gravel drive. We reach the boatlike rental car, nosed in between two Monterey cypresses. I wish my brother no harm and hope he knows it, but I say nothing. We both feel it's better this way.

Brian opens the door and half-turns again. His mouth works to speak, another set speech perhaps, but all that comes out is "Take care."

I stand with my hands in my pockets as he fishes the keys. We will never see each other again. No drunken promises to visit, no embrace to pass on to my nephew, no jokes. This is a surgical procedure, the final separation. And then the key turns in the ignition, and there's a clunk. Brian tries it again, this time pumping the gas. Nothing.

It is so ludicrously a symbol of the deadness between us, I want to laugh out loud. But it's so clearly not funny, the useless click of the key as he tries it over and over, because now my brother is stuck here. I know this a second before he does. In fact I can see the bloom of shock in his face as he remembers there's no phone. It's nine o'clock on a Saturday night, and the nearest pay phone is two miles south at the Chevron station, which closes at six, country hours. I have no car and no jumper cables. Our mogul neighbors with Uzi guard dogs are not the sort you bother for a cup of sugar.

Brian looks at me, dazed and slightly foolish, like a man who can't get it up. He seems to understand instinctively that he's trapped. "Fuckin' piece o' junk," he grumbles, so raw you can almost hear the brogue of Gramp Shaheen.

"You'll have to walk down to the Chevron in the morning. When's your flight?"

"Noon."

"Oh, you'll be fine. Don't worry, there's lots of room." My own voice amazes me, so solicitous and chummy. I open the door like a bloody valet. You'd think the bile and snarling never happened. But this is different, a matter of hospitality, like laying down the guns on Christmas Eve. Brian grabs his brief-case from the backseat, and we head back to the house. The skunk is nearer, or at least sending out a stronger warning. The silence between us is comfortable. We both appear to agree that this part can be handled in purely practical terms, no frills and no demands.

In the house I douse the downstairs lights, and Brian follows me up the spiral stair. "This is where I sleep," I say, pointing into Foo's room. Then we cross behind the stairwell, and I throw open the door opposite. "Cora's room," I inform him as we enter, by way of historical orientation.

In fact, this is where Gray stays when he spends the night, though he's never done that during my two months, so assidu-ous not to intrude. I snap the light on the bedside table, bathing the room in peach through the old silk shade. This room's not so tatty, though, its green wicker furniture crisp as Maine. Brian nods approval, soberly indifferent, even when I open the balcony door at the foot of the bed, the beckoning shine of the moonlit sea.

"We share a bathroom," I explain, pushing through yet an-other door. Even as I flick the light I wish I'd had a minute to tidy up. It's pretty gritty. There's prescription bottles all over the sink and counter, like Neely O'Hara in *Valley of the Dolls*. Funky towels on the floor and underwear strewn haphazardly. The plumbing hasn't been scoured in ages, and green blooms around the fixtures.

"Beautiful tile," Brian says gamely, as I snatch up shorts and toss them into my room.

"Look, you don't have to go right to bed. Maybe you want a drink or something." I'm rattling on as I scoop the prescriptions and push them to the far end of the counter. I open the cupboard above the tub, and *Eureka!* There's one clean towel. I present it to Brian. "I think there's vodka in the freezer. Whatever you like. It's just that I get real tired."

"Sure, sure, you go to bed. I'll be fine." There's a crease of worry between his eyes as he studies my face. "I'll just do a little work and then turn in myself."

"I bet you were supposed to call Susan."

"No, that's okay. They know I'll be home tomorrow. I'll be fine."

As he repeats this ringing assertion of life, he lifts his free hand in an awkward wave and backs out of the bathroom. Gently he closes the door. I who will not be fine turn and blink in the mirror above the sink, which I usually avoid like a nun. All I can see is the lesion on my cheek. My sickness is palpable, and indeed I'm completely exhausted. I splash my face with water, then use the hand towel to scrub at the smegma on the sink. It's hopeless.

I stand at the toilet and pull out my dick—oh useless tool, unloaded gun—and dribble a bit of piss, not a proper stream. The virus does something in the bladder to tamp the flow, or else there's lesions there as well.

I leave the light on for Brian and close my own door. I don't even bother to turn on the lamp as I shrug the crewneck and kick off my jeans. I duck into the bed and under the covers, the old down comforter that's shredding at the seams and spilling feathers like a wounded duck. Moonlight streams in, blue-gray on the furniture.

And I lie there, I who sleep like the dormouse now, nodding off into naps two or three times a day, ten hours solid at night. I stare at the ceiling, and the rage comes back. My father with the strap, my useless mother whimpering, "Don't hit his head." Brian on the field swamped by fans at the end of a game. Laughing with his girlfriend, horsing around with his buddies. My memory is split-screen, the Dickensian squalor of my woeful youth against the shine of Brian. No slight or misery is too small for me to dredge up. I am the princess and the pea of this condition.

I don't know how long it goes on. At one point I realize I'm clutching the other pillow as if I'm strangling someone, and my teeth are grinding like millstones. Then I hear Brian and freeze. The water goes on in the sink, right through the wall behind my head. I can hear him scrubbing his face—can *see* it. Because it's as if the fifteen years have vanished since we shared a room in Chester. I in my scrawny body have finished brushing my teeth, and Brian the god, a towel at his waist from the shower, steps up to the sink to shave. At sixteen he's got hair on his chest. His stomach is taut, the muscles cut like a washboard. I am so in awe of him that I have to force myself not to look, for fear of the dark incestuous longing that licks at my crotch like the flames of hell.

The water goes off. There's a shuffle of feet on the tile, and then I hear him pissing. But with him it's a geyser, a long and steady stream that drums the bowl like a gust of tropical rain. I am spellbound by the sound of it. I can feel the exact shape of my brother's dick—heavy and thick with a flared head—more clearly than my own. The pissing is brutally sensual, beyond erotic, and I'm not especially into kink. The stream abates to spurt, gunshots in the water. Then Brian flushes. The bar of light under the door goes out, and there's silence.

Still I stare at the ceiling, but now the rage is replaced by an ache, just like the empty throb that followed my little heart attack. Not that I want my brother anymore—not his body anyway. At least my own carnal journey has brought me that far, slaking the old doomed hunger. I used to jerk off sniffing his underwear, the uniforms he'd peel off after practice. But even with the incest gone, a darker yearning wells up in me, undiminished by years. I still want to *be* him. He's what a man is, not Tommy. From seven to seventeen I walked around with a sob in my throat, the original crybaby, mourning for what I would never become. And now it's come back like a time warp. I'm still wearing the glove I can't catch with, a Wilson fielder. I'm flinching in the middle of a scrimmage, terrified someone will pass me the ball.

This goes on for maybe half an hour, a sort of anxious misery, leaving me wired and desolate. I'm sick, I need my sleep. Eventually the rage comes back around like a boomerang, because it's also Brian's fault. I get up and grope into the bathroom, flicking the light, my ashen squinting face looking dead and buried. Fishing among my prescriptions I palm a

Xanax and down it. Neely O'Hara again. I turn off the light and take a silent step to Brian's door, cocking my ear. I don't even know what I'm doing. *Go back to bed*, I order myself, but that is the voice I have always ignored, the one that used to tell me not to pull my pud or stare at boys.

By inches I open the door into the darkness beyond, barely breathing, craning to hear. And there it is: the deep rolling surf of my brother's breathing, a soft whistle at the end. He sleeps a hundred fathoms deep, he always has. Please, I slept in the twin bed next to him for seventeen years. I step inside and stand there a moment to orient myself. The moonshine is strong, though it throws deep shadows on the clutter of wicker, crazy expressionist angles.

Brian in the bed is lit up clear, the white of the sheets like a luminous ground. He's turned on his side and facing me, one arm under the pillow that cradles his head. Bare to the waist, the top sheet drawn up only to his hips, so I can see the waistband of his briefs. He doesn't even bother with a blanket, for the Irish side is very cold-blooded. Unlike me, who's always shivered in the California nights, shrouded in quilts and comforters.

Yet the cold doesn't bother me now, even in just my underpants, as I move to the wicker armchair by the bed. Though I sit carefully, perching on the edge, still it creaks and rasps under my weight. I scan Brian's face for any stir, but he sleeps right through. Now I am only three feet from him, so close I could reach out and touch him.

But I just watch. His red hair is silver in the moonlight. The arm that's crooked under his head has a bicep as round as a melon. The other arm rests on his side, and now that he's bare I see that his chest and stomach are still in shape, if not so finely chiseled as when he was young. All evening I've been trying to find him battered and soft, but it's not true. He's beautiful still, and even the puffiness in his face has soothed in sleep. If anything, the greater bulk and mass the years have wrought have only made him more of a warrior, king instead of a prince.

Am I still in a rage? Yes, livid. The last thing I need is this mocking reminder that life goes on for straights, mellowing and ripening into an ever richer manhood. In the glint of the moon

Brian's skin fairly radiates with health. The bristling hair on his belly is thick with hormones. He'll be fifty, sixty, seventy, and still be winning trophies. And I'll be dead, dead, dead. Of course I know I can't blame my illness on Brian, but I can still hate him for being so alive. And the deep, deep irrelevance of his shiny life, with the peewee games and the goldens, I can hate that too. The white-bread sitcom cutesiness and the lies of the Nazi church.

I'm leaning forward with gritted teeth, my face contorted with nastiness. I'm like a bad witch, rotten with curses, casting a spell even I can't see to the end of. And maybe Brian picks up the vibes, because at last he stirs. A soft murmur flutters his lips, and he rolls from his side onto his back. His hands are on the pillow on either side of his head, so he lies defenseless. You could plunge a dagger into his heart.

Except I have shifted position now too, the roller coaster of my feelings bringing me up from down. Perhaps it's the Xanax starting to work. But suddenly it's like I'm guarding him, watching over the last of my clan, the only one whose luck has held. Oh, I still want him out of there. Back to his sweet vanilla life, every trace of him expunged, all the torrent of stinging memories he has brought in his glittering train. I wish to be left to die in peace. I don't need a brother—it's far too late in the game. But I stand watch anyway, keeping him free of harm as he sleeps, from curses and daggers.

Tears are pouring down my face, silent and futile, without any reason. Crybaby. Finally I think I will sleep. I stand, creaking the chair again, and I'm superconscious of every broken thing in my body. My six lesions, my old man's bladder, my nerve-warped knee. I wrap my arms about myself, huddling in my smallness. I take a last long look at Brian, and on impulse I lean above him, hover over his face and brush my lips against his cheek, just where my own cheek bears the mark. I've never kissed my brother before. He doesn't flinch, he doesn't notice. Then I turn and stumble back to my room, pleading the gods to be rid of him.

MYTHS

• WILLIAM HAYWOOD
HENDERSON •

1

WHEN I WAS still a young boy, my mother moved us off the reservation to the edge of town, out where the only thing beyond us was dry buffalo grass full of tin cans and bedsprings and socks dried in stiff clumps. I walked out in the long, early morning shadows and looked across the fields to the line of mountains that ran toward our old place. Stickers poked through my soles—I never learned the magic that protects your soles if you're Indian. On open ground, I faced away from the sun and shifted my little hips. I did a snake dance on ten-foot legs.

The air was clean and empty. I could hear a car coming up the road from miles away, see the silver gleams across the brown flat fields and wonder who it might be. For a few months it had been a federal worker with a white shirt, yellowed mother-of-pearl buttons, and a tie so tacky he should have been hung by it, choked blue. He'd smell as if he'd just eaten a short stack of pancakes with an ice cream scoop of whipped butter and a lake of blueberry syrup. He'd say, "Morning," as if we hadn't figured that out yet. He'd say, "Just want to make sure you all are eating well and so forth."

Mother waited at the back door. She smelled like corn. Like beans. She would watch me approach, then back into shadow, and enter sunlight again at the kitchen table. She'd sit there, quiet, unmoved, as if her hair wouldn't go gray.

She painted her lips. I took the red, painted my own, and stood beside her in front of the mirror to make sure we looked alike. She said, "You're mine."

I said, "We could be the same person."

She laughed. "You think so? I think maybe you have a lot of your father in you. But you have me too. My color."

"And Father? Tell me again."

"Your father is a beautiful man."

"A beautiful man."

"With yellow hair."

"Yellow."

"And blue eyes."

"Blue."

"And he came from across the ocean."

"The ocean."

"And he loved your mother."

"Loved you."

"And I love my baby."

"Love me."

"And you'll be the best of your mother and the best of your father, so nothing can hurt you. Nothing in this world."

"Nothing."

Through dry mornings, we ate with the window open. A fly buzzed around the food or landed on the edge of the orange juice pitcher, if we had orange juice, and the warming breeze brought in shreds of cottonwood fluff, the only sound the song of a bird or a car from far down the road. The cars turned off the state route, took the curve fast past the yellow warning markers, and came straight and humming along the road as if there were nothing but morning and horizon ahead, nothing but sun always rising and hills like temples to be skirted.

For hours, I'd stand in the shade beside the house and listen for the whine of tires on the gray asphalt. In the next car would be a lady, maybe one of my mother's employers. She'd have feet that could take a shoe with a heel and eyebrows so perfect they'd seem painted. I drew pages full of eyebrows. She'd drift to a stop in front of the house, and the grass would bunch against the car door. I'd lean in at the window from the passenger side and inhale the scent of her powder. She'd turn to me.

"Aren't you a beautiful boy," she'd say. "You come with me. You'll be mine."

2

People took our picture. Traffic flowed through town all summer, heading up into the mountains, over toward the national parks. The people wore plaid shorts. Mother and I had matching ponytails, a spot of turquoise on a wrist or finger. We held tightly to each other's hand as we were backed up against a storefront. A man ran his hand over my hair, shook my shoulder, and said, "Ain't you cute as the devil."

Mother decided to take me to church. "A good balance for what you are, what me and your father are." The night's cold moisture evaporated around us as we walked through the stark summer morning, down to the state route then straight toward the big square shadows of the buildings. Flies fought in the air over the trash bin beside the A & W. A truck passed, rumbling slowly, the only vehicle on the road this early, waiting to rev out into the vacant miles beyond town. I looked back. A few round clouds sat on the spine of the mountains. Cottonwoods shimmered along the river.

We sat at the back of the long, narrow room and pulled our shirts out from our damp skin. There was no clean light—our hands, laps, the necks of the family sitting in front of us, everything, was colored through pictures in the windows. A white man in a silver dress held his arms out toward the people, his fingers pulled into fists, and he spoke in a deep, tight voice, not letting a sound miss our ears.

". . . the wicked bend their bow, they make ready their arrow upon the string, that they may privily shoot at the upright in heart."

In the building behind the church, I sat at the end of a table and listened to the woman with the gold cross and the stiff, copper hair tell us a story about fire raining on a plain and burning away cities and people and plants. I thought I smelled sage burning. If my mother were turned to salt, would she be a stack of the pink mineral blocks the ranchers put out for their herds? Maybe she would be white and pure.

The woman bent at my shoulder to hand me paper and crayons. She smelled of flowers and cigarettes. She said, "Do you know how to draw?"

"Of course."

"Okay. Let's see what you can draw to show us the story of Lot."

The other children hunched over their drawings. I tried to imagine what the men of the city wanted with Lot's two visitors. They wanted to know them—they wanted to know them enough to get struck blind. They didn't want Lot's daughters.

"What do we have here?" the woman said, taking my drawing. "Where did you learn this?"

I reached for the paper. She held it higher, glanced down at me. I pulled at her elbow, stood on my toes. She jerked out of my touch.

3

My grandmother's house on the reservation was a whitewashed square at the edge of a gully. Beyond the bare dirt that surrounded the house, prickly pear, sage, and short grass grew on clumps of their own refuse.

I'd sit by the back door and watch for Uncle Gordon. Granite spires rose around a fissure in the face of the mountains. I took a scrap of paper and drew petroglyphs for the walls of that high gate.

Copulating waterbugs. Strings of stars tangled. Figures frozen in dance, in flight.

My grandmother had dark teeth. She took me to where I would sleep during my visit, pulling me past walls hung with heavy blankets. Spirits watched me from the pottery designs and the bunches of herbs hanging from the ceiling. My room had no windows and smelled of tanned hides. I could reach out in the dark and stroke a deer's back or run my fingers through a bird's slick feathers. The animals waited with me. They heard what I heard, the sounds focused in the complete blackness.

It wasn't my language the adults spoke, the calm, slow expressions, Gran almost in a whisper, punctuated now and then by a clucking laugh or a light slap on her thigh, and Uncle Gordon talking as if he were about to cry, unable to say anything harsh. I imagined his lips moving. He would close his eyes as he spoke, as if his voice came from his sleep. The edges of his body—the shoulders solid, and his limbs loose and gangly and soft. His voice fell into the rhythm of footsteps.

He would follow the tracks of an antelope up through a stand of aspen, across rocky barren stretches, around the edge of a pond. When he finally approached the antelope, it watched his zigzag from cover to cover, and it stood its ground, waiting, curious. He stopped close and set his arrow, keeping eye contact. He said, "Please. I won't hurt you," just before he killed it.

Nothing moved in the house. I tried to sleep, but the sound of my own breathing made me kick my legs, back and forth, beneath the blankets. The dead air against my face forced me down into my own warmth, away from the silence.

I imagined my uncle standing outside the house, the sun hazy on his arms, his long fingers, calves. He grew smaller out in the fast-moving shadows of clouds. I tried to keep him close to me so that I could see the rough skin on his elbows or his profile if he glanced to the side. Long strands of hair fell between his shoulder blades.

He walks toward me, and I wait in the shade beside the house, looking out into the glare where he moves. With the sun behind him I can't see his expression, just the mass of his body, so much larger than mine, like an idle space out in the rush of rising heat. He enters the shadow of the house, stands above me, and his face makes my breathing fast.

Our clothes lay in a heap among the roots of a tree. We slid down over the carpet of pine needles and entered the water. Steam rose around us. Uncle Gordon's prick submerged and floated out from his body.

We sat on the bottom, on the rusted, slick rocks, at the edge of the warm spring, only our faces out in the air. I rolled onto my side, a casual move. Uncle Gordon shifted into my embrace. We rarely talked, just fell to it. Now I was almost as tall as him, and I could hold him under water, throw his weight over.

We spread out on a slope of granite, crumbling black lichen, and water ran off us, pooled under us. The breeze traced along our exposed spines, our necks, between our legs. He flopped

his hand onto my back and turned his face toward me. Bits of
pebble and lichen clung to his cheek. With his eyes closed, he
said, "You should live here. On the reservation. It's the only
place."

"I'm not all Indian."

"Of course you are. Every bit I've touched is pure Indian,
and I've touched every bit."

"I think about others sometimes. White boys."

"That's not right. You can think of me. You can think of
other Indians. That's the only way. Look at what's happened to
your mother."

"She's fine. She loved my father."

"Do you love him?"

"I love what I know of him."

"What do you know?"

"He's beautiful. He loved my mother. He was from across
the ocean. He gave me my life."

"What life is that?"

"My *life*. My breathing."

"But he's not in you. I'm in you. Your mother's in you.
Gran. We can give you the life of our people. You're berdache.
You're magic here. That's the only way. With us."

"White boys."

"They're not for you."

"They were for my mother."

"Not for you."

4

Ray. I'd thought of offering him money to pose. I gave him a
square of hard cornbread at lunch. He took it without looking
up and ate it in three bites. I would have laid my hand out flat
on his forehead and pushed his hair out of his face. I would
have picked the crud from the corners of his eyes.

My friend Louise was big at a young age. Her breasts moved
like dangerous waves inside her clothing. We sat in the fields
out past my house and picked stickers from our socks. "All you

do is take what you want," she said. "No one is going to put up
a fight."

Louise was feeling ballsy. She picked me up in her Dart, red
interior, Saturday night, and we headed out along the dark
roads, the lights of town always off to the side, obscured,
fenceposts flashing past in the headlights. We passed the dump
road and pulled onto the shoulder. She shut off the engine, and
we sat in darkness, listening to the car settle and pop, smelling
the sage and the last of the exhaust fumes. "I can hardly stand
it," she said, passing the Schnapps. "The air is so warm, it's
like it's part of your skin. It's got me all tight. I've got to heat
up or cool off, fast. I'm in trouble. Help me fix my lipstick."

I held the lighter while she looked at herself in her pocket
mirror. Her lips took the greasy red. Then she reached over and
placed a red dot on my upper lip, on my lower lip. A final swig
of Schnapps.

We started out, across the ditch, through the lines of barbed
wire, into the fields of short grass, the scattered humps of sage,
the invisible cactus.

"You sure this is right?" I said.

"Never fails. Every Saturday night, all summer. You must
know that. They'll all be stoked. I can't believe you haven't
been out here before."

We walked in silence, came to the top of a broad, steady
slope. The land dropped away in a shallow plain, the horizon a
line of distant hills, flattened by the moonlight. At the center,
a small flame burned.

As we continued, in step, our arms swinging and almost
touching, the flame grew, became a bonfire of crackling dry
sage. When we could just begin to see clearly the boys' faces,
we knelt behind a low sage.

Bodies moved around the fire, stepped to the cooler, bent at
the radio to increase the volume, bring up the bass. Ray, I was
sure, in a stiff, off-balance swagger, passed across the fire. He
held his arms over his head, his beer bottle glowed through
with red from the flames, and then he spun around and shouted,
howled, out into the darkness that the fire blinded them all
against. His voice was familiar to me, but the howl, taken up
now by the other boys, had an alien intensity, something they

hadn't shown me, hadn't invited me into. I opened my mouth and tried to imagine the sound rising from my lungs, but all I felt was the dust and smoke blowing through my throat.

"This is it," Louise said, heaving herself up into a squatting position. "See that?" A boy had broken out of the circle of fire and wandered off to the left. "Good luck," she said, and she kissed me on the mouth quickly, stood up, and circled off, skirting the fire, in pursuit. The taste of liquor stung my lips. She faded, was lost, and then the close, huge noise of the bonfire faced me.

I felt heavy on the ground, unable to focus, as if her kiss had hammered my drunkenness straight between my eyes. Forcing myself up, grinding earth into my palms, I squatted there, watching. Another boy broke out and stumbled off to the right. On my feet, I moved quickly, without thought, pursuing, and the steps seemed natural. The moon opened the ground out before me, and I ran, long and wild strides, a hundred yards, and then I slowed, moved up, silently, to the boy, his legs spread in a rocky stance, far out from the music and the light. Another step and I reached around his waist from behind him, pulled his body against mine, ran my lips up his neck.

He arched back into my advance, his hands suddenly on me as he lurched around to face me, pulling my hair out from its ponytail, pulling me down to the ground with him, speaking in urgent commands, but I couldn't be sure of the voice, couldn't pull enough light from the surrounding darkness to recognize the features. He rolled on top of me, his weight and the liquor of his breath falling through me. Pain forced my voice out, but he continued.

Then, for a moment, the touch of flesh, the warm air drifting across us, the rhythm of breathing, my nose pressed into the hollow of his neck, light enough on his face above me that I knew it was Ray, knew suddenly the smell of him, knew he would settle into me, slowly, and we would laugh, and his voice and his skin and his life would be close to me.

A sharp pain in my gut, his fist, my shirt yanked out, and the sound of voices. Not my own voice, not Ray's. He wouldn't stop, kept at me, his hard fists. His mouth was open, strange, an animal choking, eyes rolling into its head.

A burning branch, flashlights, approached with a whoop of

voices. I fought to wedge myself out from beneath the weight, but my escape was cut off, my hands caught in his hands, legs tangled with his legs. They surrounded us. The light was full. His face, strong, sharp, pulled up from me, descended again. He shouted into me with the crowd's voices. The voices all aimed at me. And I heard nothing I recognized but the crackling of sage, the rich bones consumed by fire.

5

My uncle had always wanted me to live on the reservation with him, but we'd soured our luck. Things don't happen the way you want them.

Mother lets her fingers linger on her breast as she watches herself in the mirror. Her skin seems somehow altered. She closes the front of her cotton blouse—she won't look at herself anymore. She paints her lips, names the window, the door, in English, walks out onto the hot surface of the earth, steps up onto the gray asphalt as if it were a path, walks quickly to town. Inside the woman's house, Mother faces her employer with a strong smile, sets to her task, as if it is natural, as if she likes the scented cleaners, as if she appreciates the money, as if she has something to prove. She polishes white porcelain, tries to ignore her reflection looking up at her, as if it is confused with alien images, strange continents, as if she has betrayed her people, won't look up.

6

Uncle Gordon loved a boy who played on the green fields behind the school. He followed the kid out along the dirt roads. One day, he got courage and caught up with the kid and told him that he had money, that he had come up with a magical name for him, that he could cook and weave. The kid let him. Touch him. Once. Then the kid beat him. Maybe it was my fault. Gordon and me—we had no business being together, uncle and nephew. What could go right for him when we'd already gone wrong? The kid couldn't have known that Gordon was a prize.

Uncle Gordon died. He was in the hospital for a few days before he went. I brought Gran to see him. She rubbed the backs of his hands as they talked, their own language, never harsh. When he died, Gran loosened her braid and her hair came out in a wavy mass on her shoulders. She kept patting his hands. She cried when I drove her and the body back to her house. She cut her hair and ripped a sleeve from her dress, then laid them both at the foot of Uncle Gordon's bed. We dressed him in his Sunday suit, a dark brown cotton with wooden buttons, put his whitest shirt on him, and his red tie with the American flag clip. He seemed handsome, dressed as he was in the photo on his dresser, with me beside him in my mortarboard, high school graduation.

After a day of waiting—my mother wouldn't come onto the reservation—Gran and I took the dead body up the hill to a hole I'd dug. We got him down in there and Gran put her cut hair in his suit pockets before we closed him off. Then we piled on rocks and some thorny branches to keep the coyotes from digging.

Gran and I walked along the foothills to the hot spring and took a swim, rubbed each other's backs and arms with black dirt from the bottom, rinsed off and then dried in the breeze.

We sat at the grave each day and Gran cried. At night she burned some leaves in a clay pot. She only made a little food. No one came to visit. One morning, when she had finished crying, she brought me a bowl with thick red liquid in it and asked me to paint her. I spread the color on her face and hair. She sat out in the sun all day. Then she braided what was left of her hair.

7

A berdache would dress like he wasn't male and he wasn't female. A man would take a berdache as a wife as if it were something special.

A berdache was magic, the center of ceremonies, making

rain, healing, spiritual power. To ensure a good crop or rain showers, take a berdache, at night preferably, and light a fire. Put the berdache in the center of a circle and bring out the warriors, start the drums, young warriors. They start dancing around the berdache, and then they screw the berdache to make the magic.

Not like I've ever made it rain or brought anyone luck.

Uncle Gordon and I wandered slowly down from the hot spring. I placed my arm around his shoulders, brushed my lips against his ear. Broken veins formed a delicate web on his nose. He laughed. Aluminum glinted along the creek.

BLOND DOG

• ROBERT HAULE •

WHEN HE WAS five years old he traveled the far west with his parents. His mother made him pastel satin pants and sequined waistcoats. He tap-danced at state fairs throughout the summer. His success was due not only to his talent but also to his air of confidence and broad smile. The way he'd place the little patent leather top hat on the side of his head and give it a tap with his miniature tin-tipped walking stick won him the hearts of the small-town crowds. He saw it in their adult eyes, and adult eyes never lied.

His mother talked incessantly when they were together. She talked about food and sewing and everything and nothing. Everything was, ". . . nice." "Just so nice." "Beautiful." "Darling." "So nice." "How nice." "Isn't that nice?" Her eyes registered little more than anxiety, if that. There was no indication what she was saying held any particular significance to her. There was very little reason to listen to her, so he learned not to. His father didn't answer her. Didn't look at her.

When Morty danced his father drank. After the performances they always spotted him within a few yards of a beer concession swaying, but still on his feet. He saw them coming and went on out to the parking lot ahead of them. He started the car and sat silently, his hat pulled low over his eyes as if he were hiding. Morty got in the back, and his jabbering mother got in the front. She talked in her brightest, happiest voice about how nice the crowd had been and what nice things people said about Morty and his darling outfit and his nice smile. Morty looked out the window at the desert scrub and the mountains. He knew better than to make any of his own observations. She never heard him, but he could count on his father to snicker at him and mimic him.

The two of them were talking in the front seat one night as they were all returning from a fair in the next county. His mother had said the day had been such a wonderful success. The crowd had applauded for two encores, and Morty had run out of things to do for them. So he'd come out the last time, and oh how his aqua-sequined jacket had caught the sun and sparkled almost as brightly as his big blue eyes, and Morty took off his top hat and held it in his left hand down by his side. He placed the tip of his little cane on the toe of his right tap shoe and waited for the crowd to grow silent, and then to everyone's surprise he sang the theme song from "The Phil and Flo Show," a popular television cartoon program. He sang it without accompaniment all the way through to the last lines:

. . . Go toe to toe with me and Flo
And grumpy Phil, the so and so
And we'll have a gay old time!

His mother said, "He was so darling, and it was the perfect little song to sing. The crowd went just wild. It was so nice!"
His father said, " 'Gay old time,' indeed."
Morty's ears grew hot in the backseat. He shrank into his corner of the car, small and revolting like something you don't want to know about, but you just can't help catching a quick glimpse of it floating there as you reach for the flush lever. Down he went through a cold white hole and ran out under the desert floor where no one would have to see him.

As the car sped along the straight stretch of road at twilight, Morty became equal to the bushel of zucchini on the seat beside him. Two bundles of bland awful flesh no amount of dressing up could help. Eighty pounds of slick, watery, tasteless squash. What was the difference between his side of the car and the other? He was branded a dreadful human being, and he knew it the same way that he instinctively knew how to please throngs of farmers and cowboys. He knew just what to do to make them think he was adorable, and he knew because he'd had a lot of practice trying to conceal his unacceptable spongy mess of blond hair and pink skin from his father. He'd tried and tried for as many years as he was able to draw himself up on his hind legs and spring around the trailer back home pretending he was his father's prize little man. Sometimes there were rare moments when his outrageous shenanigans drew a faint smile to his father's lips. Then all the sodden twilights like this one were worth it. One smile from him was like holding his breath too long. The top of his head would grow light and take off for the ceiling while the living room spun around him and seemed to sink down beneath him, and he felt tall and strong and powerful. Just like he did that afternoon on stage. Just like he didn't feel now as the land outside the car flattened in the fading light. He looked out beyond the low cacti at the mountains bunching up at the edge of the lilac sky and thought he saw something moving out there in the foothills. It looked like a lion perhaps, or was it a large dog? A blond dog that loped gracefully along and appeared to be jumping to unnatural heights, clearing big clumps of scrub and then boulders the size of houses. It jagged, heading straight for the range in the distance and leaped right over it and disappeared beyond. There were puffs of dust all along the trail it had made. They shifted into the landscape, and a cool, dry peacefulness settled down with the dusk. Morty slept all the rest of the way home.

He always tried to please his parents, but he learned to please them in ways that brought him pleasure too. He cut their hair and gave his mother permanents. He brought her color up gradually until, by the time he was fourteen, she was winter white. On special occasions he would rat one side of her head out into a big Virginia Graham wing and empty a whole can of Aqua Net on it. All the women in the trailer park were after him to do theirs too. Often he obliged them and stood behind them in their kitchens, brushing and spraying and chattering with them about their neighbors. He told them horrid lies about their friends and marveled secretly as the rumors spread like grass fires throughout the encampment. He got into trouble frequently over his mean mouth, but when confronted by an angry housewife, he accused her of spreading vicious gossip and refused to do her hair anymore. "That's all you want from me anyway is a free hairdo," he said. "What have you ever done for me? You just think I'm an awful person," he said. "Well, I think you're dreadful, and you've got should'a been hair. Should'a been on a cat's ass!" His venom surprised her, and she ran from him in tears, his delighted laughter chasing her home.

He refused to visit relatives. No coercing could make him budge from the house on one of those excursions. They left him alone there in a huff, and he made it up to them by manicuring the lawn and straightening up the house. He had a way with rooms. With just a slight angling of a table, perhaps tossing an old serape over the back of the couch, maybe a big bucket of hollyhocks next to the TV, and the whole place was transformed. One day they returned to find he'd cut all the legs off the furniture and covered the living room floor with white sand. His mother screamed, and his father grabbed him and shook him yelling, "You're nothing but a clown—a goddamn clown!" Morty broke away from him and ran outside. A little later his mother was at the sink when she saw her best red high-heel shoes go by the window. She went out on the patio, and he was walking clear round the trailer on his hands. "I'm a clown, Momma," he said. "Are you laughing, Momma?" She was.

They made him move out to the tool shed. He fixed it up by erecting a green tent inside and covering the floor with an orange faux-Oriental rug. He had a mattress there and a set of weights and an old victrola on which he played old 78's at top volume and bellowed along. ". . . There's a girl in our garden, Marie . . . ," he sang as he emerged onto the back lot with a rose print sheet tied beneath his arms and a bath towel wrapped around his head. ". . . She's the loveliest flower I can see . . ." He danced about the petunia bed with one hand on his hip, waving at the neighbors with the other. When he had their attention he slowly let the sheet slide down around his waist and showed off his pectoral muscles, flexing them, one and then the other, to the music.

School was torture for him, because the other kids constantly taunted him and called him a queer. He fought dirty, pulling hair and scratching ignorant faces with his long, sharp nails. He got expelled for wearing mocha frost lipstick. He refused to return on his sixteenth birthday, so they sent him to beauty school. He learned quickly there. Even the names of the nerves and muscles of the head stuck in his memory, though he could barely read. He graduated at the top of his class and immediately got a job at a big hotel in Reno. Before long he was working on the show girls, pulling together wigs and pastiches, yards of costume jewelry roped through masses of banana curls, pin curls, turd curls. They loved his work. They confided in him. He told them what men want: "They want a pretty plastic pussy to piss in. Am I right?" he asked, and they answered by allowing him to dye their pubic areas pink and shape them into hearts.

Every night he visted mysterious, hidden homosexual bars and went home with a different man. "I'm lookin for an airtight fuck," he said. They bought the pretty boy glass after glass of champagne, and he said, "I like 'em with big mushroom heads on 'em, honey, so's they squeak when they go in, and I can feel the vacuum pressure all the way up to my throat!" He bagged out his cheeks and sucked them in, bugged his eyes and shrieked with laughter.

He bought a 1964 Bonneville and drove it through a stop sign in Virginia City. His jaw was shattered, and all his front teeth were destroyed. He was unconsicous for two days at the hospital. He thought he'd driven the car right under the ground somehow. He dreamed he'd been thrown from the car and his body had almost rolled off a cliff, when at the last moment a big dog—it looked a little like a golden retriever—grabbed his head painfully between its teeth and dragged him to safety. When he tried to get up, the animal placed a heavy paw on his chest and held him down. Morty started to cry hysterically, but the dog barked so loud the horizon all around began to boil up orange into the lilac sky, and Morty shut up and fell into a sleep from which awakening proved difficult.

During the weeks of his recuperation and reconstructive oral surgery, Morty frequently had similar dreams. He found himself sitting on the edge of that same cliff. The big dog was always there with him, a few feet off to the left, settled on its haunches, its chin on its forepaws, keeping an eye on him. Several times Morty attempted to get up, but the animal growled low. He didn't dare move. There was nothing to do but look out over the valley below. There were trees and brown hills that rolled out as far as he could see. In the distance to the left there was a shifting mist. He often found his eyes drawn to that subtle movement. Up above and behind him a steep wall of rock rose twenty feet or so. He could hear a sound coming off the crest like a stiff breeze running through a field of wheat.

He was quiet in the company of his parents. He spent a lot of time walking alone in the desert. In the trailer he rarely heard his mother's endless strings of familiar words. His father, who had found Jesus and stopped drinking, cornered him and tried to talk to him about redemption. Morty nodded, but his eyes were focused on the window above the café curtains and the hilltops in the distance. The older man exhorted him to give his life to Christ and renounce his sinful ways. Sometimes the rocks up there looked as if they might be moving; maybe one of them was an animal or something. One early evening in the living room, before his mother came in and switched on the lamps, his father's voice came up gently from a dim corner where he'd been sitting in his Barcalounger silently watching his son polish off a bottle of Chablis. He said, "I think I've finally begun to understand you." Morty emptied the bottle into his glass, raised it to his lips and met the older man's gaze over the rim. He spoke in a way that invited no response. "Just what is it," he said, "that you understand?"

His new front teeth were of an off-white color that he jokingly referred to as "The Golden Gateway" when he offered comely gentlemen blowjobs in the Greyhound bus station. It was a successful come-on, so he took it as an omen and bought a ticket for San Francisco. He took a sparsely furnished room in the Tenderloin that he could only face when he was exhausted or drunk. He haunted public restrooms in hotels, department stores, and parks. It was an activity he enjoyed and performed with characteristic seriousness and flair. He bought a handmade, Native American, horsehair satchel in which he carried a drill with a three-inch bit. He perforated wooden toilet stalls at the appropriate height and then spent long loving hours lining the holes with scraps of leather and fur. His days were spent in a pilgrimage to the sites of his handiwork. His ears grew sensitive to the slightest indication of approaching visitors. Frequently while attending to the details of his craft he stopped and cocked his head to one side like a mongrel detecting the whir of a distant can-opener. Quickly he stashed his tools in his bag, dropped his pants, lifted up the seat and sat down, quietly calming his breathing while he listened for the familiar sounds of someone using the facilities. He knew just how long it took the average person to relieve himself, wash his hands, and leave. Beyond that time, anyone still in the restroom was either biologically dysfunctional or fair game for the hunt.

One afternoon in the main lobby gentlemen's room of the Olympia Hotel, Morty had become so engrossed in a project that he lost all sense of time and place, until a deep voice startled him so that he dropped his needle-nose pliers. "You look beautiful sitting there like that," the voice said. It came from a large head the size of a basketball perched above the varnished hardwood door of his cubicle.

Morty, recovering himself, snatched up the pliers and gestured with them at the walls and said, "You're deceived by the darkness." He no longer felt attractive with his yellow teeth, crooked jaw, and all the weight he'd gained from alcohol consumption.

"Well, then, you look beautiful in the dark," the voice said.

Morty said, "Tell you what, you stick your dick through this hole here and I'll tell you if it's as lovely in the shade as I am."

The man answered, "Why don't you just come home with me. I promise to keep the lights off as long as you keep your clothes off."

Morty got to his feet and pushed through the door to get a look at the man. He was very tall—probably six-foot-five and of medium build, no doubt a frequent shopper at Rochester Big and Tall. Big feet too. Long fingers and nose. A nine-inch plus prospect if he ever saw one. He said, "All right, but let's not make it a party. I don't want to meet your goddamn friends."

He emerged from a hole in the wall of rock on the edge of the narrow cliff again. Before he could begin to think about what was happening to him, he felt the dog's loud vocal report pulling him into the valley below. He jumped up and off. A sharp breeze ruffled the hair at the top of his scalp, and then he dropped like a stone, feet first. Treetops and light brown earth rushed toward him; he landed gently on his toes in a clearing surrounded by chaparral. The dog stood on a rise five hundred yards further down the valley. It looked at him over its shoulder and let out one more thunderous bark that bounced around the cliffs above and surrounded him with echoes that rippled back out toward the animal. Morty set out in its direction, as it scrambled away in the dust down into the forest. At least it felt like a forest, but when he looked directly at what appeared to be a stand of eucalyptus, the masses of leaves became vague and slipped off to the edge of his field of vision as he padded along the hard-pressed ground in his bare feet. His body was entirely bare. His penis flopped against the soft down of his pubic hair—pubic hair the same golden color as the dirt, as he looked down. The same color as the dog, really. And then he realized the middle of his body was every bit as uncertain as the trees, and he couldn't tell just where he ended off and this place began. Another gruff blast from the animal drew him up short. Sand and grit blew up around him at his sudden stop, and he found himself in another clearing—a depression in the forest floor. At the far edge stood a small gray building surrounded by a garden of hollyhocks and a weathered picket fence. The dog stood expectantly next to a gate in the fence, but when Morty approached and reached out to push through it, a familiar growling threat stopped him. Hackles sprouted from the creature's spine. It backed up three or four feet down the length of the fence and sat looking at the sky. The sky that was the same color as the forest floor and his wild companion and his own skin was silently crossed with darkness as if they were looking down at the yellow clouds from above, instead of from below, and a huge ship in which they were traveling was casting an immense shadow. Momentarily they were plunged into night.

The afternoon sun was beating hard against the window shades of the basement apartment, when Morty woke up. The man, who'd revealed his name was Bob—right after he'd mercilessly and satisfactorily mounted Morty in the prescribed airtight manner—was asleep with his head on Morty's arm. Morty looked over at the meaty, slack face and remembered that "coyote ugly" meant you'd rather gnaw off your arm and leave it there than wake someone who looked like that. Still, he carefully withdrew the arm and rolled out of the bed. God, the apartment was tacky. Avocado green carpeting and Sears furniture. It would all have to be tossed, and it probably wasn't even paid for. The cement block bookcase room divider would have to be ripped out of the floor. Didn't the queen have any pride? He went into the bathroom and giggled to himself as he sat on the commode to abort his baby. The room smelled of mildew, and the towels! Cabbage roses with ragged edges. Even the toilet paper was a disgrace. It smelled of cheap perfume that reminded him of Evening In Paris, and it was so soft it disintegrated and balled up on his sore asshole. He heard Bob through the open door stir and groan on the bed. Morty gave a long buzzing fart that echoed off the porcelain, and he yelled, "If I'm moving in here all this shit's gotta go!"

They hadn't hauled the dumpster away before the ceiling had been freshly flocked, the walls had been repainted in Nightfighter Gray and the short pile industrial carpeting had been laid, completely obliterating any sign that the living and sleeping areas had ever been two separate rooms. The aluminum windows were disguised by Levolors that blanked them out into the walls. A putty-beige leather couch was boldly accented by two powder-blue upholstered cube chairs and a shattered glass-topped coffee table. Eventually, once the cabinets had been removed and replaced by natural fir stair shelving, the kitchen was done in plum that set off Bob's robin's-egg blue pots and pans—rather good kitchenware and appliances redeemed Bob's otherwise appalling taste in home furnishings. Behind that was another small room whose door was in line with the doors from the living room and kitchen so that when Morty painted it lavender, a pleasing progression of color could be seen from one room to the next, as the viewer sat on the couch and looked over the cube chairs while drinking a tall cool beverage.

Morty consumed plenty of tall cool beverages during the day, after his last hairdressing appointment had left. Locks of hair, the colors of which were rarely found in nature, littered the kitchen floor when Bob came home from tending bar at the Black and Blue to find Morty already plastered and peevish. He cheerfully cooked far too much food for any two humans to consume, while Morty laughed derisively at him from the couch. "The sow comes home to her sty," he heckled. "I turn your home into a showplace, and you just get uglier, don'tcha, sugar. All day I turn housewives into call girls, and then I go out to the passenger lounge and watch the Graf Zeppelin come in for a mooring. Look at you! You're twice the size you were when I met you, and, honey, you were doing a fine job of filling Ralph Kramden's pants then."

Bob pointed out that Morty'd put on a few pounds too. Morty's tumbler of gin arced through the living room and landed on the linoleum, and the house resounded with Morty's scream: "Who crowned you carbohydrate queen anyway!?"

Their mornings put balance into their lives. Morty always awakened refreshed. He never appeared to have a hangover, and he usually looked serene when he arrived at Bob's bedside with a mug of brewed coffee. He made excellent coffee too, for someone who never drank it himself. Bob headed off to the bar while Morty washed the dishes from the night before and recalled pleasant old tunes: ". . . Boil'em er bake'em er cook'em up sweet, m'ams . . ." Morty scraped the Yorkshire pudding into the wastebasket and sang, ". . . No way you make'em is I gonna eat yams! . . ." He tap-danced back to the sink, holding the greasy platter above his head with both hands and executed a smooth pirouette.

He was out in the yard turning fertilizer into his prize dahlia bed one afternoon when Larry, one of the bartenders from the Black and Blue, appeared on the deck looking frightened. "I brought Bob home, Mort, he's real sick."

Morty dropped his spade and vaulted up the stairs past him into the house. Bob lay on the bed clutching his stomach. His face was ashen, and tears filled his eyes, but he said, "It's just constipation. I haven't been able to go at all lately. Get me one of your codeine pills, will you, honey?"

Morty went to the medicine cabinet and located the old bottle of pills he'd been given by the dentist several months earlier when he'd fallen drunk on the sidewalk in front of the Castro theater and knocked his teeth out again. The bottle was empty. "Bob? They're gone! How long have you been taking them? Bob?" He hurried back to the bedside.

"Jesus," Larry said, "he's fainted. We'd better call an ambulance."

They scheduled him for exploratory surgery in the morning

and sent Morty home. Larry called from the bar and asked him what the doctors had said was wrong.

"I know what's wrong," Morty said. "She's full of shit; that's what's wrong with her. All she ever does is eat."

Larry laughed and said, "And drink bourbon and soda and do cocaine from the moment she gets to work until she goes home."

Morty was shocked. Bourbon and cocaine? He knew Bob tipped a few, but he hadn't any idea the man he'd lived with—for how long?—was smashed and zonked every night when he got home. He bounced around the kitchen, rattling pots and pans, always cheerful, always what? Immune. Unfazed by Morty's deprecations. He could see him standing in front of the refrigerator in his big blue bathrobe, the one Morty'd had to have made special for him because he was such a hog, standing there with the door open looking at the shelves and picking his nose while Morty grew more and more disgusted. He was so fat that the skin on the sides of his heels was covered with broken blood vessels, and Morty said, "Look at the sweet young thing with the blue feet. Isn't she purty?"

Bob wiped his nose on the sleeve of his robe, slid out a package of pork roast, Morty's favorite, carried it over to the coffee table and placed it in front of him and said, "Look what the Magic Boar brought for his favorite piglet. Now get up off your corkscrew tail and dance with him." He pulled Morty to his feet and crushed him in his arms. As they turned around the room quickly, and then more quickly, Bob began singing lightly, and then more loudly, into Morty's captured ear:

Oh, give me a turn.
I'm beginning to burn.
I'm on fire with unspeakable pain.

If you'll wet my whistle,
I won't pull my pistol
And shoot you as surely as Jane.

And shoot you as Shirley
Or chew few as curly as Shirley, or surely,
To queue few as early. Oh, fuck you as Shirley! I'm Jane!

They collapsed onto the couch, Morty trapped under Bob's bulk. "Uncle!" Morty wheezed.

"Uncle who, Buster?" Bob boomed.

"Uncle Shirley?"

The surgery was scheduled for nine. Morty arrived at the hospital at ten with a bouquet of white dahlias wrapped up in aluminum foil with a pale blue velvet bow. They sent him to the intensive care unit and told him to wait in the lounge. After ten minutes a handsome man in hospital green came through the door and introduced himself as Bob's surgeon. Morty rose to shake his hand, and he saw it in the man's eyes before a word was spoken. It was going to be very bad news, he could see that. But then what did he expect after knowing now about how Bob had obviously been trying to kill himself? How was he to have known what went on with Bob? Morty hadn't slept with him since early on. He'd grown irritated by that bulk snoring next to him, and finally he'd put a bed in the lavender room behind the kitchen and slept there. Bob had even furnished a second color TV with a remote control. He didn't complain about anything. He must have been in pain for some time. All that codeine he took, and he didn't say anything about it. They didn't say much of anything to each other really. Well, he did talk a lot of the time, but it was just quacking. Morty hadn't listened to the silly queen ever, but he'd made an effort to do things. He made quiet additions to Bob's collection of crystal snails and slugs. He frequently made up Bob's bed with elegant new linens. Little bottles and bowls filled with pansies or whatever was in season appeared next to Bob's favorite chair or alongside his electric razor or on the shelf with the cookbooks. His actions seemed to say that Bob deserved a life that held the correct textures and colors—a life through which he might be careening and stumbling, but at least his fingers would be feeling and his eyes would be open. And now this. Well, things were just going to have to change. They were going to have to take better care of themselves and actually talk to each other.

He said, "Yes, I'm Bob's roommate Mort."

The doctor told him that Bob had died of a heart attack moments before. He told him that his liver had been destroyed by alcohol and that part of his intestines had disintegrated. Morty fell to his knees and blacked out.

He couldn't think where he was at first, and then he realized he was in the backyard standing among the dahlias. He took hold of the big white one—the one Bob liked the most with its huge white blooms like moons, like Bob's face—and yanked it out of the ground. He got down on his hands and knees and slid head first into the hole. The earth inside was white and silky smooth and moved him along like a turd traveling through an intestine, only faster than that so that momentarily he was fired out of the anus with a resounding blast of warm air. He'd come out of the wall of rock and gone right over the cliff. He stretched out his arms in front of him and executed a loop in the air that brought him up to the top of the escarpment where he'd never been before. He landed in a field of tall grass that was being raked by a strong wind. The grass tossed green and silver in waves as the breeze passed through it. Morty struggled several yards through the dense growth, batting the flora away from him as he moved along. His feet sank into cool muck, and he stopped and looked down. There was a figure buried in the grass and mud in front of him. He reached down and stuck his hand into the wet soil and took hold of an arm. He pulled on it, and the body in the field turned over.

Bob's eyes blinked open in the mud, and then earth fell away from his mouth, and his mouth said, "I missed this part, Morty; this is the part I missed the most." He reached down and cleared the dirt away from his midsection. There was a tube of flesh attached to his navel that curved down into the earth. "It's a home," he said. "It's a home I can breathe into." He turned away from Morty, and his body sank halfway into the slime and became still.

When he came into the silent apartment and shut the door he felt like he was closing the lid on a box. He stood in the middle of the living room for a long time, staring at the furniture and the walls. He was struggling, he realized, to get air into his lungs. He went around and jerked up the blinds and opened all the windows and then the door to the yard. The dahlias were brilliant in the late morning light. The big colorful heads shimmered in the heat. They were the only things in the world that seemed alive. His attention was broken by the ringing of the phone. It was Larry again. "Well, Larry," he said, "Bob died."

Larry was a short, broad man with a full beard and thinning hair. He hadn't worked at the Black and Blue for long, but he was already well liked by the clientele because he listened when people talked and consequently had a ready reply for them. A lot of them came there out of loneliness, and Larry served them their drinks with an air of camaraderie. He'd liked Bob and had gently suggested to him that he lay off the drugs. Bob gently suggested Larry go try and fuck himself. Many times he'd watered down Bob's drinks when the big man wasn't looking, but in the long run it was a minor dilution of a major problem. He knew this day would come, but that didn't lessen the tragedy. When he heard the shrinking sound in Morty's voice, his heart went out to him, and at the end of his shift, he hurried over to the apartment.

Morty looked so tiny there in the hallway that he hugged him and cupped his big flat hand around his head. Morty shook for a moment and then went limp. Larry put him to bed and washed the liquor glasses in the sink and straightened up the kitchen. He laid on Bob's bed for a while watching TV and then fell asleep around midnight without turning it off.

Some hours later he opened his eyes. The television hissed, and the blizzard on the screen lit the room in a gray half light. Morty was sitting on the edge of the bed. He looked like a little kid in his white sweatshirt and red undershorts with blue palm trees all over them. Morty said, "Bob sure is dead." Larry pulled him into bed and wrapped himself around him, rocking him.

After that night the two of them talked on the phone nearly every day. Morty felt it was important to Larry that he let him know how he was doing. During the days he continued to keep his hair appointments. He noticed that the women kept their voices down now in the apartment, as if Bob's body was still in the next room, even though he and Larry had spread his ashes in the bay. Frequently he gave haircuts out in the yard, and the women would remark about the glorious dahlia bed and ask him what his secret was. He usually sent them home with a sampling of the flowers from the giant plants, except for the white ones. He began to experience cramping in his right hand, the one that held the scissors. He pounded it on the patio table to get the paralysis to let up. There were also odd outbreaks of small sores on his neck and on the insides of his thighs. Heat rash troubled him, and he had to continually change his shorts and put baby powder in them, and then he noticed his pants were too big for him.

One night when Larry came over to make spaghetti and spend some time visiting, he found Morty standing with his back to the bathroom mirror, looking over his shoulder at his butt. "In a few more weeks," Morty said, "it'll be behind my knees."

On Larry's insistence, he went to the city clinic. The doctor found white spots on Morty's tongue that he called "hairy leukoplakia." Morty said that sounded like a cheap Greek restaurant. He asked him if he'd experienced any night sweats over the previous six months. Morty said, "Yes." He asked him if his appetite was poor. Morty said, "Yes." He asked him if he ever had a black tar stool. "A what?" Morty said.

"Black tar stool," the doctor said.

Morty said, "Yes, kimo sabe."

He got smaller and weaker so that soon he was taking fewer and fewer haircutting appointments. Those who still came found themselves purchasing his furniture, because the prices he asked were so reasonable and because he was an insistent salesman: "I think you should have the coffee table, Dianne; I know you've always admired it so the price is low because it's you. If you don't want it, fine; I know I can get twice that for it in time, but I really need to get the rent together right away so I can still be here for those of you who really appreciate my work. Now if you want to take the aurelia there, it's yours for twenty bucks, and I'll throw in the dyed wicker basket under it for nothing."

He printed DECEASED across the bills that came for Bob's bedroom set and sold all of that too. By the time he had the terrible seizure that left him blue, all that was left was his twin bed parked in the center of the living room. He'd recovered enough to be lying on his side with his head resting in his hands when the men from the ambulance arrived. "Here she is, boys," he said. "It's Cleopatra on her barge. Do her a big favor and tug her up the Nile."

"This is the third time you've been in the hospital with pneumonia," Larry said, sitting beside Morty's bed. "Still you've kept your sense of humor and your courage intact."

Morty, leaning against the pillows Larry had freshly fluffed for him, was wearing purple eyeliner, blue shadow and plenty of rouge. "Well," he said, as he pulled the oxygen tube from his nose and pushed it into the curls over his pallid forehead, "I always say to myself: 'These things happen.' I used to know an old queen up in Reno who always used to say: 'I'll get over it.' Well, Larry, you don't get over it. Nobody gets over anything; it just becomes a part of you, so I always say: 'These things happen.' She also used to say: 'Honey, when you're pretty it doesn't matter how you wear your hair.' She was right about that."

When the doctor revealed that a tumor in Morty's brain was going to kill him within three months, Larry announced he would go along when Morty went back home to his parents' trailer. He finished emptying out the apartment, and then he performed the final task on Morty's list. He went out to the yard and pulled up the last withered dahlia bush. According to his instructions, he spent a long time memorizing every detail of the hole it had left in the earth.

They brought him pancakes for breakfast again. Good. And lots of syrup, as he'd indicated on the order form the night before. He was reaching for the plastic fork when a rainbow appeared around the tray and a popping noise like ginger ale went off in his head. He fell back against the pillow, and his eyes rolled up. When the pancakes hit the floor, Morty was riding a turbulent down draft that left him on the porch of the gray house in the hollyhock garden. Everything was as he'd left it the last time he was there, which must have been just yesterday. How beautiful the hollyhocks were. He really liked them far better than dahlias, but he'd had such a hard time getting them to grow in San Francisco that he'd finally given up and settled on the others. It seemed to him that these old-fashioned flowers gave a home a special warmth that no others did. They were sort of proof of permanence. They came up year after year. When his parents pulled the trailer into their lot so many years ago, hollyhocks were already there, and they'd still be there when they left. They'd still be here when he left too, he was absolutely sure about that. They seemed to vibrate color in the heat as they teetered back and forth in the sudden breeze. A shadow fell across the amber clouds up above, and a brief night engulfed him. He sat patiently for a few minutes and listened to a rustling in the pitch-black yard that moved into the trees beyond, and then the shadow passed, as always. At first there had been a terror in the recurrent event, but after experiencing it several times with no ill effect, he no longer associated it with danger. Not imminent danger, anyway, more like the discomfort he had with the low-grade pneumonia when he was away from the hospital. The sort of thing that is just a drag now, though it will probably kill you later on. The worst aspect of the phenomenon was the disappearance of the dog. He'd not seen it again since the first time the darkness had occurred.

He got up from the stoop and walked into the house. It was a one-room cottage, actually, and the room held no furniture. The floor was of the same weathered wood as the rest of the place. The doorway was in the center of the front wall, and there was a glassless, unadorned window in the center of each of the other three walls. There was nothing to do but sit on the floor, cross-legged and naked and look out at the flowers and the sky behind them. The size of the room, he discovered, depended on his needs. If he felt lonely and fearful, the room would shrink down almost to a skin around him. The brats of blooms in the windows became a multicolored cloak that caressed and warmed him. This day he felt bold and expansive. The place broadened into a ballroom so large that the floor curved away from him as if he was seated at the northern pole of a planet. He could feel himself absorbing power from the spot. He looked down at himself in the bronze light filtering through the great floral portals and witnessed his shimmering body take on a fullness that belied his emaciated state. His muscles gathered tone and started to ripple, especially along his thighs, where sparse hairs had given way to dense, butterscotch growth. He stood up, flexed his legs and then settled into them. They felt most comfortable slightly bent at the knee so that there was a reserve in the length of the tendons. He took a step toward the door and sprang all the way out of the vast room and onto the stoop. One more step took him over the garden and through the gate in the fence. He remained there for a moment breathing deeply, slabs of pectoral muscles inflating and squeezing together with each inhalation and exhalation. He was so excited that his penis became erect, the head of it pink and glistening. With a roar of exhilaration, he bounded down the path in front of the house that led to some dunes.

Beyond the dunes he had observed, in earlier, timid explorations, was a beach at the edge of a wide pumpkin ocean of gas. This time he scrambled over the grainy hills and took long sliding strides down to the curling body of mist. He galloped along the beach, letting out deep, guttural blasts of joy. He thumped his chest and laughed at himself in his new embodiment of strength and fearlessness. And then he caught sight of a figure in the distance further down the stretch of umber sand, a figure occasionally obscured by waves of gas that swept in from the ocean and dissipated against the dunes, a figure draped in aquamarine, gliding toward him quickly and effortlessly.

It was a tall, slender woman with small firm breasts and a round face, partially in shadow like a sliver of a moon. He saw one side of an aquiline nose, half of an amused magenta mouth and one familiar almond eye. It was Bob in a satin fishtail gown. They leaped into each other's arms, and their arms blended together and separated and blended together again, as did their bodies. "Humor me by celebrating our reunion with a dance," Bob murmured. His voice to Morty was breathy and delicate against his neck, yet the sound seemed to be coming from his own throat. They moved as one in the advancing and retreating fog. Bob hummed a tune, and the tune ran up Morty's neck into his ears. Morty picked it up and spoke the words:

. . . When I'm alone with only dreams of you
That won't come true,
What'll I do . . .

He'd just made his way from the bathroom, with the help of a walker, back to the bed and was standing next to it when a group of residents and interns swarmed into the room. "This is Mr. Mortimer Finger, ladies and gentlemen," an elderly doctor announced peremptorily. A few of them nodded at him, and one or two said, "How do you do?"

Morty shoved the walker aside and, leaning against the bed for support, waved his hands over his head and sang:

> . . . There's a place in France
> Where the women wear no pants
> And the men go 'round
> With their hammers hangin' down . . .

He finished by pulling up his hospital gown and shaking his dick at them. One of the physicians said to another, "Wasn't he here about a year ago?"

Larry purchased an old Cadillac for the trip to Nevada. It had a decent stereo system, air-conditioning and a large backseat on which Morty could stretch out when he felt tired. Originally it had been a battleship gray, but Larry had taken it to a cheap auto refinisher and had it spray-painted mauve. When Larry opened the door for him there was a lovely used mink coat on the front seat. "In case you get a chill, sweetheart."

They made the trip in quiet elegance. Morty found some dove-gray kid gloves and a pair of rose sunglasses in the pockets of the coat and put them on. He leaned back and fluffed his hair and said, "Bless you. This is how I was meant to make my comeback: smack dab in the middle of a fashion alert!"

His mother thought the car was really nice. She said it was nice of Larry to bring Morty home. Larry could see her eyes were full of pain. She chattered about the doctor in the trailer park who was going to look in on them in a while and how nice of him it was to do that. She said she hoped Morty would feel strong enough in a few days to bring her hair up the way he used to. "It looked so darling that way, and of course Mr. Finger needs a little trim too. Does anyone want a steak sandwich and a soda? Mort's dad and I ate a while ago. Seems like all we do is eat!"

Larry and Mr. Finger set up a rented hospital bed in the living room, because it was too large to fit into the spare room. Larry noticed how agile the man was and how his hands looked exactly like Morty's. He imagined kissing the tips of the fingers as he had done to Morty when he lay unconcious after a seizure. The thought brought it home to him how very odd this situation was. Here were two couples from different planets come together for an event that transcended their differences. Morty said it was a "transmogrification party" that would go on to all hours, and despite the terror of being left alone on his own world without this special being, Larry felt excitement welling up inside himself. There was a machine, also rented, that manufactured oxygen. It had a wood-grain finish, and, since it was about the same size as an end table, Mrs. Finger put a lamp and a little dish of candy on it and ran the tubes behind the couch and around to the bed, where they unobtrusively ran under the sheets and out onto the pillow.

In the morning Morty wanted to go for a ride into Reno to look at the desert along the way and check out the casino lights and the crowds of tourists in the city. As Larry was dressing Morty, Mr. Finger said that he prayed continually now that Morty would accept Jesus into his heart.

Morty said, "Is that the same Jesus who had tantrums in church, performed sleight-of-hand tricks before adoring crowds, who had such gorgeous hair and azure eyes and so lovely a figure that he was stripped, fastened to a billboard and planted on a hilltop so his public could watch his silken skin turn milky white like the fair maiden moon, while members of the military fought over his fabulous red cocktail dress; and nearly a dozen of his boyfriends went mad with fear and locked themselves in the main ballroom of the Holyland Hilton to find comfort in each other's arms all weekend? All except for his one true love who gave the whole lurid secret away by kissing him in public and then killing himself in a fit of passion and remorse? If it's that Jesus, yes I surrender to that Jesus, because that Jesus and no other died during a glamour attack that rivaled any other in history, and I worship glamour!

"Don't let me hear you talk that foolishness in front of Larry again," Morty whispered as the room rocked in a sudden desert gust, "or I'll take a page out of your precious boy-god's book and rise from the dead and make the rest of your life miserable."

At the outskirts of town Morty said he felt tired and had to go back to bed. That night when his parents were asleep, he gave Larry his instructions. At the moment Morty died, Larry was to close his eyes and picture the hole the dahlia bush had made in the backyard in San Francisco. He was to imagine diving headfirst into the hole and sliding through the earth until he arrived at a special place. All he wanted Larry to do was try his best. If he couldn't find the place, it was all right. He'd find it someday. That was certain. He pointed out the window above the café curtains at a hill in the distance under the moon. There was a certain group of rocks up there that appeared to take on a life of their own when the sky turned lilac at twilight. "Go up there and dump my ashes. Mind you, keep your back to the wind so's you don't have to have me for lunch like we did Bob. Everything is going to work out just fine, Larry, once this last shadow passes there will be nothing but light."

The next day Morty had stopped speaking. His mother waved to him down at the end of the room as she walked through the kitchen area, and Morty's arm came up from the bed and waved back. Later on, the arm came up briefly and then sank back down. By evening, as she was watching her husband pop some corn—a regular evening ritual in their lives—she turned once more and waved. He didn't move, only followed her across the room to the bed with his eyes. She adjusted his tubing and smoothed his colorless forehead with her dry hand. She said, "There's my boy. You danced so beautifully for me, and I'll always love you for it."

She smelled burning popcorn and turned to see smoke pouring from the pan on the stove. She rushed to take it off the flame and then ran into the bedroom. Her husband had one hand on the bureau next to the bed and was bent over, holding his stomach with the other. "What is it, Harley?" she said, coming up beside him and putting her hand on the small of his back.

"It's me, Pearl. I've got to break into a million pieces and take them all in there and show him how much I love him."

"He knows all about that," Pearl said. "Why'd you think he came back up here? It weren't the trailer he came to see. It's us in it."

Around seven in the morning Larry went over and changed Morty's diaper and put a fresh towel under him. The night before when he performed the task, Morty had screwed up his face and tried to fluff his hair like a beauty queen; but now his arms remained motionless, and his mouth was slack. Larry smoothed the sheets and adjusted the pillow. He sat down next to the gasping face and said, "I'll be seeing you, honey. See you in my dreams."

After a long pause, the left side of Morty's mouth twitched into a half smile, and then relaxed. There was a movement in the center of Larry's chest, and he caught his breath. The sound of the oxygen machine amplified a sensation that the room was under water, slowly losing all its air from a leak somewhere. Larry controlled his fear and closed his eyes and remembered the hole in the backyard. He got down on his hands and knees and put his face in the dirt that he imagined was there and wept.

A long time later he opened his eyes and set about fixing up the body. He put a clean sweatshirt on him and changed the diaper again. The body was still peeing in the bed. He thought maybe he should tie a knot in it, and he choked off a laugh. He got out the curling iron and went to work on the hair the way Morty had taught him, being careful not to burn the scalp or, as Morty said, ". . . the smell will make everyone absolutely ill. . . ." He put the pair of kid gloves in one of the hands, but he couldn't bring himself to place the rose glasses over the eyes. He went into the bedroom and woke up the Fingers. "Come and look at Morty," he said.

Larry sat on the boulders atop the hill at sunset and opened the cardboard box. The ashes were a creamy color, a color that pleased Morty when they first looked at Bob's ashes. Morty said they were pure and clean and light like Bob's heart, and they would fly easily. Morty tossed them into the air over the side of the boat, and they were hit in the face with grit. Their horror turned to laughter when Morty said, "I guess she owed us at least one good slap in the face." This time Larry checked the wind direction carefully and then waited for the sky to take on the lilac hue that Morty loved. At the right moment he dumped the box into the wind. A bright flash blinded him as the white arc caught the last rays of the setting sun. He blinked and lost his balance on the rocks.

He slid quickly into the dahlia hole and felt himself being sucked into the earth. When he opened his eyes again he was sitting on another hill, and he was looking down at a wide beach before a field of churning vapor. There were two figures down below dancing in each other's arms. One was a tall blue-finned woman, and the other was a barrel-chested, fawn-colored, cloven-hooved man, yet he knew instinctively who they were and yelped as he started down the side of the hill at a gallop. At his approach, the dancers broke apart and fell to their knees to greet him. They laughed and hugged him and told him he was, on Earth and any of the worlds beneath it, the fiercest and most magnificent blond dog of all.

GREAT LENGTHS

• JOE KEENAN •

"IF YOU TEASE me, I'll leave."

"I won't."

"And you can pay for your own beer."

"Then I really won't."

"I'm miserable enough as it is without your making it worse."

"I'm sorry," said Gilbert. "It's just I've never seen you this way."

"Stop smirking!"

"I'm *smiling*, all right? Because I'm happy for you. So what's his name?"

My voice as I replied was level and dignified, all but daring him to laugh.

"His name is Humphrey."

Gilbert's eyes widened as he gripped the side of the table, causing veins to rise on the back of his hands.

"Have to pee!" he murmured through tightly compressed lips and, rising quickly, fled to the downstairs john. He returned some minutes later carrying two more beers and looking flushed.

"Well, congratulations!" he said, toasting me.

"Congratulations are premature."

"This Hum—" he began but stopped, overcome by a series of esophageal convulsions, like a dog that's just been given medicine. "This Hum—Hum!—Hum!—s'cuse me, hiccups! —this friend of yours, is he nice?"

"He's wonderful."

"You're sure it's love? I mean, you're not the type that falls easily. Maybe you just have the hots for him."

"I think I can tell the difference," I said stiffly.

"So can I," he said. "After a month or two. So, *tell*," he said, leaning forward eagerly, his blond forelock tumbling over one eye, "what are the symptoms?"

"Oh god, let me see. Well . . . I think I see him on the street when it isn't him. I begin to call him fifteen times a day and have to stop myself. I go to the Lower East Side every afternoon and walk around his block, hoping I'll bump into him."

Then, reddening somewhat, I added that the night we'd met I found myself unable to resist stealing his cigarette butt from the ashtray when no one was looking.

Gilbert's brow furrowed. I could see that he viewed my case with new seriousness.

"Took it home, did you?"

"Yes."

"Puff on it, thinking about where it had been?"

"I might have."

"Were you naked?"

"Who remembers! The point is I'm completely obsessed with him. But him! He doesn't even—" Realizing what I was about to say, I stopped myself and shuddered.

" 'Know you're alive!' " finished Gilbert, grimacing tragically and brushing an imaginary tear from the corner of his eye.

"I told you I'm in no mood to be teased!"

"Well, too bad! You *always* tease me when I'm in love which is a lot more often than you are. Now you finally fall and I'm supposed to sit here all hushed and attentive like you're the fucking Bolshoi Ballet."

"Fine! Go ahead, tease me!"

"HUMPHREY?" he bellowed, for the benefit of the entire café.

"Go easy, all right? I'm really—"

"In love with him! I know," he said and patted my hand maternally. "And you want my advice on how to get him?"

"Well . . . yes, I suppose."

It embarrassed me to admit this. Gilbert, you must understand, is not the sort of person you normally look to for counsel when making a vital decision (unless, of course, you want to be sure you *shouldn't* do something, for Gilbert's endorsement is the acid test of a bad idea). When it comes to matters of the heart, however, Gilbert has skills that cannot be lightly dismissed. Like Lola in the musical *Damn Yankees*, whoever Gilbert wants Gilbert gets, and while his romances are often short-lived they are never unconsummated.

"How old is he?" asked Gilbert.

"Our age. Twenty-seven, eight."

"Good-looking?"

"He's a god."

He took a thoughtful sip of beer. "They can be difficult. Well, if I'm going to be any help you'd better tell me everything."

"All right."

"Omit *nothing.*"

The frank salaciousness of his tone filled me with uneasy speculation as to how widely broadcast the details might become once I'd confided them to him. Gilbert, I knew, has long been of the view that while his own secrets are sacred confidences, meant to be carried to the grave, other people's secrets are different and similar in concept to currency. Still I knew that if anyone could tell me how to conquer the affections of my aloof beloved, Gilbert was the man.

Taking a deep swig from my glass, I lit a cigarette, and unfolded my tale.

Some weeks ago I had received a phone call from an actress friend named Nancy Malone. She had joined a theater company operating out of a basement in the East Village and offering a repertoire of what she termed "stunning and innovative new works." Under the guidance of its brilliant Artistic Director, the company was engaged in a spiritual quest to distill the very essence of theater, to strip away centuries of artifice and convention and arrive at something true and primal and shattering.

"I'm not sure this is my dish," I said.

"Don't be so close-minded, Philip. It's very exciting stuff. I've only been doing it for a few weeks but already I'm getting in touch with all these places inside me."

"Ah."

"The problem is audiences. We don't have the budget to advertise so the houses are really small. I guess word about what we're doing hasn't gotten around yet."

Restraining a natural desire to remark that perhaps word *had* gotten around, I swallowed hard and asked when I might attend a performance. Nancy has recorded many a free demo of my songs and this seemed a simple if not entirely painless means of repaying her.

Two nights later I located the address and, tiptoeing over several gentlemen in diminished circumstances, approached the box office and purchased a ticket for the evening's offering, which was titled *Hors d'Oeuvres in the Abattoir*.

Performed by an inexhaustible company of twelve, the piece was a vivid exploration of warfare, both modern and ancient. The director, in his desire to insure that the full terror and brutality of combat would in no way elude his audience, had staged the work environmentally. As a result the spectators were encouraged, and at times obliged, to feel that they were not mere observers but instead full-fledged participants in the battle of Vicksburg, the Crusades, the siege of Troy, the fire-bombing of Dresden and, judging as best I could from the accents, the French Revolution.

My fears of a long, dull evening could not possibly have been more misplaced. So unceasing were the cast's efforts to discomfort us in the name of pacifism that boredom was not for a moment among the options. We were deafened by screams, sirens, and gunfire, blinded by searchlights and asphyxiated with smoke. We were assigned roles to play, whether we cared to play them or not, and the roles alternated dizzyingly between those of victims and those of oppressors.

Drill instructors barked commands at us. Cossacks raced among us brandishing plastic scimitars. Terrified peasants wrapped themselves around our ankles and pleaded for mercy, then blood-spattered Centurions saluted us, dragged them away and stabbed them repeatedly, as if at our instruction. Infantrymen fired on us with toy machine guns as the lighting booth bathed us in garish red floods. At one point we were poked rudely with bayonets and forced to walk several times around the playing area for reasons that had something to do with the Bataan Death March.

As one of those theatergoers who feels resentful if he's expected to clap along with a reprise during curtain-calls, my reaction to these impositions can be readily surmised. I simmered with rage and spent every unhectored moment devising poisonous things to say about it to my friends, especially my collaborator, Claire, who shares my belief that people go to the theater to be engaged, not ambushed.

After two uninterrupted hours (for the director had not been so foolhardy as to provide an intermission) the cast finished by drenching themselves in blood and chanting the lyrics to "She's A Grand Old Flag" while squatting in front of tombstones. After the lights rose Nancy rushed over to ask my opinion. I told her that if she would meet me at a local bar called Phebe's, I would be more than happy to share my thoughts.

I hastened to the bar. Taking a table in the back, I ordered a scotch and began eagerly sharpening my withering comments concerning the show's abrasive simplemindedness (though I planned to tell Nancy, as is the invariable custom on these occasions, that her own contribution was beyond praise and that it pained me to see a luminous talent like hers wasted on such twaddle).

I was perusing my program, devising unkind puns on the names of the creative team, when I gazed up and saw that Nancy was standing in front of me and she had brought Michelangelo's David with her. He was wearing jeans and a black turtleneck, the hair was darker if not the skin, and he'd left his pedestal at home, but apart from these minor discrepancies he was certainly Michelangelo's David or, barring that, a close relative of Michelangelo's David, possibly Michelangelo's David's handsomer brother.

"This is Philip," she said to him, "my writer friend I told you about. Philip, this is Humphrey Snow. Humphrey's the Artistic Director of the company and he's completely responsible for the piece you saw tonight."

"Nice to meet you," said Michelangelo's Humphrey, extending a large, perfectly shaped, powerful yet sensitive hand across the table.

I get to touch him! I thought and, grasping it firmly, did my best to give the sort of handshake that would convey equal measures of warmth, intelligence and immediate sexual availability.

"A pleasure to meet you, Humphrey!" Such music in the name! "I was very impressed with your work."

This was certainly true in the literal sense. My heart might have been aflutter but I saw no reason to totally betray every critical standard I had developed in a lifetime of theatergoing.

"You really liked it?" he asked, his bottle-green eyes boring directly into mine.

Oh, what the hell.

"*Liked* it! Humphrey, I don't know when I've ever felt as moved as I did watching your piece. I was completely overwhelmed."

"You *looked* sort of overwhelmed," said Nancy. "In fact, I was worried you were really hating it."

"Really?" I asked, amazed at the suggestion. "What could have made you think that?"

"You just had this look on your face. There was one scene where I was screaming at you because I was a Vietnamese woman and you were Lieutenant Calley. I could have sworn you were about to hit me!"

I mumbled something about attempting to enter into the spirit of the moment by "probing the Lieutenant Calley within me." This was apparently the right stuff to give them because they immediately became very excited and said yes, *yes,* this was *exactly* what the evening was about. *Hors d'Oeuvres in the Abattoir* was not just a play but an "interactive exploration" of the roots of warlike behavior. It had been carefully crafted to give the audience numerous opportunities to confront and act out their own feelings of hostility or victimization. How refreshing it was to find someone willing to surrender to the experience! Most people just got annoyed.

I could see that Humphrey, apart from being beautiful, was a man of considerable charisma. Nancy had been working with him less than a month yet here she was earnestly spouting opinions of a sort she'd never once voiced in ten years of summer stock and *La Cage* tours.

"The problem is that the commercial theater has trained people to be voyeurs. They only want to watch. They're not used to being asked to respond, to give."

"Yes," nodded Humphrey. "And if you give them anything but what they're used to, they turn right off on you."

"Well, people are like that," I offered weakly.

"Not all of them," said Humphrey.

He smiled an approving smile at me, and lightly patted the back of my hand.

That was all it took. Before I could stop myself I was off and running, talking Grotowski, and Artaud, spitting on Broadway, and describing with passionate reverence every bad rage and leotards show I'd ever been forced to squirm through.

I did not have to dissemble at great length. Humphrey quietly seized the floor, taking up the topics I'd introduced but speaking with much more fervor and insight, for he believed in them all as much as I merely pretended to.

As I listened to his low musical voice I found all my smug disdain for the avant-garde melting away. Here, I realized, were artists trying to break free from the shackles of tradition; sincere, dedicated, attractive people attempting to rekindle a jaded audience's sense of the primal mystery that is life. How could I be so small-minded as to scorn their efforts which, while at times imperfectly realized, were still far nobler in intent than a thousand of the slickly produced entertainments I not only enjoyed but sought to emulate?

Midnight came and went and I sat mesmerized as Humphrey discoursed ever more thrillingly on theater's ability to carry us away to ancient uncharted places, far from the stifling grind of daily existence.

He could cite no more poignant proof of the theater's power to transport than the case of his own sister. Confined to a wheelchair since childhood, she'd become an eclectic theatergoer who never missed one of her brother's plays. And, unlike those far more severely handicapped by conservatism and timidity, she had always proved eager to participate fully in these innovative productions. By so doing she had many times been released from her captivity and borne away to sacred places, there to feel and share with others the full measure of joy and pain that is the human condition.

Entranced as I was by Humphrey's speech, there were moments when I lost the thread of it, so transfixed would I become by some small detail of his physical person. The pink fullness of his lips, or the light stubble dotting his jawline would render his words inaudible, or else his shoulders would drown out some point he was making. His cheekbones were positively deafening.

Still, enough of his words got through for me to realize with some pain that he belonged to a far higher species of being than I did. Indeed, so compelling were his arguments that I even found myself reevaluating *Hors d'Oeuvres in the Abattoir.*

How searing and magnificent it all seemed now. How dynamically he had made his themes come alive for the audience. How cleverly he had demonstrated the banal sameness of war by having those Confederate soldiers sack Troy. What a genius he was! What insight he displayed! What nice hair he had!

The hour grew late and Nancy began fading. The check was requested and paid. Humphrey stood, yawned and stretched so that his shirt rode up and bared his stomach, a hard flat surface traversed by a single raised vein that made my heart stop. They walked toward the door and, seized by an uncontrollable impulse, I reached down, snatched his just-extinguished cigarette from the ashtray and dropped it in the pocket of my jeans.

Fears raced through my mind as I followed them to the sidewalk. Was he straight? Were they, in fact, an item? Would Nancy, an Upper West Side neighbor, bid me good night and, shooting a "nyaah, nyaah" look in my direction, stroll away, triumphantly clutching his arm?

"I'm sorry if I've been a bit of a bore," said Humphrey, favoring us with the smile he'd rarely displayed in the course of our discussion.

"No," I protested, "it was fascinating! I'd like to discuss these things more sometime if . . ."

The sentence hung unfinished in the air as I executed a brisk, involuntary Charleston on the sidewalk.

"Jesus, are you all right?" asked Nancy.

"I'm fine!" I said, slapping at my thigh where the cigarette butt had ignited the lining of my pocket. "My leg's asleep!"

"There," said Humphrey. "I've even put his legs to sleep!"

Though not what's between them, I thought.

A cab pulled up.

"You want to share this, Philip?" she asked, clambering in.

She was going home alone! They weren't an item! There was hope! Shaking Humphrey's hand I assured him that the evening had been a profound experience and that I couldn't wait to see the company's other works. He thanked me prettily for my compliments, turned and walked downtown. It was only through the most superhuman effort that I tore my eyes away from his retreating posterior and climbed into the cab.

"Interesting guy," I said, wondering how to begin the delicate cross-examination that would determine where my chances stood.

"Isn't he wonderful! I think he's maybe the most special person I've ever met."

"Well, he seemed pretty fond of you. In fact, I assumed you two were an item."

"I wish! No," she sighed, "Humphrey likes boys. Just my luck."

"Too bad," I exulted.

My exultation did not last long, as the question of prior claims suddenly reared its head. Surely a man of such rare qualities would be besieged by swains offering far greater inducements to romance than I could hope to match. At this moment he was probably racing home to some affluent Nordic ballet dancer with a ten-inch cock, a certificate from Cordon Bleu, and a three-book deal with Knopf.

"So . . ." I said, yawning, "Humphrey's gay?"

"You're surprised?"

"No, it just never crossed my mind that he might be. Um . . . I suppose his boyfriend is that tall good-looking guy who played Vlad The Impaler?"

"No. Arborio is straight. I don't think Humphrey's attached just now. He had a lover but they broke up a few months ago. So, did you *really* think what I was doing worked? I'm still incredibly insecure about that scene where I'm the Statue of Liberty but instead of a torch I'm holding the Uzi . . ."

That night I thrashed sleeplessly on my bed for hours, kept awake by a dull, persistent nausea that was partly due to my keen longings and feelings of inadequacy and partly due to having swallowed the cigarette butt. But by morning the nausea was gone and in its place was a firm resolve. I would change in whatever way it would take to be worthy of Humphrey. I would make him love me as I loved him.

"So what did you do?" asked Gilbert. "I mean apart from diet and exercise and all the usual stuff?"

"Well, I rushed right off to see the company's other two shows."

"You *are* in love."

"They were good," I protested, deciding it would be unwise to elaborate. The specific details of the shows—one, an all-male *Trojan Women*, and the other a collage based on Eskimo creation myths—were not germane to my dilemma and would only provide a person of Gilbert's facetious nature with more fodder for satire.

"You couldn't drag me to one of those things! So have you seen Humpy again?"

"Several times. In fact we're collaborating."

"That should help. How'd you pull that off?"

"I was out with the cast after one of their *Trojan Woman* performances—Humphrey's actually in that one, as Menelaus—and he was saying how he thought the show needed music and maybe some of the big speeches might even be songs. I said I was a lyricist and I'd be happy to see what I could do and Humphrey said he'd have a go at the music himself."

"He's a composer?"

"Not really, but he has a good ear and he knows a lot about ancient instruments."

"Claire will be thrilled to hear this."

He referred my collaborator, Claire Simmons. I usually seek Claire's insights on all matters, personal and creative, for she is a great dispenser of astute advice, solicited and otherwise. I had, however, kept her completely in the dark about Humphrey. This was partly because I felt that, given her hidebound views on experimental theater, she would not soon take to him, but mainly because I knew she'd be incensed at my taking time from our own efforts to write with him.

"I haven't told Claire. She'd only get mad. We're supposed to be writing a club act for this rich old would-be chanteuse and I keep putting it off. But I have to work with Humphrey. It's the only way I can be alone with him."

"You get to be alone with him?"

"Yes."

"Then why don't you make a move?"

"There's no opportunity to—he's all business."

"Have you tried to make him laugh? You're good at that."

"Not with him, I'm not. He's more the serious type. Besides, all we ever talk about are the shows and if I make jokes he'll think I'm making fun of them, which I'd never do because they're really—"

"Searing and brilliant. I know. And I'm Claudette Colbert. Have you tried flattering him?"

"To a point."

"What do you mean, 'to a point'?"

"Well, I don't want to seem fawning or obsequious. There's such a thing as laying it on too thick."

Gilbert's eyes Ping-Ponged off the ceiling.

"*Not* where experimental artists are concerned, dear. Believe me—I've wooed my share of trailblazers and there is not a *thing* you can say to them about their work that will strike them as the teeniest bit excessive."

"You're sure?"

"Absolutely. Pile it on. Of course," he continued, "flattery by itself isn't enough. What you really need is something to create some special bond between you."

"We're working on the show together."

"You and him and a dozen other people. What you need is something you share with him and you alone."

He paused awhile in meditation, the feverish contortions of his face reflecting the cerebral gymnastics transpiring just behind it.

At length he squinted a bit and said, "This sister of his, the one in the wheelchair—is he very close to her?"

"Oh, yes. Extremely. He's over at her place two or three times a week, looking after her, cooking dinner, that sort of thing."

"So she's important to him?"

"Yes."

"Good. Tell him you've got one, too."

I blinked.

"One what?"

"A handicapped sister. Say you have one. You don't tell many people because it's difficult for you to talk about her. Of course, it can't seem *too* big a coincidence, so be sure to make her handicapped in a different way than his is. Not much worse though—he sounds awfully competitive."

I stared at him, waiting for the burst of laughter that would prove he was joking. It didn't come.

"Gilbert, that is the most appalling suggestion I've ever heard."

"What's wrong with it? It will give you something really personal to discuss together. You can compare notes, swap stories . . . talk about how guilty you both feel that she should have to suffer while you're all right. It will make him think you understand things about him no one else can. And then one night when you're talking about it, start to cry a little. He'll hug you—and that's when you pounce."

"That is *despicable!*"

"Why! You'll be happy to have him. He'll be happy that you can empathize with him. I mean, Christ, Philip, do you want him or not?"

"Gilbert, you jerk! You can't build a relationship on lies."

"Oh, *no!* And you really *adore* big long antiwar collages!"

"That's another kind of lie altogether," I said indignantly. "I tell the sort of lie *you're* suggesting and for the next year I'm lying in bed awake every night worried half to death!"

"And who's lying next to you?"

In the next week I saw Humphrey several times to work on the *Trojan Women* songs. While naturally determined to scorn Gilbert's outlandish advice concerning tragic siblings, I felt that his point about flattery was perhaps well taken. I praised Humphrey extravagantly at every opportunity, even when it made me feel guilty to do so, as praise was not entirely warranted. This was particularly the case during our songwriting sessions, for it was soon apparent that Humphrey's gifts, so abundant in other areas, did not extend to composition.

Gilbert, however, had been remarkably prescient in asserting that no compliment, however immoderate, would strike him as more than his due. He even seconded my opinion that his melody for Hecuba to wail after the murder of Astyanax, was "soaring and heart-rending" even though the tune was, if truth be told, wrong for the moment and uncomfortably similar to "How Do You Solve A Problem Like Maria?"

But the strategy, while guilt-inducing, was undeniably effective. I grew in Humphrey's favor and he seemed eager to have me around. He even returned my compliments, and sought out my opinions in front of the cast (having already, I suppose, a fair suspicion as to what they might be).

Still, if Humphrey was often willing to praise me, he was equally willing to offer gentle criticism of those aspects of my character he felt were in need of repair. He was especially appalled by my taste for light entertainment, a taste which, though I attempted to play it down, was betrayed by his first glance at my bookshelves and record collection.

"Philip! Such an appetite you have for this garbage!" he said as he poked among the show albums. "Don't you listen to anything else?"

I tried to draw his attention to the bottom shelf where he would find a smattering of jazz vocals and an album of "Best Loved Melodies of Chopin," but he was already perusing a small bookcase the contents of which were heavily weighted toward film star biographies.

"Really, Philip," he said, frowning down at Mary Astor, "you have such a wonderful, perceptive mind but what good does it do you if you stuff it full of glitz and nonsense?"

I made some lame remark about Hollywood films being the mythology of our time but he countered that this was exactly what was wrong with our time, adding sadly that he expected better from one who had shown such keen interest, not only in the exalted poetry of ancient Greece but in Eskimo creation myths as well. I assured him that I'd found my recent foray into Euripides far more compelling than a hundred old films and that I couldn't wait to broaden my studies.

By the time he left I'd arranged to borrow *Hesiod's Theogony*, *The Golden Bough*, *Death in Venice*, plus several other volumes I probably wouldn't have requested had Humphrey not been wearing cutoffs. I ploughed dutifully through every book and peppered my conversation with quotes.

Despite these efforts, however, romance did not seem to be blossoming. If Humphrey was aware of my feelings he never in any way acknowledged them. At times it seemed he simply took it for granted that I, like most of the men in his life, suffered passionate longings for him which we would all, poor dears, have to cope with as best we could. I was not the only man in the company with a thing for him. Two of the actors treated me with a veiled hostility that grew less veiled the more time I spent in his company, and the atmosphere of competition only increased my fears and misery.

Work continued on the songs and soon two were ready to go into the show. I'd mentioned them to Gilbert, confessing my chagrin at the way they'd turned out, and he was unable as such to resist attending the performance on the night they went in. Never a master of the diplomatic response, he fled right after the curtain and left his machine on for a week.

One Monday night I was at Humphrey's trying to find a delicate way to suggest to him that his melody for Cassandra's mad scene might strike some as unduly reminiscent of "Stormy Weather." We were interrupted by the phone.

"Well, how are *you?*" said Humphrey in a warm, coquettish voice that made my throat close in panic.

"Yes, I had a nice time, too," he said. "You were right—the food there is excellent."

I sat at the table, trying to seem absorbed in my rhyming dictionary while inwardly straining every cell in my brain, listening, interpereting, probing the nuance of each word and inflection.

"You are completely *shameless!*" he said, and laughed.

The tone was flirtatious but not intimate, like one pursued but not yet captured. But if my rival was indeed "shameless" how far away could conquest be!

"I would too, really, but this is a very bad week for me. I'm putting more changes into my production. Why don't you call again Sunday and we'll plan something then?"

He paused and then spoke in an absolute purr.

"Well, we'll have to see about *that*."

Returning to my side he picked up his lyre and started plucking out feverish variations on his melody. A minute later I pointed to the wall where there was a photo of a pretty woman in a wheelchair.

"Is that your sister?" I asked.

"Yes. It was taken several years ago. She's even prettier now."

I asked him why she was in a wheelchair. He told me that one day when they were children they had been riding their bikes together and she was hit by a car. He spoke of how brave she had been and of how much he admired her courage.

I stared for a long moment at the alabaster bicep protruding from the sleeve of his polo shirt. Then I swallowed hard and said, yes, I felt much the same way about my sister.

And so Betty was born, emerging from nothingness a detail

at a time as Humphrey, his tone alive with curiosity and compassion, probed for fresh information. Each innocent query posed some new conundrum about which I had no time whatsoever to think before responding. Indeed, her biography was improvised in such blind haste that I felt less like the instrument of her creation than an appalled spectator.

"You never told me you had a sister!"

"Well, you never asked."

"You say she's handicapped?"

"Yes.

"Like Marthe?" he asked, referring to his own.

I recalled Gilbert's warning against excessive coincidence. "No, not like Marthe. She never had an accident or anything."

"What's the matter with her?"

"She's mentally retarded," I said.

What? Whoa! Wait! Back up! Rewind! She's blind but only in one eye and I only brought it up because—

"Is she severely retarded?"

"It depends on what you call severe."

"I mean, is she helpless and incontinent and—?"

"Oh, no! Nothing like that! She's just   slow. I mean, she's practically my age but—"

"She has the mind of a child?"

"Yes. Five or six. Somewhere in there."

"Philip, you never mentioned this. Even when I spoke of my own sister."

"Well, it's not that I'm ashamed or anything. It's just, you know, some things are private. I don't share them with just anyone."

"Am I just anyone?" he asked, injured.

"Of course not! That's why I'm telling you now."

Humphrey's questions continued and I could not help but notice that the more poignant were my replies, the more physically demonstrative he became. Some affecting detail would cause him to sigh gently and touch my hair, or give my knee a tender little squeeze. And so agreeable were these caresses that I soon found myself spouting horridly calculating reminiscences of Betty's childhood, detailing her slow progress under dedicated tutors, her heartbreaking setbacks and her tiny, hard-won victories which brought such joy to my family. Now and again, a nervous astonishment at my own mendacity caused a tremor to creep into my voice. He asked if I thought a glass of wine might calm me and I said I'd be pleased to have one if he would join me.

As the October light faded Humphrey lit candles and we sat drinking wine and sharing stories about the struggles of our sisters. We spoke of our love for them and our purposeless but nagging remorse at having been spared their afflictions.

It wasn't hard for me to describe the most agonizing guilt for every lie I uttered filled me with fresh pangs. Several times I was ready to blurt out the truth and try to pass the whole thing off as some playwright's exercise in empathy. But then Humphrey would rest a hand on my shoulder and I'd hear myself telling the story about when Betty found the puppy under the Christmas tree. Soon there were tears in his eyes and seeing them there brought tears to my own. He brushed one of mine away, and as he did I took his hand and held it against my cheek. We stared at each other.

The stare, among other things, lengthened, and soon we were rolling about on the sofa, necking furiously, and his hands began fumbling with our belts. A shrill voice within me seemed to cry out, "*Stop this!* You can't possibly let yourself have him under these circumstances!" But as I mentioned earlier, Humphrey's physical charms had an uncanny way of drowning things out and by the time he'd unbuttoned his shirt I couldn't hear a thing.

The next morning I awoke to find Humphrey gone and in his place an affectionately worded note explaining that he was buying breakfast and would soon return. I scrambled down to the bathroom and performed those morning ablutions which take on a special urgency after a first night with a new paramour. These completed, I sank down on his sofa and pondered my situation which seemed, to say the least, fraught with distressing complexities.

Having longed to win my beloved's affection by being worthy of it, I had won it instead by being as unworthy as could be imagined. I had resorted to tactics so dishonest, so unscrupulous, so Gilbertian in nature that my conscience fairly screamed to confess the deed and be cleansed of it.

Yet how could I do so? If it was painful to contemplate the guilt I would suffer if I continued deceiving him, it was more painful still to imagine the hatred he would feel for me if he discovered I'd seduced him with a lie.

And what about the sex! I recalled the previous night, small details of which flashed enticingly through my mind, coming attractions, so to speak, for nights yet to be. Yet one honest word would be all it would take to ensure that I would never taste such delights again!

My reasoning, from that moment on, grew even more elaborate and contorted than the lovemaking had been.

Clearly I had proven unworthy of Humphrey's affections. But this was due, not to any innate flaw in myself but rather to Gilbert's corrupting influence. I now had to prove to Humphrey that I truly *was* worthy of his love. But since I could not prove *anything* to him if banished from his society, the only thing to do was to continue with the ruse.

I would, however, while prolonging this one relatively minor deception, strive to be, in all other respects, Humphrey's vision of the ideal beau. By doing so I would prepare for the inevitable confession, accruing great stores of love and esteem which I could then squander on forgiveness.

In the weeks that followed I worked tirelessly to achieve this goal. I read virtually every volume in Humphrey's theater library and what I could not comprehend I asked him to explicate, realizing in short order that the less I understood the better, as he dearly loved to explain things. I exercised daily and lived on fish and raw vegetables. My demeanor became more earnest. I was sensitive, empathetic, less quick to judge and more open to unconventional ideas and forms of expression. Whenever I felt my old sarcasm threatening to return—as I often did—I suppressed it ruthlessly. Friends commented on the change in me, sometimes in rather disparaging terms. I tried to see where they were coming from and forgive them.

Humphrey often visited his sister and he began taking me along occasionally. I leaped at this chance to show what a caring person I could be and whenever a visit was impending I searched for some small gift I could bring Marthe to brighten her day.

Marthe was a small woman of twenty-six with a lovely, frail beauty. She was always pleasant to me but from the first moment we met I sensed a wariness from her which, coming so immediately, made me wonder about my predecessor. Either she adored him and resented the substitution or else she loathed him and was thinking, *Oh, God, here we go again.*

Her attitude toward Humphrey also puzzled me. I could see that she cared deeply for him, but he had spoken often of her passionate interest in his work and this interest was not apparent.

"Philip," he said, introducing me, "is a lyricist."

"Musicals?" she asked brightly.

"A few." I blushed.

"Right now he's working with me on songs for my *Trojan Women.*"

"Oh."

"The last two go in next week—you can come see it at last!"

"Oh, good. Though you've told me so much about it I sort of feel like I already have."

"The cast is wonderful," I said.

"Do they leave you—I mean, is there much participation?"

During our visits Humphrey would fuss and cluck over her, cooking and fetching things and performing simple tasks she was obviously capable of doing for herself. I could see she was annoyed by this but she seldom betrayed it. She suffered his ministrations in silence and even thanked him, till it was not clear who was doing whom the favor. Her patience and good humor made me like her very much and want to do things for her, which was, of course, just what she didn't want, but she forbore my kindnesses as patiently as she did Humphrey's.

My fondness for Marthe brought me closer to Humphrey, but it had troublesome consequences as well. My rapport with her only increased his eagerness to meet Betty.

I originally thought I'd gotten around the problem by placing Betty in a cozy group home upstate where I visited her once a week. As his queries about when he might accompany me grew more frequent I did my best to make the notion unappealing, claiming that the trip took four hours each way and involved changing buses twice in dreary little towns. This put him off for a while but in time he began to feel guilty at begrudging the effort and grew more insistent.

My evasions left him hurt and, worse, suspicious. Was she worse off than I'd let on? Was I ashamed of her? Was I ashamed of *him?* Did I feel he would not know how to behave, that he would be insensitive to her limitations and try to discuss Pinter with her? I fielded his questions as skillfully as I could, claiming always that this particular week wasn't good for one reason or another. But I could tell that although he accepted my explanations, his suspicions were growing daily. Either an introduction would take place soon or all would be lost.

"Well, what do you want *me* to do?"

"*Something!* I wouldn't have this problem if it weren't for you, Gilbert!"

"No, and you wouldn't be fucking your brains out with Humpy three times a week either. I think if anything a little gratitude's in order."

"Thanks ever so much. Now what the hell do I do about Betty?"

Gilbert's shoulders shrugged noncommittally as he buried his face deeper into my refrigerator.

"Tell him she moved. Tell him she died."

"After all my stalling? He'd know I was lying and he'd never trust me again!"

"And God knows he ought to. You *know* I hate Swiss cheese and it's the only kind you ever buy."

"Gilbert, this is serious! I've never had anyone even close to this good. I mean, God—you saw him."

"When?"

"In *Trojan Women.*"

"Oh, right," said Gilbert, a little too casually. "He's okay, I suppose."

"*Okay?* You're *seething* with jealousy and you know it. He's perfect—and I don't want to lose him over some ridiculous lie."

"Then find a Betty!"

"Oh, *thank* you. No problem! I'll just phone Bellevue Hospital and arrange for a rental!"

"I mean get someone to impersonate her."

"Who am I going to ask to do a thing like that? The only woman I'm close to who's the right age for it is Claire."

Gilbert frowned.

"I don't suppose she'd do it."

"She'd find the idea completely deplorable. Besides, she's mad at me because I owe her material."

Gilbert took a container of chicken salad from the fridge and began eating it with his fingers. The kitchen was silent but for the sound of his meditative chewing.

There was merit in his suggestion that Betty could move away. I might invent, say, a pair of religious grandparents living in Arizona who had expressed a sudden desire to look after her. But if Humphrey's suspicions were ever to be quelled, her departure would have to wait until he was at least satisfied of her existence.

I looked to Gilbert and saw that a smug smile was spreading slowly across his face.

"What?"

"You're haven't told Claire about Humpy yet?"

"Don't call him that. And no, I haven't."

"Well," he beamed, "then your problems are solved."

He proceeded to outline a suggestion that I found tenuous in the extreme. I told him this and he replied that if I had a better idea then he would very much enjoy my sharing it with him, though I would, he trusted, excuse him if he declined to hold his breath while waiting. I ushered him out of my apartment, fell onto my bed and spent the better part of six hours applying every ounce of intelligence I possessed to solving the dilemma.

Then I phoned Gilbert and said, "So what was this plan again?"

That night I greeted Humphrey with the news that I was bringing Betty into the city one afternoon next week. Could he swing by my apartment and have lunch with us? He responded exuberantly in the affirmative and I named a day, making certain to choose one on which he had already scheduled a rehearsal of his new piece, a Kabuki *Timon of Athens*. He regretted how brief the lunch would have to be, but felt, quite mistakenly, that it would be the first of many.

Then, muttering a nervous prayer, I called Claire. Everything depended on her.

"Hi!" I said cheerfully. "What have you been up to?"

"I've been stalling an irate, aging soprano who paid up front. It's great fun. You should try it sometime."

"I'm sorry. I have the opening done."

"What about the patter song?"

"Umm . . ."

"Swell. I'll just phone and say you've been captured by pirates."

I groveled a bit, then explained that I hadn't gotten around to it because I'd been busy with volunteer work. I'd joined Project Boost, an organization that provided services for the mentally challenged, and I was now spending several hours a week as a companion to a retarded man in his twenties. This revelation was followed by a moment of silence.

"Are you still there?"

"Yes. Forgive me for saying so," said Claire evenly, "but this doesn't sound at all like you."

"I know." I squirmed. "But a few weeks ago I was watching PBS and I saw this documentary about their work. It seemed like something I'd find really rewarding if I could just get off my duff and do it. I kept thinking, I spend so much time fucking off and how hard would it be to give a little of that time to some poor disadvantaged . . ."

I continued in this vein for some minutes, racking up hours in hell, and at length Claire seemed convinced.

"Well, Philip, I think that's wonderful. I'm really very proud of you."

"Thanks." I winced. "Anyway, what I wanted to ask you is would you like to come to lunch next Saturday and meet the fellow I'm working with. His name is Humphrey."

"I'd be happy to."

"Good," I said, and proceeded to give her strict instructions (garnered from my hours in Project Boost's training program) as to how she should behave when she met my young charge.

She should speak slowly, as slowly as she could manage, providing little spaces between words so that he would have time to comprehend. She must confine her vocabulary to simple words of not more than two syllables and avoid abstract concepts entirely as they would only baffle and upset him. Humphrey, I told her, had the mind of a four-year-old and a tremendously fragile ego. He was aware that most people were brighter than him but became hurt and even hysterical when he felt they were going out of their way to demonstrate this to him. Violent tantrums were not out of the question, and as he was physically quite robust all care should be taken not to induce one.

And, oh yes—he sometimes got odd ideas into his head, but she should not consider these small misapprehensions alarming or strange as they all had clear roots in his formative years. In childhood, for instance, he seldom met anyone outside his immediate family and so continued to assume that all the people he met were related by ties of blood. In more recent years, a constantly shifting array of institutional nurses had left him easily confused about names and given, as such, to whimsically addressing others by whatever name entered his head. She should be flattered if he called her Betty, because that had been his mother's name.

The intervening five days passed in just under twenty minutes. When the joyful morning arrived I rose late, breakfasted on half a pint of Mylanta, and quit the apartment. I had instructed Humphrey to let himself in around noon and I could not be there since I was supposed to be fetching Betty from Utica.

I stopped by Claire's place at one. I had advised her not to wear makeup as Humphrey had a way of wetting his finger and trying to paint with it, so her round face was completely unadorned. As we walked the few blocks to my place, I nervously reiterated my instructions until she grew rather waspish. Why, she exclaimed, to hear me go on one would think *she* was the mentally handicapped one! I stared, appalled at her perspicacity and Claire, taking this as a rebuke, lowered her eyes and said she was sorry to have uttered such a "dreadful flippancy."

I opened my door and there sat Humphrey, smiling beatifically and wearing the Mickey Mouse sweatshirt I had loaned him, explaining that Mickey was a great favorite of Betty's.

"Hi!" sang Humphrey, waving, as if to a child of two.

"Hi!" sang Claire, waving right back.

"Look who's here!" I said to Humphrey. "Look who's here!" I repeated, avoiding Claire's name. He was allowed to get it wrong but I wasn't.

"I know who *you* are!" said Humphrey, rising and extending a hand. "You're Betty!"

"That's right!" I said, shooting a surprised look at Claire. There! it said. He's taken to you already!

Claire pumped his hand happily and said, "Yes, I'm Betty. And I know your name. You're Humphrey!"

"That's me!" he said with a grin. "I'm Humphrey!"

"And that's Mickey!" said Claire, pointing to his shirt.

"Yes!" concurred Humphrey. "You like Mickey?"

"Oh, *yes*," said Claire. "I like Mickey a lot!"

"Me too!!" said Humphrey.

"Me three!" I said in a high squeaky Mickey voice and we all had a good laugh over that.

Humphrey beamed at me and announced that he'd already made lunch. I had instructed him that Betty was devoted to fluffer-nutters, a virtually inedible combination of peanut butter and marshmallow fluff. I'd hoped that their dense gluey consistency would serve as a nice impediment to conversation and I smiled to see a large platter of them waiting on the coffee table.

"Who wants some nice cold milk?" I asked and both my guests responded enthusiastically. Betty said she would get it and cheerfully bustled off to the kitchen.

Humphrey took the opportunity to turn to me and mouth the words, *"She's so sweet!"* His look was so gentle and lovestruck that even in my panic it made me melt. *Oh, lord*, I thought, *I want him always to look at me that way!* Then a cold dread overcame me when I thought that his continued affection depended entirely upon my ability to keep two opinionated highly articulate adults talking to each other like five-year-olds for the next forty minutes.

Claire returned holding two glasses of milk and it was then that a merciful providence intervened. Claire, grinning madly at Humphrey and saying, "Nice cold milk!" tripped on my throw rug and sent one glass shattering to the floor. She gave a little gasp and stared down at the spill with a flustered look. Humphrey, his heart bleeding for poor Betty, who had, after all, only been doing her best, fixed her with a look of tragic empathy, his bottom lip distended in a furious pout.

"Awwwwwww," he said, then looking down at the spill. *"Bad* rug! *Bad* rug!"

"Bad rug!" agreed Claire, and stamped her foot angrily on it

several times. And as I cleaned up the spill I thought, *forget it!* I'm a *genius! I'm home free!*

We sat for fifteen minutes or so, exchanging big smiles and chewing our fluffer-nutters, muttering the occasional "Yum yum!" while rubbing our tummies with pleasure. There were a few efforts at communication but so dense and mucilaginous were the sandwiches that each incomprehensible effort at speech dissolved into giggles, further enhancing the general air of arrested development.

By the time lunch was finished Humphrey had only twenty minutes left. I knew that these minutes would be among the trickiest but so breezy was my confidence that I started the ball rolling by informing Claire that Humphrey had made the lunch especially for her.

"All by yourself?" asked Claire.

"Yes," said Humphrey, beaming. "Just for you!"

"Thank you very much," she replied. Then she rose, took the platter and began placing all our glasses and the milk carton upon it in a somewhat precarious fashion.

"You made the sandwiches, Humphrey, so *I* should do the dishes."

Humphrey, fearing another clumsy mishap that might prove ruinous to Betty's self-esteem, rose sharply and said, more loudly than he intended to, "*No!* Let me do it!"

Claire, taken aback by his outburst, and warned of his violent and irrational temper, dropped, panic-stricken, to the sofa.

"I'm sorry!" she gasped.

"No, *I'm* sorry!" said Humphrey, himself in agony at having scared her.

"No, *I'm* sorry!"

"Don't be sorry!"

"Okay I'm not!" said Claire, terrified.

"Why don't we just leave them for later?" I asked. Both nodded vigorously and a rather strained silence descended.

At length Claire broke it by saying that she thought Humphrey was a lovely name. Humphrey replied that Betty was nice, too. Claire, her phrasing slow and cautious, remarked that there was a very famous movie star and his name was Humphrey Bogart. Humphrey smiled proudly and said that he knew this.

"Is Philip a nice brother?" he asked.

Claire turned to me, puzzled, and I gave a little nod.

"Oh, yes. Philip is a very nice brother."

"And Betty's a very nice sister."

Claire asked Humphrey in a voice of concern if he liked where he lived.

"Oh, yes. It's on the Lower . . . East . . . Side," he said, pronouncing it as if it were some exotic Mandarin province. "It's big and sunny and I like it a lot."

"What do you like to do there?"

He said that he liked to listen to nice music, and sometimes he painted pictures. He also liked to make up plays.

"You make up plays in your head?" asked Claire eagerly.

"Yes. It's fun."

"I like to make up songs," she said.

"Good for you, Betty! Would you sing me one of your songs?"

I flashed a warning look at Claire and her eyes widened with the realization that our songs were a trifle sophisticated to be grasped by Humphrey. She sputtered something about her songs not being very good. But Humphrey would have none of it.

"I bet they're real good!" he said, and looked to me to goad her.

"Betty is shy!" I said. "Hey, who wants to play Old Maid?" I asked, suddenly remembering that I had a purchased a deck of the appropriate cards in anticipation of just such stickiness as this. I produced these now and all talk of culture was mercifully banished.

The game did not proceed swiftly. Claire, terrified that a loss might provoke Humphrey into another hysterical tantrum, was doing her best to lose, and Humphrey, seeing how extraordinarily inept a player poor Betty was, grew equally determined not to hurt her feelings by winning. As a result, minutes ticked slowly by as the lack of pairs matched defied all odds of mathematical probability. This was fine by me as each second brought closer the moment when I could rise and announce that it was time for Humphrey to go.

I had just happily matched one ballerina with her twin when the phone rang. My heart fairly exploded at the sound but then

I remembered that the machine was on and I could simply ignore the call.

"Don't worry," I said. "The machine will answer the phone. Oh, look, Betty—here's the other fireman!"

The machine clicked on and my heart stopped as I heard the voice of an excited Nancy Malone. She was speaking very loudly to be heard over the actors' warm-up, which was going on in the background.

"Philip! It's Nancy! Is Humphrey there now? It's important!"

Humphrey rose sharply as did Claire's eyebrows since Nancy was a friend of hers as well.

"Is that Nancy *Malone*?" she asked, forgetting, in her surprise, to speak in the Mister Rogers tone she'd employed all afternoon.

Humphrey stared at her, baffled and Nancy breathlessly continued.

"We just got a call from this *Village Voice* reporter! He wants to do a piece all about you and the company, and he says—"

Humphrey bounded over my sofa with a swift, surefooted agility that Claire would not, I feared, ascribe to his many years of experience competing in the Special Olympics.

"Yes, yes, I'm here!" he said, snatching up the phone. "What about the *Village Voice*?"

I looked to Claire, doing my best to wear an expression suggesting delighted astonishment at the strides, literal and figurative, my young charge was making, but the effort soon proved overwhelming and I turned hopelessly back to Humphrey.

"Well, it's about *time!*" he said, snorting indignantly. "We've been doing the most dynamic work in the city for two years now and all they've written about is mainstream crap and the so-called innovative bullshit those assholes in Soho have been doing. Do you think this may be in response to my letter? Oh, hold on—" he said and turned to us. "Excuse me, I'll be with you in a minute. This is wonderful!"

He looked at Claire and said in an utterly infantile voice, "My friend has nice news! It makes me happy!"

"If Humphrey happy, Betty happy too."

He babbled away for another moment then hung up, crossed to where I stood and gave me a huge ecstatic hug. I clung to him tightly, feeling that the opportunity would not, in all likelihood, present itself again.

"Happy news!" he gushed over my shoulder. "A man who works at a newspaper"—he grabbed a copy of the *Times* and waved it for Claire's edification—"he wants to write a story all about the plays I make up."

"Nothing like exposure, is there?" said Claire pointedly.

"Exposure!" said Humphrey, impressed. "That's a very good word."

"Sit down, dear. I have a bunch of them."

"Oh, wow," said Gilbert. "Were they really pissed?"

"Oh, *no!* We all had a huge laugh and then we went out for pizza."

"I mean, he didn't actually get violent, did he?"

"Not unless you count ransacking my apartment, toppling bookshelves in an effort to take back everything he ever gave me."

"Poor baby!" clucked Gilbert, and signaled for two more margaritas.

"And of course Claire will never speak to me again."

"Oh, she'll get over it. Just tell her it was my idea and she can blame it all on me."

"What I don't understand is the stupid *Voice* interview. Nancy says it was all a hoax."

"A hoax?"

"They called the reporter back and the number he left turned out to be a pay phone."

"Probably some idiot Humphrey didn't cast in a show," said Gilbert, sagely. "Anyway, Philip . . . you'll get over him. I mean, you weren't really that compatible."

"I know we weren't. But I loved him!"

"A passing infatuation. It would never have lasted. You know that deep down you can't stand Eskimo plays and Kabuki Shakespeare. It would only have been a matter of weeks before— what's the matter? You look funny."

"I don't believe I ever mentioned that Humphrey was doing a Kabuki Shakespeare."

"Didn't you?"

"No."

"I must have heard it from someone else," he said, pushing his chair a bit back from the table.

"Who?"

"I'm not really sure. I've been so busy lately—"

"Doing what?" I asked, leaning forward over the table. "Writing on theater for the *Village Voice?*"

Gilbert smiled weakly and inched away. I made a grab for his collar but it was no good. Gilbert, vastly more experienced than I in the mechanics of sudden flight, was out of the bar before I'd even stood up. He'd left his shoulder bag on the floor and, searching through it, I found, as I'd suspected, paperback editions of *Timon of Athens, The Oresteia Trilogy* and *Lives of the Scandinavian Dramatists.* I sat there, asthmatic with rage, more at myself than Gilbert, since I should have known, from the moment he'd laid eyes on an armor-clad Humphrey onstage, that he was no longer to be trusted.

But after another drink my rage subsided a bit and as I leafed through the three books, plus a thick hardcover tome entitled *Learning Esperanto*, I began to feel a certain sense of relief.

A smile bloomed on my lips as I thought of Gilbert, whose tastes ran toward early Judith Krantz, slogging dutifully through page after page of Euripides, Grotowski and Joseph Campbell, Humphrey quizzing him constantly to make sure that he was absorbing it all. And the smile broadened when I saw that Gilbert had left not only the books but his wallet as well.

An hour later I was humming happily as I stood at the register in Tower Records.

"Goodness me!" said the short, cute clerk. "You sure you can carry all these?"

"I'll manage," I said, handing him Gilbert's American Express Card.

"We certainly like our show music, don't we!"

MEETING IMELDA MARCOS

• CHRISTOPHER BRAM •

THREE WEEKS AFTER his return to the States and the dank chill
of Washington in winter, Jim Goodall drove down to Virginia
Beach for his nephew's wedding. The occasion only deepened
his low spirits. He was forty-five years old and useless in the
world. Marcos had seized power by declaring martial law and
Kissinger supported the ruse, despite everything Jim and a few
others had reported from Manila. Robbie dropped out of college and married a nice girl who worked in a Fotomat, despite
Jim's years of hoping for something original from the boy.

At the reception at the Ramada Inn, his sister's family exiled
Jim in his perfect Hong Kong-tailored tux to a small table with
his niece, Meg, her new boyfriend from William and Mary,
and a wet-eyed old woman in a beige wig whom nobody
seemed to know. The rest of the family shared the big table up
front with the raucous new in-laws. Jim had learned over the
years one can't improvise a personal life through someone else's
family, but it hurt to be reminded again how superfluous he
was.

"Poor old Robbie," Meg scoffed. "So proud and smug up
there. Like marriage was the Nobel prize. Well, even dork
brothers deserve to be happy."

She sounded more good-humored than nasty about it, a
witty twist to her mouth. Meg seemed to be at an age where
she saw through everyone, and wanted people to know. Jim
wondered if she saw through him. He had to remind himself
repeatedly she was nineteen now, because he couldn't look at
her baby-fat cheeks or large brown eyes without seeing his
niece at fifteen, ten or seven, as if she would always be the little

tomboy who admired him without reason, who disappeared a half hour before he ended each visit because goodbyes embarrassed her. Today she wore a velvety blue dress with a high womanly collar, but her long straight hair and lack of lipstick suggested a girl in jeans and a sweater.

"You feeling okay, Jim?" She'd been dropping the "uncle" all day, as if toying with who they were to each other.

"I always cry at weddings," Jim teased.

"If they really were in love," said Meg, "they would've eloped. This is like they need to act it out in front of people to tell themselves it's real."

"Bad faith," said the boyfriend, nibbling a wingette. "This must seem rather comical, sir. After embassy parties, dinners with dictators."

"Not at all," Jim replied. "This is family."

The boyfriend, Doug, was terribly polite and respectful, but phrases constantly popped out, which suggested he thought Jim was the enemy. His dull blond hair tied back in a ponytail, anemic sideburns and faint stars of acne on his pale face, he looked like the kind of cocky student who'd consider anyone with the Establishment the enemy. His mouth kept closing in a placid, lipless smile.

"Doug read your piece in *Foreign Affairs*," said Meg. "Before he knew we were related. Doug reads almost everything."

Doug smiled at Jim. "I'm just curious. Power fascinates me. Corruption, too."

There were the usual rituals after the cake, but Meg didn't join the girls jumping for the bouquet, and neither Jim nor Doug got up for the bride's garter. Dancing followed and Meg and Doug sat that out too, but Jim went over and asked his sister for a dance.

"It's almost over," Ann groaned through her grin while Jim gingerly steered her around the floor. Looking lively and inexhaustible from across the room, she appeared shell-shocked up close, her grin a weary baring of teeth. "You're welcomed to come back to the house afterwards. But Rick and I are just going to collapse."

"I should go back to the motel and collapse myself, thank you."

"Might be best all around." Ann sounded relieved. "You been having a good chat with your niece?"

"She's becoming quite the woman," Jim said automatically.

"Still waters run deep. I don't know what to make of this Doug. Two of a kind, eggheads both of them. You were like that at their age. What do you make of him?"

"He seems nice enough. Well-spoken. Polite."

"Too polite," said Ann. "I wish he didn't remind me of Eddie Haskell."

The music changed and Jim and Ann stepped off to the side to make their goodbyes. Ann patted Jim's stomach, a new gesture. His brother-in-law's stomach bulged badly in his rented tux and Jim wondered if Ann missed the presence of a flat male stomach in her household.

"But you had a nice time? Did it make you feel sorry you never got married?"

"A little," Jim lied. He loved his sister and needed to humor her. He kissed her goodbye on the cheek, thanked her for inviting him and returned to the table to say good night to Meg.

"We were leaving too," said Meg. "In fact, Doug and I were wondering if you'd like company. It's going to be a regular marriage morgue back at the house."

Jim had thought he wanted to be alone, but he liked the idea. Ann was concerned about Meg; maybe she needed his advice. He invited them back to his motel, warning them he was in no shape to do anything except sit and talk. On their way out, Jim noticed Robbie dancing and laughing with his bride and long-haired buddies, having too good a time to notice old Uncle Jim's departure.

His motel was down at the oceanfront, ten miles away. Meg rode with Jim, Doug following in his yellow Volkswagen bug. It was cold in Jim's car and Meg kicked off her shoes to sit on her nyloned feet.

"Good to see you again, Meg-wump. Been what? Almost four years. And now you're in college. I can hardly believe it. Where have all the flowers gone?" Jim used to know how to talk to his niece, but tonight he heard himself babbling.

"God I hate family," said Meg. "Oh, not you, Jim. You were smart to go off on your own. My nuclear family. There's times I'd like to nuke *them*."

Meg claimed Robbie's wedding had given her parents marriage fever. All through Christmas break she'd been feeling everyone thought she should be the one dropping out to make grandchildren, that money for a college education was wasted on a girl. Jim enjoyed being an ear for her unhappiness; it made him feel tender.

"They don't think that," Jim assured her. "Your mother finished college."

"And look what she did with it," Meg muttered. "What do you think of Doug?"

"Doug? Well-spoken. Polite." Jim decided he should return Meg's trust with a little honesty. "I just met him, but he seems bland to me. Unformed. Young."

"Really?" Meg sounded intrigued by his disapproval, not hurt. "You know, he really wanted to meet you."

Jim hesitated, then snorted. "The family eccentric? The black sheep?"

"*I'm* the black sheep," Meg insisted. "But seriously. Doug was curious about you. He's interested in foreign policy and life overseas. I kind of used you as bait to get him down here for the wedding."

He wouldn't visit without bait? What kind of boyfriend was that? Jim looked in the rearview mirror and saw the yellow Volkswagen puttering close behind them. A streetlight swept overhead and there was a glimpse of Doug at the wheel, pale and vague, his mouth lightly sealed in that catlike smile. "I take it *you* like him."

"Oh, yeah." Meg had roped some hair around her fingers; she gave it a tug. "I think I'm in love with him. Or something."

Ocean boiled and snored in the darkness out beyond the empty parking lot of Jim's motel. As they stepped inside, Jim found himself irritably conscious of Doug. Ponytail whisking from side to side, the boy walked with Meg with his hands in the pockets of his bulky army jacket, showing more interest in the layout of the motel than in Meg or her uncle. The boy wasn't unattractive, yet there was nothing lovably solid about him. He seemed self-effacing, yet something about him suggested he smugly believed he would never be invisible.

"What did you guys want to do?" Jim asked in his room. "Watch television? Talk about weather? I'm afraid there's nothing I can offer you to drink."

Meg and Doug said they'd drunk too much already. They sat together on a bed.

Jim opened the curtains. The ocean was barely visible through the reflection in the sliding glass door, rows of silent white breakers floating through the image of a motel room. Jim watched himself there while he undid his bow tie and shook off his black jacket. His red hair was thinning, his face still burned from Manila. Jim never tanned, only burned, peeled, then burned again. He expected Meg and Doug to hold hands, but they didn't. This generation must express love—"Or something"—differently.

They talked. Actually, Doug and Jim did most of the talking, Jim seated in a chair at the vanity table, Doug at the foot of the bed. Meg sat beside Doug, leaning back on her elbows, calmly watching the men.

"But you were mainly in Manila, Mr. Goodall? Never Vietnam?"

"Oh, made a few inspection tours of the embassy in Saigon when I was with INR. Odd city. More like an American service town than anything Asian, until recently. You hardly know there's a war going on until you get out in the countryside." But Jim couldn't talk about that. "No, Manila, Singapore for six months, Bangkok. A year in Finland to keep me from going native."

"Do you think the Paris Peace Accords are close to getting signed or did Kissinger say that just to get Nixon reelected?"

"They'll get signed. Soon." Which was what made Kissinger and the rest so blindly confident about their other decisions. Jim couldn't discuss that either.

"Doug and I are going up for the Inauguration next week," said Meg.

"You don't say. Seats in the President's box?" Jim teased.

Meg frowned.

"There's a protest rally," Doug explained. "A kind of anti-Inauguration on the Mall. They're expecting hundreds of thousands."

"I see." Jim hadn't pictured his niece taking part in any of the demonstrations and rallies he read about overseas. He wondered if this were Doug's doing.

"Do you disapprove, Uncle Jim?" Meg used his title mockingly.

"Not at all. I came to the conclusion years ago this war was a mistake. To protest now is to flog a dead horse, I feel, what with the talks in Paris. But no, if you believe in this rally, you should go. Just be careful."

Meg's mouth remained budded in an angry pout. What other response had she wanted from him? She suddenly locked eyes with him and said, "Uncle Jim? Do you smoke grass?"

He blinked, but refused to be intimidated. "Why? Do you have some?"

"As a matter of fact—"

She grabbed at Doug's army jacket heaped on the bed behind her. Doug smiled sheepishly at Jim and nervously watched Meg, who took a cigarette pack from one of his pockets. She dug into the pack with two tiny fingers and brought out a tightly rolled joint.

"What're you doing, Meg-wump? You out to shock poor Uncle Jim?"

"Not shock. Share. I always thought you were someone I'd like to get high with." She placed the joint in her mouth and lit it, smiling at him.

Doug glanced around the room, pretending not to be there.

She passed the joint to Jim, who sniffed at it, tasted it, then took a deep toke. He didn't understand what game she was playing, but he played along, flicking ash like a connoisseur and saying, "Harsh. We get better over there." He passed the joint to Doug.

The tips of Doug's fumbly fingers were very cold and soft.

They passed the joint around, Meg watching Jim, pleased with him, intrigued. Her calm brown eyes disturbed him, as if someone else scrutinized Jim from the back of her head. He tried winking at Meg to break the stare. Not looking at what he was doing, his hand stumbled around Doug's hand, until Doug had to grip Jim's fingers to take the joint. Touch lingered like a mild electric shock in his knuckles.

"That's enough," said Jim the next time the joint came to him. He wetted his fingertips and snuffed the thing out. "You two have to drive back."

He stood up to crack the sliding glass door. An icy jet of salt air reminded him where he was. Everything he associated with this burned muddy smell was on the other side of the world. He wasn't stoned; he was remembering.

Sitting on the bed, Meg held Doug and grinned into his armpit. Doug looked only uncomfortable, indifferent, vague. He gave another sheepish smile to Jim, as if he were more concerned with what Jim thought than with what Meg was feeling.

Jim suddenly understood. Meg loved a boy who didn't love back. And the first reason Jim could imagine for any man not to love his niece was that the man must be just like Jim. A feeling of indignation came over him, and protectiveness.

He returned to his chair. With a note of reprimand in his voice, he told Doug, "I love my niece."

"A terrific person," said Doug, parking his hand on her shoulder.

"Guys," Meg groaned. "Can we talk about something else?"

Jim finished his challenge. "And I'd hate to see her hurt in any way."

Doug looked blank.

Meg looked annoyed. "Why're you getting so sanctimonious, Jim? Just grass. You smoked some yourself."

Jim loved the girl and wanted to protect her. But just as one had to be careful saving a small country from itself, one had to be doubly prudent with a niece.

"I'm not a dope-a-holic," Meg insisted. "I thought it'd be fun to get high with you. And I wanted you to see I'm not naive little Meg-wump anymore."

"I wasn't referring to the grass," said Jim. "I meant only . . ." He looked into Doug's eyes. He smiled apologetically at Meg. "Just showing my concern for your future. In a clumsy, uncle-ish manner."

Meg laughed at him. "Are you stoned? I'm not stoned. Doug, are you? We didn't smoke enough to stone a hamster. Did we? No. We're *not* stoned."

Doug was boyish without being pretty, pale and thin without grace or effeminacy. Jim knew appearances meant nothing, but he looked for something to support his suspicion. The boy's eyes were a washed-out blue, his eyelashes long and colorless.

"We should be heading back," Doug told Meg.

Jim needed to know. He had a responsibility to Meg to learn the truth and protect her with it. She didn't know men the way Jim did. "When you came up for this rally," he asked, "were you coming up for the day or did you plan to spend some time in D.C.?"

They were planning to spend the entire weekend, staying with Doug's family across the river in Fairfax. Jim should've guessed Doug was from inside the Beltway; he had that suburban Washington knowingness about politics, unlike the cynical indifference of people down here, such as Jim's brother-in-law. Perhaps Doug's sociable ambiguity was merely the result of growing up among bureaucrats.

"Did you want to come with us to the rally?" Meg asked.

"That's an idea. Or another possibility: I've been invited to a round of parties the night before the Inauguration. All Democrat, of course, but lots of bigwigs. Would the two of you be interested in that?"

Doug looked interested. Meg asked, "Would we have to dress up?"

"What you wore today would be fine. It would give you a chance to see your uncle's world firsthand, Meg." It would give Jim a chance to study Doug. "And Mrs. Marcos is coming to town. I could introduce you to her."

Imelda Marcos was not quite a household name in 1973, but Doug knew who she was. His eyes lit up and he told Meg, "Imelda herself! Wouldn't that be wild? Can't you just hear Harry and Jane when we tell them we met Imelda?"

Meg was already tempted and Doug's excitement convinced her completely. Everything was arranged. Still on semester break, Meg was riding up to Fairfax on Friday afternoon to join Doug. They'd come into town that night, meet Jim at his apartment near Dupont Circle and he'd take them on a tour of parties inside the very government they'd be protesting the next day. The duplicity was part of the night's appeal. Meg became more excited. Doug became hesitant for a moment, perhaps wondering why a grown man wanted to share an important evening with two college kids. Jim wondered himself.

Doug gave Jim a firm handshake at the door—"Been a pleasure, sir. We'll look forward to next week"—and Meg kissed Jim on the cheek, importantly, almost gratefully. They went down the hall with their arms around each other's waist, Doug holding on to Meg very, very tightly.

Jim closed the door, sat on his bed and said aloud, "What in blazes are you doing, Goodall?" Now that Meg's boyfriend was out of sight, he could find no reason for suspecting him. It was like a temporary insanity brought on by the wedding, anxiety over his return to Washington, and the fact he could no longer fly out to Bangkok for a weekend whenever he felt like it. He didn't think he felt like it now, but after a lifetime of celibacy followed by the past three years of controlled indulgence, Jim understood his libido well enough to know sexual frustration was in there somewhere. Not that he was sexually attracted to Doug. The boy was too unformed, bookish and familiar, too American. Jim seemed sexually attracted to the idea of protecting Meg, even though she might not need to be protected. He should forget the whole thing.

Driving back to D.C. the next day, through the dreary grayness of Virginia in January, Jim thought more about Doug and Meg and found his sexual interest gone. All that remained were the abstract questions, the problem-solving aspects. If this Doug were homosexual, what then? Did he tell Meg? Did he confront Doug and persuade him to break off with his niece? Knowing the truth was just the beginning. Jim was relieved the entire business existed only in his unhappy imagination. He went to the State Department gym as soon as he got back, worked off his tensions in a good game of racquetball with a divorced bureau chief and felt much better.

The week passed slowly. Jim was walking the corridors since his return from Manila, in limbo between assignments. He had so little to do he was pleased when one of Imelda's Blue Ladies, her entourage of hired friends, called to ask for help in getting into the Inaugural Ball. Jim had a few last-minute regrets about the task of chaperoning a niece through a night of stuffy parties, but decided it'd be good to have someone with whom he could share the jokes and comments he usually had to keep to himself.

Friday arrived and he picked up the tux he'd had cleaned and pressed after the wedding. Cleaners all over the city were swamped with evening clothes that week. Jim preferred the simpler life of his studio apartment here to the complicated households he had to keep overseas, yet there were nights like tonight when he missed having a couple of servants to launder his clothes or shine his shoes. He sat on a stool in his underwear and polished his shoes himself, then washed his hands and finished getting dressed.

The doorman buzzed to say there was a Mr. Brattle to see him. It took Jim a moment to remember Brattle was Doug's last name. "Send them up, Zack."

A minute later Jim opened the door. Doug stood in the hall, wearing the same navy blazer, wide necktie and ratty army jacket he had worn at the wedding. He was alone. "Hello, Mr. Goodall."

"Where's Meg?" said Jim.

"Ah, Meg. Well, sir. Meg's running late and"—Doug explained how Meg's ride from Virginia Beach left later than scheduled and she wouldn't get to Doug's house until after midnight—"she said we were to go ahead without her and I'll see her tonight when I get home. Oh, and I'm supposed to arrange for us to meet somewhere tomorrow, at the rally or parade, whichever makes you more comfortable."

Doug spoke quickly, smiling his placid smile, arrogantly looking Jim in the eye. He had both hands in the pockets of his army jacket.

"Dammit, is that the only coat you own?" Jim barked.

"What?" Smile and arrogance disappeared; the boy looked frightened. "I'm sorry. I didn't think—"

"Here." Jim went to his closet and grabbed the tweed overcoat he bought twenty years ago when he thought he'd be in Europe. "Out of style, but they'll think you're a damn terrorist in that thing," he said, trying to sound more friendly. "Come along. We're cabbing it tonight."

Jim hurried them downstairs and out into the cold. He remained angry with Doug, not for the coat but for coming without Meg. He didn't know what to say to Doug, how to talk to him. Meg was their only bond. Doug, too, seemed lost without her. His self-assurance was gone and his tone changed wildly. "I'll try not to embarrass you," he said in a small pathetic voice during the cab ride to the Cosmos Club. "The powers that be," he smugly declared, looking out at the large wainscotted room full of important people in expensive clothes. "Drinking champagne out of plastic globlets."

Not until they were at the first party did Jim realize what people might assume about him and this boy. Everyone knew

Goodall was a bachelor. He considered introducing Doug as his nephew, until he remembered "nephew" was also a euphemism. Then Jim noticed other young people in the room, a scattering of males and females, some dressed as elegant miniatures of the adults, others looking as shaggily collegiate as Doug. The boy did not stand out. If only he would mingle on his own and stop following Jim like a nervous puppy.

"The bar's over there, Doug. That's the buffet table if you're hungry. You'll have to excuse me, I have business to discuss."

Actually, Jim had nothing to do tonight except make appearances at three different parties. To escape Doug, he let himself be trapped in a conversation with Mrs. Weed, wife of a former ambassador to Burma. She wore an odd metal collar that went up to her chin with what looked like a bit of tractor tread hanging below. Jim didn't know her well enough to ask if this were fashion or a neck injury. Listening to stories about Mr. Weed's hunting trip in Kenya, Jim glanced past the cogwheel earrings and watched Doug down drinks at the bar.

The next party was in a hotel ballroom. They spent more time checking and unchecking their coats than they did among the guests, union people and the few Congressmen the unions still elected. The backslapping was loud and incessant.

"Fascinating. Very fascinating," said Doug while they waited in line outside for the doorman to find them a cab. Doug's cheeks and ears were pink, his thin lips relaxed in that meaningless smile again. "Like wandering in and out of scenes from *War and Peace.*"

"With disposable cups," Jim reminded him. But he found Doug less irritating now, almost pleasant to be with. He had had a few drinks himself. "I'm glad to hear you're enjoying this. It's still a pity Meg couldn't join us."

"Yeah, well, Meg's great and all that. But there's times she can be a drag, always needing to be the center of attention. This is more fun without her."

And Jim was annoyed with Doug all over again. "That's a strange way for a man to talk about the woman he loves."

Doug shrugged inside the enormous overcoat and smiled at Jim. "I guess I'm not a conventionally passionate person."

Which was similar to the excuses Jim had given himself in college and law school before he understood his real reason for not looking for a wife. At least he'd been considerate enough not to mislead anyone before coming into knowledge. Doug seemed less considerate than Jim had been, more selfish.

"Hey, Jim," said Doug as they climbed into a cab. "You promised me Imelda Marcos."

Alcohol made the boy terribly forward. "Maybe the next stop," said Jim. "If we're not too late."

The last party was in a posh residential neighborhood off Wisconsin Avenue. A fleet of matching limos parked up and down the tree-lined street announced Imelda and her court were still inside the enormous Tudor house surrounded by boxwood. Jim immediately saw her from the entrance hall. She sat in a wing-backed chair, which had been moved to the center of the living room, circled by laughing men and women. Her olive-skinned hand with its gold bracelets gracefully twisted and turned like a charmed cobra while she spoke.

"Is that a boyfriend behind her?" Doug asked much too loudly.

Jim whispered, "No. Just Jack Valenti. A family friend."

"We going to talk to her?"

"In a minute." Jim assumed Imelda was doing the entire circuit, Democrats tonight, Republicans tomorrow. He hoped she might leave before he had a chance to approach her. She made him oddly nervous tonight, perhaps because he no longer had the armor of an official role to play with her. He motioned Doug toward the grand piano, where a sulky pianist played jazz variations on the Philippine national anthem.

"But she *will* talk to you," said Doug. "Even if you're her husband's enemy?"

Jim grimaced. "Not enemy," he whispered. "Critic. A foreign service officer can't afford to be anyone's enemy. Besides, she can't imagine they have enemies. Only misunderstandings, which she thinks she can sweet talk you out of." She had tried it a few times with Jim, on a lewdly narrow loveseat. His colleagues came away from this treatment nervous wrecks, but not Jim. You can't sexually intimidate someone whose compass points elsewhere. Yet it was all a game that affected nothing.

Thinking about Imelda, Jim found himself staring at Doug. He had to confront the boy about Meg. He would not be as ineffectual here as he had been over there.

"Let's go meet Imelda," he said and grabbed Doug's arm. He led him across the room, wanting to get this over with as quickly as possible so he could be alone with the boy.

"*Jeem*. How nice to see you again."

A gracious winner, Imelda was her sweet, genially corrupt self tonight. She looked up at him with perfectly stenciled eyebrows and smile, still Miss Manila of 1953 and incapable of showing an honest emotion. Her face was on too tight.

"We were *so* sorry when they took you from us," she said poutily. "Washington must've needed you *so* badly." No trace of sarcasm came through. She offered him a handful of bright red beetles, her enameled fingernails.

Her touch shamed Jim with memories of failure and helplessness. "I have someone who'd like to meet you, Madam President. Douglas Brattle, a friend of my niece."

"*Imelda Marcos!* Madam President, I mean. This is such an honor!" Doug bowed when he took her hand, looking ready to kiss it. He was as fulsome and fawning as Imelda herself.

"Douglas? That is our favorite American name in my country. I didn't know Jim had a niece. That's good. Family is important to us too."

Jim stood by while Imelda flirted and Doug gushed. The boy was so slippery. If Jim confronted him about his sexuality in words, Doug would deny it, just as Imelda had denied artful accusations about her husband's ruthlessness and her brother's greed. Words were good only for diplomatic courtesy and lies.

"We won't take up any more of your time, Madam President. I trust you'll enjoy the weekend festivities." Jim set his hand on Doug's knobby shoulder to lead him away—and suddenly knew what he had to do to protect Meg.

"Thank you so much, Jim. And it was a pleasure meeting *you*, young man."

Doug grinned goodbyes and final compliments and Jim had to push him toward the door, resisting an urge to grab his ponytail and drag him out. His hand pressed against the bone and muscle beneath the boy's clothes.

"The dragon lady herself," Doug clucked while they pulled on their coats. "This year's model, anyway. What a weird, seductive woman."

"Only with those who want to be seduced." Jim had never

seduced anyone in his life. Even in legal arrangements, he simply presented the facts and stood back, making no attempt to charm or bully his way through. Did he actually intend to seduce Doug? He was irritated enough to feel ruthless for the sake of his niece. Without knowing how far he should take it, Jim looked for a way to begin.

They took a cab that had dropped off two laughing Navy officers and their dates. Jim gave directions to the driver, then turned to Doug and said, "You've had an awful lot to drink. Are you sober enough to drive home?"

"Am I?" Doug touched his cheeks and forehead, grinning. "I'm so excited right now, I don't know what I feel."

"I'll fix some coffee when we get back to my place. I don't want to have to worry about you on the road." Jim spoke brusquely, harshly. "If worse comes to worse, I suppose you *could* sleep over."

"Oh? Oh," said Doug. "No. I'll be okay," and he went off on Imelda again, asking if it were true she sang "Hello, Dolly" at the White House for LBJ.

When they arrived at Jim's building, Doug swayed when he got out of the cab. "Damn. Maybe I did drink too much."

"I thought so," Jim scolded. "Well, come on up and I'll make coffee. You have to get your coat and give me mine back, anyway."

"Right," said Doug and he followed Jim inside. "Maybe I should call the house and see if Meg's there yet," he announced in the elevator.

Upstairs, Jim put the kettle on and took off his tux while Doug called home. The apartment felt much too warm. Jim tried to plan his next move. In the Patpong in Bangkok, just being on the right street said it all. A middle-aged American wearing sunglasses in bars, Jim knew he looked like either a secret agent or a blind man. The "gift" of crisp baht notes afterward made it as natural as buying dinner. Jim felt like an awkward teenager in more personal, informal transactions.

"Uh-huh. Uh-huh. You don't have to wait up for her, Mom. Can't Barney? You're not excited I met someone famous? No, she's Argentina, Imelda's the Philippines. It's like meeting Mrs. Adolf Hitler! A few drinks, yeah. Champagne, some bourbon. A little, but—" Doug glanced over at Jim, who stood half behind the open door of his closet. The boy sounded more drunk on the phone than he had in the cab. "Sure. But what about my guest? No, we're riding in tomorrow with Harry and Jane."

Jim kept his trousers on but hung up everything else. He tucked his shoes into their pocket of the shoe bag on the inside of the door. His undershirt fit snugly over his shoulders and flat stomach. When he came out from behind the door, Doug was off the phone and looking thoughtful on the sofa.

"Meg's still not there?" Jim asked.

"No. But the people she's riding with live on Old South Time. They do everything a couple of hours late. Uh, my mother thinks I'm drunk and wants me to ask if I can spend the night." Doug rolled his eyes over his mother.

"I said you could." That the boy's mother *wanted* him here put a different light on what Jim intended. But Jim was doing this for his family, not Doug's. "You won't be needing coffee then." Jim stepped into the kitchen to turn off the boiling water. "Would you like a nightcap?" he called out.

"Sure. Why not?"

Jim never drank alone, so his kitchen cabinet was full of bottles of liquor given as presents over the years. He filled two tumblers with Dutch herb-flavored gin, which should be enough to keep Doug loose without making him pass out. He wanted to seduce the boy, not rape him.

"Here's a new experience for you," he said, gave Doug a tumbler and told him what it was. He sat on the sofa beside Doug. It wasn't a loveseat, but sitting a foot from the boy should suggest something.

"Different," said Doug after taking a sip.

Jim leaned in closer, setting his arm on the back of the sofa. He was at a loss as to what to say or do next. He was no Imelda Marcos.

Doug smiled at Jim and took another sip. His ponytail flopped over his shoulder and Doug gripped it with one hand while he held the tumbler with the other.

"Your hair," said Jim, seeing a subject. "I thought only fire-breathing radicals wore their hair long."

"I'm radical," said Doug. "In my fashion." He stroked his ponytail. "I just like the way it feels."

"Do you wear it loose or tied up when you go to bed?"

"Tied up. Or it gets all tangled. Will I be sleeping out here on the sofa?"

Jim narrowed his eyes at Doug. "There is no in and out here. It's a studio apartment. And *this*"—he patted the back of the sofa—"is a sofa bed."

Doug looked over the square-armed, salmon-plaid sofa, then at the rest of the neat, spartan apartment. "This is all you can afford?"

"It's all I need when I'm in the States." Jim was confused by the boy's calm, his failure to be disturbed by Jim leaning over him, his easy acceptance of the fact they'd be sleeping together. Attempting a suggestive gaze, Jim lowered his voice and said, "Maybe we should be going to bed?"

"Okay." Doug calmly finished his gin, stood up and began to undress.

Jim wondered again if he'd misread Doug. The boy took off his blazer and unknotted his tie as matter-of-factly as someone who thought only of sleep. Jim stacked the sofa cushions and set them in their corner. He gripped the handles and unfolded the bed across the room. He presented the fact of a bed, and even that failed to make an impression.

"Right out," said Doug and he went into the bathroom and closed the door.

Jim hung up his trousers and removed his socks and garters. A man in garters was too absurd to seduce anyone. The whole situation was absurd and Jim didn't think there was going to be a seduction. Maybe the boy wasn't homosexual after all. Or maybe he was, but so indifferent to old men Jim didn't register as a sexual possibility. Jim looked down at himself, his undershirt tucked into his blue silk boxer shorts, his arms covered with copper hair and the seams of dried skin left by all his burnings and peelings. Jim felt too old to be playing this game. Waiting for Doug to finish in the bathroom, he turned off all the lights except the reading lamp beside the bed.

The toilet flushed and Doug came out, yawning. His shirt and undershirt were in one hand, his pale chest ribbed and hairless. He saw Jim standing importantly beside the bed. He padded around to the other side, tossed his things on a chair and stood there, shyly looking down at his belt buckle.

"You know," he said, "I've never been to bed with a man."

The sudden acknowledgment of sex startled Jim. His first reaction was to turn it against the boy. "Is that a disclaimer, Doug, or a proposition?"

Doug looked at Jim, his mouth pulled straight, his eyes nervous and apologetic. "I just wanted to know what was going on here."

"You tell me." Jim pulled his undershirt over his head. If Doug could be bare-chested, so could Jim. They seemed to be daring each other to declare himself; Jim refused to declare himself further than Doug had. Mystery was power.

Doug frowned, then shrugged the matter aside and unbuckled his belt. "I'm zonked," he said, stepped out of his trousers and draped them over the chair. His white briefs hung across his hips like a loose bandage. He stood flicking the waistband with his thumbs, looking down at the bed, not looking at Jim. His thighs were pebbled with goosebumps. He pulled off the briefs and slid under the blankets.

Jim pulled off his shorts as he turned off the light. Climbing into the dark, he wondered if Doug meant to trick him into making a fool of himself. Or if the boy intended to submit passively to the old man out of fear and good manners. Or if Doug always slept nude and was simply declaring his innocence.

You think too much, Jim told himself two seconds later.

They were instantly all over each other. Hands, legs and mouth, Doug turned into a different person, his kissing all tongue and teeth, his long bare length wildly three-dimensional. The world was usually so flat and remote.

"Ah! Never held another guy's dick. Hold mine. Oh, yeah."

Unafraid of seeming depraved or corny, Doug was in a hurry to touch and try everything, even scooting down to try that, timidly at first, then ineptly, his breath and long hair tickling. Jim was accustomed to more Buddhist lovemaking, leisurely and proficient, and a different set of smells. Doug smelled strongly of baby shampoo and faintly like butter. Jim palmed the small bottom in one hand while the boy eagerly humped himself against Jim's groin. Even his finish felt new and Western, a grimace followed by groans, a sharp cry and the tossing back of his head. The face was so close Jim needed his reading glasses.

He fell on Jim's chest, rolled off and lay on his back, rib cage heaving.

The blankets were thrown on the floor and Jim's eyes had adjusted to the dark. He wanted to finish too, then the strangeness of it all began to catch up with him. This was different from his friendly, professional encounters, dreams of sex where he went to bed with nations, not individuals. This was someone Jim knew in the real world, specific and familiar. It felt like incest even without the involvement of a niece. Jim was remembering he had intended to do this for Meg.

Doug lay there with one hand over his eyes, gasping like a landed fish. "I'm sorry," he said in a hurt voice. "I feel awful all of a sudden."

Jim was uncertain how to respond to that; it sounded as excessive as Doug's finish. "You seemed to enjoy yourself," he said dryly.

"I guess." He lifted his hand and smiled weakly at Jim. "So. You are gay, aren't you?"

"Like you," said Jim, although he found that word too slangy, too coy.

"I don't know," Doug sighed. "I feel so bad I must be straight."

"After sex all animals are sad." Jim spoke from experience.

Doug took a deep breath and worriedly asked, "There, uh, something you want me to do for you?"

"Be honest with Meg."

Doug lay still a moment. "I meant so you could have an orgasm."

"I know what you meant." Jim was afraid of what he'd feel after sex. And he wanted to use his failure to finish as proof to himself he really had done this for Meg. He wasn't convinced.

"If you're sure you don't want anything, is there something I can wipe off with?"

Jim went to the bathroom to get a towel. He remembered other conversations after sex, all the cheerful questions about American music, appliances and farm animals. This was going to be more intimate and unpleasant.

Jim sat at the foot of the bed. Doug shyly rolled away while he used the towel.

"What's Meg told you about me?" he asked Jim.

"Very little. That you're smart. Book smart anyway. And that she's in love with you."

"Yeah. Well." He reached down for his briefs, then decided he didn't need them. His ponytail had come undone and he used both hands to draw his weeping willow of hair behind his shoulders as he sat against the sofa part of the bed. "She's told me lots about you. How you're the one interesting person in her family. How I shouldn't be misled by the way you sometimes talk like a used car salesman. How you took her to *Lawrence of Arabia* when she was ten years old and she caught you crying in a couple of scenes." Doug drew his knees up to his chest. "She thinks you might be gay, you know."

Jim froze. He didn't want to believe anyone in the family knew, not even Meg. "A common assumption about a bachelor uncle," he muttered. "A cliché, in fact." Yet something in him was thrilled Meg guessed at him correctly.

"But you are gay," said Doug.

"Does she suspect you are?"

"She knows men fascinate me in a way women don't. Intellectually, sometimes emotionally. Maybe I'm just horny and curious. I don't know. But Meg gets threatened and angry about that. She's kind of a feminist, about herself. She doesn't particularly like other women."

Jim listened with half an ear, wondering why he should feel pleased Meg knew about him. He felt less alone in the world, which was frightening.

"Meg's very perceptive about other people. But she was only half right about you." Doug smiled. "She thinks you're gay, but so moral and repressed you probably don't even know it."

Hearing how he looked in Meg's eyes finished changing her in Jim's. She was an intelligent, emotional adult, capable of understanding what had happened here, capable of judging him. The rules had changed since he was their age, but not that much. The idea of Meg hating him gave her a solidity and importance she had never had before.

"I sure proved her wrong on that one," Doug crowed. "Oh, she doesn't look down on you for being innocent. She might even envy you. Despite everything she says, Meg has very mixed feelings about sex."

"You've slept with her?"

"Oh, yeah, several—" Doug stopped, remembering who Jim was. Then he laughed and shook his head. "This is too weird. It's not like you and I have anything to hide from each other," he said, lowering his knees and uncovering himself. "We have sex. Not very often. I feel funny not feeling about her the way she feels about me."

He was so blithe about it, his guilt or depression completely gone. Yet Jim couldn't feel indignant for Meg's sake. The angry protectiveness that had brought this about was numbed by his awareness of Meg and confusion about himself.

"You don't have to worry about Meg," Doug insisted. "She's on the pill. But see? I can have sex with women. I must be pansexual."

Jim stood up and went into the kitchen. He turned on the light and was blinded. When he could see again, he opened the refrigerator and saw only beer and Gatorade.

"You're in good shape for someone my father's age," Doug called out.

Jim had forgotten he was still naked. Annoyed, he looked out and saw Doug sprawled on the bed, a very white, scrawny boy, hair peeking from his crotch and armpits like mattress ticking. He insolently sat there, too shameless to cover up, talking to Jim as an equal. What was it about this nebulous cipher that put him in bed with both an intelligent girl and her blundering uncle?

Jim left the kitchen light on when he returned with a bottle of Gatorade.

"Thank you." Doug swigged from the bottle and passed it back to Jim. "Does anyone in the State Department know about you?"

"Why?" Jim said flatly. "You won't tell on me if I don't tell on you?"

"No." Doug looked surprised. "I assumed we weren't going to tell anyone."

"Not even Meg?"

Doug made a face, puffed his cheeks full of air and blew the air from a corner of his mouth. "Damn. I've blanked that out all evening," he said indifferently.

"I intend to tell her," said Jim. Did he?

Doug looked at him skeptically, worriedly. "The thing is,"

he said, "Meg might figure it out just reading my face tomorrow. Especially since she didn't want me coming into town without her."

"You said she did."

"It was more like, 'Go ahead, see if I care.' She said she was afraid you'd like me more than you liked her. But she was running late and I really wanted to meet Imelda Marcos." Doug was grinning sheepishly. "And maybe I was curious about what would happen without her."

Of course. The boy had come here to be seduced. Even Meg had sensed that possibility. All the time Jim felt this was something *he* did, he'd been just a gear in a machine of other people's experiments and accidents. It was as bad as his career in the foreign service, only this time his own body had been one of the chief conspirators. He wasn't a hero, he wasn't even a good villain. He regretted not having finished his sex. He could not feel any more guilty or helpless.

The telephone rang.

It was almost one o'clock. Jim and Doug looked at each other.

The second ring sounded more accusing than the first. Doug gritted his teeth, miming fear, mocking it. Jim was genuinely afraid. His guilty voice would give them away. He wanted it to be his voice, not Doug's. He stood up and walked toward the telephone.

"Dreams of virtue breed monsters," Meg said—in a letter from graduate school several years later. Long after Jim freely resigned from the State Department, after Meg had forgotten Doug and forgiven Jim, she periodically needed to pick apart that night in an effort to make herself a full participant in it. "Your old monsters fascinate me. 'Curious George' did it out of sexual selfishness. You, on the other hand, did it not for sex, and not (as you once proposed) out of a confused need to get closer to your niece by hurting me. I now suspect you did it as an act of revenge against my family, who never needed you the way you wanted to be needed. I don't hold it against you. Blood is thicker than water, spilled blood thicker still."

ENROLLMENT

• PHILIP GAMBONE •

EVERYONE SAYS THAT my second cousin Monica's was the first mixed marriage in the family. Technically, this isn't true. Not if you count all the cousins in the previous generation—my first cousins—who married non-Italians. There was Angela, who married a Greek, and Denise, who married an Irishman, and Robert, who married a girl of indeterminate extraction. (My grandmother always referred to her as *l'inglese*, "the English-woman," a phrase that delivered more disdain than you might imagine.) In the late fifties, my oldest cousin Johnny even became engaged to a Protestant, though apparently that doesn't count either, because she converted some months before the wedding. So what the family means, then, by mixed marriage is this: that Monica Scarpetto—the daughter of two nice Italian parents—married a Jew.

This was two years ago, and when Monica and David announced their engagement, though there were raised eyebrows and whispers about how they would raise the children, everyone was essentially happy for them. "Hey, Nicky, times change," my mother declared, as if I were the one who still needed convincing. And then she proceeded to tell me, for the umpteenth time, about the "antique days," when all a girl had to do was smoke to become persona non grata with the family.

We'd all come to expect this marriage. Monica and David had been dating since college, and, by the time they graduated and were out in the work world—David as a financial analyst, Monica as a buyer for a large department store in Boston—he was showing up at all the major family gatherings. It didn't matter where we got together: at Monica's parents' or Aunt

Carmella's, or my mother's. Whatever the occasion—Fourth of July, Thanksgiving, Christmas even—David would be there, well-dressed, well-mannered, and charming. He praised everyone's cooking, told appreciative stories of the summer he traveled in Europe—Italy was his favorite country, he said—and, but only when asked, gave sound, conservative advice about financial investment.

You could tell, Aunt Carmella said, summing up all the evidence, that David came from a good family, which, as she later explained in one of those tête-à-têtes that aunts in my family are always having with me, was as important to Jews as to Christians.

For our part, we learned to wish David "Happy Hanukkah" at Christmastime and "Happy Passover" at Easter. And when they announced their engagement, my father even congratulated them with a *Mazel tov*, chuckling at himself afterward the way one often does after using someone else's language for the first time.

If David's good upbringing—his *educazione*—made him eminently acceptable to the women in our family, what made him acceptable to the men was the fact that he was also a "regular guy." After dinner, he would join my uncles around the TV to watch football or basketball. And when the dining room table was finally cleared—dessert and coffee, nuts and fruit and confetti being an hour long affair after the games—he would sit with the men for several rounds of cards and Sambuccas.

I was always the first to leave these parties. Even if it was Christmas. Even if it was my parents who were hosting. There we'd be, maybe fifteen or twenty of us—aunts, uncles, cousins—a kind of Italian Bob Cratchit and family, full of holiday *festevolezza*. I'd stay through the sweets and coffee and then, just before the card-playing got going, make my excuses: papers to correct (I taught school then) or other friends, perhaps old acquaintances from college, to whom I'd promised a drop-in call. After all, it was the holidays. None of this was a lie, though there were stronger, less explainable reasons why I really wasn't staying.

"Eh, Mr. Russo," my mother would call out to me, throwing up a hand, like a jilted soprano. In our family's personal mythology, Mr. Russo was another person from the antique days, a family acquaintance—a *cumpare*—who was forever having to be somewhere else. According to my mother, you could be enjoying a cup of coffee and a nice conversation with Mr. Russo when all of a sudden he'd put down his cup and announce that he had an appointment elsewhere. "He never stayed in one place for more than ten minutes," Aunt Carmella added.

Everyone who remembered Mr. Russo, called him a "curious" man. He might as well not have been Italian, I was led to believe, for all the regard he gave to the social customs of his own people. And now they were telling me—but jokingly, of course—that I was the new Mr. Russo. Aunt Carmella once even explained to David who Mr. Russo was and why it was such an apt name for me. She wanted him to understand everything about being a part of our family.

Mr. Russo was long dead and buried before I came on the scene in the mid-fifties. But in time I came to have my own speculations about his odd behavior. Speculations I shared only with my "roommate" Josh, the other—but unacknowledged—Jew in the family.

For Monica and David's wedding, my parents offered to buy me a new suit. "So that you make '*na bella figura*," my mother told me over the phone one night. "You know *bella figura*—a good impression?"

This had been one of my grandmother's expressions. Since Nonna's death a few years back, my mother was more and more echoing her own mother's Old World idioms.

I told Mom that I knew *bella figura*. And that I hardly needed their money. At thirty-three, a math teacher turned computer programmer, I was doing fine.

"We just want to make sure you look great," Mom said. "We're proud of our son." She paused, then added, "And this time don't you dare do like Mr. Russo. You stay for the whole reception. I want several dances with you."

As it turned out, everyone—Jews and Christians alike—dressed to cut a good figure. And while I've never been the kind of guy who makes free with words like "stunning" and "ravishing," that's exactly how the women, especially the women in my family, looked. It was hard not to feel proud. A lot of my cousins and aunts, even the ones in their sixties and seventies, have aged well: "because of all the olive oil," my grandmother used to claim. And, though we're not a wealthy family—florists, dry cleaners, chefs being the family professions—still the women know how to dress. At Monica's wedding I felt caught up in all the enthusiasm they had for making *'na bella figura.* I wouldn't have pulled a Mr. Russo for anything. Not that day.

The ceremony took place, not in a church or temple, but in the ballroom of a swanky new hotel in Boston. Despite the little canopied pavilion under which Monica and David exchanged vows—Josh later taught me the name, *hupah*—the ceremony was an ecumenical affair. Monica and David had both a rabbi and a priest officiate. Apparently, it took quite a lot of doing before they were able to find two clergymen who would agree to such a service. The priest, Father Joe, was a silver-haired man in his middle fifties, the kind who had probably entered the seminary right out of college and who—I was guessing all this, trying to figure out what had brought him to this wedding— had probably, maybe during the Vietnam War, had an affair or a bout with alcoholism, or some crisis of faith, and come out of it a lot more relaxed about all the rules. In short, a guy who had come to see that love could make everything—rules, tradition, even family—irrelevant. The rabbi, too, it was reported, was sympathetic. He came from a liberal synagogue in one of the suburbs west of Boston. They were my heroes that day, even more so than Monica and David, who, I felt, didn't really know (not as well as I) what they were getting themselves into.

"Did they smash the wineglass? Did you dance the 'Havah Negilah'?" Josh asked me late that night when I crawled into bed. He'd had his back to me, but now he rolled over, letting me hold him in my arms.

"All of that," I told him, cuddling up close. "I wish you could've been there."

"Me too," he said.

"Eventually they'll figure out who you are," I told him. "I give them another six months. Wait till next year."

"Next year," he said, then chuckled. "Next year in Jerusalem."

It was a warm evening. We were both naked. I buried my nose in Josh's shoulder and breathed in deeply. We'd been together about a year, but I was feeling—all over again— something like that first rush of falling in love with him, the thrill of another's body, at once so alien and so familiar, being offered to me.

Last month, Monica and David had a baby, a little girl whom they named Danielle Louise (part David's family, Daniel being his grandfather; part Monica's, Louis—"Louie"—being her father's name).

"Save the twenty-fourth," my mother told me over the phone one evening in early October. "Monica's going to throw a party for the naming of the baby. She's sending you an invitation next week." In the family network, my mother is the clearing-house for invitations. "I don't think they're going to have her baptized," she went on. "Monica's calling it a Naming Party. It's like what the Jews do for baby boys, you know a *bar mitzvah*, except it's for a girl."

"Well, not quite," I said. "A bar mitzvah is for when the boy turns of age, like Confirmation. Josh's nephew just got bar mitzvahed."

In the two years since David and Monica's wedding, I had taken every opportunity possible of keeping Josh focused in my family's mind. I hadn't actually spelled it out for them, what kind of a relationship we had, but I knew he had come together for them—in much the same way that objects begin to come together for an infant—as a distinguishable and significant "ob-ject" in their field of vision, as the person I was sharing more than just an apartment with, as the man, in fact, who had foreshadowed David and Monica's mixed marriage by almost a year. About six months after the wedding, we had taken a big step and invited my parents over for dinner. And when Uncle Rudolph died and Josh voluntarily attended the funeral, I think that clinched it.

"Well, whatever it's called, that's what they're doing," my mother said. "I think they're inviting Josh, too." In my moth-er's way of talking, "I think" means "I know." I tried to imagine what kinds of conversations had occurred to bring this invitation to pass. "I guess the rabbi will be there," my mother continued. "Remember the one who married them?"

"Sure," I said.

"But no Father Joe," she told me.

"Okay," I said, trying to sound as copacetic as a pear on a plate.

"What do you think?" she asked.

"About what?"

We were each waiting for the other to go first.

"I don't know . . ." She sounded discouraged by my not taking up the ball, and I suddenly felt guilty, as if she'd asked for something and I'd refused. "I guess it would have been nice if the baby could have been baptized too, that's all."

"What about times changing?" I asked. "Isn't that what you said when they got married?"

"Oh, but you understand, don't you?" There was confusion and annoyance, and a tinge of panic in her voice.

"Let them do what they want," I told her.

"Nicky, it's not a question of letting them do what they want." Now she sounded just plain frustrated. "It's just that it looks like Monica's giving everything to David's family and nothing to ours."

"She's inviting all of us, isn't she?"

"Sometimes," my mother said—she was laughing, but I could tell she felt exasperated with me—"sometimes I just wish I'd had a daughter. She'd understand what I'm trying to say."

The Sunday of the naming, Josh and I took the Turnpike out to Monica and David's. The directions they sent us—a computer-generated map that David had printed up at work—were written as if the only places from which guests might come were the towns around Route 128 or Interstate 495, the circumferential highways that ringed the city. On this map, Boston existed only as an alternative directional marker—"To Boston"—somewhere off in the east, an undisclosed bull's-eye at the end of the sure, true arrow which was the Massachusetts Turnpike.

"Where *is* this place?" Josh joked as we passed the exit for Framingham.

"One of those M towns," I said. "Millis, Medfield, Middleborough, Marlborough. I don't know, they all sound alike to me."

We laughed. The suburbs were not our thing. Josh and I had been renting in the South End, the gay ghetto, for three years now. We had begun to ask realtors to show us property for sale, town-house condominiums as close to downtown as we could afford. Even Cambridge felt too rustic.

We got off at the next exit. The sky was overcast: gray and sooty-white like pigeons' feathers. And although it was just after noon, the sun, a dull glowing behind the cloud cover, sat low on the horizon. Sunday afternoons in winter we usually spent in one of three ways: curled up on the sofa reading the paper, giving or attending a brunch, or at the gym working out.

The directions took us through an old manufacturing town and then out beyond a sprawling high school. The road became country-ish, stone walls and large old maples flanking both sides. Maybe as recently as fifteen years ago this had all been farmland. On the hill to our right and through the leafless branches of the trees we could see the new development where Monica and David lived: one- and two-acre lots planted with large contemporary colonials.

"The next turn is ours," I told Josh. "Apple Creek Road."

He looked at me. "This isn't going to be one of those developments with names like Wisteria Way, is it?"

"Two hours," I reassured him. "I promise we'll stay just two hours."

"And then make like Mr. Russo, right?" he added, grinning.

David greeted us at the door and we stepped into the warm, tinkly, humming world of the party. Handsomely dressed people, none of whom I recognized, were coming and going through the tiled entrance foyer, itself almost a room, decorated with furniture one might call "sharp"—all chrome, glass and marble. Descending the staircase from the second floor, where presumably they'd gone to leave coats and freshen up, were still other guests. Everyone seemed headed for the back of the house, from which I could hear the noise of the party in progress.

As we were unloading onto David our coats and gifts and congratulations, the doorbell rang again.

"Go on in," David told us. "I'll catch up with you guys later." He was beaming. I wondered if having a son could have made him any happier than he was at that moment.

The living room, a large, cathedral-ceilinged space with a white brick fireplace at one end, was packed. I didn't see anyone I recognized. What I had thought was to be a small family affair had turned into an enormous party. There were lots of young couples, and lots of children. It was the kind of party a couple of gay men would try to be anonymous in.

"I'm going to get a drink," Josh told me and headed off to the far end of the living room where a bar, complete with hired bartender—a young man in a crisp-fitting red vest—had been set up.

As if she'd tracked me on radar, my mother now appeared.

"You're here!" she said and gave me a kiss on the cheek.

"Mom, you look terrific," I told her before she could start in on the never seeing me bit. She did look great. Her hair, a strawberry blond that in the last few years has emerged as her color, was done up in soft, sweeping waves. She was wearing a new cocktail dress, a bold flowered print on silk, and gold jewelry. Though I knew she'd be sixty-eight in February, she could easily have passed for fifty. I hate the pretty boys at the gym, but when Mom dresses up she makes me realize that looking great often has more to do with generosity than vanity.

"Isn't this wonderful?" she gushed, as she absentmindedly fingered my sport coat. "Do you believe how much space they have?" She kept firing questions at me: had I been given a tour of the house? had I seen the new baby? "Look, over there." She pointed to the sofa where Aunt Carmella was cradling Danielle in her arms. "Isn't she adorable?"

In her exuberance, Mom seemed to have forgotten her dismay that this wasn't a baptism.

"Let me go over and say hello," I said, pulling her fingers off my jacket.

"Did Josh come?" she asked.

"Sure," I said. "He's here somewhere." I looked about casually, as if his whereabouts wasn't that big a deal: the same casualness I tried to affect whenever I pulled a Mr. Russo.

I gave Mom a so-long-for-now kiss and made my way over to Aunt Carmella, greeting people I knew, nodding and smiling at the others. Josh, I noticed, was chatting with the bartender.

"Eh, Nicky!" said Aunt Carmella when she saw me. She's my mother's sister, but the differences between them are amazing. Aunt Carmella's eighty-one, the oldest of my grandmother's eight children. She's got the heavy, doughy figure that Mom would have if she didn't watch her weight; and the bulbous Renzulli nose, a nose my mother had reshaped back in the fifties. "I haven't seen you in ages," Aunt Carmella scolded. "Where have you been?"

I never have a good answer to this question, not one that can do justice to both of us. As if she understood this, Aunt Carmella shifted her attention to the baby. "Look," she said.

I squatted down. Danielle's tiny face, smooth and pink, was folded up in sleep. "Isn't she adorable," I told her. It seemed ridiculous to be echoing my mother's very words, but I wanted to say the right thing. I wanted to do the right thing. I couldn't tell if I—but *who* was I to this new one? the second cousin once removed?—if I was allowed to touch Danielle, take her in my arms. Maybe that would have been too feminine, the kind of thing only men who say "stunning" and "ravishing" can get away with.

"You make a beautiful great-grandmother, Aunt Carmella." This time I used my own words.

In the past, such a statement would have been an occasion for Aunt Carmella to suggest that it was time I got married and started having a family too. I had handed her the perfect opening. Instead she just blushed. "Three times a great-grandmother," she said.

Apparently, we were all learning to say our own words. Then Josh came over, a tall drink in his hand, looking like the Cheshire cat.

"Eh," said Aunt Carmella when she saw him.

I could tell that she recognized his face but couldn't quite come up with a name. That was okay; she had just done one wonderful thing. That was good enough for now.

"*Josh*," I said, loud and clear as a shofar, "I'll leave you and Aunt Carmella to visit awhile."

"Go get yourself a drink," he suggested, and gave me the Cheshire look again.

The young man in the red vest was standing, hands behind his back, waiting for business. When he saw me approaching, he immediately took a more formal stance. Then, just as quickly, his whole bearing relaxed. He smiled, and in an instant I knew what Josh's grin was all about.

"Hi," I said. He looked to be about twenty-six, twenty-seven—handsome, clean-cut, friendly looking—the kind of guy I see all the time at the gym, except without the attitude. "A brandy and soda."

"Sure," he said, giving me another friendly smile, and set about mixing my drink. He had brilliant blue eyes, the kind I've heard guys say are "to die for," except I'm a brown-eye man myself.

"It's quite a party, isn't it?" I asked. An innocuous enough question, but under the circumstances it had the ring of openers I used to use in the bars.

"Yes, it's a beautiful party," he said. He might have been agreeing with me out of a sense of professional duty—the customer is always right syndrome—though the way he said "beautiful" sounded too genuine for that.

When he finished making the drink, he held it out to me but didn't release it into my grasp until I'd looked up at him. Then he kept watching me as took my first sip.

"Perfect," I said. There was an awkward pause. Our business now over, I was free to wander off. Instead, I took another sip. I was the only person standing at the bar: nobody else was looking for a drink. "I'm Nick," I said.

"Dennis." We shook hands. It felt daring—and thrilling—to be making this contact under the eyes of all my relatives.

"The baby's mother is my cousin," I told him, though as soon as I said this, I realized I was babbling, just as in the old, pre-Josh, days when I would try to keep alive whatever ember of a conversation I had managed to kindle at the bars.

But Dennis seemed happy to talk. And so we did, occasionally interrupted by other guests wanting drinks, which he mixed with a bartender's quick efficiency.

He told me that he came from a large Irish-Catholic family on the South Shore. Eight brothers and sisters.

"Nine kids," I acknowledged. "That beats anyone in my family, and we're Italian."

After we'd both chuckled over that one, he told me, "Usually on Sundays I'm at my mom's, unless of course I have to work a job like this. She does a big dinner for all of us who can come." He looked so happy telling me this.

"Every Sunday?" I asked. "Brother, would my mother love to have you for a son."

Someone came up to order a drink. While Dennis was mixing it, I tried to imagine spending every Sunday at my parents'. It was a tempting idea, all that family togetherness. And though I didn't think it could ever be more than a tempting idea, it made me want to know Dennis even more.

"So where do you live now?" I asked when he'd finished making the drink.

"Out this way," he said. "We moved here from the South End last year." He was handing me all the rest of the clues I needed.

"Funny we never ran into you," I said, handing him all the remaining clues he needed. "We've been in the South End for three years now."

Josh wandered over, taking casual mouthfuls of ice from his otherwise empty glass. From the way Dennis smiled at him, I could tell a couple of things: that they'd already introduced themselves, and that Dennis had already linked us.

"So," I said, "this is turning out to be quite an occasion." We all laughed. And then it was time—according to an announcement the rabbi was making—for the ceremony to begin. "We'll catch you later," I told Dennis. He nodded, and I winked.

Josh and I moved away from the bar, positioning ourselves with the other guests—there must have been sixty by now—to face the corner of the living room where the rabbi was standing. Monica and David had joined him, along with Monica's parents, David's parents, and a couple whom I did not recognize.

Because we were toward the back, and therefore inconspicuous, Josh took the opportunity to whisper to me.

"Isn't Dennis cute?"

"Adorable," I mouthed, then whispered, "but I still go for dark-eyed Jews."

I took my eyes off him and looked out over the gathering. It was clear that most of the people here were not Jewish. Of David's family, only his parents and his brothers and their wives had come. Most of us were goyim—friends, neighbors, relatives of Monica. And yet, in the midst of this party, this innocent enough Sunday afternoon gathering, we were all about to stand witness to a religious ceremony with origins that went back five thousand years.

I brushed my hand against Josh's.

"In the traditional Jewish family," the rabbi began, "the birth of a male child is a cause for high celebration. In accordance with the covenant God made with Abraham, the ritual of circumcision—we call it the *berit milah*—is performed eight days after the baby is born to mark his enrollment as one of the Jewish nation."

It seemed strange to be holding a drink, like holding a drink in church. I glanced to my right where a large potted houseplant, a rubber tree of some sort, stood. On the Spanish moss that covered the base, I set my drink down.

"Good boy," Josh whispered to me.

"We in the reformed tradition," the rabbi went on, "think that the arrival of a girl should be attended with as much joy and celebration." A few people laughed.

He explained that, in addition to the baby, there were four people present who were most important in the ceremony: the godfather and godmother—he nodded to the couple I hadn't recognized—himself, the rabbi—again a few people laughed—and the prophet Elijah. "The empty chair here," and he gestured to a large easy chair, "is for Elijah."

Josh leaned over to me. "It's in case the baby is the Messiah. Elijah's present to announce the arrival of the Messiah."

"But this is a girl," I whispered back. "Girls don't get to be Messiah."

Neither Josh nor I are against religion—I go to Mass a few times a year; he does the high holy days—but right then I couldn't control the urge to enjoy with him that little irreverent conspiracy. I needed it against all the family stuff. Against this family embraced couple who, a generation ago, would have represented a greater blasphemy even than the sin—of Sodom! of Gomorrah!—which Josh and I performed weekly.

"Pay attention," Josh whispered.

Now David was reading from a book:

" 'In accordance with Jewish tradition we present our daughter to enter into the Covenant of Abraham and to be part of the Jewish people. We praise You, O Lord our God, King of the Universe, who has permitted us to reach towards holiness through observance of Mitzvot and commanded us to bring our children into the Covenant of Abraham our father.' "

There was something both foreign and familiar about this prayer. There were phrases—"King of the Universe," for example—that seemed lifted right out of the words I remembered of the Mass; and others—"Covenant of Abraham," "Mitzvot" —that gave off an exotic perfume.

" 'We are mindful that we have come through a time of uncertainty into strength and joy.' "

Monica was holding the baby, bouncing it slightly in her arms. I recognized it as a nervous gesture, a way of trying to calm herself. One hand went up to her eyes; she was wiping away tears.

A time of uncertainty, I thought. What was that for them, for her? Lots of possibilities occurred to me. Maybe my mother knew, or at least guessed, though I knew I would never dare ask.

Josh whispered, "At a briss we pray that the boy will one day get married, too."

"Typical Mediterranean fertility anxiety," I whispered back.

David was finishing with a prayer in Hebrew: ". . . *she-heh-chi-yanu v'ki-y'manu v'higi-anu lazman hazeh.*"

The rabbi then took up a crystal goblet into which had been poured ceremonial wine, blessed it, dipped his finger in the wine, and touched Danielle's lips. She cried out, and everyone laughed. The ceremony ended with the passing of the cup to Monica and David, their parents and the godparents.

"Don't we get to drink, too?" I asked Josh.

"What do you think this is," he said, "communion?"

What's left to tell is this:

After the ceremony everyone seemed more relaxed. The party got louder and friendlier, the caterers laid out quite a spread on the dining room table, Dennis was doing a brisk business at the bar.

I made myself a hefty sandwich and wandered about, happy to do some catching up with people, just as happy to blend in with the crowd. Once, out of the corner of my eye, I saw Josh checking out the prints and paintings Monica and David had hung on the walls; later I saw him talking to Dennis at the bar. I wanted to join them, but felt that where three were gathered eyebrows might be raised. And then Mom found me again, and our conversation turned to when I was coming home for a visit.

"Isn't this a visit?" I said.

"Nicky, we never see enough of you."

"How about Thanksgiving then?" I asked her. "It's only a month away."

"Well of course Thanksgiving." She sounded annoyed. Apparently, Thanksgiving didn't count. Visiting at Thanksgiving was a commandment.

"Who's doing Thanksgiving this year anyway?" I asked. "You, or Aunt Carmella?" I knew that the plans would already be under way.

"We're going to Aunt Carmella's." Then she added, cautiously, "Monica and David won't be there this year."

"Aha!" I said, jumping at the opportunity to tease her. "So I'm not the only Mr. Russo in the family!"

My father joined us. He, too, looks younger than his years: ruddy face and a head of thick, silvery hair that Mom loves to tousle. Whenever I think of Josh and me being together forty years, I think of my parents and how they still get a kick out of each other. I want that, too.

"Where've you been?" my father asked me.

"Dad, do you know how many people have asked me that today?" I said, laughing. I was enjoying all these opportunities to tease them.

"Well, just don't be such a stranger," he said. He was trying to be brave and feisty, like Mom, but I could tell he had really missed me.

"Do you think Josh would like to be invited?" Mom asked. She glanced quickly at my father.

I could still see Josh chatting it up with Dennis. The two of them looked like they were having a good time.

"Gee, maybe," I said. "I'll find out."

"And call once in a while," my father added.

"*Oy vey*," I said, raising my eyes heavenward. We all laughed.

Josh and I have friends who every year throw a big gay Thanksgiving party in the South End: fifteen, eighteen guys. We've been invited the last two years, and doubtless will be invited again this year, but again we'll decline. Josh will either come to Aunt Carmella's, a first, or he'll go to his folks' in New

Jersey. We've often fantasized what it would be like to be with our "gay family" for just one of the holidays, and now, as my parents kissed me goodbye—the first time ever that they'd left a party before me!—I thought about this again. I knew that even at that moment Dennis was being enrolled into our—Josh's and my—other family, and that one day we would invite him and his other half to dinner. And that that would lead to their meeting other friends of ours, and our meeting other friends of theirs. And so it would go, on and on, *in secula seculorum*, as some of us used to say. At the same time, I couldn't wait to tell Josh that Aunt Carmella was inviting him for Thanksgiving.

I started making my way over to the two of them, then noticed, on a coffee table in the middle of the living room, the crystal goblet from which the rabbi and all the parents had tasted of the wine. It was still half full—a rich ruby color—and seemed, for that richness, sadly abandoned. I picked it up, drank, then carried the rest to Josh and Dennis at the bar.

A HAPPY AUTOMATON

• BRUCE BENDERSON •

1

I WAS TREADING water in New York City when I hooked up with Custard the black albino, by way of Oklahoma, in Times Square. For two years I'd been combing hustler bars near Forty-second Street. I'd slowly dumped a career, taken up my savings, found a room in a hotel, and dropped out of a circle of well-meaning friends. Now I wandered this small maze around Eighth Avenue where no one knew my last name.

I'd seen him—Custard aka Rambo (viz tattoo on left arm)—a few times before, I suppose. Those hollow cheeks, pinholed saucer eyes, scruffy goatee were far from unusual in the places we frequented. What set Custard apart from the others, besides the fact that he was an albino, was a kind of violent yearning or dread coating every word or action. I was soon to learn that it could take control of the tender, wiry body.

But I'm getting ahead of myself. It isn't just that the chain of events is tangled in my mind, it's the fact that the beginning seems hidden and ongoing at every moment. For example, eight, maybe nine, years ago. A time of normal, banal, unrestrained pleasure seeking. Talk of a new illness that is probably sexually transmitted races through the grapevine. I am lying in bed alone, with a fever that undulates and a splitting headache. It marks the moment when I decide that I am being invaded by a deadly virus. No sense in trying to corroborate it medically or to stem its tide by a change in behavior. The sickness growing inside me has a slow will of its own.

And years before this watershed, there is a hallway in an Art

Deco building. Orange light from new fifties fixtures illuminates the camel-hair cap that matches my towheaded older brother's little overcoat. He is eleven. He has come to pick me up at the optometrist, and a sudden surge of brotherly sentiment makes him put his arm over my shoulder. The gesture makes my skin crawl. Later my brother will become sadistic to animals and other children, but especially to me. I am convinced that it is all based on my repulsion of that single gesture in the hallway near the optometrist's office.

A fatal outcome of both these incidents lies far in the future—last year, in fact. His name is Sphinx. Aliases Shadow, Joey. He has a way of calling forth new tricks by arching his eyebrows quizzically. His liquid, encircled eyes remind me of a Velázquez painting. According to his story, he has no memory of his real parents. He was taken away from them while still a baby and sent upstate to a foster home. There on the farm, the Sphinx quickly became little more than one more pair of hands. On the day of his sixteenth birthday he told the old farmer who had raised him that he wanted out. He planned to go back to New York and find his half sister. The old man thought it was a dumb idea. Go, if you want to, he sighed. So Sphinx left and it was obvious they would never see each other again.

This is the probably true story he tells me the night of our first meeting under seven thousand watts of fluorescent light in Time Square's McDonald's. I am listening carefully, frozen over coffee, watching the shreds of lettuce spill over his blackened fingers. In this shadowless light his face is as blunt as a feline's, the snout almost as foreshortened.

I am walking into a dim bar perhaps a couple of days later. The person called Sphinx is sitting up front, hands in pockets, face in a deadpan. His eyebrows trigger up, and his eyes fix mine in the mirror. I buy him a drink. His fingers tremble as he takes the glass from my hand. The fingers of his other hand drum impatiently on the bar while a foot taps incessantly. He keeps talking. Whenever he pauses, his teeth begin to grind.

About a year and a half after he came to New York he got sent back upstate to a correctional facility. Maybe it was just a question of hanging out with the wrong people. There was a friend of his who had a gun. They kept talking about what it would be like to have a lot of money . . .

"*Over here's the methadone clinic, Sphinx. There's this doctor works here gets paid once a month, on a Wednesday. He's a black dude, see. During lunch this doc will always cash his paycheck over there across the street, then go back on the job till four. Then he comes back out, walks to that blue Mustang over there . . .*"

Sphinx is telling the doctor—a trim black man in his forties—to unlock the door of the blue car. Both he and his friend are grinning as if they have just run into a pal. Under the friend's jacket the gun remains jammed against the doctor's back.

Sphinx is lying on top of the doctor on the floor in the backseat of the car. The friend is watching outside with the gun. Sphinx finds the wallet against the man's ass, ties him up. They run.

What happens to the three or four thousand they get this way? How long will they have to enjoy it before getting caught? Sphinx's big eyes blink, not registering one word of my question. He lights a cigarette and suggests we take a walk. He leads me down a dark path of broken street lamps toward Tenth Avenue. Passing a park, he hops over a railing into bushes and unzips his fly, motioning me over.

The next night he says, Want to get high?

We go back to my hotel, I give him twenty dollars, and he leaves to get the smoke. Lying on the bed, I let my eyes float to the wavy lines of the TV. Hard to believe that giving into uncertainty can make anxiety retreat. Then only repetition is left to be dealt with.

He is taking out a glass tube. Fitting one end with a wire screen. Then he opens one of the two tiny plastic vials. "Where's the reefer?" I ask.

"Reefer? This is crack, man. You got a lighter?"

Sphinx scowls at me when I tell him I don't, but he digs out a book of matches. Having never smoked crack, I watch him.

He does it by taking one of the "rocks" out of the little vial and putting it in the end of the glass tube, against the wire screen. As the crack is heated and melts, turning to smoke, it actually does make a crackling sound. Then you heat the sides of the tube to turn the melted part to more smoke.

His pouting lips suck the glass stem. He takes a long pull and holds it, then lets the white smoke stream out. It smells like plastic. He takes a second pull and puts the stem down to cool. He jumps up suddenly, runs his hand through the hair on his neck, goes to the door to check the lock, sneaks back to see if the pipe is cool, hops to the window to peek out of it.

When the stem has cooled, he holds it shakily to my lips, tells me to pull slowly. He puts a match to the other end, and the white smoke begins to stream into my throat. It feels burning and numbing at the same time, like dry ice. As the smoke enters my lungs, my heart starts pounding almost instantaneously. It is a strange sensation because the tangible smoke is so immediately connected to the racing feeling of getting high.

After I take a second drag he gets up again. He strips off his tank top. Lanky arms and chest. With shaking hands, he begins to caress his crotch through the black jeans. Suddenly he lunges at me, and I collapse backward onto the bed. Our mouths fasten together as he unbuttons my shirt, kneads my chest, his hands streaming with sweat. Bulky and wide-hipped as I am, my body fits into the lithe puzzle of his—hard, bony, covered with scars and scratches. We struggle for control over one another, stopping every few moments to light the pipe, inhale the smoke, and exhale it into each other's mouths.

When I wake up he is gone. I have a rapid pulse, short shallow breathing, aching muscles, raw nipples. This will be followed, surprisingly enough, by weeks of intense well-being. Someone has pulled out a stop. Pounds begin to melt, and daily routines, like dressing myself or styling my hair, become effortless, creative, for the first time. Yet I deny that I am becoming a "crack-head." The "crack attacks," as Sphinx begins to call them, are few and far between, less than four or five a month.

. . . I'm going to rape you. Are you ready? It will be the only "man rape" in the whole history of crime. Let me get those hands behind your back and pin you to this couch here. You're not going to get away. Now I'm going to rip off your clothes and rape you.

He certainly plays along, laughing with delight as I pin his arms behind his back. And he is still laughing, but derisively, when I look up from our entwined bodies into the grim eyes of our parents. Heart pounding with embarrassment, I leap off my brother, run down the hall into my room.

Now they know.

There is the creak of the bathroom door and animated whispers of my father; laconic, bemused answers from my brother: Just don't encourage it, that's all . . . I'm not . . . We're really worried about him.

And years later I would not be exaggerating to maintain that this is one of the lenses through which weeks with Sphinx will slip by. Weeks that have a semblance of days without incident. I mean to say they have a seeming reasonableness. I may make a quip about chaos or out of nowhere admit the importance of being organized. At that moment, someone who knew me intimately would be able to see something peel off and drop away . . .

From time to time friends come to see me and Sphinx, though *friend* means something else out here. People know that I have money, but they also have to respect me because I have protection. Supposedly my boyfriend is taking care of that. *Boyfriend?* Then do we love each other? Perhaps. Sentiment, jealousy, and resentment are all extended states of mind in another, more familiar story. In that story they stretch consciousness out like pulled taffy into a narrative. Out here where I am now, the same feelings exist as spells, only for the moment and in a relation of discontinuity . . .

Sphinx is nonetheless worried about my state of mind. I'd sent him out to score get-high and he'd come back with a single vial. We opened it and found that it contained only tiny chunks of macadamia. "Shit," I heard him mumble, "ripped off by fucking Freddy."

I knew whom he meant. Freddy is a spittle-lipped Polish boy who dresses in fatigues and shaves his head. Sphinx went out to look for him but came back empty-handed.

According to Sphinx, weeks will pass before what I will tell about is supposed to have happened. We're sitting at the bar when I realize that Freddy is sitting at a table across the room eating a bowl of chili. I can feel myself leaping to my feet, pointing an accusing finger at him. "Hello, Mr. Rip-off!" I am shouting across the room for all to hear. "Sell any macadamia nuts today?"

There is silence in the bar as everyone turns to watch. Freddy's jaw freezing as he asks if I am referring to him.

"Who's else?" I spit.

Freddy's body is convulsed by trembling as mine is inflated with a sense of omnipotence. As the tip of his tongue darts over his lips, he seems to lunge toward me while men on either side hold him by the arms. One is shakily trying to calm him. "Forget it, Freddy boy."

Freddy's big knuckles are growing pale on the edge of the bar stool, but I have not gone back to my seat. The Sphinx, my protector, has become ashen. As awed whispers begin to erase the silence, he leads me out. I've never seen him look so upset before.

"I can't believe how dumbass you are!"

"What do you mean? He's the one who ripped us off, isn't he? I mean I know it wasn't you holding out on me."

"Sure it was him. But that was a month ago and nobody around here remembers anything. Even I forgot about it."

"Fuck it. He's a cocksucker."

"Listen, Bruce. About a year ago I used to carry around this piece. It made me feel good. Like I used to play with the idea in my mind, if anybody looked at me funny I'd just take it out and blow 'em away."

"I don't give two fucks. I don't get ripped off!"

"Listen, Bruce. You got five dollars so I can get something to eat?"

"Sure, Sphinx, sure."

And a week later, had he really forgotten? When I mentioned the incident, the eyebrows flew into their quizzical arch, and the mouth went slack. It was the dull, wry look of a gentleman.

"Well, I'm going home," I told him. His face remained without expression.

"I mean just for a couple of days. My mother has cancer."

I flew upstate the next morning. Some of her hair had fallen out from the chemotherapy, but her eyes were aglow with the abstract idea of having a son home.

We sat in one of the more expensive local restaurants with

Dad, eating canned asparagus tips under hollandaise. Mom began a conversation. "See him?"

She meant a middle-aged man who was sitting across from a pregnant woman. He looked bottom-heavy too. His thinning hair was neatly clipped in back, but his sideburns were long and fanned. For some reason he reminded me of a lawyer during the Nixon administration.

"Yes, I see him."

Mom nodded toward my black leather jacket. "See him, see you."

"What's that supposed to mean?"

"I know his mother. You're about the same age."

"Okay."

"Look how decently dressed he is. How neat his collar is." Suddenly Mom's sad eyes leapt desperately into mine, mascaraed lashes trembling. "Couldn't you try to look more like him?"

"No, I couldn't."

"Why not? I know it isn't living in New York that made you change because I've been around too. People are basically the same wherever they live. But he's sitting with his wife, isn't he? And you're sitting with your sick old parents. Wouldn't you like to be sitting where he is?"

"I don't think that would be too appropriate, Mom."

"And why not?"

"Just because."

"Because why?"

"Because I am middle-aged like him, and college-educated too. But I'm also a cocaine-using homosexual living on the fringes of crime with a nineteen-year-old ex-offender hustler. Now you tell me. Is where that guy's sitting really appropriate for me?"

Dad piped up. "Clown. Eat your asparagus."

It is probably in the very same frame of mind that I see myself standing in her garden without my shirt, looking at her enormous roses. "I was just admiring the flowers you planted," I hear myself say.

"Well, you got quite a burn, son."

"I did not, Mom."

"You sure did. Oh, my God. What's that on your arm? It's not AIDS, is it?"

"What are you talking about?"

"Good God, it's worse than AIDS. Does my son have a tattoo? Why, Bruce, why?"

"Because I like tattoos."

"You *like* them?"

"They're romantic."

"I'd hate to be the girl you go out with."

"I mean like literary romantic."

"Literary? My son the writer. He writes all over his arm, disfigures his body. Won't they love that at the Pulitzer committee."

"Did it ever occur to you that some people could find a tattoo on a man's arm sexy?"

"Sure. I know what kind of people you're talking about. I know more than you think I do. You wouldn't think, would you, that your old mother would know anything about that. But I'm going to let you in on a little secret, son. I got something to show you on my left buttock. Excuse me for hiking up my dress and pulling down these panty hose. Go ahead. Look."

"Oh, my God, you've got a tattoo!"

"That's right. Now come close. Don't be afraid. I want you to read it."

" 'The door you open to cross my threshold of pain' . . . pain? I don't get it, Ma."

"I'm talking about ass fucking."

Bathed in sweat, I come to in the middle of the dream abruptly, to the sound of a slamming door. Sphinx has walked in with a girl of about fifteen. He says her name is Oklahoma. She has unbaked white skin, bluish-circled eyes, and stringy, dirty-blond hair.

"I was wondering, Bruce, if Oklahoma can stay here tonight since she's got no place to stay."

"All right."

Sphinx packs up the crack pipe for us. He hands it to Oklahoma, who takes a drag and begins to rap. Apparently she really has come from Oklahoma. She claims to have forgotten her real name. She remembers her arrival in New York at Port Authority in search of her boyfriend, about a month ago, where she immediately looked for a pay phone to call a shelter that asked no questions for a bed.

The number she dialed was called by many runaways. But a pimp had been able to have the calls rerouted to his own number. (A week later the ruse would be found out and reported on the evening news.) He told Oklahoma where to wait for him so he could take her to the shelter. She ended up in a hotel, where she was raped after being injected with heroin.

The pimp must have misjudged the dose because she fell into a coma. When she came to alone in the hotel, she had a vivid memory of the incident, but no recollection of her own name.

As we get high, Sphinx and Oklahoma start to kiss. He will cradle her in his arms, lavish her with caresses, lull her into believing in him. The maneuvers are far different from any he has ever tried on me during our acquaintance and lovemaking. The two get naked and climb into the bed next to me. At some point I must have fallen back asleep.

Cathy!

I awake with a start, the name ringing in my ears. Oklahoma has claimed to have discovered her real name! We are all naked in bed together. Rolling away from Sphinx, Oklahoma Cathy curls up against me. "I owe you," she sighs.

"For what?"

The Sphinx's naked body doubles up with laughter. "You don't remember, man?"

How many nights later do I come to again, feeling like the wrong thread ripped out of a fabric by the weaver, the room dark but light streaming from the open bathroom door? Squinting into it, I think I see Oklahoma Cathy's naked silhouette. Then a male body coming out of the bathroom. He glances at the bed and leaves.

"Where's the Sphinx?" I manage to call out. My mouth and throat are so coated that I can hardly speak.

"He went out. Now go back to sleep."

But when I wake up this time, I am even less than a single thread in a vast, empty grid. The sheet feels wet and grimy, caked to my thigh. A more emaciated Oklahoma Cathy in halter, short-shorts, and a different hairdo is smiling down at me. I open my cracked lips to try to speak, but a pattern of needles shooting across my face prevents me. Running my fingers over the skin around my mouth, I feel the tiny lesions.

"Don't touch," says Cathy. "They're goin' away."

"What happened?"

"You just had one toke too many. One moment you were on a roll, you helped me figure out what my real name was. Then bingo: out like a light. Do you remember yesterday? You came to then, had us laughing all night long doing imitations of your folks before you passed out again. All them sores popped up when you were sleeping, what are they, herpes, right, Custard?"

Bare-chested under his leather jacket, his face serious and pale under a tight yellow natural, Custard, aka Rambo, comes to sit at the edge of the bed. His saucer eyes keep getting lost in shadow. With a bruised-knuckled hand he touches my face lightly. "That's right, bro. Herpes. They ain't nothin' to worry about. I had a case of 'em in jail when I got knocked on the head. They'll be goin' away before you know it."

"What's he doing here? Where's Sphinx?"

"Don't talk about Sphinx," says Oklahoma Cathy. "Don't you remember how he went away soon as you got sick? And he took your bank card with him, I think."

"I want to talk to the Sphinx."

"You seen the Sphinx around?" Cathy asks Custard with a nonchalant sigh.

"Lasts I seen him was with Shorty," says Custard.

How can there be theft in a thieves' world, where possession is a parody? To whom do even our bodies belong, when self-possession exists only in the instant and when possession is only pursued for pleasure? At the bar, Shorty raises his tiny claw, which is missing part of the thumb. "Yeah, I seen Sphinx. I got something to show you." With a flourish he whips off his little baseball cap and sets it on the bar next to his Southern Comfort. Then he lowers his head to show me a four-inch bald spot with stitches.

"Tell Sphinx thanks for me, will you?"

"Sphinx? Come on," I say. "He didn't do that to you."

"No, bro, you're right. He didn't," squeaks Shorty. "But the Sphinx sent a friend. The Sphinx sent him."

"I don't believe you."

"I was coming out of the Marriott with this john, a senator always gives me ninety. They seen me walking out there with him. The friend beaned me with a lead pipe and Sphinx comes for the ninety."

"Like shit he did. I'm going to ask the Sphinx."

Shorty pulls the cap on quick again. "No, don't! It'll only cause trouble. I don't want them coming at me again."

"Okay, Shorty, don't worry. But who's this friend of Sphinx's?"

"I don't know him, pop, but I seen this dude before. He's a what-you-call-it . . . albino."

A dizzy spell dips me backward, and my face falls into a shaft of light for a moment. Shorty sees the sores.

"Yo, how come you got weird sores all over your face?" He peers up at me curiously, while my mouth remains sealed. I am only a thread in this amorphous, shifting tapestry.

I live to perpetuate the laws of the world.

2

There is no pause to put down the briefcase or take off his suit jacket. "Something's wrong," he says. "Something's wrong," says Dad again. Instinctively he goes toward the hall where the thermostat is located. Then he backtracks, goes to the kitchen and gets a flashlight. "What's wrong in this house," I hear him mumble again as he snaps on the flashlight and beams it at the thermostat. Then he bends close. Like a jeweler working through an eyepiece, he squints and trains one eye on the dial. He shifts the dial less than a millimeter. "Somebody's been fooling around with this," he says.

"Isn't it set for seventy-six?" I ask. "That's how you always have the air-conditioning. I remember it was put on seventy-six."

"It's not set for seventy-six," he says.

I am drawn to the thermostat. I peer at it over his shoulder. "It's set for seventy-six," I say.

"Ah ha," he snorts, "so you think so. But if it is left like that, it'll keep going until it gets seventy-four. The idea is to put it *here*." He shifts the dial to seventy-seven, but it really isn't seventy-seven, either. It is an infinitesimal space below the mark for seventy-seven, a position so precise that no one can find it but him.

"*There*," he mumbles, moving the flashlight closer. "There!" Suddenly he whips around with uncharacteristic abruptness. "I know your mother couldn't have done this because she's too sick to get out of bed. But you, you don't understand. You're wasting energy. Were you hot in here? You're crazy, it's not hot in here. Do you think it was hot in here, something is wrong with you if you think it is hot in here, go ask your mother, because it was seventy-six!"

"I—I'm not hot in here," I answer.

"Good," he sighs. "I'm glad you're here, son. Your mother is so sick and she's glad to see you. Stay for a week, why don't you."

"I won't be able to, Dad."

"I understand."

Though Custard's hands and feet are peeling from eczema, the rest of his body looks smooth and yellow, like custard. He is sitting on the edge of the bed in his underwear. He's got my shaving mirror and is trimming the edges of his sparse blond goatee. He is trying to convince me to buy some crack so that he and I can get high. His girlfriend, Oklahoma Cathy, went out about three hours ago to try to turn a trick, and there is still no sign of her.

I am unwilling to buy crack, as Custard well knows. I was out for five days the last time I smoked. I must have gone into convulsions or something. And then the herpes. Herpes is a bad sign, I explain, it has to do with the immune system. Besides, money is running low.

Custard puts the mirror down so he can rest a hand on my leg. He explains masterfully, with a smile, why I am mistaken. Did he tell me about getting the herpes all over his ass in jail after a fight? And now he's A-okay. It depends on how pure what you smoke is. None of that stuff made with ammonia. That's poison. I know where to get some pure shit. Just lay twenty or thirty on me, I'll be back.

When he gets back, he takes out the new glass stem and jams the screen tightly into it. Gallantly puts the first rock in for me. Begins to tell me about him and Oklahoma Cathy, before taking his pull. She's been his woman since she was thirteen. Then he had to leave her in Oklahoma to go West with his brother.

In his underwear again, the smoke streaming out of him, Custard struts back and forth across the carpet as the words spill out. Life is a fuckup. I fucked up my hands in Death Valley, working in a borax mine. It gets into your skin and burns cracks into it. Saw people crushed by falling slabs of borax. Me and this little Mexican cunt living in a trailer near the mine. You know those pincers on poles they use to get the cans down in grocery stores? We tightened one up. Caught rattlesnakes with it and cut off their heads and tails, chicken-fried 'em.

Reggae on the radio. Custard is talking politics. Those Jews, man, who think they can let a land go then come back to claim it, kick everybody out. And that fucking Reagan, who thinks all people have to be like him, somebody should teach that asshole a lesson and blow him away. What about poor people who don't got ranches in Santa Barbara?

Station changed. Custard is dancing. Doing an R-and-B stroll. Singing along with the words as he mimes with his hands. We used to do this in jail.

Stops. Eyes go far away. Mouth tightens into a grimace. That's right, man, I was in Sing Sing. The saucer eyes get even bigger and the pinholes look tinier. Fucking two and a half years because I had a happy trigger finger. I'm fucking not going back to that fucking place, man. I made up my mind about that. I want to get a job, go back to school.

Anger begins to flood Custard's pink, blank-eyed face. Is it jail or a job? Cathy? The mines? Does it matter?

"Tell me what's happening to you."

"I don't know, Poppa. I feel funny. I feel like I could take somebody's head and smash it, you know what I mean?"

"Of—course—I—know—what—you—mean." It's hard to speak with the crack building up in my head, inflating spaces between each word. I pull the eczemaed hands into mine, massage them. Feel the once broken, ill set bones.

"There."

"That's right, Poppa," says Custard. "It feels good, don't stop."

"I'll take care of it for you."

"Harder, I can't feel it."

"I'm massaging your hands as hard as I can, Custard."

"It feels good."

Violence shuddering through his muscle-addled spine, he has sprawled facedown on the bed, legs kicking. "Fucking goddamn, it's not fair. Massage my legs harder, bro."

"I can't take it all away from you, Custard."

"You can, Poppa, you can."

He kicks off the shorts, struggling for breath, cursing threateningly. My hands are aching from the effort of massaging his buttocks. "I can't feel it," he says.

"Yes, you can, baby." He has turned on his back now, is holding up a hard-on and trying to push my face down on it. But I am refusing to suck it without a rubber. So my hands, trembling from crack and limp from fatigue, manage to rip open the package and fit one on him. The wave breaks soon in one gigantic convulsion that takes us with it, legs closing around my neck in a scissors lock, ferocious pumping . . .

He leaps to his knees on the bed. Rips the rubber off and holds it up to the light from the television. His face is streaming sweat. His hollow eyes triumphant, exultant.

"Look! Look! How many sperm! A million? A billion? Enough to start a whole nation!" He ties a knot in the end of the rubber and throws it in my face. "Put it in the sperm bank!"

A few days later, as his head is resting on my thigh, the telephone rings for the first time. Custard wanted a telephone. Of course, it's not Oklahoma Cathy calling. She's been gone more than a week since that day she went out to find a trick. She would have no idea that there is now a phone in the room. I pick up the receiver.

"Hello?"

"Hello, little brother."

"How did you get my number?"

"There are ways, when you work for the government in Washington."

"But I'm not listed."

"I told you, there are ways, that's all."

"So why are you calling?"

"I want to know how my little brother is."

"Fine."

"Are you? I doubt that. I doubt that you're fine."

"Do you now."

"Yes. And I thought I would just try to call you now because even though it's two P.M. on a Thursday, well—I didn't expect you to be at work, no, I didn't expect you to be working."

"What business is it of yours?"

"Well, as it turns out, brother, it is very much my business. What you are doing with your valuable time is very much my business, some people might say."

"Those people are wrong."

"Are they? Well, I don't know if they are. Because I think it would be very much my business how you spend your time when you will be living off the money our parents slaved for. And I am out here trying to support a family."

"Your fucking family doesn't concern me, big brother. Nor am I interested in what you think of the way I spend my time. And as for that money our parents slaved for, I am not living off that precious money but on my own savings, for your information."

"Well, it's a whole new ball game now, kiddo."

"What do you mean?"

"I mean that Mom is dead and for some perverse reason she has left you a rather substantial trust which both Dad and I tend to oppose to the bitter end."

"Mom is dead?"

"That's right, kiddo. Be talking to you."

"Rub my ass harder, man . . . Give me that stem."

"How's that?"

"It's all right. Keep rubbing it . . . Yo, Bruce, when you first saw me, did you think I was white?"

"I don't really think about what color people are, Custard."

The pale-eyed, pink skull-face looks at me with annoyed contempt. "You mean you didn't think about was I white or black?"

"I just didn't think. Could I have some of that pipe?"

"Wait a minute."

"Jesus, Custard, you're hogging it all for yourself. Give me some of that."

"Open your mouth one more time and I'll let you have this."

"Give me that pipe."

"Don't get me mad, man."

"What would happen if I did?"

"You ever been worked over before getting cornholed, Bruce? Kind of opens you up first. Happens all the time in jail. Keep rubbing my back, rub my shoulders for me."

"I don't like violence, Custard."

"Nobody does, Poppa, but sometimes it's necessary."

"When would that be?"

"Keep acting wiseass and you'll find out."

"Maybe I just will, maybe I'd like to find out."

"You know I wouldn't hurt you, Daddy, long as you keep looking out for me."

"Hmm, hmm."

"Feels good, don't stop."

"Who do you think I am, your wife or something?"

"That's right, baby. Why don't you put on Cathy's panties and walk around for me, like a real wife."

"Very funny."

"And don't talk back to me, neither. I hate a white female talks back to me."

"Whatever you say, darling."

"Keep rubbing my legs like that. Give me that pipe. C'mon, put on Cathy's panties for me, would you?"

"I'd feel silly."

"No you wouldn't. Now put on some lipstick."

3

Way back when . . . We're back at the beginning again, when the stakes were not so high. Life was a banquet then. People who were around in those days would know what I mean. Our libidos found a free, expansive structure. You know the rest. I'm talking ten, twenty years ago, before pleasure got detoured into dread. You had sex or got high when you wanted to and tried not to give it much conscious value. You wanted to be directed but thought about it as something that was just happening to you . . . So let's get high again, baby. This time it's me saying it. Custard's been out like a light since he got back at five. Why won't he wake up? The moving job must be taking a lot out of him. Too bad we need the money. Cathy had disappeared. I'm stone broke and any money from the will is years away. So c'mon, baby, wake up. I want to get high.

I walk over to the pile of clothes on the floor and pick up the industrial stapler lying next to it. The thing weighs more than an anvil and spits one-and-a-half-inch staples. Custard says he uses it to put together wooden packing boxes.

Get up, baby. You don't even look like you're breathing. Playfully I aim the gun at his ass and start to pull back the trigger. He flips around and jerks to a sitting position. "Chill, bro, I need my rest, man."

"And we're going to rest, baby. We'll get high while we rest."

"Why don't you go out and get it?"

"You know I'm no good at that, Custard. You always get the good stuff."

With a grudging sigh he puts on his jeans, his work shoes, and his leather jacket, takes twenty out from under the rug, slams the door.

I lie back with a sigh. It is almost a sigh of luxury. For the first time I am . . . But how to explain the luxury of a life virtually without choices? It is an automatic life and I am a happy automaton.

Then why must the following happen?

Custard comes back and tosses two crack vials on the bed. I pop one open and dump it into the stem. I light, I pull, there is no crackling sound. Tipping a rock from the stem into my hand, I taste it. Macadamia nut.

"Who sold you this?"

"The Sphinx," says Custard. His tone is hollow, almost dead. No clue as to whether or not he is telling the truth.

The Sphinx?

It is not the Sphinx, or Custard, or even myself pulling me off the bed, putting my clothes on. I slip the stapler under my coat. It is not my mother, my father, or my brother who brought this pain, this suffering, this betrayal down on me.

Sphinx is easy enough to spot, weaving in front of the crack house on Ninth Avenue, wobbly-kneed high, his hand jerking from the back of his neck to his pants, then back again. Those familiar old eyes. As I come toward him the eyebrows arch quizzically, just as they did that long-ago day in the mirror. But this time my hand has a plan: to fly out and cover his face and slam it against the wall of the building. Starting at the Adam's apple, the other hand begins punching its neat row of staples all the way down to the navel.

IN MY FATHER'S CAR

• GEORGE STAMBOLIAN •

THERE, ON THE road ahead of us, a boy of sixteen is walking backward with confident strides, one arm extended, thumb erect. An Italian obviously, newly ripe and cocky, with flushed cheeks and limpid eyes. He is wearing one of those mesh jerseys that stops just below the chest, exposing a woolly stripe descending from his navel into his jeans. He bends his head as we pass, looks in, and smiles with a seductive mix of arrogance and pleading. A moment later he is an image in the rearview mirror, a torso locked neatly into hips, fierce buttocks pumping against denim on this hot August day.

What did he see? A man with glasses askew and a cloud of white hair slouched in the passenger seat. A gaunt driver with a black mustache who stared back at him hungrily. Two men together. Two old men.

"A hitchhiker," I say as though it mattered now, but my father remains silent. He is brooding over other images, thinking of no one's body but his own.

"Are you okay, Dad?"

"Sure, I'm okay. Why shouldn't I be okay?"

He is lying, of course. He would rather be driving himself, if he could. He would rather not be making this trip at all. And he considers it an insult to his manhood that he has to ride in the passenger seat, the woman's seat.

I am taking my father to the hospital where they are going to examine his heart and remove the catheter he has been wearing in his penis for over a month. Despite his impatience to rid himself of this humiliating tube, he almost called them this morning to cancel the appointment. "Doctors!" he muttered while I helped him into the car. I knew what he meant: Doctors are devils fooling innocent people just to make a fast buck. Doctors are idiots who couldn't fix a leaky faucet let alone a human being. What do doctors know about real people who work hard and don't take vacations every six weeks?

This is one of the few subjects on which my father and I agree, even though I am a doctor of sorts myself. This is how I remind myself that I am still, inescapably, his son.

My father thinks his troubles began when he started getting headaches threading needles in his tailor shop. Then a man sent back a jacket because the lapels were uneven. A woman complained noisily about a crooked hem. One day, while cutting open a seam with a razor, my father's hand slipped and deeply gashed a suede coat. My mother argued with him for months before he finally agreed to see a doctor who told him that the nerves in his eyes had begun to deteriorate, that one had already frayed to nothing.

"What are you telling me," my father shouted. "I can't work without my eyes. Work is my life."

"If you keep working, you won't have any eyes at all," the doctor said.

That night my father sat at the kitchen table with his head in his hands and refused like a child to eat his dinner.

"Quit while you're still the champ," I told him. "Look at Man O' War. Look at Muhammed Ali."

"Look at Garbo," my mother added, hoping to make him laugh.

My father clutched the edge of the table until the veins rose on his hands. "I was the best tailor in the world," he said. "There'll never be another like me. Never."

"Can't you go any faster?" he asks now despite the line of cars in front of us. He wants it to be over so he can return to his house, sit in his armchair, and watch his television. He must have a bet to make on a baseball game or maybe a horse race, and I am denying him a chance to win, reminding him perhaps, just by being here, of what he has already lost.

"Do you want us to have an accident so you can go to the hospital in an ambulance?"

He looks at me as though he were amazed I could imagine that scenario, then nods disdainfully at the traffic. "For Chrissake," he says, "why are these guys on the road? Don't they have work to do?"

He is an impatient man, my father, a stubborn man, and superstitious enough to drive one mad. He thinks that death has its own geography, its list of favored places where it congeals and waits: condominiums in Florida, funeral homes, and especially hospitals—go there and its bony hand will reach out for your throat. That is why he avoids attending the funerals of his friends. He is afraid he might catch death from the flowers or the embalming fluid, from the creaking chairs or the tears of wailing women. That is why he balks at the idea of a will and refuses even now to buy a cemetery plot.

"Please, Dad," I said to him a few months ago, "Lakeview is almost full. In another year or two there won't be any room left. Your parents are buried there, your sisters and your brother. All the Armenians are there and all your friends, Mr. Verelli, Mr. Syzmansky. Do you want to be put someplace in the suburbs with the WASPs?"

"Don't rush me," he said. "A man with a plot is a dead man." And when I told him I would buy it myself, if not for him then for my mother, he grabbed my arm. "Buy it and you'll kill me. Is that what you want, to kill your father?"

The truth is my father believes in miracles. He thinks he is never going to die. An afterlife of hymns and shining angels does not interest him. It is this life of flesh and corruption he intends to keep. People who think he is a religious man are mistaken. My father does not rely on faith. He has something better—overwhelming proof, irrefutable evidence that he will present point by point to anyone who asks:

At the age of ten, while bathing his father's horse in the sea, he swam out farther than usual and began to flounder. He went down once, twice, and then a third time. He said to himself, "I'm going to die," and saw his life pass before his eyes just as he had heard it would. But then, miraculously, his foot touched a smooth round stone, and pushing hard against it he burst up into the air gasping and happy to see the horse again.

At twelve he had a box kite he had made himself that was more beautiful and could fly higher than all the others. Some of his friends were jealous, and one day the meanest of them snatched the string from my father's hand and ran away. My father chased the boy along the shore, through the alleys of the city smelling of cumin, and finally onto a busy street directly in front of a Jewish undertaker's wagon with four horses. My father's body hit the center post and fell tumbling among the hooves and wheels, but somehow he got through with only a bruise on his chest that quickly healed. An undertaker's wagon!

Then it was the day Greek soldiers landed in Smyrna after the Great War to retake their ancient city from the Turks. A crowd was waiting at the harbor to greet them—Greeks and Armenians waving flags and cheering. My father was there too, next to the first line of soldiers, when a boy he had never seen before touched his hand gently and said, "Your mother wants you to go home and milk the goat." "What do you mean?" my father said. "Can't you see, the Greeks are here." "Your mother will be angry," the boy said. "You shouldn't make her angry." So my father gave the boy his flag and started to walk home when he heard a sudden volley of shots. Turkish patriots hiding among the roofs had fired on the crowd, killing several people. Despite the confusion my father struggled back to the place he had been and saw the boy's body on the ground, his eyes open to the sky. He was dead. He had died for him.

Finally, God spoke to my father. His spirit entered his seventeen-year-old body while he was walking home one day from the marketplace. It filled his chest with a dizzy heat, rose up and exploded from his mouth forcing my father to shout, "I want to go to America! I want to go to America!" People thought he was crazy. "Why do you want to leave?" they asked him. "The Greeks are here now, and everything's going to be fine—no more massacres, no more wars." Even my father doubted his sanity because he had never thought about America and knew nothing about the place. But his demands were so relentless his parents decided at last to send him across the Atlantic along with his brother Charles, and soon they also left to join their children after selling their house for a good price. The next year the Turks reoccupied the city, subjecting it to fire and vengeful slaughter. Those who survived lost everything.

"So I saved my family," my father says, "because God spoke to me, and He spoke because He loved me and because He knew I would hear him."

I have listened to these stories so often they have made a home for themselves in my mind. I see my father's head breaking through the waves and watch him as he bends almost lovingly over the pale face of the unknown boy. I repeat the horse's funny name—Muddy, and follow the magnificent kite as it soars above the Aegean. And if I asked my father now, in this car where he is slowly fading, he would tell those stories again, not to please me but to erect them once more into a fortress against death. He might even use them to ward off my doubts and questions because he knows that less fortunate people have told me other stories from those terrible years before the fall of Smyrna, and have filled my mind with other images—twisted bodies rotting along roadsides or half-swallowed by the desert, decapitated heads with gaping mouths impaled on spikes, skeletal women and children huddled in doorways silently screaming from hunger.

I was thirteen when I went to our city's murky library and found a forgotten book with photographs. One showed a mound of earth covered with the naked, freshly killed bodies of men all in their prime. Turkish soldiers were standing next to them led by a handsome officer who looked like George V or Nicholas II. And it struck me that the faces of these soldiers resembled those of their victims—the same mustaches, the same cropped beards. I had to remind myself that the languorously sprawled bodies were Armenians, uncircumcised Christians, until I realized they had probably been posed in this way—on their backs, their legs slightly spread—to draw attention to this difference. So I studied their nakedness, their white bodies against that black earth, until nausea and the ache of my erection forced me to close the book.

That night I asked my father why God had saved him and not the others.

"All those Armenians who were massacred," I said, "they must have prayed to God to. But God didn't hear them, or at least He didn't do anything to save them. And they didn't just die—they were starved to death and bludgeoned to death; they were drowned and burned alive, babies and children too, hundreds of thousands of them, all praying for nothing. Even those who killed them still say it never happened."

"I don't know about them," my father said. "God saved me. Be thankful for that."

"But that stone in the water, it was just there. Some people make it and some don't. It's just chance."

"Chance!" he shouted. "One time is chance, maybe two, but four times, that's not chance, that's destiny. God knows everything that will happen."

"Then why does He *let* it happen?"

"That's God's business," he said. "Do you think you can know God's business? Now shut up or He'll hear you."

A rush of coolness enters the car. Dappled sunlight crosses my father's face and makes him rub his eyes. We are going along the vast park that was given to the city a century ago by a wealthy industrialist. His statue stands at the entrance, an elegant man in a frock coat defiled by graffiti and bird droppings. Not far from here there is an abandoned quarry filled with water where naked boys used to dive off the rocks to prove they were men. A fat boy in my sixth-grade class named Willie Korda told me about the place one afternoon when we were alone in the cloakroom. "They've got hair already," he whispered, "and you can see everything." He moved his hand across my fly and offered to take me there, but I found it myself. I crouched in a thicket of laurels and watched them leaping, their genitals catching the sun as they floated for an instant in the bright air. I imagined they were the young heroes in my comic books, Robin or Boy, their secrets revealed at last.

As soon as I got my license a few years later, I drove my father's car into the city and found a boy my age with curly black hair walking along a side street eating a candy bar. He had pulled up his T-shirt so that it hung from the back of his neck like a small white cape. I asked him directions to a nonexistent street then invited him for a ride. He wanted to drive the car for a while just to see how it felt, but I told him it belonged to my father. "Then let's cruise around for girls," he said, but I suggested something else. I took him down the tree-shrouded road that ends at the quarry, and he showed me what he had even before I could shut off the engine. "Sort of looks like a Coke bottle, don't it?" he said. When I sank down on him, I could hear his heart pounding and smell the chocolate on his breath.

Willie became a florist when he grew up and served for many years as the scoutmaster of our local troop. He would see him every Fourth of July proudly marching his boys down Main Street, banners flapping around his head. He married a shy woman as fat as himself but never had any children. And he never abandoned the habit of taking solitary walks in the park whose hidden paths he knew since childhood. One night a gang of teenagers trapped him in the bushes, tore away his clothes, and took turns beating his pink body with fists and chains until his heart gave out. In court they testified that Willie had made advances and had tried to molest them. His wife said that was impossible: Willie had been a loving husband, a leader in the community. She begged the jury to punish his murderers severely, but they won their case.

The quarry is surrounded now by a high metal fence posted with warning signs. Too many of those strong leaping boys split open their skulls on the jagged rocks below the surface.

"Do you remember the last time we rode this way, you in the passenger seat and me at the wheel?"

"I always drove my own car," my father says. "I never asked anyone for a favor."

"I was sixteen. You were teaching me how to drive. We used to go to the park on Sunday afternoons. You had the Chrysler then. Don't you remember the '51 Chrysler?"

"That was a beautiful car," he says. "They don't make cars like that anymore."

"Every time I made a mistake you'd pound the dash and yell, 'You never were any good, and you'll never be any good.' Do you remember?"

"What are you talking about? Why am I listening to you?"

"I went to a driving school. They told me I was the best student they ever had."

"So you learned, didn't you? And I sent you to college to get a good education—something I never had."

"You looked so sad the day you gave me the keys I thought

you were going to cry. You asked me if I knew how hard you had to work just to earn enough for the down payment, if I understood the value of a dollar. Then you said, 'Driving a car is like having a gun in your hand, so when you're out there don't forget that the other guy's got a gun too, and the other guy can be a crazy idiot.' "

"That's right. There are idiots everywhere just waiting for another idiot to come along."

"At the end you rubbed your hand along the fender and said, 'She's a beauty. Take good care of her and remember I need her.' "

"I loved that car," he says. "I wish I still had her. This Mercury is a lemon."

My father's memories are not my memories. He thinks of the old country and recalls how sweet figs could taste in the morning when they were still cool and covered with dew. He always says, "There are no figs like Smyrna figs," and buys them whenever he finds them even though they are brown now and not green, dried and wrapped in cellophane.

He remembers the time he took all his savings, including the money my mother had hidden in a cookie jar for my sister's birth, and bought shares of Morman Motor Cars six weeks before the Crash because someone had told him it was a sure thing.

He relives the day a man came into his tailor shop who had fought in Vietnam. The man's right leg had been amputated below the knee at a field hospital in Pleiku. His left arm was paralyzed and had shrunk by a quarter. Shrapnel had twisted his spine. He asked my father if he could fix his new suit so he wouldn't look too ugly at his daughter's wedding. "I'll make you look like a king," my father said. He took out his tailor's chalk, lifted here, pulled there. "I'll be back in a couple of weeks," the man said when the measuring was finished. "What do you mean?" my father said. "Sit down. Have a Coca-Cola. It'll be ready in an hour." My father kept his word, and when the man put on the suit again he looked taller, straighter, even his shrunken arm seemed longer. "How can I thank you," he said. "Now I *am* a king." That night my father told everyone he had performed a miracle of his own because he had made a broken man whole again.

I see my father crouched at the kitchen table in our old house listening to race results on a radio station so garbled by static I imagine he is a spy picking up messages from the Germans or the Japanese whose secrets are encoded in the dollar figures for Win, Place, and Show.

I see him talking with others, making everyone laugh with his jokes, always the same, always successful. My father, the comedian, who still shows off his profile and says, "John Barrymore!" because someone once told him he looked like the actor, and because his name too is John. But in my mind he speaks to me only in monosyllables, commands or refusals, made harder by unsmiling eyes and cigarette smoke pouring from his mouth, yellowing his teeth, staining his fingers, and more present to me than his own body.

And I remember this scene at a church picnic when I was nine. The men are sitting outside in shirtsleeves admiring little Stevie Krikorian as he talks endlessly about his sacred Yankees while tapping his bat on his toe or punching his oversized mitt. He is their prince, the new generation in a new world, the pride of immigrants, practically a friend of Joe DiMaggio's and Yogi Berra's. "And what about your son, John," someone asks my father. "What does he like to do? Does he like ball too?" Their eyes turn to me, and I look to my father, but he only shrugs his shoulders.

I light a cigarette and blow the smoke out the window so it won't tempt him, but he catches the smell and savors it with flared nostrils. Then in a stern voice he believes is fatherly he says, "Don't inhale. It's not so bad if you don't inhale."

"What would be the point of it?" I ask him. "And how would I look smoking like that?"

"I'm giving you good advice," he says. "I'm speaking from experience."

"I know. The doctors had to scare you to death to make you stop so you wouldn't kill yourself."

He clenches his jaw and releases it with a hiss of breath. "So

I made some mistakes," he says. "Does that mean you have to make the same mistakes? Is that some kind of law?"

The traffic light suddenly changes, forcing me to stop the car so abruptly it frightens an old Puerto Rican woman at the curb who is carrying brightly printed shopping bags filled with groceries. Although the light is now in her favor she still hesitates, uncertain of what I will do. She studies my face cautiously then sees my father—another person with white hair burdened by life and ungrateful children. Reassured, she grabs her bags more firmly, bows her head as though we were the lords of this place, and crosses the street with a heavy shuffle.

"She looks like Nene," I say, meaning my grandmother, my father's mother. "Nene used to come down to this neighborhood to buy bulgur wheat and halvah and those dried apricots pressed in sheets I liked so much."

"Oh, yeah," my father mutters, making me wonder if he remembers this street of small shops and sagging tenements that has taken on the appearance of a frontier town.

"Look over there," I say, pointing out the place to him. "That's where Assouni's market was where she shopped. And two doors away where it says *Comidas Latinas*, that used to be Angelo's Pizzeria. They made the best pizza in Connecticut."

I say nothing about the night the Syzmansky brothers barred the entrance to Angelo's, grabbed their crotches, and told me, "We don't want you in here, faggot." Jimmy the younger brother, pursued by all the girls, who liked to "fool around" with me in the basement of his house while we looked at dirty pictures. Mike the older brother, the star of our high school basketball team, who would call me on the phone sometimes, his voice trembling, and say, "No one's home. Why don't you walk over?" Both of them the lanky, blond, and smooth-skinned sons of my father's dearest friend.

I remain silent two blocks later as we pass a corner bar boarded up with plywood that once had a neon palm tree above its door and was called the Bermuda Lounge. At seventeen I hid in the darkness across the street and watched the men come and go—men with mascara and puffed-up hair who seemed to belong to another race, to have dropped from a doomed planet—until one of them discovered me with his blinking eyes and said, "Don't be afraid, sweetie. Come on in. No one's going to hurt you." My father will never know how I ran away that night and drove his beautiful car through the city telling myself, "I'm not like that. I'm not like them."

"They're gone now," I say, "the Lebanese, the Italians, all the people who used to live here."

"That's what it's all about," he says. "That's America. You make money and you move."

"Well, you made a little money, but you never got rich."

"Who says I wanted to be rich?"

"You wanted it all your life. That's why you played the horses with every dollar you could spare."

"So how many times did I win? Once or twice."

"And you spent years calculating the ups and downs of the Dow Jones so you could crack Wall Street. You filled stacks of notebooks with your figures. Einstein would have been impressed."

"It was just a way to pass the time, to occupy my mind. A man needs to occupy his mind."

"You could have passed the time talking to your family, but instead you dreamed of hitting the big one, finding the secret treasure. You wanted to be the Count of Monte Cristo."

My father's eyes open wider. His body seems to rise magically from the seat. He tilts back his head and proclaims, "*The Count of Monte Cristo!* What a story! Who makes movies like that today?"

"No one, Dad."

"It was the best. It still is and will always be."

"You're right, Dad."

He smiles at me with a rare look of pride. For this moment I am his ally, his pal walking arm in arm with him toward some glowing horizon. Then he lets his body sink again, his shoulders hunched, his eyes on the road.

The Count of Monte Cristo with Robert Donat—my father has seen the movie at least a dozen times, and I have watched it with him almost as often on the old Admiral in our living room. Of all the stories he has ever heard, this is the perfect one: Edmond Dantès, a handsome young sailor, is falsely accused of treason by three greedy men and condemned to the prison of Château d'If where for fifteen years he struggles with the old abbé Faria to dig a passage through the thick rock walls. Before dying the abbé reveals the secret of a fabulous hidden treasure, and Edmond finally escapes by placing his own body in the abbé's burial sack, which the guards then hurl into the sea. He finds the treasure with the help of pirates, becomes the Count of Monte Cristo, and thanks to the immense power of his wealth proceeds to destroy his enemies utterly, damning each one by name—Danglars, Mondego, De Villefort.

"It's a story about justice," my father always says, "and I believe in justice, and so does America. Look at Hoover, that bastard! He was robbing the people, taking the food out of our mouths until Roosevelt came along and kicked him out. And look at what the Japanese did at Pearl Harbor. America was just sitting there minding its own business, but we got back at them, didn't we? We smashed them. It's the same story."

It does no good to tell my father that Roosevelt probably knew of the attack in advance, or that Hoover never planned to steal the gold from Fort Knox. "What do you know?" he says. "Were you there? I was there." To make his point he has never bought a Hoover vacuum cleaner even though we have laughed and explained that it is not the same family. He doesn't want that accursed name in his house, especially on a vacuum cleaner that could suck the change out of our pockets and mow us down on the carpet. Hoover is the Evil One, the bloated capitalist in pin-striped pants. Roosevelt is the eternal friend of the working man, the Great Crippled Father.

One winter night I asked him why he never talked about the way the abbé becomes a father to Edmond while they're in prison:

"Remember that scene just before the old man dies? He says, 'I leave my mind behind in your possession. Use it for justice.' And later Edmond protects his enemy's only son, the young viscount de Mondego, who's afraid he'll become a coward like his father."

"That's the way it should be," my father said. "One generation helps the next."

"But you don't understand, Dad. The real fathers almost kill their children. It's the other fathers, the ones without children, who save and teach."

My father started to laugh. "If you're looking for a better

father, don't waste your time," he said. "I'm the only one you're ever going to have."

"So that makes us even," I said, "because you'll never have another son. It'll all die with me—your name, your stories, everything."

"Is that what you're learning?" he scowled. "Did some man teach you to talk like that?"

Then, two years later, after watching the movie again, my father surprised me. He leaned forward in his armchair and confessed that his passion for *The Count of Monte Cristo* went beyond its associations with the Depression or the war.

"You see," he said, "I know what that story is all about because when I was young I was also falsely accused."

"Accused of what?" I asked him.

"You know, when people say you did something you didn't do, when they say you're something you're not?

"But what was it? Did they say you stole something, that you lied?"

I waited for my father's answer, but it never came. He stared at the shifting images on the television screen until his expression, which had softened, became hard again. "Forget it," he said. "That's all in the past. I don't want to talk about it anymore."

For years I tried to lead my father back to this question without success, so for years I thought his refusal to speak meant that his "crime" was in some way sexual. Perhaps while playing with a friend in the shade of a fig tree one of my father's gestures had been misinterpreted by the boy himself or by a malicious observer. Perhaps a wandering merchant, plump and perfumed, had tried to seduce him with gaudy gifts and after being rebuffed had made accusations in order to defend himself. Whatever the cause, the results would have been the same: taunts and hateful names. I even imagined my father's story about the goatboy might be more dream than reality, that the boy was not unknown to my father but a beloved friend who had betrayed him, at once a savior because of my father's continuing love for him, yet someone to be punished by an imaginary death. And so my father's desire to come to America would not have been inspired by God but by his own desperate need to escape an unbearable situation and to save his family from further shame.

I wanted this interpretation to be true so I could tell my father I understood him in the hope that he would understand me. Hadn't I been taunted and maligned like him, called names on the street and in the halls of my high school? And like him wasn't I still dreaming of justice, or rather inventing impossible scenarios of revenge against my enemies in which I would threaten them with exquisite tortures only to forgive them with an outstretched hand? But I never spoke of these dreams to my father because I would have had to explain to him that some accusations can be true and still unjust. I would have been forced to confess that of all my enemies I considered him the greatest.

Just as my father had escaped to America, I went to Europe as a student and hitchhiked my way to Smyrna to see his birthplace with my own eyes.

"Did you find our house?" he asked eagerly when I came back. "Did you see the fig trees?"

"While I was looking for the house I met a Turkish boy who offered to guide me," I said. "His name was Genghis, and he had blond hair and blue eyes. I didn't know Turks could look like that. He was just fifteen so I bought him ice cream, but later he bought me tea to show he was grown up. We spoke German mostly because his father had worked in Munich. I told him my parents were born here and that they were Armenians. He didn't really know what that meant, I suppose because he was too young and because there were no Armenians left."

I thought my father would be bitter. Here was proof, once again, that the massacres would never be acknowledged by those who had committed them, but he said, "I'm glad you met that boy. Turks can be good people. They were our neighbors. We ate the same food and played the same games. Things didn't go wrong until the end."

I never told him the boy and I made love that night as easily as we had eaten ice cream while watching the boats rock in the harbor—so easily that I realized my father might have done the same without a thought in a culture so unlike my own. But I have not abandoned my theory because I am afraid if I do my father's secret will elude me forever. Whatever the injustice he suffered, it must have been very great to give him this enduring thirst for revenge, to make him want to be the best tailor in the world, to make him dream of finding at last a fabulous treasure, and to fill him at times with longing for a son better than I. Once he may have wished to stay young forever, handsome as a movie star, but now he knows his last chance for justice is to escape death, to become a wonder for succeeding generations—old certainly, blind perhaps, unable to move someday, but eternally alive.

The hospital is a new tower of steel and glass on a hill overlooking the city. All that remains of its old structure is a squat wing of faded brick where, according to my mother, I was born a healthy baby, just the right size and weight. I mention this fact to my father as we leave the car, but once again he has no mind for these matters. Now that we have arrived, his strategy is to get in and out as quickly as possible before some hovering creature has a chance to carry him off. Yet when we reach the entrance he stops and examines his reflection on the heavy glass doors. "When did I get so old?" he asks and repeats the question: "When did I get so old?" I don't think he would be surprised if a voice said to him: "John, remember the time you missed lunch so you could finish that wedding dress? Remember the day that truck cut you off on the highway and you cursed until your head ached? That was the day you got old. If you'd eaten your lunch, if you'd started out five minutes later or five minutes sooner, you'd still be young and strong."

As for me, the evidence is clear—I am beginning to look like my father. And now that he is dying, my metamorphosis has accelerated. He seems to be hurling his traits at me in a mad effort to guarantee their survival, or something in me is sucking them from him against my will. All I conceded to him before were my long legs and the line of my nose. The rest, or most of it, I credited to my mother. But now he has invaded every feature and has found a passage into my bones to give me the same slight stoop, the same forward thrust of the head. "Stand up straight," my mother would warn me. "Look at your father. He never learned to stand straight." For years I slept without a pillow on the firmest mattress I could find, I pressed my back against walls. What good did it do?

When we enter the lobby, my father sniffs the air to find what he expected—the sterile, chemical smell of death seeping from the pastel walls, rising from the hard gray carpet. He looks at a man shaking with palsy who is kissing the fingers of a nervous little girl with pink ribbons in her hair. He stares at the tumble of multicolored teddy bears in the gift shop window, their eyes black and bright, forever open. And as we stand waiting for the elevator, he studies the faces of the people around us to see if their fate is written there, to see if he is still the exception, the only one here by mistake.

The elevator arrives at last, and the crowd pushes us in, presses us back. The congestion is even greater when we reach the next floor. I maneuver my father into a bit of empty space, and as I try to regain my footing, my knee strikes something hard. "Excuse me," I say before realizing that I have hit the metal frame of a wheelchair. The man seated in it returns my smile, looks at my father, and smiles again. We have recognized each other instantly like compatriots in an alien land. He is young, no more than twenty-five, but his youth survives now only in the defiant curve of his dark lashes and in a milky tenderness on the side of his neck. The rest of him looks as though he had been exposed to a rapid succession of violent seasons, malarial heats and paralytic colds, wearing away the flesh, curing it down to the skull. I am tempted to touch his hand and ask his name, but we continue to stare at each other as I read our common language in his eyes: "I was handsome once," he is saying. "You would have wanted me. If you can choose, if that's possible, then choose to look someday like your father, not like me." A moment later an orderly forges a path for him out of the elevator. The wheelchair rattles then moves soundlessly down a long white corridor.

By the time we reach our floor my father is sweating despite the air-conditioning. I can smell the heat of his body, a hint of urine.

"Is that the only elevator they have in this hospital?" he asks. "Do they think we're sardines?"

"A lot of people are sick, Dad."

"Who's sick?"

"That guy in the wheelchair. He's dying, and he's just a kid."

"Okay, maybe him, but the rest of them have been fooled by the doctors. They've got to pay for this place, don't they?"

He continues to mutter complaints until we enter the doctor's office where we are greeted by a buxom nurse in an immaculately white uniform, her shoes like clouds at her feet.

"Well, here we are," she says with a wink. "Right on time."

"I'm always on time," my father answers." "A man should be on time."

"I'll tell that to Dr. Chin," she says, "but while we're waiting for him let's get you into a smock and do a few tests—a little blood, a little urine."

"I've got the tube on," my father says. "I've got the bag."

"The catheter. We'll take care of that. Don't worry, your son will be here waiting for you."

"I don't worry," my father says.

The nurse smiles at me as though we were the only grownups present. "Come along," she says, and my father plays his part—a child again, following his mother to the fearful first day of school.

From this height I can see almost the entire city stretching down to the Sound, and in the far distance the faint, reassuring silhouette of Long Island. This is still an industrial city of immense brick factories producing brass and corsets and handguns; a working-class city of innumerable taverns and churches: St. Augustine, Sts. Cyril and Methodius, and our own Church of the Holy Ascension, sold years ago to Black Baptists who have retained its octagonal cupola and trefoiled cross. I was an altar boy there. I sang in the choir about God's mercy.

When my father reached America he came to this city and got a job in a lace factory. He worked six days a week, ten hours a day, and every night went to Mr. Jacobian's shop and learned the tailor's trade. Then he made love for the first time with a woman thanks to his worldly cousin Harry who had connections. My mother revealed this to me one night after quarreling with my father. "He went to a prostitute before he married me, did you know that?" she said, crying. "That's why they made him get married, to save him from hell, to stop him from wasting his money." I asked my father later if it was true. "I was young," he said. "I didn't know English very well." I wanted to know what she looked like, the color of her hair, her age. Had he been afraid? Had she helped him? Was he trying to prove something to himself? My father glared down at me. "Men don't talk about those things," he said.

Well, I have become a man who does talk about those things, but not to my father, never to him. Even before he married his world was his neighborhood and his home where the women cooked for him and washed his clothes. But the day he gave me the keys to his car, this city became mine. The economic boom hadn't changed the landscape yet, and on summer nights the streets were filled with people, mostly boys like myself and young men with nothing to do. I would see them hanging out in front of drugstores, smoking lazily on park benches, hitch-hiking without embarrassment. They would look at me as I passed. They wanted what I had, a car to kill time, and I wanted them.

A week after finding the boy with the candy bar, I saw two others fighting in a vacant lot, kicking and whipping each other with their belts. One was tall and stocky, the other wiry and quick. Both had crewcuts and were wearing identical red shirts with green collars. Finally, the big one fell clutching his belly, and the other stood over him slapping his belt against his thigh until he was sure it was finished. As he walked away I followed him in the car and asked if he needed any help.

"Help with what?"

"With anything you like."

He directed me to a street of decayed buildings and to an abandoned house with rusted balconies. We made our way over shards of glass until we reached the kitchen where the moonlight revealed a bare linoleum floor patterned in false mosaic. A cracked, blackened sink still hung from a wall.

"This used to be my house," he said. "I come here sometimes when I want to get away. It's peaceful. No one bothers you."

He drew me closer and put his arm around my shoulder. He had a bruise on his cheek and a streak of drying blood by his ear. I was surprised by his height, a full head shorter than mine.

"I need some relaxation. Would you like to be a buddy and give me some relaxation?"

He took off his clothes and arranged them neatly on the floor, then stretched out on top of them, his small white buttocks slightly raised. I stood next to him unable to move.

"What's the matter?"

"I've never done that to anyone before."

"It's easy," he said. "Just use lots of spit."

He moaned when I entered him, but I came in a shudder after only a few seconds.

"I'm sorry," I said.

He looked back sorrowfully then buried his head deeper into his damp shirt. "You can't win them all," he sighed. "But will you do me a favor? Will you please just stay in there for a while?"

After that I hunted every night I could and found a mechanic with greasy tools in his pockets I was afraid would stain the seat, a sailor from Wisconsin who stripped but kept his cap on because I asked him to, a handsome deaf-mute who lived with his mother in a trailer camp and thanked me with signs. I found college students who sometimes felt guilty and workers' sons who never did—Poles, Slovaks, Greeks, and especially Italians with names like Sal, Tony, and Vinny. I caught boys in summer whose bodies tasted of sea salt, and boys who steamed up the car in winter so that I had to wipe the windows before going home. Boys fresh from dates whose lips were still red from kissing, and boys desperate to escape their lonely nights. Some who asked for money, no more than a dollar or two, and those who offered, incomprehensibly, to pay me. The ones who had to be reassured that I expected nothing in return, and the ones who reciprocated every act with a hunger that surprised me.

And on those nights when my father needed the car I would walk to the main road, stick out my thumb, and let myself be caught by others. Most were married men who, I imagined, had sons of their own—factory workers with lunch pails tossed on the back seat, businessmen stiff with dignity, nondescript men so timid their hands would shake at the wheel. I would sit through their game of innocence waiting for the opening line:

"There's this guy down at the plant . . . You should see him in the showers."

"You're a good-looking kid. Do you have a girlfriend?"

"Boy, I'd like to do something tonight, anything."

At times I would have to encourage them, prompt them with a line of my own:

"I'm not going anywhere special. Just out for some excitement."

"I was just checking. I thought my fly was open."

When I spoke this way I would try to sound tougher, less intelligent than I really was. I would slouch in the seat, open my legs wider, and let them see what they longed to see, even turning my head away so they could look more easily. Whatever those men saw, I knew they wanted me, and that desire rushing beneath their words and glances made me feel as powerful as those slim-hipped street boys who so excited me.

It was after one of these hitchhiking adventures that my father offered the only sexual advice he ever gave me. He was sitting in the living room watching a baseball game on which he had confidently bet and would lose fifty dollars.

"How did you get home last night?"

"My ride didn't work out so I hitchhiked instead."

"I don't want you doing that."

"Why?"

An outfielder was staggering backward for a catch, but the falling ball was just beyond his reach.

"Damn it! He should've had that."

"Why shouldn't I hitchhike, Dad?"

He looked at me. The inning was over. "Because you can get into trouble."

"What kind of trouble?"

"You're a young kid. People will take advantage of you."

"How?"

"Some men look for kids like you."

"What men?"

"Men. Bad men."

"Why?"

"What do you mean why?"

"Why are they looking for kids?"

"Never mind why. I'm just telling you not to do it. Do you understand? That's all."

Had my father listened more carefully he might have heard the irony in my voice and realized that more than a baseball game had been lost. I had gone through a rite of passage far more important than his giving me the keys to his Chrysler. I knew more than he did, not just about my life but about the world, and I thought he could no more comprehend me than he could transport himself onto that grassy field in Chicago where the winning team was celebrating its victory. Sitting there in his armchair he seemed to shrink away, to become as tiny as the figures on the television screen. I held the truth. I was the master. I could destroy him with a word.

What desires do I have now that friends I loved have died or are dying like the young man in the wheelchair, when others have been killed on the streets like Willie Korda by those who might have been their brothers or their sons? And what power do I have now that my father has armored himself with frailty and approaching death? Two years ago my mother made another revelation to me. We were drinking coffee in this hospital after a visit to my father who was recovering from a prostate operation. "Your father still comes to me at night," she said, "and it frightens me because he tries so hard. I told him, 'John, that's all right. Don't worry if you can't finish,' but he keeps trying and then he cries. 'What good is a man if he can't work anymore,' he says. 'What good is a man if he can't be a man.' "

Sometimes I wonder if my father's death will miraculously give me new life. Other times I imagine that he can still guide me, can teach me things the way the old abbé teaches Edmond Dantès in the dank prison of Château d'If. Like a good student I have questions for him that I have refined over the years. They have a place in my mind next to his stories about Smyrna. Here they are, the questions I will never ask:

If he had not escaped the old world in time, and if I had been born there, would we have been killed someday together? Would our naked bodies have been displayed together on a mound of earth or against a riddled wall?

Will we reveal our great secrets to each other before it is too late? Will we find a hidden treasure that will enable us to seek justice against his enemies and mine?

And will his God save and protect me too, even though He

has failed to save so many others, and even though I have cursed him for forsaking them?

The nurse leads my father back to me. He looks weaker than before as though some nourishing fluid had been drained away, exhausted. His hair needs combing. He hasn't rebuttoned his shirt correctly.

"What did they do?"

"They took the tube out," he says. "They looked at this and that."

"How's your heart?"

"It's not my heart so much, it's my blood pressure. He gave me more pills. They always give you pills."

"What else did the doctor say?"

"He said I'm old."

"What does that mean?"

"Old. It means old. What else do you want it to mean?"

Once outside the sun presses down on us, almost blinds us as it glints fiercely off the windshields in the parking lot. My father raises a hand to his eyes and lurches toward the car. He attempts to open the door himself, forgetting that it is locked.

"Relax, Dad. We'll be home soon. You can take a nap and still have time to watch your game."

"I don't want to go home," he says. "What do I have to do at home? I want to see my tailor shop. Take me there."

"But, Dad, I don't even know if the building's still standing. They're tearing down that whole section of town for a shopping mall or something. They've blocked off most of the streets and ripped up the sidewalks. It's a mess, believe me."

"Did you hear what I said? This is my car. Take me or I'll drive there myself."

We go as far as we can and abandon the car two blocks from the site of my father's shop. The space in between is a jagged landscape strewn with slabs of broken concrete tilted at mad angles and rusted pipes jutting treacherously through the debris. Here and there remnants of softened macadam show treadmarks like the traces of prehistoric bones. We make our way together across this wasted land, sometimes side by side, sometimes with me a step ahead pointing out obstacles, suggesting footholds. My father wipes his brow and grunts in reply, determined to reach his goal. There are no workmen about, no sounds of machinery. Except for a haze of rising dust, the sky is cloudless. We are alone.

We come at last to the edge of a broad depression that was once an avenue. My father's shop is on the opposite side, its windows cracked, its door caked with mud, but still intact despite the demolition that has already devoured most of the structure housing it. The only way to reach it now without making a tortuous detour is to cross a makeshift bridge composed of narrow planks resting precariously on dented steel drums. I start to advise my father against following this route but he is already talking, telling me another story:

"There it is, my old shop. This is the old neighborhood. Emeric Verelli had a luncheonette next door to me. He served great blueplate specials—meat loaf, turkey, whatever you wanted. I used to eat there all the time. And across the street, right where we're standing, was Bill Syzmansky's tavern. In the summertime, when it got really hot and I was sweating over the pressing machine, he'd send one of his boys over with a cold bottle of beer. We were all friends, it was like a family with good times and bad times.

"I remember his boys. We went to school together."

"Do you know what it was like during the Depression? Roosevelt said, 'The only thing we have to fear is fear itself.' And he said it because people were afraid. I was afraid. Do you understand that? Every time I left the shop there'd be somebody outside trying to sell me an apple. 'Please, mister, buy an apple—just five cents, just two cents.' Old guys, young guys with kids at home looking for a piece of bread. Guys who used to be rich—bankers, big shots. It made no difference. Nobody had work."

"I know what fear is, Dad."

"But I wasn't afraid to work. I had to take care of your mother, your sister was a baby. I had my parents to support, my father was too old and sick to work. One day a man brought in some fabric, beautiful English worsted, and asked me to make him a suit. I was young then, still learning my trade. It took me three weeks to make that suit, and do you know what my profit was? A measly five dollars, and I was happy to have it."

"And now they're tearing the place down."

"So now they're tearing it down. John the tailor? Who was he? Maybe they'll build new shops for other people to work in, or just smash it all into a parking lot. What can I do about it? What can anyone do? But I want you to remember this—that shop put food on the table and clothes on our backs. We had a roof over our heads. Can you understand? It kept us alive."

My father does not expect an answer. He continues to stare at his old shop, caught in his memories, oblivious to everything else. Then, suddenly, his body stiffens, turns to stone. He has seen what I have already seen—a man with blond hair swept high on his head walking nimbly over the debris a hundred feet away. He is wearing large sunglasses with glittery ends, a flowing white shirt open to the waist, tight powder-blue pants that show off his fleshy rump and taper to a stop just above his ankles. His left arm is swinging in shallow arcs to balance his weight while his right hand remains firmly attached to the strap of his leather shoulder bag. He knows who he is—a queen of the old school preserved against all odds, an outrageous survivor, and now in this desolate arena almost an acrobat as he steps blithely onto the bridge without missing a beat and gives us a brief, regal nod.

My father has not moved, has hardly blinked his eyes. He is probably reviewing names to identify this creature in all the languages he knows—Armenian, Greek, Turkish, English. Or perhaps these words are too shameful for him. Perhaps the only thought he can permit himself is this: "He's one of those men, one of those bad men." And now my old anger returns fueled as always by the silences of the past. I want to say to my father, "Why stare at him when you can look at me, your son? Why search for names when I know all the names in even more languages than you do? Haven't you realized yet that I could die before you?"

"Oh!" my father shouts.

The man has slipped, has fallen with a bounce on his ample behind. His queenly legs rise and spread above him in the flawless sky. His arms become wings fluttering on either side of the narrow bridge. His bag drops from his shoulder and swings dizzily in the void.

"Oh, look!" my father says.

The man is up. He has lifted himself with a single agile leap. A quick brush to his buttocks, a quicker tuck to his hair, a final adjustment to his shoulder strap, and he is on his way again with undiminished energy—across the bridge, toward my father's doomed shop, and beyond to a place of his own, to a bar still open on a forgotten street where men laugh together under neon trees.

"Come on, Dad, let's go home," I say, anger lingering in my voice. "He may fall again, and then what will you do? You may have to go over there and help him, lift him up."

My father turns his tired face to me and lets me see the blue circles in his eyes. He puts his hand on my arm and leans his body against mine. He weighs me down yet seems about to fly away.

"Don't worry about him," he says. "He's still young like you and can take care of himself. But hold on to me, will you, so I don't fall too."

POPULAR MECHANICS

• CRAIG LEE •

"PLEASE, RICHARD, LIVE with me for just one year. You should be in a more normal kind of environment, don't you think? Just try it for one year."

Maybe Dad was right. He was tired of his mom's apartment, tired of how it smelled of patchouli and cat box, singed hair and Alice B. Toklas brownies stinking up the kitchen with a sickly sweet promise of pleasures he wasn't interested in. Dad's house had its own smells; water-logged mold, dust, Lemon Pledge. Somehow they were comforting. Outside his father's house there were avocado orchards, a freshly mown lawn, not continuous fog and uphill concrete. His mother bragged about how lucky they were to be able to live in San Francisco, how it was such an understanding, free atmosphere, not like that small-town "squaresville." But sometimes, when he'd watch his mom stumbling back home with her friends, guys that read poetry or played saxophones in North Beach cafés, deadbeats laughing at him because he was up watching "The Beverly Hillbillies" and TV was "just uncool, man,"—sometimes he'd think about how, whenever he visited Santa Juan, he and his Dad and his stepmom could watch TV and nobody complained and nothing was said because they were busy eating freshly made popcorn, not hash brownies. So maybe it would be all right to spend a school year in Santa Juan.

It wasn't. He realized that after a few weeks. His dad was pleased at first, but soon he faded away into the shoe store routine. They didn't go the Lake Roja like before, when Richard visited for two months every summer. Now his dad was even thinking of selling the boat. His stepmom was either indifferent or slightly contemptuous; "Oh, is that how they do things in San Francisco?" she'd continually say in a mocking tone. But the biggest problem was that he wasn't a Chuke, a Sosh, or an Okie.

Everything had been set and regulated at Santa Juan High long before Richard Manz entered ninth grade. If you were rich and white you were a Sosh. Poor and Mexican, a Chuke. White trash, Okies. He wasn't any of these things. The Soshes were Peggy's and Jimmy's and Billy's drinking Tabs and sneaking dry kisses in their parents' playrooms during parties where they'd assemble paper flowers for the annual homecoming parade's class floats. These parties were the social high point of the year and you weren't anybody unless you regularly went to, and held your own, float party. The Soshes were confident in their destiny and secure in their procedures. They knew nothing of where Richard had come from, knew nothing of Human Be-Ins or City Lights Bookstore. They were like an old family show rerun. Richard wrote in his diary: June Cleaver and Grace Slick are competing for my soul.

So he decided: I will ride this out and just observe. This place is too weird for me and I am too weird for them.

He went through the motions of his classes. Some of his teachers, recognizing an intelligence, an understanding that reached beyond their regular charges, attempted to draw him out. It didn't work. He'd retreat behind the shelter of his indifferent gaze, spending class time doodling portraits of his teachers, of other students. He would be a cartoonist one day. His favorite subject was the boy's vice principal, Mr. Rudoff. He resembled a wiry little terrier. He had a square head, with a flattop spread of kinky, fuzzy hair. Some of the students called him Pube Head. Pube Head was constantly smiling, especially on Parents Day, a Pepsodent grin cracking the reddening edges of his overgrown baby face. Richard assumed he had tomato skin because he wore his neckties so tightly that they cut off the circulation between his head and the rest of his squat body. At the weekly school assemblies, Richard would scribble in appalled fascination, observing the fleshy neck folds straining against the choke hold Rudoff had placed on his collar. Mr. Rudoff always wore three-piece suits. And it was rumored he had three paddles in his filing cabinet, including one with holes in it to give a little extra zing to those bad asses he had no alternative but to administer corporal punishment to.

Sometimes Richard would imagine Rudoff smiling like that and spanking someone at the same time. It would send a nervous chill through his body as he rushed home after school, ran up the stairs of his father's house, closed the bedroom door, turned on the AM radio, and flopped onto his bed, staring at the ceiling for a while and thinking about things. Then he would reach under the bed and pull out his stack of comic books. Between the comics and the radio he lived in a superexaggerated world of X-Men, ? and the Mysterians, Dr. Doom, fantasies bigger than life to take him away from the mundane Rudoff-like terrors of tiny town.

Lying on the bed, watching the way the wind would rustle the thin curtains, he'd think about his favorite comic hero, the Sub-Mariner, an Atlantean prince running around in a tiny green scalloped bikini. Slowly he'd submerge himself, to join his prince, into a deep, dark, mysterious pool, 20,000 leagues beneath his dreams. As if sleepwalking, he'd find himself getting up, moving toward his chest of drawers, opening the top drawer, taking out that jockstrap his gym instructor had required for P.E. His stepmom, Sue, had taken him to buy that jockstrap. It had been humiliating to buy something so personal with his stepmom. And he had the feeling she knew it too. But that first night, when he brought it home, he had this incredible urge to try it on in the middle of the night. Something about it excited him, just like something about the Sub-Mariner excited him and he found his hands running wilder than a shark frenzy over his body as he lay there, wearing nothing but his brand new jockstrap and thinking of Atlantis.

He knew that jerking off had to do with sex, but he wasn't quite sure what sex really was all about, why he felt the way he did, why he did things a certain way. He looked to his comic books for advice, but comic books did not explain these things. Comic books could only offer him the comfort of knowing that, despite all odds, the world was governed by a pure and true moral code. One might have to wait three or four issues, but eventually Thor would save Valhalla and Captain America would send the Red Skull into oblivion. Balance and rational order would be restored. This was something he desperately needed to believe.

He made no attempt to seek out new friends in Santa Juan. So it was surprising when Roger Smight came up and sat down next to him in the courtyard during recess. Small and scrawny, Smight had thin, pressed lips. Fish lips, Richard thought. A nerd. But nerds could turn into superheroes when you weren't looking. Smight peered carefully at Richard through his heavy horn-rimmed glasses and said, "You know, Manz, I'm luckier than you. I've lived here all my life. I know everyone here. And they know me. I'm friends with the Soshes. Not like you. Nobody can figure you out. That's why nobody invites you to float parties. I bet I'll go to more flower-making parties than you this year," he finished, a slight sneer spreading like an oil leak across those fish lips. Richard was dumbfounded by this intrusion. Why was Smight doing this? Roger, sensing his confusion, pressed on with the methodism of a curious child pulling the wings off a fly.

"And anyway, what are you? Jewish like your Dad? Or a Catholic like your stepmom? Could help determine if you go to any float parties this year!"

"I don't follow any religion," Richard said, thinking of the philosophies he'd heard his mom expound on. "I just follow my own spirit."

"Bad answer. You're too weird for Soshes," Smight snorted, walking away. It was the last time Smight ever tried talking to him. Until that day he wore the shoes to school.

Next Saturday he was in a local department store looking through the single records. He noticed another kid from his school across the aisles. Rudy Nunez was a big bull of a boy, bushy black pompadour riding shotgun on a bronzed face polished by a thin veneer of swarth. He scared Richard in the way that all fascinating and compelling terrors did. Looking at Rudy, the way he stood, all contemptuous cool, sunglasses and tight pegged jeans, started a wave of those Sub-Mariner kind of feelings, as if he were being sucked into a whirlpool. He felt the black water swirling around, felt like he was going down, down, down.

"Hey, man, whatcha buying? Get that Love record, it's all

right. Better than that Cher, man, that's for Wussies." Startled from the deep, Richard resurfaced.

"You like Love?"

"Yeah, it's all right."

And he and Rudy started talking about music. He discovered they had this tenuous, yet tangible connection, something that had to do with Rosie & the Originals and The Midnighters and the Dave Clark Five.

Rudy wasn't a comic book, but he was almost like a superhero. Not that he was someone Richard could talk to. It had been all right that day in the department store, but it wasn't all right when he saw him the next day in school. He couldn't go up to him and his crowd. No big tough Chuke was going to hang out with some little Wuss weirdo.

It was better to forget Rudy, concentrate on something else. There was this girl who sat behind him in American History. She'd crack gum through Philadelphia and Sitting Bull and whisper to her friends and pass notes. Tall, skinny, pouty goldfish mouth, cat-eyed with some serious Cleopatra/Liz Taylor eye shadow bringing out a Chicana of the Nile countenance, Yolanda Delgado was working a pair of tight Capris into the currents of Richard's dream pool. She resembled other women in his pantheon of Goddesses, like the lead singer for the Ronettes or that comic book heroine, Wanda the Red Witch. With pleasure, Richard noticed that, as with Wanda and Ronnie Ronnette, Yolanda was of Spanish blood. Wanda in her sexy cape and cowl, sassy New York beehive, queens in gin-sling dresses like Ronnie Ronnette and local cha-cha girls like Yolanda Delgado had become founts of inspiration to the kind of person who wasn't getting invited to float parties. And frankly didn't care.

One day he noticed Yolanda standing by the front of his father's store, the Santa Juan Bootery. He usually went to help his father with inventory after school. Yolanda started gesturing toward him. She wanted him to come outside. "Listen, boy," she said, "can you do me a little favor, please?"

"My name is Richard."

"Okay, Richie, you wanna be my friend, huh?"

Of course he did. And he could be if he would just get her a little bottle of shoe dye, just take it when his dad wasn't looking. He was deeply honored by this sudden interest from a Goddess. Soon he began regularly swiping little accoutrements for the betterment of Yolanda Delgado: black fishnets, Ultrasuede shoe dye, knee socks, any accessory that could be lifted when Dad wasn't looking. He'd run outside and around the corner to find Yolanda opening those incredible be-shadowed eyeballs, laughing in a slutty purr as he handed over the booty from the Bootery.

"You got this for me? You're so nice! Listen, can you get me some more later? Aw, come on, I know you can! C'mon—be my friend, Richie. I promise I won't forget you." And she'd laugh and call out to Alicia and Conchita, and they'd go click-clacking down the street in those nail-thin stilettos they kept in their purses to put on after school, snapping gum and giggling while he stood there, slack-jawed, in awe of the miracle of B-girl.

Often, as he walked to school, he'd think about Yolanda, wondered what her house looked like, what her parents did for a living, whose pictures she had on her walls, what records she had. Maybe he was part Chuke and didn't know it. Adrift in a sea of Yolanda, one day he floated by a junked-out Impala parked near the school. Its occupant, a foul-mouthed Okie named Buddy Spike, leaned out the window, blew some ciga-rette smoke and yelled, "Hey, junior, why you wiggle your hips like a girlie when you walk?" Spike started laughing. Richard stopped for a moment. That night in his diary he wondered: What was I supposed to say?

The only time the Okies and Soshes and Chukes came to-gether was at the football games. The Soshes sat in center bleachers cheering Steven Patterson. Chukes on the left yelled for Jose Lozano. Okies on the right roared for Bill Gump. Sitting with the school band, Richard played Sousa on a pic-colo. He noticed Rudy Nunez and Yolanda Delgado, under-neath the bleachers, touching, laughing. He blew his piccolo twice as hard as the cheers rose for every touchdown.

It was during the game that he noticed Rudy's shoes. Rudy must have bought them at the Bootery. They were black and tan, with a fake alligator skin pattern, high boot heels, pointy toes. They were flashy, crass, low class. Richard suddenly coveted them. No Sosh would have been caught dead wearing shoes like those. The day after the game, Richard told his father he wanted a pair. His father was quietly appalled in his gentle shoe-salesman way.

"Richie," he replied, "those shoes are for . . . well, you know, the ethnic types. Guys that wind up pumping gas or picking avocados. You sure you want those?"

"Yeah, Dad. They're going to be in fashion for everybody real soon."

He had him there. His father, hopelessly outdated, was a conservative, formal brown leather Florsheim man in a time when casual suede Hush puppies ruled the planet. His father often looked to Richard as a barometer of styles and fads to come. He respected Richard's instincts. Those shoes were his.

The next day Richard tottered up the street in his newly elevated, higher-heeled position. He felt a new surge of confidence, like the pilot of a yacht. As he got to the schoolgrounds he saw Yolanda and Conchita. Slightly swaggering by, he nodded in their direction.

"Hey bay-bee!" cried Yolanda, "I like those shoes!" Conchita whispered something in her ear and they both started giggling. Richard flushed. He had made a good choice.

When he got to the Math bungalow, his first class, he was surprised to find no one inside except for Roger Smight, who looked like he had gas pains.

"You're late, Manz," Roger said. "Miss Berk is ill and Mr. Roid's substituting. We're 'spose to transfer rooms. They sent me in here to monitor." Smight lifted up his glasses, took a glance in Richard's direction, and snorted. "Weird shoes, Manz."

Smight seemed to think about something for a moment and said, "You know, if you stay in here, you could probably ditch out math. I could say you didn't know which class to go to, and you could play dumb. You're still new here. No one expects you to get anything right. We could tell them we decided to study together."

"Are you sure?" Richard didn't understand Roger's sudden willingness to include him in a plan.

"Sure, I'm sure, doofus," Roger replied pulling out a coin. "Wanna flip for it? Heads I'm right, tails you're wrong."

Richard thought about it for a minute. "That doesn't work out right."

"Life is tough," replied Roger Smight.

"We're not suppose to be flipping coins," Richard cautioned. "They say it's gambling. I think that's dumb, but Rudoff made a big stink about it at the last assembly."

"Don't be a chump. Rudoff's an idiot. No one takes him seriously. Rules are made to be broken, right? Isn't that what they believe up in San Francisco? I call heads on first throw—okay?"

Before Richard could respond Roger had thrown the coin up in the air and caught it, slapping his hand over it when it came down. Lifting his palm, Richard saw an eagle. Tails. He had won a quarter!

"Beginners luck," Roger said. "Let's do it again. This time I'm tails."

And this time Roger won. So they flipped another coin. And another. Dimes, pennies, nickels, quarters, pockets emptied out as silver and copper flew through the air, waves of excitement building to a fever pitch as each flip of the coin increased or decreased prospective wealth. They become so caught up in this terminal drama of what they considered major high roller action that they didn't notice the door to the Math bungalow opening, revealing the unexpected, and unwanted, presence of Mrs. Sabina Orth, Girl's Vice Principal, who had just caught Richard Manz flipping a coin in the air.

"All right, young men, what are you doing?" she said in a spinsterish bellow. "Roger, what is Mr. Manz doing here? You were suppose to monitor the room alone, Roger, not with Mr. Manz. And Mr. Manz, what are you doing with that coin?"

Roger looked up and without the slightest hesitation, said "Manz here is teaching me a new version of the law of probability. Only this lesson is turning out to be a lot more expensive than Mr. Roid's class."

Richard felt like a kitten trapped in a closet.

"Okay, Roger, no smart remarks," Orth twittered. "I want you to escort Mr. Manz to Mr. Rudoff's office immediately."

Roger was unfazed as they walked to Mr. Rudoff's cubicle in the administration building. "Why did you fink on me?" Richard demanded, alarmed by the easiness of Roger's quick betrayal.

"Survival of the fittest. Anyway, it's your first offense. Rudoff's not gonna do anything to either of us. And you owe me a quarter—that last flip was mine."

Richard thought of Roger's prediction as he began spending the first of what was to be five days on a lunchtime detention bench, beached on a hot bleacher watching everybody, including an "innocent" Roger Smight, enjoying the freedom now denied him. "Normally I'd give you a warning," Rudoff had said with great cheer. "But I feel that, being new to our community, you don't really understand that we mean it when we establish rules here. So you have to learn this lesson."

So far his lesson included doing his best to sit as far away from the other detention bench criminals as possible. No Chukes—they probably would have dropped out of school before wasting valuable socializing time sitting on a stupid bench. No Soshes either—they usually got after-school detention in Orth's homeroom, if they were punished at all. But he, the misfit, the fish out of water, had been placed with the lowest order on the food chain. There were four of them, and they were all a few years older. Hank Gudger was considered a real mean J.D. And there was Roy Wills. And Buddy Spike— the one who had been so interested in his walk. These were the guys that hung out in those smoky Okiemobiles after school, chugalugging Gallo and Bud and saying rude things about any girls that walked nearby.

Occasionally some Okie acquaintance would saunter by the bench and say something like "Suckers!" and the benchees would yell back "Ah, go bite it." But mostly they were persona non grata, temporary untouchables; anybody caught talking to them faced the similar fate of parking their butts on that boring hell-bench.

The sun hit his face, burned his sensitive skin. Squinting his eyes, Richard thought he saw Yolanda and Rudy in the distance, sitting in the shade of the lunch tables, heads close together. Alicia and Conchita started shrieking "Hey, Ru-deee, look! That little kid from the shoe store is on the bench!" Yolanda and Rudy looked up and gave Richard a wave. Hank Gudger noticed this exchange and muttered, "Chuke lover," growling like a Doberman pinscher.

To relieve the tedium Hank Gudger started punching the shoulder of Buddy Spike, who punched him back. That quickly got dull. Then they started talking about what girls they had fingerbanged. After this subject wore out it was time for a spitting contest, seeing who could hawk lugies the furthest. That too soon lost its appeal. Then Gudger looked sideways and gave Richard a deadeye glare.

"Hey, scrub, why you on this bench, anyway?"

"I'm not a scrub," Richard said with as much courage as he could muster. "I'm an A9, not a B9. I got caught flipping coins."

"Baby stuff. Scrub stuff," Hank Gudger snapped. Then he became aware of something else. "Hey, look at those shoes. Those are some butt ugly shoes you got on. Don't look right on you. Look better on a girl."

"Then they ARE right for him," Buddy Spike of the junked-out Impala says, laughing. "Because he's got a little sissy walk like a GIRL!"

"Yeah, and he probably puts on his mama's old rags when he gets home," adds Wills.

"Probably just one of them fairy boys," said Gudger. "Fairy boy with fairy scrub shoes. Where did you get those ugly shoes, huh, scrub? Answer me, you little twerp, or I'm gonna be waiting for you after school."

"I got them at my dad's store."

"Ohh, so you got 'em from DADDY? Your Daddy goes to that Jew temple, doesn't he, scrub? With that fairy shoe store on Main? Huh? Are you a Jew too, scrub? Must be. Only a Jew or a Chuke would wear UGLY CHUKE FAIRY SCRUB shoes like those."

Now all the Okies were laughing.

Richard said nothing, stared into space. If only Sub-Mariner would rise out of the ocean and tear them apart. But visions of superhero salvation meant nothing to the Okies. They were on a hate roll, and they were feeling good.

"Do they let you wear those fairy Jew shoes in that temple?" Buddy Spike said. "Hey, don't you know the Jews killed Jesus. Man, I bet if Jesus saw those shoes, he'd die all over again."

"You know I think those shoes look kind of dirty," Gudger said slowly. "They could use a cleaning. A spit shine, eh?"

"Yup—they're dirty like a Jew." And with that Roy Wills

collected a wad of saliva in his mouth and spat at Richard's shoes.

"Hey, you didn't get them clean enough," replied Gudger, who aimed and fired a viscous gob of snot that hit Richard in the neck.

"Hey, stop that," cried Richard.

"Oooh, I missed. Too bad," Gudger cackled. Soon everybody on the bench began swishing their mouth juices around before starting up another round of fire, hocking and spitting as he flinched and jumped, trying to avoid contact with the phlegmatic projectiles. John Callen, who was suppose to be the bench monitor but had thoroughly ignored everything until now, told Richard to "sit your ass down or you're on report to Rudoff!"

Now some of the Soshes were watching. Kids began laughing and screaming and pulling their friends over to see that weirdo from San Francisco who was sitting on the bench and getting bombarded by Okie phlegm. Richard felt sick to his stomach. Too small to fight back, no allies, no friends, his sense of right and wrong outraged. Where was Wanda the Red Witch when he needed her? He put his head in his hands, felt another piece of spit hitting him, heard laughter echoing in his head. He just wanted it to end.

"Hey, you punks, leave the little kid alone," came a voice from the distance. He looked up. It was Rudy Nunez! Yolanda was standing next to him, laughing. The bench Okies were furious.

"Hey, Chuke, this little Jew a friend of yours?"

"No, man, but if you punks want to maybe tangle with someone your own size, you're welcome to meet me and some of my people after school, know what I mean, man?"

Okies were bad business, but nobody wanted to mess with Chukes. So that was it. The game was over. The Okies just stared ahead, sullen and furious. But not as furious as Richard. Something overwhelmed him. He suddenly stood up, turned to his tormentors and screamed, "You goddamn Okie trash fuckers go to fucking hell!"

They were stunned for a moment. Then John Callen rose up, ready to give orders. But he was too late. Richard walked off the bench. He suddenly felt invincible. Rudy Nunez had defended him. He had power now. Justice could be served. People were yelling threats at him as he walked away. But he just didn't care anymore.

He walked straight to Rudoff's office and sat down in the waiting room. He had a right to appeal. He had a legitimate complaint. He had to avenge his honor. People had no right to spit on him just because they didn't like his shoes. Mr. Rudoff, in a position of power and authority, would understand that he had been the victim of a great, saliva-filled injustice. He knew that after hearing his case, Rudoff would set him free from sitting on the bench and enduring that kind of public humiliation.

Rudoff looked up from behind his desk and smiled.

"Mr. Manz," he responded in that gruff, squeezed, tight-neck voice of his. "What are you doing here? Bench getting too hot for you?" And he let out a little lighthearted chuckle.

"Mr. Rudoff, I don't like to be a tattletale, but everybody on the bench was spitting on me. A lot. Look at this," Richard said, showing a gob stain on his shirt. "It's not fair. Roger Smight was flipping coins with me, and only I was punished. I know it was wrong and I was breaking the rules and everything. But being spit on isn't fair, either. It's like cruel and unusual punishment."

"Well, well, my, my. Cruel and unusual, eh? Good vocabulary you have there, Manz," Rudoff said, a slight twinkle in his eyes, bushy eyebrows knitting, cheeks flushed with blood. "Now why don't you tell me who was spitting at you on the bench."

"I don't know their names—just the guys on the bench." Richard suddenly hedged at naming his attackers. He thought of junked-out Impalas following him down empty alleys after school.

"I don't want to get anybody in trouble. I just don't want to be spit on. That's not supposed to be part of my punishment, is it? Isn't there some other way I can make it up? Can't I take after-school detention?"

Rudoff's eyes sparkled like little Christmas lights.

"Well, you still have some time left," he said with an easy-going tone. "And the after-school detention room is already filled . . . you know, I can't let you off the bench. It's not the regular procedure. But . . . I think I'll make an exception since you feel this punishment is so CRUEL and UNUSUAL . . ."

"Oh, thank you!" Richard began to cry out.

"You can get off the bench," Rudoff replied. "If you take three swats now."

A red flag went up. In one day Richard had been deceived by Roger Smight and victimized by Okies. Now he had to get a beating as well? All because he flipped a few coins and wore the same shoes as Rudy Nunez?

"Why does it have to be swats? I think I've made up for flipping coins, I mean by being spit on and everything. You usually only give swats to people who have multiple offenses."

"Multiple offenses!" Rudoff gleefully chortled. "You should be a lawyer, Richard! And if you were a lawyer, you'd understand that there is something called due procedure. And in this case, if you want out of your time, you're due three swats." His eyes narrowed, as he leaned back in his chair. His voice sounded like it was coming from the end of a long hallway.

"You know when I was your age I was a little hell-raiser myself. My father used to beat the crap out of me sometimes. And at the time I hated him for it. But now I realize it did me a world of good. And I'm sure it will do you a world of good too."

Richard suddenly felt like he had a hollow hole inside his body. He felt like a glazed donut. Something was dropping out of him. It was like he was somebody else watching a strange movie that vaguely resembled his life.

Rudoff walked over to a filing cabinet, opened the top drawer, and brought out a hard wooden paddle. "Look, Richard," he said, like a father talking to child terrified of his first trip to the barber. "It's not so big. Just three swats, it's over, and you're free to join your friends during lunch. It will only take a second."

"Mr. Rudoff, I'm not really sure I want to do this."

Pube Head now gave him a steely appraisal, then offered that automatic grin. "Richard, you need to understand my authority here. You did something wrong and you need to receive the appropriate punishment. Now either go back out there on the bench and suffer whatever happens to you or take the three swats. You have to serve your sentence."

His sentence! Rudoff was crazy! Now he realized what was going on. It was a trap. He was being held by a double agent. He had no choice but to endure this sacrifice. This was the first of a three-part adventure. Manz against the Rudoff empire of Santa Juan. He thought: I have to go through a ring of fire to find the magic box with the secret map and it will set me free on the way back to San Francisco headquarters. I have to make a sacrifice—all superheroes do.

Yes, that was it. This was all a test. And he would get through it. It would make him stronger. And he would be careful to never end up in this madman's quarters again. He'd call his mom up tonight, go back. He really didn't mind if her kitchen smelled after all.

"All right," he said, "I'll take the swats."

"Good boy!" Rudoff said with ruddy cheer. "I promise you, it will only hurt for a moment."

But as he got closer, Richard suddenly found himself tensing and backing off.

"Okay, Richard, I want you to bend over and grab your knees."

But he couldn't. He just couldn't do it. Which seemed to infuriate the boy's vice principal of Santa Juan Union High.

"Now, Richard, listen to me. I want you to listen to me. Pretend that it's like a game. Like statues. Listen—just pretend you're my robot! Do you understand? You are now my robot."

His robot! Rudoff's speech was getting thicker.

"Now I want you to listen to my command, robot! On the count of three, you are going to bend over and grab your knees."

Rudoff was standing behind him, close. He could feel hot breath on his neck. He could almost sense the paddle behind him, poised to strike.

"Are you ready? Okay, here we go. One—Two—Three. BEND OVER, ROBOT!"

He couldn't bend over. This robot could not compute the message.

"Did you hear me? I said . . . BEND OVER ROBOT!"

He turned his head, and looked at Rudoff, puffing out his pink cheeks like a furious bullfrog.

"Richard, what are you doing?" Rudoff's voice was starting

to rise. "I'm not playing any games with you. You are not obeying me. Do exactly what I tell you or you are really going to know what it feels like to be hurt! Okay? Are you going to play? Are you going to be a good robot? C'mon, bend over, robot! BEND OVER, GODDAMNIT! BEND OVER, YOU SON OF A BITCH!"

"No," he heard himself screaming. "I am not your robot. I'm not anybody's robot. No, no, no, no, NO!"

And he runs.

He runs out of there as fast as his pointy-toed imitation alligator shoes with the high heels can take him, runs down the hallowed hallways of Santa Juan Union High School, past rows of lockers and classrooms filled with Soshes and Chukes and Okies, past the parking lot filled with Mustangs and Oldsmobiles and Impalas, runs out onto the street, toward the Main Street Bootery. And as he keeps running he suddenly sees a familiar car—a red Chevy. Rudy's car! Rudy's red Chevy with "Darling Baby" written in white script lettering on the back window, and Rudy's sitting there listening to Brenda and the Tabulations singing "Dry Your Eyes." Richard is opening the door to the car. He is jumping in and hiding his head below the dashboard, right in front of Rudy's lap, in front of this bulge, and as he puts his head there, suddenly he understands. He KNOWS. He knows why he likes the Sub-Mariner, knows what it is about Rudy that he is fascinated by, knows that he loves Rudy, Rudy who is looking down at him, surprised, yelling "Hey, what the fuck you doing, weirdo?"

THWACK!

"I'm ditching that fucking school and hiding from that fucking Rudoff. I'm sick of this shit. Let's get the fuck out of here!"

"Hey, all right," Rudy says with a laugh. "You a little rebel now, kid?' "

"Fuck that, man, let's split," Richard says.

And BOOM, they're off in their Red Chevy space bomb, hurtling through the galaxies, geared up to explore the outer ionosphere as Rudy presses the pointy toe of his imitation alligator Chuke shoes on the accelerator and

THWACK!

They race through the lemon groves, singing "Pushing Too Hard" at the top of their lungs until, all of a sudden, Rudy slams on the brakes, looks hard at Richard and grabs his head, pushes Richard's head against his crotch, yelling "Suck it, punk" in a hard, strained voice, a mechanical voice, like that voice gruffly shouting "Bend over, Robot!" in his ears and Richard goes limp, he surrenders, he's dead meat, he was wrong, sometimes good guys don't wear white, and the voice yells "Suck it, Robot" and he's among the machines now, he's a machine himself, with knobs and dials being twisted and twirled by the Black Commander Rudy Rudoff and

THWACK!

There were tears in Richard's eyes when he stood up. But he didn't make a sound.

"Very good, Richard," said Mr. Rudoff. "You were very brave. His mouth looked juicy red, like he had just eaten a watermelon. "You took it like a man. Just like I did when I was your age."

That night, when Richard got home he could still feel the muscles wiggling around his butt. He thought of maybe calling his mom. But what was the use? His backside tensed as he lay down on the bed. He must have just lain there for about thirty minutes, staring at the ceiling. Then he jumped up, ran downstairs, took his new shoes off and threw them in the garbage can. He didn't ever want to see those ugly things again. Only a stupid Chuke like Rudy Nunez would wear shoes like those. Tomorrow he would ask his dad if he could have a new pair of Hush Puppies. Maybe then he might get invited to a few float parties.

WHEN MARQUITA GETS HOME

• BIL WRIGHT •

MARQUITA WAS TIRED of wiping sweat from between her breasts. The little hankie she'd had since seventh grade was too damp to do any good, but Marquita kept it in her fist, letting her own body's water trickle out through the cloth and down her dirty fingers.

She wasn't working hard. If she'd been working hard, everything would be sweating. She'd have taken off her cross and pulled her hair up off her neck. No, she just wanted to be out here looking busy. She was waiting for Gabriel. She wanted him to try to leave this house tonight so she could tell him just a little bit of something. Something he could take with him.

When men from off the avenue would walk up behind her and talk about her backside and ask about her Saturday evening plans, Marquita would straighten up quickly from the front stoop weeds she'd been halfheartedly pulling and grab the dampness of her skirt from between her legs.

"Bastards." It might've been for the men who'd passed, but Marquita knew damn well who she meant it for. All day, knowing Gabriel and that other boy was layin' up in that room had caused her lunch to repeat. She allowed herself one more sponging inside the bodice of her dress. "I'm about to choke to death out here."

Her hand slid up to her neck. "I shouldn't even be in all this weeds and crabgrass and mess."

Still, the strength to go inside would not come. Climbing the subway steps, Marquita had become so unsteady on her heels, they seemed to want to run out from under her, leaving her in midair with this awful gagging feeling in her stomach and throat.

"But it's my house, damnit." She'd made her way upstairs to the stoop, jabbing key after key into the brownstone door. It flat refused to open, as though it had been given orders not to let her in. She stood away from it, glaring, when she heard footsteps coming at her from inside. She stumbled backwards like she'd been punched, and her purse opened up with all the change and tokens running every which way. She'd have to wait till morning to go hunting and searching through the grass, though—probably before she left for church.

Now, she just wanted to know what was keeping them so long. She wanted them to come through that door so she could put Gabriel's tail on real straight before he took it wherever they were going.

Inside 490 Ansonia, Gabriel Goodney grinned at having to turn back into his room.

The boy had laughed softly in his ear with his tongue and said, "Don't feel like you got no drawers on, mister." Gabriel had forgotten himself. True, nearly a half-hour had passed since they'd started out, but dusk had brought shadows to the boy's face that Gabriel had not seen before, and he'd wanted him naked again. Then, in the time he thought they had before Marquita came home, he'd combed the boy's hair and washed his face with kisses.

"I've never had anybody in my own bed before." He thanked himself, smiling into the boy's stomach. "We've got to get out before Marquita gets home." Coming down the hall, he heard his sister's keys beating against the lock. He heard her drop them and curse. He knew she was out there waiting. "Damn." Gabriel grinned. "If only we hadn't got started that last time."

"I hate summertime," Marquita spit down at the dandelions. "Summertime, people get so foolish from the heat they cause Jesus to look the other way. That's what Daddy would say." It was the only reference Marquita remembered her father ever making to Jesus. Even with curse words, Ernest Goodney didn't use Jesus' name. Most people Marquita knew called Jesus when they cursed. Ernest Goodney didn't.

Jesus was looking the other way when Marquita's daddy wrapped himself and his truck around a railing on the Concourse in the Bronx only two Augusts ago. He'd been trying to avoid killing someone too drunk to drive and too stupid not to.

Marquita winced and thought again of her brother. "I done the best I could to take care of that fool." She pulled at the elastic on her panties. "But I won't work my body to the bone and him layin' up like a woman with some man. Not in my daddy's house."

When Gabriel came through the door he looked like his daddy. He stepped out onto the stoop chest first, sneakers untied and his shirttail out.

"Bastard," Marquita called at him without opening her lips. And when she did open them she said only his name, and the sky in Brooklyn looked like rain.

"How ya doin', Marquita?" Gabriel turned a penny from heads to tails in his pocket. The boy stood behind him like a pretty shadow.

"I'm tired, Gabriel, and I dropped my stuff all out of my purse in the grass." Damnit, why did she sound like she was whining? She wasn't supposed to be whining.

"We could help you, Marquita. Betcha we could find it all."

"No." She wasn't sure if it was the sound of her voice or thunder.

"Well, we're going to the movies, then."

Marquita looked down into her dress. For the first time today her skin looked dry, parched, ready to crack and tear away from her body like dried mud.

You been layin' up with that sissy since four o'clock this morning. Her teeth bit down so hard her gums ached. Still, she could not open her mouth. When you go outta this yard with that boy, don't you ever bring him back. A wind picked up her skirts and her legs looked suddenly at the street. Marquita belched up a sneer. Don't give a damn. Let the whole world see my ass.

"Well, go then, Gabriel. You and your friend go on to the movies."

Gabriel thought he must still be asleep. Must be dreaming with the boy's legs wrapped too tight around his head. He and the boy seemed to move out into the world like the wind was carrying them too fast to move any one part of their bodies. He did look back once before they flew down into the subway. Marquita reminded him of a postage stamp stuck in the corner of a big, brown envelope, unable to move or turn around.

Marquita Goodney felt like the girl with the pigtails in *The Wizard of Oz*. Here she was with a tornado coming and wasn't nobody home. She was scared in an hour or two the roof would blow all over the damn place. Everything she owned would be upside down. She didn't have a dog to tell or take with her. Marquita fell back on her stoop, folding and unfolding her hands around her handkerchief.

She was waiting for the tornado.

Once inside the Forty-fifth Street Cinema Grand, Gabriel watched Carl push through the turnstile and into the darkness; a maroon satin baseball jacket with a gold stand-up collar, an elasticized waist over a tight Levi'd butt. Gabriel padded behind him down the aisle of the mid-city movie house and reached suddenly into the blackness. He knew that he was not reaching for Carl, but back in time. Preceding Gabriel down that aisle in the dusty mist was a trembling shape in a navy cotton dress. The belt was twisted, revealing a torn cardboard backing. The wrinkled pleats of a long skirt rode over a pale slip that was even longer. As the shape before him paused, he heard his sister whisper, "We got to go further front. We need to be further front."

Brooklyn Christ Zion was an enormous cave with an aisle down the center of its belly. Marquita weaved and stumbled down that aisle like a delirious drunk. Gabriel knew she'd had only cup after endless cup of tea from the one tea bag she could find before she lifted herself away from the table and told him they should proceed to the church. Silence accompanied them to Christ Zion as it had two nights before to the morgue.

The morgue called it claiming the body, as though very simply Gabriel and Marquita could have said, "That man belongs to us. He's ours. We've come to take him home." Gabriel thought maybe some families did claim bodies that way. It was not the way it had gone for Marquita and him.

In the morgue, his sister had put both hands on their father's chest and then his face, which seemed to spread from end to end atop his shoulders like a melting mask. Ernest Goodney, Jr., lay there looking crushed and bloodied, surprised and dead.

"Put your hands on him. Touch him. You'll never touch him again," Marquita said. He'd never heard her sound like that.

Cold. Metallic. Her voice found his insides like a fish hook and pulled through him.

At the end of the aisle in Brooklyn Christ Zion, tight-lipped and gray, in a white shirt (though frayed at the collar), in his brown suit (with a cakey yellow stain on his lapel) was the man Gabriel could not touch.

It was Marquita who'd screamed long and loud and wept over her father's corpse. As a child, she hadn't cried out loud about anything that he could remember. Instead, when she'd wet her pants or tripped on a jump rope and fallen, she'd hidden in the closet they shared where she sniffled like a small animal until she drifted off to sleep in a corner on an old duffel bag that held their dirty laundry.

Gabriel remembered a time when he had just turned nine and Marquita was not quite thirteen. Ernest Goodney stood over her and barked at the rumpled, whimpering dress in the corner of the closet, "I did the best I could by you, girl. And you still snivelin'. Snivelin' all the damn time."

He unbuckled his belt and slid it through the loops around his waist.

"I'm gonna give you somethin' to snivel good about, girl."

Gabriel stood behind him, barely half as tall as his father, afraid to move. He hoped his sister might cry out, crawl through their father's legs and escape into the streets. He imagined her running in some blinding shaft of divine light straight into the arms of their mother; the mother Ernest Goodney claimed they'd never see because she did not care, had never cared, had left them indeed to snivel like strays on a doorstep or in dark corners of closets.

"Touch him. Put your hands on him."

And Gabriel heard himself answer, "Run. Run, Marquita." And he could tell she couldn't hear him. She was used to corners. Used to crying on old army bags. She'd been raised on her daddy's belt buckles being the best anyone could do for her. "Run, Marquita. Run before we both get closed in here with him."

And Gabriel felt sorry he'd never said it out loud.

Inside the morgue and again in the church weaving down that long padded aisle, Gabriel heard his sister scream in a language he dared the dead to understand.

*　　*　　*

Inside the Forty-fifth Street Cinema Grand, Carl bit Gabriel's shoulder, oblivious to the others in the movie house.

"You wake?"

"Yeah."

"Whatsa matter? You haven't said much of anything since we left your house. You all right?"

"I'm okay."

"Maybe we should stay uptown tonight. Tomorrow's Sunday. We could stay in bed all day." Carl reached for Gabriel's hand but could not seem to find it.

"There's no need for me to run from Marquita. I live there too. It's my house just like it is hers."

"I was just thinking we could be together."

Gabriel answered in a voice that was low and even like the voice of the man he'd been picturing in the coffin at the end of the aisle. He said, "We can be together in my house. In my room. Marquita can't tell me who to bring into my room. I got mine. She's got her own."

Carl looked at Gabriel who sat next to him, close enough to kiss as he'd done just an hour or so before. That was what he wanted now. No matter where they were or who might see. But Carl knew it would be senseless. Because Gabriel was not there. It would be, Carl thought, and did not even know why, like kissing a dead man.

It was at least eight-thirty Monday morning before Marquita was able to leave the house. Her one good slip, a yellow nylon, was too long to wear without pinning it up. As she checked the hasty job she'd done in the hall mirror before leaving, Marquita noticed a tea stain on the skirt of the pale green dress, also nylon, she'd ironed late Sunday to start her week in. "They promised to get this mess out!" she moaned in exasperation, remembering her conversation with the man at the cleaners. "Well, I got to pray nobody sees it cause I'm too late to change. Maybe I could throw a little dusting powder on it though."

Dusting powder continued to fall from her as she tiptoed past Gabriel's room and out the front door. Marquita did not even really know if her brother was inside. Still, preparing herself for the day to come had been trying enough. Marquita had not seen Gabriel since Saturday evening. Sunday there'd been church and he was never home Sunday mornings anyway. Dusk had barely fallen on Sunday evening when Marquita cold-creamed her face, rolled her braids, ironed her green nylon dress and read from the book she'd bought at the drugstore along with a new lipstick.

Now, as she double-locked the apartment and passed through the tiny vestibule and into Monday, Marquita was grateful it was too early for her neighborhood to be stirring.

Marquita stared around at the buildings of Ansonia Avenue. "Fig bars," Marquita mumbled. To her the buildings resembled the same quarter-for-two molasses fig bars she'd grown up eating.

"Nothin' but cracks and chips. Pieces falling away. Rot out your teeth and ruin your appetite for anything good later on." She yawned into her purse, slipping her keys inside. If it had not been for Ernest Goodney's legacy, Marquita's own crumbling fig bar of a house, she told herself, she would have left this neighborhood not a moment after he'd been taken away from her.

In 1971, Ernest Goodney, Jr., moved his children Gabriel and Marquita to Ansonia Avenue in Brooklyn from a housing project in The Bronx. Ernest told the men at the garage that he wanted his kids to have a better grade of company now that his daughter was coming into womanhood and his son was getting to be a young man.

He also told this to his children. Marquita, just turning fifteen, thought it sounded practical but irrelevant since both she and her brother kept pretty much to themselves anyway. They came and went obediently, following the schedules laid out for them. They padded quietly around the house, appearing in hallways and disappearing into rooms as though sleep-walking; spoke in tuneless whispers if at all. Marquita remembered being shocked when she first realized Gabriel's voice had changed. Somehow when she had not noticed, Gabriel the boy had slid into the mouth of his room. The room swallowed him and spat out the beginnings of what sounded like a man.

During that time of her fifteenth year, Marquita went often to the corner of the kitchen and sat, her legs wrapped around the cold chrome legs of their eating table, her hands fingering its splintered vinyl top.

She stared slowly from corner to corner. Her father had taken almost a full week to cover the walls in a flat lemon yellow which, in order to make themselves more interesting, reached hungrily for thumbprints of jelly from Marquita's toast, splatters of spaghetti sauce from Gabriel's sloppy frying pans, engine oil from her father's trousers.

Her eyes focused on the photograph of Coretta King in a mourning veil that Gabriel had cut from *Ebony* magazine and framed. There was a child, a little girl, lying across Coretta King's lap. Marquita knew that this was the youngest daughter of this woman and of the man she mourned. Sometimes, however, alone in the corner of the kitchen with her eyes half closed, Marquita imagined that it was not the King child at all, but Marquita Goodney stretched across this veiled woman's legs. If there was comfort to be found in the folds of these skirts, Marquita needed comfort. Marquita claimed her place on this woman's lap.

Marquita stared at this photograph late one Saturday evening as the rest of the house lay sleeping. Her eyes never lifted from the grainy black-and-white images as the Saturday night sounds of Ansonia Avenue teased her in young folks' tongues through the kitchen window screens. Her jaw wrenched slowly open and her body's water fell from her face to her fingers tracing and retracing the jagged outline of the vinyl tabletop. From her legs wrapped fiercely around the table's chrome legs, from her shapeless aching body came a long and hollow moan. Mama, where are you? It tore at the veils of the woman in the photograph. Where? It was the moan of a body plunged deep into the waters of a baptismal font. Where? It was the only baptism Marquita had ever known. Tears of blood stained the tabletop. Two small breasts strained against a cotton gown. Oh God. I hurt. Daddy. Oh, God. I hurt.

Gabriel shuffled into the apartment and let the door slam behind him. He hummed on an unsteady pitch in a high, vibratoed tenor. He stopped, as if in a tunnel, waiting to hear an echo.

"Marquita! You home?"

He knew that she was; that she had to be. It was Monday night. Monday night was a work night. As long as Marquita's belongings were in this house, she would be here. For supper.

For a cup of after supper tea. To make a bag lunch for Tuesday and roll her hair. Marquita would be here.

From the entrance to the apartment, Gabriel could look ahead down the hall. The door to his bedroom was ajar. He knew he'd been careful to close it when he and Carl left two nights before. He strode ahead, pushed it open with force.

"Damnit," he mumbled suspiciously. "Marquita," he thought, "better not've done nothin' crazy."

All day at Websterbooks, Gabriel had thought of Marquita doing something crazy. Overseeing a shipment to the West Coast, handling an uneven exchange at the register, even at lunch Gabriel had a look in his eye that made Stax the floor manager kid him.

"You look like somebody's gonna be waitin' for you after school, boy. Somebody with a big stick."

Now, staring down at his sheets, Gabriel could make out Carl's sneaker prints.

He remembered that the first time they hadn't even gotten out of their pants and shoes. Gabriel had taken Carl's shirt up over his head and wrestled him to the bed, licking his chest, his armpits, nuzzling his navel and biting the hair just below.

Yet from the time they'd left the house on Saturday, gone to the movies and then to Carl's, Gabriel knew he'd treated his friend like a stranger and not one he was particularly pleased to be with.

Sunday Carl dragged Gabriel to Central Park where Gabriel continued to distance himself, hands in his pockets, staring down at the pavement. By Sunday night even Carl seemed relieved that the weekend was over and sorry he'd convinced Gabriel to come home with him.

"Shit," Gabriel mumbled. Carl was wonderful. Truly wonderful. And as pretty as any man Gabriel had ever wanted. Too brown to be called yellow. Flirty brown eyes and a smile that made you want to eat his lips and swallow his tongue whole. Gabriel laughed now to think it had taken him two weeks to lay a hand on him.

For two weeks after Carl had wandered into the store ("Do you have Baldwin's *Giovanni's Room* in paperback?"), Gabriel dreamed his face across the store. They'd lunched together. Carl had even come in a couple of days when he knew Gabriel was on a break.

He was not only bright, he was vigilant about finishing up his Master's at City and moving ahead to a doctorate.

"It doesn't make sense to waste time," he said firmly to Gabriel. "It only means you're out there begging again, with nothing much to show for it." It was a tone that Gabriel found patronizing at times and it made his uneasy. He was self-conscious about seeing someone who was more educated than he. Gabriel was still paying off tuition loans on a bachelor's degree that by now was worth less than the balance of the loans. He admired Carl, who seemed to be swimming in pretty deep financial waters himself, and somehow making it toward shore.

It was not admiration however that stirred Gabriel the Friday night he asked Carl to come home with him. It was the feel of his torso under that satin baseball jacket and the hard-on fighting against his jeans.

They were supposed to be watching a special showing of *Cabin in the Sky* at Theatre 80. Gabriel decided he hated *Cabin in the Sky*.

"I'll put a bandanna on my head and sing you a hundred choruses of 'Old Black Joe' if you come to Brooklyn with me."

"Damnit, guy, it was either Brooklyn or Harlem tonight. I'd already decided." Carl laughed and it was agreed.

Gabriel brushed his hand over Carl's sneaker prints on the sheets. He remembered thinking he was going too far that Friday night as they took the train toward Brooklyn. He was going too far, but he refused to turn back.

Everything else in his life seemed to be on Indefinite Hold. The day-to-day tedium of Websterbooks was becoming depressing. ("Gay section?" He'd laughed openly to Carl's second inquiry that first day. "Hell, Websterbooks just got around to Black Studies this past year. Their corporate headquarters are located at the turn of the century.") Four-ninety Ansonia had become a setting for avoiding Marquita's glum moods and stern looks of disapproval when he came in or went out. He couldn't decide what might change his feeling like a boarder in a house he deserved to feel was home.

No, he said to the bed beneath him. No, he had not made a mistake. He was sure of it. He had not been acting out like a child who knew better. He'd been acting like a man who paid rent and bought food and had the right to make love in his room with the door closed. He was damned if he'd allow himself to be buried in an old brownstone in Brooklyn.

"Marquita!" Gabriel strode toward the kitchen. There sat his sister, hands folded quietly on the kitchen table, staring up at him helplessly. She swallowed once, twice. Then, as her fingers slowly straightened out toward him she shrugged and said, "Such a mean headache. While I was trying to shop dinner."

Marquita laughed weakly, but without looking at her brother. "This is as far as I got. Just overtired I guess. Workin' and not sleepin' and all."

Gabriel reached across the table for the Fairway shopping bag. He saw Marquita flinch. Suddenly he wondered if she was afraid of him.

He took the bag to the sink and emptied it: frozen peas, a package of hamburger meat and an onion spilled out onto the drainboard.

"I was gonna put a lot of onion in the hamburger the way you like it."

"I can make dinner, Marquita." He was curt, not altogether friendly. He didn't mean to sound unfriendly.

"I'm not even sure I'm hungry. Back of my neck feels so tight, feels like my head's 'bout to fly off." There was that sound that she made, as though she was sniffling or laughing maybe, through her nose. Gabriel felt uneasy, as though they were not alone. He half expected that this was not really Marquita slouching just across the room, but an image superimposed, a foil. His sister, he suspected, was waiting just behind him, or in the cupboard or the oven ready to spring.

"I was . . . ," he started slowly. "I was thinking about inviting my friend Carl to dinner, but I knew I hadn't . . . hadn't said anything about it."

"He was in here the other night, I didn't know anything about it."

He was right. She'd been waiting, just outside herself. Her voice sounded full now, like a horn with lows and highs and middles.

"You're right. But if he comes to dinner, I'll buy food. So there'll be enough."

"You haven't been buying food, Gabriel. Long as we've been together in this house. Except when there was something special you wanted."

"But I haven't had . . . somebody . . . here . . . before."

Marquita now looked up from the table and focused directly on her brother. Her whole body asked him, "You gonna keep on having somebody here, Gabriel?"

Gabriel swallowed. His eyes darted from corner to corner before he said, "I want Carl to be able to come back here." When he looked at his sister, the muscles in his chin jumped but he knew he had to ask, "Is that gonna be all right with you, Marquita?"

Marquita slowly pushed away from the table and stood. She came toward him. She was huge and black, horrible and ridiculous, a shadow darkening the whole room, moving yet not moving at all, like a recurring grade-school nightmare.

When her face was just inches from his, he thought she might spit at him or reach past him for a knife or pair of scissors. But she spoke. It sounded as though her voice was somewhere in the back of her neck where she said her headache came from.

"I'll do what I'm s'posed to do, Gabriel. Like I always have— take care of this house and you too, for as long as you're in it. You do what you will."

Then she reached for the package of meat on the drain.

"If you're not gonna cook it, we need to put it away. Nothin' spoils faster than cheap ground beef."

Gabriel saw Marquita's nails dig through the cellophane wrapper and into the meat. The package was shaking in her hand as she turned away. A memory cracked through him and he struggled with it for a moment. "Put your hands on him. Touch him. You'll never touch him again."

The morgue. The damn morgue. "Touch him. Put your hands on him. You'll never touch him again."

Slowly, Gabriel Goodney shook his head inside his head. Slower still, his eyes kissed his sister above each brow. Gabriel had been right not to touch him. He wasn't wrong then. He wasn't wrong now.

Marquita walked slowly out of the kitchen and down the hallway to her room. She closed the door quietly behind her. Leaning against it, facing into all that was truly hers, Marquita stared at the world. She slid out of her slippers and stood beside them, in her stocking feet, her eyes still surveying the room. She padded silently several feet to her dressing table.

It was old decaying wood, painted many times over, the last a pinkish ivory that reminded Marquita of nail polish. Her fingertips searched its surface slowly, looking for lumps, bubbles in the polish or places where it was still wet.

Marquita's mouth fell open in a wide silent grin. She'd run her fingers over this surface a thousand times, each time vaguely surprised to find it dry. Thumb to middle man to pinkie, she placed her fingers hard against it. Then quickly to the mirror above it and away again. No fingerprints.

"It's dry," she thought. "It's all dry." She closed her eyes. "It's been dry for years."

Marquita looked toward the bed. Like freshly ironed linen, she placed herself upon the bed, her legs curled under her, her arms up over her head against her pillows.

My bed is cool and the sheets are smooth and dry. No wrinkles in my sheets. She closed her eyes and opened them again. She put her hands over them and said to her room, "There are no damn wrinkles in my sheets."

She lay there without moving, her hands covering her eyes. She thought she heard Gabriel humming in that funny, pretty voice of his. It was closer. It was farther away. She heard him moving in the hallway.

But her father's voice was nearer, in her room, inside her head. "Take your hands away from your face, Marquita. Stop that damn snivelin'."

She saw her father's face on the ceiling.

"Take your hands away from your face."

She heard the front door close. Marquita took her hands away from her eyes and stared straight up. On the ceiling, where the face of her father had been, Marquita could see her brother walking slowly away from the house. And she could hear him. Humming.

ENGLISH AS A SECOND LANGUAGE

• BERNARD COOPER •

"YOU MAY BE wondering," said Mr. Rowlands, "why I am wearing this hat." I, for one, was wondering. Except for a conical party hat with crepe paper fringe, Mr. Rowlands was the picture of officiousness—starched white shirt, drab navy tie, shoes shined to a high gloss. He paced among tables of attentive faculty, some of us new to The Institute of Fashion, others veterans. "I intend to show you," Mr. Rowlands continued, "that appearing foolish is not only easy . . ." dramatic pause, his party hat askew, "but is also necessary for successful teaching. After all, what is it that a teacher does?" Silence from the assembly. "A teacher, my friends, goes out on a limb." He drew a tree limb on the blackboard behind him, slashed an X at the furthermost end. "A teacher takes risks, introduces new ideas to a room brimming with formative minds. As one philosopher put it, 'A teacher affects eternity.' " I glanced at my watch. "I tip my hat to you all," he said. The hat flew back with a snap of elastic.

Mr. Rowlands was not a regular member of the Institute. He was a Group Spirit Facilitator, offering his services to schools and corporations wishing to extract a sense of goodwill from their reticent employees. He'd breezed onto "campus"—the sixth and seventh floors of the Barker Brothers furniture outlet in downtown Los Angeles—in order to lead forty teachers through the Get-To-Know-Your-Fellow-Faculty game, a round-robin during which we were asked to announce our names, areas of expertise, pet peeves and favorite colors.

"Red," chirped the cheerful Miss Bartlett, instructor of Color Theory I, II, and III, dressed in red from head to toe. "And human pyramids," she said, crimson lips curled in disdain, "I hate them. All those people piled up. What's the point?"

"Excellent," crooned Mr. Rowlands.

Miss Bartlett blushed and took her seat.

"And you," he said, pointing at me, "up, up, up."

I stood, heart heaving beneath my wrinkled shirt. "I'm Richard Cole. I'll be teaching English. I like gray . . ."

"Gray is not a color," murmured Miss Bartlett.

". . . and I can't stand cold spaghetti." It was delicate; I wanted to participate in the game, to charm these strangers, and yet I hoped my ambivalence would show, would send out a signal to potential allies who found the proceedings as absurd as I did.

It took more than a half hour for everyone to introduce themselves. Mr. Rowlands seemed pleased by each response, liberal with his grin. The atmosphere had, I must admit, turned genial, and sensing that his mission was accomplished, Mr. Rowlands gave us over to the president of the Institute, Barbara Bundy.

Large Barbara Bundy strode to the podium, clutched the neck of the microphone and wrenched it into position. Her black hairdo was sliced in two by a streak of gray. "First," she said, after mild applause, "let me share some exciting news with you. The Mayor visited our facilities just last week. He was terribly impressed by our new architectural carpeting. You know, I told him, this will be the first opportunity for many of our minority students to function in a carpeted public area."

I left the room to get a drink of water, to breathe and stretch, to reassess my livelihood. I was followed out the door by a tall black woman, Janet, who shook my hand and told me she worked in the Research Center. "Call it the library," she said. "That'll drive Bundy crazy." Lit by yards of track lighting, we faced one another in the corridor. Suddenly, Janet gazed at the carpet and drawled, "Whut is dat, Porgy? Some kinda fungus?"

The Sunday before school began, I sprawled on an old foam chair—it sagged beneath me in a sorry heap—re-reading the poems I'd use for my class, Introduction to Literature. I'd stop between stanzas, convinced I had nothing insightful to say. At least not these days; after teaching literature for five years at various schools, I'd never grown accustomed to the harsh remarks that greeted my favorite works. "Spray him with Raid," was one young man's reaction to Gregor Samsa's metamorphosis. After what I thought was an aptly impassioned lecture on the deprivation and death of Akaky Akakyavitch in Gogol's "The Overcoat," the daughter of Hollywood celebrities looked at me in wonderment and said, "Like, get a grip. It's only a coat." Not a titter had hailed the humor of Dorothy Parker or James Thurber. And—when I'd made the mistake of reading surrealist verse—if eyes could make noise, their rolling would have been heard for miles.

I put down my book and drifted out to the porch. The neighborhood children had gathered on Sunland Avenue, and above the distant mariachi music and the clatter of cars grinding up the hill, I could hear them argue.

"I bet there's a ton of blood in a body," said one boy rocking on his rickety bike.

"Don't be stupid," shouted the girl next to him. "That would mean you'd weigh a ton."

"Ton of blood, ton of blood," sang a set of twins.

The bungalows of my apartment complex—pitched roofs, clapboard walls—glowed with the last of autumn light. On the stoop next door, Ricardo was combing his cat, Titanic, and laughing at bits of the escalating argument. Titanic tried to dart from his arms.

"I guess," said Ricardo, snatching at cat hairs drifting through the air, "we're all nothing but big bags of blood."

"A pleasant thought," I said. Titanic finally freed herself, raced to the nearest patch of dirt where she writhed and raised a cloud of dust. Ricardo and I sat on our steps. We craned our faces into the sunlight, continued to talk with our eyes closed.

"I'm horny," said Ricardo. "Or maybe I'm lonely. Do you ever get to the point where you can't tell the difference?"

"There must be a word for that."

"Desperation?"

"An even better word."

"You're the word man," he said. "You suggest something."

The sun felt good on my skin. Optical dots flashed under my eyelids. I didn't want to think about loneliness, my own or anyone else's.

"Do you think Trent ever gets lonely?" Ricardo asked after a long silence. Trent lived across the street. Every evening he walked to his mailbox dressed in a pair of skimpy shorts. Trent was a one-man geometry lesson, his physique a marvel of volumes and planes.

"Ricardo," I said, "I can't even look at Trent—he wants me to look, wants everyone to look."

"Those thighs, those biceps," said Ricardo. "Forget fondling. I'd be happy just to measure them. Tell the truth. Wouldn't you?"

My eyes were still closed, but I pictured Ricardo seated on his stoop—brown skin, black hair. Since he'd moved next door in October, I'd welcomed his endless, ingenuous questions, and never felt obliged to answer.

On the first day of the Fall semester, I found Janet in the faculty lounge, guzzling cups of coffee and tugging at the shoulder pads imbedded in her sweater. "Are they even?" she asked me.

"Perfect," I replied. "Are you trying out for quarterback?"

Miss Bartlet, dressed in a red jumpsuit and squinting at color swatches in the corner, said, "Those are called Pagoda Shoulders. They're absolutely darling."

"They weigh a ton," said Janet. "I think these pagodas are made of cement. I'll never shrug again." She poured more coffee into a Styrofoam cup and looked me up and down. "Honey," she said, "a word of advice: Bundy hates it when her teachers wear jeans."

"Unless," Miss Bartlet broke in, "they're clean and ironed with a neat crease."

"Betty," said Janet, turning to Miss Bartlet, "no one *wants* a crease in their jeans."

"I think a crease in denim is quite chic," said a woman wearing the most elaborate earrings I'd ever seen. They were like Caulder mobiles, tinkling and turning and catching the light. "I have a wire insert you just slip into wet jeans for an even crease. So convenient."

"Isn't Valenti coming out with pre-creased jeans?" someone asked.

Janet grabbed my hand and dragged me to a sofa in an empty

section of the lounge. "Look," she said, "there are two rules for survival in this place. One: talk only with people whose names don't rhyme."

My eyebrows bunched.

"Haven't you noticed that everyone here in a position of power has a rhyming name? Barbara Bundy. Frank Fox. You're an English teacher; isn't there a word for that?"

"Alliteration."

"Right. William Pope, Dorothy Layton; *they* can be trusted. "And Two," she said, batting at her shoulder pads, "dress the part. That's all that counts." Janet gave my knee a squeeze, rose and dashed for the door.

Before the door could close, Barbara Bundy swept into the room. "Attention everyone. The Student Finance Association has created bumper stickers to be given to those children delinquent on their loans." She held up a strip of paper that read, *If you're late with your loan, you won't have anything to stick this on.* "Aren't they just . . . what's the word I'm looking for?" She turned to me.

"Adorable?" I offered.

I got lost on the way to my classroom. The halls of the Institute were long and spotless, each named after a famous designer. The Edith Head Hall contained large blowups of Miss Head's sketches, women in voluminous skirts, some as fluffy as cumulus clouds. The Bill Blass hall was painted dark green, and hung along its walls were party dresses in metallic fabrics, pressed under glass like giant flowers. When I finally found room 702 (I'd confused the Calvin with the Anne Klein hallway), my students—twenty girls and one boy—were quietly waiting.

I fished the roll sheet from my briefcase. As the readout unraveled, I noticed the boy had raised his hand.

"Yes?"

"Can I go?" he asked.

"Go?"

"Yeah. Can I leave?"

"Aren't you enrolled in this class?"

"Yeah. But it's going to rain." I gave a sidelong glance out the window. Ominous clouds slid over the city.

"I'm afraid I don't understand."

The boy lifted the lapel of his jacket. "It's suede," he said. "If I leave right now, it won't get wet."

"I'm sorry," I said, "but I think W. H. Auden, the writer whose work we'll examine today, is every bit as important as your jacket." I imagined a giant silver scale: on one side sat Auden, legs crossed, nursing a cigarette; on the other lay a crumpled jacket. The scale seesawed up and down.

After everyone was accounted for, I passed out Xerox copies of Auden's poem *Musée des Beaux Arts*.

"Isn't this an English class?" grumbled a girl in the front row.

"Of course," I said through thirty-two teeth. "I'll translate the title in a moment. But first let me give you some biographical information."

When I turned to the blackboard, I distinctly heard her snap, "Thank you, daddy." I wrote down the dates of birth and death. I filled in Auden's early history—doctor father, Oxford pranks—then walked around the room with a photograph of Auden, wrinkled and wry, at the age of fifty.

"Assuming that a person's history shows on his face, what kind of life do you think Auden led?"

"Not enough moisture," guessed a dewy, fair-haired girl.

"You're probably right. Auden drank a great deal and smoked four packs of unfiltered Camels a day." But my statement was lost in a flurry of talk erupting in the corner.

"Excuse me," I shouted. My glasses slid down my nose. "Is that conversation pertinent to Auden?"

"No," a small voice volunteered.

"Well, stop," I said, adding, "please.

"The point I'm trying to make is that, like many of us, Auden's sensibility consisted of two distinct aspects. On one hand, he had tremendously formal ideas about what poetry should and should not be. He considered poetry, as he put it, 'a game of the intellect.' He disliked poetry that was theatrical. He once went so far as to say that a poem should be like a person in a parlor—well-groomed, and well behaved. On the other hand, he was adventurous, lusty . . ." random giggles ". . . he lived by his wits. He was an ambulance driver in the Spanish Civil War. He was openly homosexual . . ." collective intake of breath " . . . and he wrote some of the most important poems in the twentieth century. His face is the record of a rich and complex life. Any questions before we read?"

"Awdeng?" said Sun Ha. "Please to spell."

After class, Sun Ha explained in halting phrases that she'd been mistakenly placed in my class instead of English as a Second Language. She promised, with a slightly fearful conviction, to work very hard if I let her stay. I told her I would, suggesting books that might be of help. She wrote down the titles and authors of each with great concentration. To seal our agreement, Sun Ha reached into her Institute of Fashion canvas carryall—every student was required to buy one—and dug out a package of Hostess Twinkies. "Sir," she asked, head cocked, "you like a Twinkie?"

"Great. I'm starved. Also," I called as she left the room, "you don't have to call me sir."

The cake was spongy, so sweet it stung. I sat on the edge of my desk, gazing out the window. Clouds obscured the afternoon sky, their dark bottoms sagging toward the skyline. There was an instant, before the first drops, when the streets beneath me gleamed gold, and the glass facades of nearby buildings burned with an otherworldly light. Then the hiss of hard rain, like whispers in a foreign language.

"How would you paraphrase," I'd asked my class, "what Auden means when he says that suffering 'takes place/While someone else is eating or opening a window or just walking dully along'?" Their answer was this: a few stifled yawns; furtive glances at the clock; a sketch of eyes in the margin of a Xerox. And then Sun Ha had raised her hand. "He mean," she ventured in a shaking voice, "pain of one not felt by other?"

"Yes," I'd said, wiping my forehead. "Thank you. Yes."

During the drive home—the traffic was wet and treacherous—I wondered if there was any difference between me and Mr. Rowlands. I pictured myself in a party hat, teetering on the limb of a tree. After a day of extracting answers, I found that what I wanted, second to an aspirin, was to hear Ricardo asking questions.

The rainfall was mild by the time I reached my street.

Searching for a parking spot, I drove by Trent at his mailbox, shirtless despite the weather. His shoulders and chest were slick with rain. He shifted his weight from foot to foot and his mammoth anatomy seemed to shimmer. Trent's head was bent toward the mail, but I saw him watch me from the corner of his eye; he shuffled through the envelopes so his triceps could bulge to their best advantage.

To avoid walking by him, I sat in my car and stared at raindrops streaking the windshield. Soon my breath was fogging the glass, my own breath, blooming before me. I thought of writing something with my finger, but couldn't think what to say. I dragged my palm across the haze and saw that Trent had gone.

The neighborhood children were gathered on the street. They bickered again. Their raincoats glistened.

"If there *are* Martians living on earth, why," asked the girl, "would they look like us?"

The boy on the bike said, "So they can go to the supermarket and become president and . . ."

"No way," said one twin.

"Is so," said the other.

The children eyed me with suspicion as I passed.

I went straight to Ricardo's. Titanic was curled in the corner of the porch, deep in a feline dream. I pressed the bell and a buzzer rumbled. *"Quien es?"* he said, and then, "Who is it?"

"It's Trent," I said in my deepest voice.

I heard water gush through the pipes, footsteps on the wooden floor, the rustle of tidying up. When Ricardo finally opened the door, his shoulders were squared, eyes expectant, hair coated with fragrant tonic. He saw it was me and bellowed, "Weasel!"

"Jesus," I said, "I didn't think you'd actually believe me."

He loomed in the doorway, disappointed. His black hair and dark eyes absorbed the evening light.

"When you recover, can I come in?" He spun on his heels and I followed him inside, closing the door behind me. Ricardo crumpled onto the couch. He shook his fist in my direction, and with his free hand patted the cushion. I sat beside him with my briefcase on my lap. Second by second, his features softened, released from the tension of wishing for Trent. The room was ripe with the scent of his tonic. We faced the dining room table, a slab of plywood lit from above. Scattered atop it were parts of the models Ricardo built for an architect: balsa wood windows, cardboard walls, rolls of paper shingles and brick. Ricardo had often asked me over to see the completed models; he'd remove the roof with care, talk about what the architect intended, his finger hovering over the rooms like the finger of a giant

"Do you think I'm a jerk?" he asked. "Wouldn't you like a visit from Trent? Knock knock. Richard, it's Trent. I have something to show you."

My impersonation, I told him, was better.

"Richard," he said. "Why can't you just admit to lust once in a while? Why can't you just ogle someone and enjoy it?"

"Like the wolf in cartoons? Eyeballs popping out on springs?"

"You're so . . . intellectual."

"Oh, goodness no," I mocked. "Not that. Isn't this the part where you take off my glasses and unpin my hair to reveal the sexpot seething beneath the prim exterior?"

He thought a moment and pounced at my glasses. I tried to grab them back. My briefcase fell to the floor.

"Why, Miss Cole," he said in a Southern accent, dangling my glasses out of reach, "you're lovely as a magnolia blossom."

The room was a blur. I sat back and asked for an aspirin. Ricardo brought me two, and a glass of wine to wash them down.

"How about a toast?" he said, reclining on the rug.

"To what?" I mumbled with the tablets on my tongue.

"*Al placer.*"

I looked at him, puzzled.

He asked, "Don't you know any Spanish?"

"Margarita. Tacquito."

"We'll take care of that," he said, draining his glass in a single gulp.

It must have been the wine. Later that night, after a shower, I posed before my bathroom mirror—head-on and profile, bemused and seductive and nonchalant—imagining how I looked to Ricardo. The task, I thought, was impossible. I'd seen my face for thirty years: straight hair, green eyes—straight, green, from every angle. How, I wondered, could Trent muster such self-regard.

The doorbell put an end to my reverie. I went to get dressed before I answered, but Ricardo had let himself in. He whistled as I ran by the bedroom door. "I didn't know you had hair on your chest," he called from the living room. I pulled on my pants in a dark corner. "I love that," he added. "It makes my *dedos del pia* curl."

"Your what?" I yelled as I slipped on a shirt.

"Toes," he said when I entered the room. "You look nice, by the way."

"What's this?" I asked, squinting at a stack of cardboard he held in his hand.

"This," he said, "is lesson one." He fanned out the cards; on each he'd printed a Spanish word in red ink. While I threaded my belt through the loops of my jeans, Ricardo rushed around the room, taping nouns to appropriate objects. *Silla, mesa, lampara, ventena, libro, reloj, cortina, puerta.* I watched muscles stretch his shirt as he ripped pieces of tape from the roll. Thunder sputtered far away. Rain drummed the metal awnings. The radiator rasped. *"Perfecto,"* he said when the last card was in place. We stood side by side and surveyed the room. "I'll come back tomorrow night and test you." Ricardo was about to turn toward the door when I caught his arm and drew him toward me. I could feel the heat within his sleeve. His broad chin was shadowed with stubble. His pulse stammered at his temple and throat.

"Can I ask you something?" he whispered as he reached for the light.

"Now?" I asked as the light went out.

"How many times does someone have to tell you they're lonely before you get the message?"

In the dark, all around me, hung unfamiliar words. "I guess," I said, "I'm a slow learner."

The following day at school, I was trying to define onomatopoeia, but all I could think about was the V of Ricardo's stomach, slowly bared as I undid his zipper. I would have pictured the folds of his pants parting over and over—a moment so sharp with anticipation, the rain had seemed to stop in abeyance—if I hadn't been interrupted by a question.

"Like, *sizzle* and *boom* and stuff," said the boy, "I get that. But couldn't any word be oma . . ."

"Onomatopoetic."

" . . . yeah, if you said it the right way?"

"Could you be more specific?"

"Well, like the word *tree*. Couldn't that be onomato—whatever if you said it to sound like a tree?"

I walked around my desk, faced the class. I bent my arms like the branches of an oak. I intoned the word tree, but drew out the e-e-e-e for as long as I could and made the sound waver like leaves in a wind. "Like so?" I said. And laughed. Alone.

"Excuse me, Mr. Cole." Barbara Bundy was standing at the door. I felt like an acorn had caught in my throat. "You look very busy and I hate to disturb you, but we have a problem."

"I was attempting to illustrate . . ."

"There have been," she continued, "several complaints . . ."

". . . oma . . ."

". . . about the window display in the Calvin Klein hall."

"Oh," I exhaled. "How may I help you?"

"I'm afraid the only access to the window is through your room." She pointed to a narrow door. Everyone turned. "Have you seen the window in question, Mr. Cole?"

I'd seen the window on the way to class. Against a bright yellow backdrop, a mannequin swung a tennis racket and beamed a wicked grin. She was dressed in typical tennis clothes except for a jacket with a map of Vietnam embroidered on the back. A sign read, Tennis Anyone?

"Frankly, Miss Bundy, I thought the effect was very offensive."

"How could one not?" She thrust a hand on her ample hip. "The yellow backdrop and black jacket—they clash something awful. I'll see to it," she said, "this instant," and disappeared through the narrow door.

"Don't worry," said Janet, laughing. "If Bundy saw this"— she yanked my tie—"she probably didn't notice the oak. You look like a real professor in that suit."

"I feel like a public accountant," I said. We had to shout; the lunchroom teemed with rowdy students parading their outfits up and down the aisles.

Janet eyed the crowd and said, "I've finally figured out the school's admissions policy: You're in if you can button your clothes."

Across from our table, a video monitor flickered with a fashion show from Europe. A few students stood before it, reverent, transfixed. "My in-floo-ence," the designer was saying in an undiscernible accent, "Iz microbiology." Women wearing flaccid hats and drooping skirts spun on the runway. "Ezpecially amoebas."

"Hey," said Janet, "look at that." She pointed to Miss Bartlett who was shoving coins in a vending machine. "Notice anything different?" Miss Bartlett was dressed in navy blue. "I've never seen her in anything but red." Janet sighed and sipped her coffee. "Kind of shakes my faith in the status quo."

"I know," I said, "I know." The weather, my clothes, my romantic life had all been altered without any warning, and Miss Bartlett—prim in blue, wrestling with a candy wrapper—seemed a harbinger of sudden change.

I said goodbye to Janet and went to collect the essays waiting in my box. The halls were noisy, jammed with people. I passed by a group of prospective students who were touring the Edith Head hall. "This is Edith Head's actual signature," said the Institute's public relations man, tapping a framed piece of paper. An *oooh* rose from the cluster of girls, but I saw they were looking into his eyes, a moist, Rasputin blue.

In the faculty lounge, two teachers were grading patterns for men's pajamas. I slid the essays out of my box and pictured Ricardo inside his apartment, seated at a slab of wood, holding the walls of a house together, waiting for the glue to dry. I willed myself to remember his scent, his compact body beneath my sheets. The night before, he'd burrowed his head into the pillow and cast an arm across my chest, incanting Spanish words in his sleep.

I was about to put the papers in my briefcase when Sun Ha's handwriting caught my eye.

Here is poem I chose by W. C. Williams:

This Is Just to Say

*I have eaten
the plums
that were in*

the ice box

and which
you were probably
saving
for breakfast

Forgive me
they were delicious
so sweet
and so cold

I like the poem. In Korea where I come from, my mother sometime put note on ice box. He have ice box. Maybe he write poem to put on ice box. He saying with really deep feeling he can't help to eat sweet plums. He had to. Sorry. No more I can say.

I looked up and the lounge was empty. A pot of coffee brewed on a burner. From the window overlooking Figueroa, I saw the tangled afternoon traffic, headlights and brakelights doubled in puddles. As I loaded my briefcase and buttoned my coat, " . . . sweet plums . . . had to . . . " resounded like an echo.

JOURNEY

• MARTIN PALMER •

AS HE LOOKED down at the wrinkled skin of the water from several miles up in the clear evening air, setting out on his long trip, he saw the islands and the harbor just as they were in photographs. He felt relieved to see that the landscape confirmed itself. An unintelligible commentary by the pilot rattled on the intercom as he struggled with the plastic wrap of his ice-cold knife and fork and looked at the food before him. The busy flight attendant's red-blond crew cut with a faint balding tonsure reminded him exactly of an actor he had admired, nude in an all-male video several years before. He wondered if the young man, in this age of contagion, had changed his occupation to something just as public but less hazardous, if he was the one.

"Is everything all right?" Later, the flight attendant smiled impersonally, leaning toward his seat to gather the little pile of garbage left on the plastic tray.

"Is it? . . . I mean, are you . . . ?" He was astonished to hear himself begin such a personal question about the young man's past, and to a complete stranger. But a bewildering and urgent need for reassurance propelled him. As the attendant stacked his tray, he saw a wedding band on his left hand, and although he knew that such a display was the flimsiest of conventions, his anxiety ebbed to embarrassment.

"Pardon, sir?"

"Everything's fine. Thank you."

Not having understood a word said to him, the young man smiled soothingly, swept the trash into the container, then turned to the opposite aisle.

He settled himself against the window once more, watching the sunlit clouds form far below, recalling how, as a child on summer afternoons, he often longed to sit in such vast billows, watching, far out of reach of everything around him until he was called in to eat his supper with his father, lingering over the ice cream they always finished with. Often they would sit together afterward in the darkness of the screened porch while he, sleepy and secure, asked endless questions about anything that came into his head. On planes he wanted only to read, doze, or daydream, and he discouraged conversation with anyone. During the long hours of this trip he went in and out of passenger lounges and the padded tubes of the large planes and was thankful that no infants were nearby. Finally, with a feeling of alert weariness and after two changes of planes in the night he reached the city where he was to celebrate a family anniversary.

Staying with a nephew and his wife until his sister and brother-in-law returned from Europe, he had a hearty dinner with several of the younger family members and had drunk a little too much of the smooth red wine he enjoyed; consequently he had reacted sharply to some conversational platitude and told a young wife whose father had been a minister, "Religion is the most destructive human invention I can think of."

She had vigorously defended her father and her faith, and though she was not a person to nurse wounds, as he lay in bed that night he accused himself of acting inappropriately and felt chagrined about it; how earnestly pompous he sounded.

"They'll think I'm an old fart," he told himself morosely, aware in the darkness of the background noise in his ears that had started last year and had finally settled into the sound of frying, though without any noticeable harm to his hearing. He sighed.

That afternoon he had enjoyed watching the light change as a looming thunderstorm cooled the thick, humid air; then it crashed and rolled about him as sheets and curtains of rain pounded the soaked ground. The stillness, then the bird songs beginning again after the storm, along with the soft tap of dripping leaves, took him back to the past. Where he presently lived there were no thunderstorms even though thunderheads sprawled around the horizon on some days. He missed them. Now, in the fragrant night that echoed with insect sounds under a moon growing full, a bird began its song, pausing between elaborate phrases as if it were drawing breath. He fell into the kind of sleep that no pill or preparation seemed able to change; a sleep that was a noisy grinding and boring through the shallows of consciousness all the hours of the night with sour, thin dreams flickering in and out of it.

The morning was sunny and hot, a summer heaviness here that came early and left only after one of the late fall storms. He had made an appointment to see a department head at the university from which he had graduated thirty years before, curious about the possibility of a teaching position. An idle curiosity, since he didn't really want to return to the city. He had a mild sense of discomfort, of airlessness, when he thought of perhaps coming back. At the same time he was forced to glimpse a small dread of being alone with aging, of losing a place in his life; an anxiety anticipated but vague. But the idea of teaching at the other university in the city, which was founded as one of the black "Agricultural and Mechanical" schools scattered through the region and which had since grown and become well known, appealed to him as having a shade of defiance. Why he felt this way he could not precisely say. He told himself that it would be giving back what had been withheld or taken away, and it didn't occur to him how fatuously romantic, how condescending his attitude was, or to question why he had it.

All nearby parking spaces at the university were taken and he had to park near the cemetery and walk several blocks in a coat and tie, which he thought appropriate for the interview. The department head was noncommittally polite and the talk, which had been arranged only the day before, soon silted in shallows of trivialities and courteous indifference, and was over. He felt shelved as he passed a teaching assistant who was on the telephone informing a student she had won a writing contest. He thought of the pleasure in her face and voice. The teaching assistant looked worn in the service of his department, older than the usual bunch, a bit wizened.

Reaching his car, he stood still for a moment in the heat and glare, hoping for any faint movement of air that would cool his wet shirt. He looked across the hedge at the thick, well-kept grass of the Old City Cemetery, and found himself examining the field of small headstones of the Civil War soldiers clustered in a slight depression of the ground that had formed over the years. The incisions were barely readable now and hardly a foot of the headstones remained above the grass. Remembering, too, that his father and mother lay inside in the family plot which he had not visited for years, and guiltily surprised that he had forgotten, he walked to the entrance. All of it looked so ancient. Broken pediments and corners from several ornate Victorian tombs lay gathered in a fort, but the effect was one of diminishing with age, with years, as if even the mottled gray stone of the plots' borders had shrunk, was dissolving slowly in time, being eaten by the carefully tended strong green grass; irresistibly. As his feet sank in grass so springy that it felt artificial and he looked at headstones in the family plot, he remembered the regular visits here with his father, bringing roses, lilies, and camellias from the garden. The place had seemed bigger then, and he almost always saw other people here and there, tending things or perhaps strolling. There were always fresh or wilted flowers or wreaths in view, the wilted ones making him think of dead pets and rain and weathers and sad things. Today in the bright glare there was only neat, devouring green, an emptiness as if the place had passed from human use into the abstraction of a monument that one passes without seeing. Some of the headstones were so remote in time and memory that he had no idea any longer of who they had been. Who was "Little Nella" beyond what was carved on the mottled stone beneath a lamb? It had the distance of a diagram of the solar system lit obliquely by a tiny sun, which was memory fading. The traffic in the nearby street shaded by a canopy of tall pecan trees, tires and an occasional honking horn, came to him. He drove to his old home feeling as if he were riding in a still, hot time capsule.

Susan and Philip Tebo, his sister and brother-in-law, had known each other most of their lives and in the course of it had married forty years ago. They had worked hard staging the wedding of their youngest daughter four months before, and their relief was so great that they had hardly thought about their anniversary. Now they regarded it as the lesser of the two events that year. This annoyed him. Having missed the wedding, he had saved time and money to come to what surely must be an occasion, and now they returned from their long vacation only one day before their party and seemed to see the event almost as an imposition. He thought, too, that it could be tinged with just a little superstition: don't draw attention to it. Because they weren't making much of it, he felt a little devalued because he had; he felt accused of sentimentality, in poor taste. The dance and reception given by their children were to be at their house, tucked with its old cemetery and enormous oaks into a section of the city walled off by green over the years so that not even the busy traffic could be heard only a short distance away. A chain across the drive by the historical marker barred casual visitors except at stated times, and only when it had been accidentally left down did the occasional tourist couple show up to find them at the dining table, to be kindly escorted out in embarrassed confusion, though some wanted to go through the house anyway. His father, a friendly and gregarious man, had sometimes even invited them to sit down to the meal, to the strained discomfort of his children. The house, which had become shabby at one point, was carefully restored in every detail and maintained like a religion, a taste in English antiques having superseded at some point the original heavy, comfortable Victorianisms of its builders. He sometimes missed the dark, bulky gold-fringed curtains with the elaborate cornices and dusty smells, ideal places to be alone in the window embrasures, watching life outside.

"Now it's Milawd Manor," he thought, looking around at the stylish, expensive light airs and graces of its present manifestation, immaculate in the day.

For him it was not connected with his life anymore. He remembered the still heat and acrid smell of the attic, an essence of time, when he could open large bound trunks and rummage. Some had held packs of useless money with fascinating engravings and mottoes. He would open the glass port just above his head and crawl out on the slate roof at the exhilarating level of the tallest trees three stories up, causing a whistling explosion of the pigeons along the roof ridge. All that had been carted away and cataloged or dumped, and the port had been sealed.

On one of the couches in the garden room lay a book opened to "Things To Do To Refresh Your Spirit," left by one of the daughters, he thought. "Bathe your temples with rosewater on a hot day," he read. "Read a chapter of Beatrix Potter to your daughter," it went on in a babbling list. Being gracious was a serious profession to some of his family. Being serious often was not. As he went down the hall a soft flash in the long mirror by the table caught his eye, and he stepped over to examine his reflection in the mild shadow. Except for a tiny cut high on one cheek he looked back at his usual face; nothing different marked him. He could live with it.

That lunch a couple of years ago with Jack, a longtime friend, came to his mind. In a crowded restaurant while they were eating and the waiter hovered around the group of tables, Jack had undone a couple of buttons and pulled his starched shirt open to reveal a cluster of dark spots near the middle of his chest, shapes that looked to him like a map of Greece and the Aegean islands, the first comparison that came to mind after he noticed that Jack didn't use underwear. The next image followed swiftly: Jack's sunken cheeks deep in the hospital pillow with his nose rising like a beak, the end wholly covered by a charred brown scab, his glazed eyes following the visitor in the darkened room, his voice a rough whisper. That was three months ago, and afterward as he walked across a small park returning to his car he was almost on top of him when he recognized the shabby, seedy man half sprawled over a bench, a stunned, drowsy expression on his shockingly aged face. Todd, who was in his forties, had been a sought-after drifter, the brightest of that group, living well on his looks. Once Todd had visited him for almost three months. In the pale sunlight, his once lustrous mahogany-colored hair now a thin straggle across his scalp, Todd squinted at him questioningly as he nodded and walked on. He felt shaken.

Lately some kind of interference had grown invisibly between his visible world and his realm of feeling; he could not make the contact, the connection, that joined them. Lines were coming down, and even anxiety wasn't getting through when he expected it; the air seemed to be getting thinner and thinner. He looked at his own reassuring face again and shut off speculation.

*   *   *

Last light was a bright pattern through the great trees as guests walked up the drive from where an attendant parked their cars. A remarkable number, he noticed, had attended the wedding forty years before and seemed to have ridden through time as in a luxurious automobile, arriving now intact, paunchy and wrinkled and with the chalky skin of age in many cases, but tended well and recognizable. Baskets, bowls, urns and arrangements of flowers filled the rooms and the flagged terrace leading to tables set up beside the pool under a large striped marquee that cast a reddish shadow in candlelight over the white tablecloths covered with crystal and silver. A three-piece orchestra played show tunes that echoed in the tree branches, dark above the lights. Susan and Philip, wearing paper crowns put together by some of the grandchildren, animatedly enjoyed themselves as they accepted compliments and congratulations. He found it hard to believe that he had been at the wedding ceremony that long ago. He recalled the crowded church and the May afternoon heavy with heat. Then the receiving line in front of the mantelpiece in the house; all the flowers then, too. He remembered the excitement, how he had enjoyed it. Now, seated between two cousins, one old and one young, from different sides of the family, he bent his head forward and fixed his eyes on her face as the older woman, slightly drunk, plowed through a long account of her son, his wife, and her grandson now in school, exceptionally gifted, sensitive to so many things, and so on and on. Like many others, she assumed that because he lived so far away and returned so seldom, he was eager to hear every detail of her concerns and activities, with only perfunctory questions about his own. Her interest in life outside the city was that of someone reading items in a newspaper. Often such things were interesting, but they were seldom important. He remembered that Cara Fontaine had no other family, and he thought, sometimes, that he might have too much. In this place, who was invited where, to what, and when, was supremely important, and slights, real and fancied, were always a consequence of consanguinity and position. He knew that Susan and Philip, naturally thoughtful within their circle and often kind, made a particular effort to see that Cara was included in their parties and in most of the larger family dinners and anniversaries.

"My goodness," the young woman on his other side breathed dubiously, "I'm certainly getting an awful lot of family history." She smiled tightly, and he knew she was bored and impatient, wanting to talk to her other companion instead.

Cara went straight ahead like a large powerboat on a small river, sloshing everything with waves of detail that only she could care about. Her eyes swam with tears behind her glasses, and she sipped champagne frequently to wet her throat. He appeared absorbed in her recitation, his eyes fixed on his plate, listening. But he was hearing the voices around him that he had known all of his life; hearing the changed timbres but unchanged cadences that had come across these years, in a kind of wonder, following the thread he found in them. After toasts were proposed, including a shakily emotional one by Cara, and after the cake was cut, the Tebos rose to dance, together first, then with every child and grandchild and into the guests, looking energetic and happy. Finally, around midnight, the tide of the party ebbed. After the combo left, the bursts of laughter were fewer in the settling night. He slowly climbed the stairs to his room and stood at the window, closed to help the circulating air, and looked out on the dark lawn where the shiny leaves of a hedge reflected glints of moonlight at the edge. The deep shadows concealed the hard edges that flatly defined the world in daylight. He thought of stage props.

His young life had coagulated into a group of set pictures that came in a series as if he were watching one of the gaudy old travelogues with voiceover. Until just a few years ago he had always had the feeling that he was the youngest person in any group, because from an early age he had been. Now when he was at an airline counter or in a department store, or when he was treated with particular deference or "sirred" by the young, he saw, in flashes, how he must appear to others: a graying middle-aged person who was "well preserved." Lately he couldn't account for how rapidly this change, this passage, had occurred; and now he could outline an old age, and even a death in his future. There the decades lay, in orderly sequence as he quantified them, number after marching number. And he couldn't find himself in them, couldn't define his place in them clearly. Anxiety crept into him as he considered it. He got into bed and finally slid into sleep.

"This is from Katie." Susan Tebo's sharp laugh penetrated as she opened letters and cards in the garden room and handed one to him across the sofa. "She knows how I feel about this stuff."

The clipping was a photograph of an elderly couple, the husband a retired appliance salesman, the wife large and shapeless in her dark dress, celebrating their forty-fifth wedding anniversary, listing their children's names and the numbers of their grandchildren as well as one great-grandchild. Across the top their friend Katie had written, "I see you both made the news." He had noticed how cartoonish and silly many of their cards had been; then he realized that all were meant sincerely as thoughtful choices. Katie aimed to make them laugh, and the put-down of her unwitting targets was the kind of thing they laughed at.

Just outside the French doors in the glare of a hot sun the daylilies looked fresh and invigorated by the heat and light. He felt distanced from them by the glass, and he could hear as though at a great distance the jays in a frenzy at a squirrel, whose repeated chirr and chatter provoked them. Susan loved working in her garden and earlier that afternoon had taken him to nearly every flower bed, shrub, and recently planted tree as if to personally introduce him to something as close to her as he had always been. As an older sister, Susan had been the person whose likes and dislikes, whose tastes in so many things, even in food, and often in people, had influenced him most from the time he could remember until he was well grown, and this hold on him could still be powerful. A lonely child who was often alone, when he was with Susan he felt wanted and had loved being around her with her friends when they were young women and he was still a kid. Along with his attentive father, she had nearly always taken time to listen to him. Once, when he was about twelve, Susan and her summer date at the time circled into a restrained quarrel. He had been talking to the young man, but later curled in the window seat, reading. The quarrel grew.

"And that brother of yours. Does he have to go to the picture show with us? I mean, his voice and the way he moves his hands . . ."

An angry Susan went upstairs, leaving the date nothing to do except stalk out without saying goodbye to anyone.

"That booby," Susan said to him the next day apropos of nothing as she sat by him stroking his fair hair. "He'll never come around here again, I swear."

Both parents died when he was young, and Susan, with Philip, had been the most immediate family he had; in the years he was away at school he had longed to be with them. Whatever his successes, he always took them to Susan. But absence had also brought about a certain wishful thinking that, when he visited, contrasted with reality. This had grown into a reserved tone in their relationship when he moved away, took up his own life and its consequences, as the years passed and they diverged. Time and distance had diminished her the way places are smaller and often simpler when one returns years afterward to see them. But he recalled with feeling how much her approval had meant to him.

Susan put a videotape of the party on the machine and after a brief spattering of black-and-white lines, the wobbling camcorder, held by one of the children, focused on couples making their way toward the house, some waving at the camera, all hanging on to each other's arms, many of the women holding their long skirts, trying not to stumble on the gravel in their high heels.

"Look at that!" Susan exclaimed. "Who are all those old people struggling up the drive?" She peered intently for a few seconds, watching them as they reached the door. "Oh, good Lord!" Her tone was rueful surprise. "It's us!" She began laughing. "Look at us, all those old things creeping around. How awful! But at least we're still here."

They watched the amateur video as Susan commented on various ones at the party, the food and flowers, the combo, the dancers. "You'd never know to look at them. Look how happy they seem." Susan leaned closer. "Alec and Peg are divorcing. Peg told me she just can't take another cheap girlfriend." Susan adjusted the videocassette. "But she's done it for thirty years. She'll get a good settlement, anyway."

"There's Cal Sinkler, Martha and Jim's oldest, right on the edge of the pool. And drunk, as usual." Susan froze the frame for a couple of seconds to see if any damage was being done. "Martha says he was shameless about the au pair from Germany. And right in front of Lallie and the children."

He had seen only couples, old and young and in between. He

wondered if their world simply pinched off singles, as Susan might prune an imperfect flower on one of her plants. Susan sipped her diet cola and watched as the camera veered broadly toward some of the dancers.

"Oh, how good you were to dance all that time with Cara Fontaine!" She sounded grateful, as if he had saved an awkward situation. She examined the older woman, whose back was to the camera. "She looks wonderful in that dress. That must have really cost her son a lot more than he can afford, poor thing." She turned to him as she took a strawberry and dusted it in powdered sugar.

"Philip has been very smart, and everybody we know has been making lots and lots of money, too, the way things have been." She finished the strawberry and dusted her fingers. "Except the Fontaines. But they dress and act like they've been making it too, and come to all the parties and have a good time. No complaints, thank goodness."

She clicked off the video then rose and walked over to pour herself another cola.

"I hate to say this"—her voice became emphatic, with a hard edge—"but I'm afraid Eddie, the grandson, is going to turn out to be gay." She sounded as if she were crossing someone off a list. "I can tell. He's fourteen."

Alerted by the distance in her tone, he was stung to hear how she felt, her guard down.

"The boy's fourteen years old, for Christ's sake. By now he already is whatever he will be. You know that." He felt the heat in his face. He wondered if she remembered her date's remarks so long ago. He had never forgotten them and was self-conscious about appearances for a long time afterward.

There was a change in her tone. She sounded surprised, as if she had just noticed someone else in the room, and she smoothed her answer.

"You know what I mean," she became conciliatory. "I meant all the"—she searched briefly—"difficult situations he'll have to put up with; that's all. And he'll have to make his own way and all that. It's just going to be harder for him. He has to go to County High now, with all those types. You certainly know what I mean. And I hear that some of those County kids and parents can get awfully strident over various things."

"Yes, Susan, I know what you mean." He looked at her with curiosity. "Do you know any of those people? Any at all?"

"If you mean gays, the ones we know have the tact to be discreet." She frowned, then laughed. "I can never forgive them for ruining a perfectly harmless and charming word." Her tone was sharp.

"Ruined?" The word hung. "You sound like one of those old biddies who used to write society columns and then bitch about the escorts they'd known about since they were born."

"Why are you so touchy? Honestly, I can hardly say . . ." She didn't finish.

"All right. All right. I guess I've been away, out of touch too long to sort people out these days. When I come, I always see the same bunch. Do you and Philip go to any other—"

"Why, of course we do," she interrupted with exasperation and relief. "We're not the stick-in-the-muds you think we are. If you came home more often you'd meet some of the others. 'Those people,' as you call them. What a snob you can be. We voted Belva and Clyde Hixson into the Lake Club, finally. He's helped Philip a lot, and she's certainly presentable. She still calls her curtains 'drapes,' though."

"But do you ever see any of the A and M college bunch? They're in the news from time to time even up where I am. Remember when Papa used to take us out to hear the singers and we'd sit here and they'd sit over there?"

"Philip and I go to the series at the new Arts Center at the university. We simply can't get to everything everywhere."

"I saw Mrs. Gladys Washington's picture in today's paper as head of the City Commission on Charities. Weren't you working with her once? Did you ever go to her house?" He was genuinely curious.

Susan, who had been examining a planter turned to face him.

"Look," she said firmly, "stop baiting me. You know I don't have to put up with anything like that anymore, ever. I don't even have to think about it," she went on, picking up the paper. "I don't want to and I'm not going to. There are a lot of whites that I don't have to put up with, either."

At that moment he looked at her as if she stood on the other side of a chill, windy little ice field that had appeared suddenly, like the ones he found on some of the hikes he took where he lived now. He felt an unexpected grief.

"These strawberries are delicious." He had speared one with a toothpick, and after eating one he was able to speak.

"Can you think of something you especially want to eat? Philip got some mullet roe for you, for breakfast. And tonight we'll drive down to Bayou Springs and have seafood." She sat by him and put an arm around his shoulders. "I'm so glad you're here."

His grief retreated to an invasive regret. He smiled at her and touched her hand. "I'm glad, too," he said. "I'm glad I came. I wanted to tell you . . ." He picked up his empty glass and rattled the ice gently. "It's good to be here," he finished.

The salt marsh smell at Bayou Springs in the evening air was pleasant, taking him back to summer days spent there on the coast, with crabbing and sudden dark squalls and the steady breeze singing through the screened porches in the night. At the foot of the concrete boat ramp a tall and elegant heron stood, swiveling its head to watch for minnows. Just offshore the springs of fresh water from the limestone beneath boiled up to the surface. Marsh grass lined the salt bayou, and pines in the distance were dark against a sunburst of light and clouds. The settlement, hardly fifty people, hadn't changed at all from what he remembered, and he was inordinately pleased and surprised to discover this. By the small restaurant stood a large live oak tree with tufts of gray moss, and across the road was a decaying cottage that appeared empty. A general store with a rusting sign and a boat shed sat on the bank of the little bay. At the restaurant they had beer with their fish and crab and oysters, and hushpuppies and fries.

"Um, tell me, mm, what's going on up there?" Philip always hesitated a bit, humming to get started. It was a familiar trait. "I mean, how are things?"

He couldn't talk economics in any knowledgeable way, but he gave a newspaper item capsule that confirmed whatever Philip was thinking and disposed of the matter.

"You never eat those things," Susan said to Philip. "Why are you doing it now?" Philip chewed his cucumber stick slowly.

"I do all the time. The redfish could be fresher."

"Mine is delicious and just as fresh as anything could be. How's yours?" Susan turned to him expectantly.

"Really good." And it was. Susan and Philip never failed to have small disagreements when they went out to eat. Years ago these often had an edge of rancor, but he noticed now that their tone was one of comfortable habit, of filling in.

Driving back in the evening light they went along a rural corridor of thick green vines almost smothering some of the bordering trees. Passing one patch of sand and scrub oak, he saw a one-room church, old white clapboard, with a small, sandy graveyard. It was an unexpected sight here, something that he thought had disappeared years ago. The sight of a few high-banked graves, some with dying flowers in glass jars, moved him. Then the memory of walking barefoot in the hot sand and the pain of stepping into a patch of sandspurs came to him; and of his father driving the car, and the wild pigs that sometimes ran out on the narrow highway before the fencing laws. The sun was low, just beneath an enormous pile of clouds with purple centers and a nimbus of golden light around the edges where the moisture created great rays scattering upward. Susan and Philip continued a desultory exchange, evidently begun some months ago, about summer plans. The radio in the car was tuned to a station broadcasting nondescript music, and the amplifier near his ear was distracting. He watched the familiar scene pass.

Planning to leave on an early plane, he put on his pajamas and robe to pack. He hoped he could sleep. The trip was a long one.

"Come on back to our room and talk to us." Susan pushed the door open after a soft knock. "We'll have a little while together. Everything has been too busy, and we really haven't spent time with each other."

He followed her down the hall to their large bedroom where they lounged on a wide bed with pillows crumpled against the headboard. He sank into a big, comfortable wing chair in bright chintz, facing them.

"Now, tell me about everything. What's going on with you." Susan straightened a pillow against her back.

Feeling as if something had unlocked, perhaps after the ride and the dinner, and coming to the end of his visit, he began to speak to them.

"Sometimes I wonder if I'll ever get down here again," he began uncertainly, not knowing clearly what he wanted to say. He smiled. "It's just been very hard now, and I've lost—I'm losing—a lot of people close to me. And even about my own self . . ."

"What do you mean, not coming down again? Don't be silly!" Susan's tone was protesting, reproving, as if he had used bad grammar. "Of course you're coming down whenever you can. We're always here." She went on, "And as for losing friends, well, you told us times are bad up there. People move away. You said they did. I know it's hard. Why don't you come back home?"

"I've been there, Susan, for fifteen years. That's where my work is, my house . . . It's not a question of moving back. You can see that, surely. And that's not what I'm talking about."

"Well, um, the way I read it, the boom's over in those parts." Philip turned on his side. "It'll be like the third world again, just as it was. I say if you're not making a profit, then why stay in?"

"And I think it's gloomy up there, and too cold and wet. Those trees were too dark. Arctic. Even the word sounds like a jagged thing. Like ice. It would get on anybody's nerves." Susan shivered a little.

He noticed Philip staring past him intently as the conversation slipped into a loop he hadn't foreseen. He half turned to see the bright screen of the large television set tuned to "Larry King Live." Larry King's mouth moved animatedly in the silence as printed words crawled across the bottom of the screen reading, "The subject tonight is incest." Now Susan's face shone in the dim light and he saw that she, too, was engrossed by the television. He leaned from the chair to touch the selector lying at the foot of the bed and turned the sound on.

"Sometimes he's pretty good," Susan said as she and Philip settled down, adjusting their pillows.

"Good night," he said. "I'll finish packing. The dinner tonight was delicious, and I enjoyed going down there so much." He stood at the door, one hand on the frame.

"Good night and sweet dreams," Susan said, looking up. "I

told Eva to fix the mullet roe for breakfast. We've loved having you here. It really made a difference." She turned back to the television and gave a small sigh as she listened, absorbed.

After his shallow sleep it was more restful to rise in the dark and then start his shower. As he dried himself, he could hear the early, tentative note of a bird in the garden. He thought of the drive down to the springs, the countryside, the familiar grounds outside. Wanting to feel the fragrant, barely cool touch of early summer and to hear all the waking sounds he missed, he tugged at the window and, after a hard push, threw it open to the morning air; with a deep breath he leaned forward into the dark. At once a deafening, shrieking, pulsing wail filled the house and echoed, blasting, through the grounds. He slammed the casement shut and ran to the door to find Philip half awake, swaying at the end of the hall, at his bedroom door.

"My God, I didn't know you had the alarm . . ." he began, his heart racing.

"We have to," Philip answered, waking now and turning the switch. "It's not like it used to be, you know. That's all right."

It was still dark at the airport when he embraced both of them then boarded his plane, a smaller commuter prop type that was to take him to a larger central airport for the longer flight. A streak of sunlight spread across the horizon as it lifted off, and he saw that they climbed through a soup of haze that hung everywhere over the landscape and which he had not seen before. They flew just at its upper edge, and beneath him the woods and towns and features seemed half dissolved in the dirty brownish smoke that looked as if even a hurricane might not be able to blow it away. The sight of it oppressed him. He felt a heaviness as if he were breathing it in the cabin.

Soon after, he boarded the larger plane for the long return, following the now bright sunlight across the continent, flying up among the chevrons of ice crystals glittering against a pale but intense blue. During those hours he ate, dozed, read, and watched. The haze thinned, and he could see the clear features of the remote earth. As they moved up the edge of the land, miles above it, he saw the anatomy of mountain ranges, bays, ice fields, and glaciers, one as large as a small state, laid out below as if a child's colored relief map had been fashioned for his inspection. He thought of the old explorers, feeling out the terrain mile by mile, sometimes almost foot by foot; their toil, their ardor, their wonder. They had to reconstruct what they found like the group of blind men in the tale, defining the fabulous elephant. Now there it was, handed to everyone on the airplane as most of them dozed or played cards or snacked, plugged into headphones. They could be strolling past the ports of some showy diorama at a regional fair; an entertainment. At last, in the bright, cool afternoon he landed, having crossed the entire continent to return still early in the long day. At this season the sun set later and later every evening, and night became a brief, chill twilight. He recalled how energizing it once was for him to wake early and find the morning sun as high and as blazing as it would be by midday in other regions; how mysterious and beautiful to bask, when the weather was fair, in hour after turning hour of light. At times it filled such days with a sense of eternity. Driving home up the hill, he saw a mist of tender green filling the branches of the delicate trees along the road, the dark firs scattered among them in somber accents. Turning into his drive he noticed a bank of alders, the small new leaves flashing in the sunlight, and he thought again of how thin it was, all of it; how only a few feet higher from where he stood, the rocks, the bones, showed through, as permanent and unconcerned with what lived and moved on it as anything he could think of. Beyond that was the blue air that showed nothing and was endless.

TWILIGHT OF THE GODS

• MATIAS VIEGENER •

IT IS A little known fact that Rock Hudson, Roy Cohn and Michel Foucault met and became acquainted in the waiting room of the American Hospital in Paris in 1984. Each of them knew he was dying, and it was a time for them to settle their scores with each other. They had to answer the Big Questions. Rock Hudson had loved Foucault for many years but he could never get close to him. Since the late fifties, Roy Cohn had chased Rock Hudson, but fruitlessly: Rock was more interested in intellectual men. In the twilight of their lives, Roy, Rock and Michel shared the same clinic and came to a profound understanding.

Roy was staying at the Hotel Georges V off the Champs-Elysées and Rock had an apartment that he bought early in the sixties in Saint Germain des Prés. No one knew where Foucault lived. While the two Americans drove up in limousines, no one could tell how Foucault came and went. The nurses said he arrived in a battered Renault and the doctors thought the drivers looked like American graduate students.

At their first meeting, Roy did not know who Foucault was. They were stretched out on leather chairs in the clinic.

"Who are you?" Roy said. "I've seen you before. I've seen your picture."

Foucault was a little dizzy. He had just received a strong antibiotic injection. "I?" he muttered. "I am the archaeology of knowledge."

"Hmpf. A philosopher. Do you know who I am? Do you?"

"Yes-s-s," Foucault said slowly.

"You do?"

"My American as-assistants told me."

"What did they say?" Roy said, shaking Foucault's arm to keep him from falling asleep. Roy Cohn was an impatient man. "Tell me what they said."

Foucault yawned. "You are power and I am knowledge," he said, shutting his eyes. He was completely bald. He wore an oversized leather jacket full of metal studs and his head kept rocking as though he were chewing on something. The napkin in his lap fell to the floor; Roy Cohn hesitated, he looked for a nurse, but then he picked it up and tucked it back into the lap of France's greatest living philosopher.

Foucault, Cohn and Hudson were all receiving extensive injections of HPA-23, a promising experimental treatment for AIDS, manufactured from Swiss mountain goats. Being that the injections were expensive and privately developed, the French were distrustful. They wanted everything paid in advance. It seems the hospital had been left too many unpaid bills by the last two years' worth of AIDS patients. Only Roy had trouble paying his bills—his money was locked in tight, labyrinthian trusts—and the French doctors paced the halls outside his room. Rock had a lot of money, but he worried about Foucault, who had holes in his shoes.

"How do you pay your bills?" Rock asked.

"I don't," said Foucault. "The University of California does. I've been under contract for years."

"They own you," Rock said. "Your intellect."

"No, my body! It's like MGM."

Rock shuddered. There was a rattle at the glass partition to the clinic, where several spectators gathered to look at them. Men and women, teenagers, even parents with children. They pressed their faces to the glass and watched Foucault and Rock Hudson, who turned away.

"Oh, Michel," Rock said. "Men have tried to own me for years. I understand."

"No, no. I *like* it. They take care of me. They buy me clothes. They buy me books, they get me dinner . . . I can devote my life to work."

Rock got very pensive. A ringlet of dark hair fell on his forehead. "I could take care of you," he said gently. "If only you would let me." Foucault said nothing. The noise of the crowd outside the partition was getting louder. A nurse came in and said, "Monsieur Foucault, it is you they want." Rock looked up. "We so rarely get to be alone," he said. Foucault sighed. He sat in his seat and the nurse looked impatiently at him. "Go to them," Rock said. "The people need you."

The biggest crowds at the American Hospital were always for Rock Hudson or Foucault. Sometimes they couldn't tell their fans apart. The people who lined up to see Foucault were all Americans. Rock Hudson always got the French, but what was difficult was that the French dressed like Americans, wearing sunglasses and bright shorts, while the Americans in dark jackets and black shoes all tried to look French. This caused no end of confusion. In fact, the French never knew who Foucault was, though they instantly recognized Rock Hudson. Many of them were convinced he was once the partner of Jerry Lewis, whom they considered the greatest genius of the century.

No one showed up to see Roy Cohn. A messenger came by to give him a notice of suspension from the New York State Bar. He received telegrams about the lawsuits his former clients were bringing against him and about the taxes the government wanted from him. Roy was a famous man. A Public Television camera crew arrived to interview him about the Rosenbergs and the McCarthy trials. "Leftists," the nurses whispered, "radicals!" The reporters heard Cohn was dying and they wanted the last story; there were things people wanted to know, information about McCarthy, Ronald Reagan, Dashiell Hammett. Seeing that Cohn couldn't run fast—his handy little legs weren't great when he was well—they cornered him in the halls with their cameras. But they didn't get a word of his on tape. Roy Cohn was used to dodging people. In America, New Yorkers often tried to spit on him from their fire escapes.

Despite all the bad news, Roy Cohn was tranquil. He gazed dotingly at Rock from his armchair. Both Roy and Foucault were shrinking. Roy, who never had good posture, began to slouch; he was so little that when he sat down his skinny legs didn't reach the floor. He gazed at Rock, who gazed at Foucault. Rock was the only one who kept his hair and did not shrink, a star to the end. Roy sat in his chair looking like the balding Picasso, or like Eisenhower, or W. C. Fields. All bald men look alike to their nurses. The staff knew exactly what was going on:

they saw Roy staring at Rock and Rock staring at Foucault, a triangle of famous men. It didn't take an advanced degree to see that they were at a stalemate. Someone needed to break the ice, otherwise they'd sit there like this until they died.

All of Roy's assets were frozen by the New York Supreme Court. When the French found out, they tried to lock him out of the clinic. He stood forlorn outside the glass doors, pressed in front of the people who came to watch that day. Roy mouthed "help me" through the glass. Rock looked at him. "Roy shouldn't wear those tank tops," he thought to himself.

"What's the commotion?" Foucault asked. He couldn't see too well because the injections that morning had been particularly strong and he accidentally wandered into a corridor of American students who flashed cameras in his face.

Roy was pressed to the glass by the crowd. There was a man beside him who seemed to be reading a newspaper, which was also pressed to the glass, near Roy's hip. Roy began to tilt. His feet left the floor and soon he was diagonal against the glass, splayed in his red tank top. His face was pushed up against the foggy glass, so even if he could have gotten something out, it wouldn't be clear. His lips looked like a pink rosebud. You could see him breathing; the foggy patch around his face began to grow, so even if he could mouth more of a message, no one could see it.

Rock tried to confer with Foucault, but the philosopher's perceptions were too muddled by the drugs. "I keep seeing flashbulbs," he said, "like asterisks. Everything you're saying is filled with asterisks."

". . . At a time like this," Rock said. "What do I do?"

The doctors passed by to make sure Roy was still locked out. The clinic had a little system by which it took two people pressing separate buzzers to allow patients or visitors through the glass portals. Sometimes it was enough if you held up a little orange card similar to the passes for the Paris Metro, but other times they had to confer and call a specialist before you got in. It was quite dirty outside. Rock noticed blue paper napkins on the floor and little balls of dust. Roy seemed to be sneezing.

Finally Rock called the doctors over and agreed to cover Roy's bills. It was against all his better judgment; he read about

how Roy would borrow money from clients and friends, even
though he had pots of it locked up in funny accounts. The
French were delighted, however. They brought the documents
to be signed, two or three of them, along with a fat Montblanc
pen, which Rock grasped with a flourish. It was like signing the
Declaration of Independence.

Roy came back inside, quivering with gratitude.

"Forget it," Rock said. "Just leave me alone, if you know
what I mean." He wanted to be alone with Foucault. Roy
acquiesced and moved to the sidelines. Foucault himself came
back to life. Through all of his encounters with Rock, he had
seen that it was tremendously difficult for Rock to reach a
decision—it was part of his intellectual nature. Since Rock had
actually made a decision, Foucault applauded him for it.

For many years, and after much searching, Rock had studied
Ikebana, Japanese flower arranging. He believed it was the
purest path to knowledge. Now he was not sure. There was
something in German philosophy that he just couldn't get out
of his mind: Rock remembered how Hegel said that all of
history was a grand progress, a kind of majestic parade that
united flesh and spirit in a glowing future. He found it deplorable in himself that he could not sustain his vision of this
two-lane parade.

"A parade?" Foucault said. "It's more like a carnival."

"You don't see it this way, do you?" Rock said. "The idea
that everything is connected doesn't wash with you."

"There is only Nietzsche," Foucault said.

"Of course, Nietzsche!" Rock said. "Tell me about Nietzsche."

Foucault began to talk. "Nietzsche taught us to question all
systems," he said, "and he demonstrated how, if we could
know anything, it had to be in parts. He made knowledge
fragmentary."

Roy listened from across the room but did not intrude. He
sat behind Foucault so Rock's gaze could overflow onto him.

"I think *The Will to Power* is seminal," Foucault said. "It is
there that you can find the fragment driven to its apotheosis . . ."
Foucault, always very precise with his English, stumbled over
this last word. His attention started to drift. "Tell me," he said
to Rock. "Were you at Elizabeth Taylor's party the night
Montgomery Clift had his accident?"

"I'm not sure," Rock mumbled.

"Not sure?"

"Those were terrible years. We all drank so much. I remember being in the car once when Monty crashed, but then he was a terrible driver. A real ditz. He had lots of accidents; most of them didn't get in the papers."

"Oh," Foucault said pensively.

"I know once I did pull him out of some wreck and his nose was bleeding, but he certainly didn't need plastic surgery that time. Anyway, back to Nietzsche. There were no cars when he was alive."

"No," said Foucault. "But if you had been in Montgomery's car for the big accident . . ."

"Do you think," Rock said, "that the fragment breaks into knowledge to remind us that we are only provisory? You know, man is only a bridge, not a goal."

"Hmm. It's true that Nietzsche says that man is a transition and a destruction," Foucault said. "You see it in so much of our lives. Think of James Dean. I've spent many years thinking about James Dean's accident and I've never really been satisfied with the findings."

"It was always hard . . . to get answers from Foucault," Rock said in his last journal. "Sometimes, when I can't sleep, I have imaginary conversations with him—my eloquence surprises both of us—and I see us spiraling higher and higher into the realm of truth. I want very much to tell him about my seminal essay refuting Schopenhauer. More than anything else, the fact of its being rejected by every serious journal in America pitched me into that ridiculous affair with Montgomery Clift. Oh, how Monty hated himself!"

It was hard to get Foucault's attention because there were American graduate students around every corner. They sat on the polished floor of the clinic and wrote down everything he said. Rock began to bribe the students to leave them alone. He gave them word processors. He offered them money to study at Irvine with Derrida. Several of them left, and the ones who stayed were all thinking about writing their Ph.D.s on Foucault. "The energy around Foucault," one of them said, "was enormous. He was a kind of Socrates of the Brave New World; he attracted every kind of fruitcake and zealot." Although Foucault claimed to be indifferent to all the attention, he began to notice the crowds dwindling. "Don't go back to those Structuralists," he cautioned the graduate students. "They'll tell you black is black and white is white. They'll fool you with bargains."

Roy watched these proceedings with some amusement. He liked the students; he remembered his own days at Columbia, where he had gone so as not to be drafted into the war. During those years, most young men were fighting fascism, so, like Foucault's young Americans, Roy got to sit in empty halls to hear men like Mark Van Doren and Lionel Trilling.

Roy was miserable that Rock wasn't interested in him. He had chased Rock since a party at Peggy Guggenheim's in 1959; everyone was there, Sartre, Ned Rorem, Jack Kerouac, even Lauren Bacall. Rock was chasing after the middle-aged Sartre, who was more interested in his Algerian houseboy. Close to the peak of his career, Rock wore a black turtleneck and kept saying "daddy-o" and "bad faith, man." Tab Hunter, who had just broken up with a promising young nuclear physicist, wanted Sartre too, but the Algerian houseboy's grip on his philosopher was unshakable.

At the clinic, Roy looked at himself in the mirror. He called the nurse, Marie-France. "I look like the aging Sartre," he said, "don't I?"

Marie-France had never heard of Sartre. "Yes," she said, "you look like him in all his late movies. Especially when you wear your top hat."

When Marie-France left the room, Roy took a hard look at himself. He had that funny scar along his nose that he got as a baby; his mother just couldn't leave it alone. A few facelifts hadn't hurt him—his skin was pulled tight around his bulldog jaw. What had changed most since he got sick was his eyes, which were a softer blue now, not as recriminatory as they once were. Roy Cohn realized he was going to die. Until now, he was the only one who had not come to terms with his mortality. He was the only one who still filed lawsuits, insulted nurses and drank cocktails. Now he saw that the students were glued to the glass window to watch them die. He saw the clerks writing up the bills, the garbage men striking outside, and the cleaning ladies sterilizing the floor.

Roy Cohn saw all these things—the litter, the dirty glass and the shiny floors—but he knew that on some fundamental level he had no idea what they *meant*, how these shimmering phenomena tied into the noumenal realms of being. Foucault and Rock were hunched over a notebook, talking quietly. It was late in the day and the light was amber, outlining the two of them like Madonna and child. Roy reminded himself that he was Jewish, and that he didn't usually have thoughts like that.

Recognizing that the power of knowledge was stronger than he was, Roy decided to join Rock at Foucault's feet. He pushed his armchair over to the other two. He was a small man and it took a long time. The other two eyed him suspiciously.

They had the answers, Roy told them. Rock Hudson and Foucault looked at each other. Roy stood next to his chair like a little soldier and bowed deeply from the waist.

"Okay," Rock said, "but no tank tops."

Our world will never know exactly what the three of them talked about. All the graduate students with their notebooks, their tape recorders and video cameras were banished from the room. This was very hard for Foucault; he knew the students would carry his name through the world, but he let them go. "One must learn to care for one's own name," he said. Foucault saw that he might have more in common with Rock and Roy than with all the graduate students, who, while not waiting for him to die, knew that they would become the authorities on Foucault after he was dead.

For many days, they hardly left the clinic. The nurses said their conversations centered on the meaning of love. It began by Roy's discussion of language, sex and truth in the 1950s, which turned into a love paean to Rock.

"Don't pull that," Rock said. "You treated me like meat. And you too," he said to Foucault, "act as though I'm insensate muscle tissue. Well I'm *not*. I have feelings, just like Roy. I get no respect. I want to be respected for my mind."

Marie-France came in with their tray of cherry-flavored protein shakes. She put them on the table and left courteously, without a word.

"What is respect?" Foucault said. "We speak of love without addressing our own constructions as subjects. Surely in this sense we are all ill, all of humanity, and all of knowledge is merely an expensive clinic."

Rock was speechless. He bent over to poke under his chair. He pulled out his journal. "All of knowledge is an expensive clinic," he wrote.

"Exactly so," Roy Cohn said. "But if we are the illness, what is the cure?"

Rock shuddered with embarrassment. "Roy," he said, "that was meant *figuratively*." He said each syllable slowly, distrusting Roy's vocabulary. "Michel was not making an equation between our being ill and the condition of the world. Were you?"

All of them were struck silent. There was nothing to say. "Who are we, what are we now and what have we been?" Rock asked in his journal. "Our construction as subjects . . . teeters daily on the balance of truth, power and language. Roy's gift is his recognition of the necessity of the 'thing-in-itself,' the language of the body, and of 'sexual' love. Michel? Ah, Michel ma belle . . . Soon I shall be able to call him *mon philosophe*."

They sipped their delicious cherry-flavored drinks. In just a few weeks, Marie-France had become an indispensable part of their lives, able to anticipate their least thoughts and most subdued wishes. How did she know to bring wild cherry and not banana or piña colada? Roy started to hum "Just One Kiss." There were some things that even Marie-France missed. In the corner someone had knocked over the oscillating fan. It was placed there because the air-conditioning was broken, and not it lay on the floor, still running and still oscillating. It heaved from side to side like an animal. Roy kept humming "Just One Kiss." Foucault watched him curiously, the fluorescent light shining off his bald head.

"Linda Evans," Foucault said to Rock, "is all right?"

"Yes, fine," said Rock.

"I was worried. All the newspapers . . ."

"I know," said Rock, "she's fine. I only kissed her once. Here, she sent me this copy of Rilke."

"*Oh*," Foucault said. "In German, too."

"I loved Rilke when I was young," Roy said.

"Me, too," Rock said. "He's so sensuous and intelligent. I wanted to sleep with him. Why have I *always* been attracted to poets and philosophers? I always hoped I'd meet Rilke at a party."

"He was dead before you were born," Foucault said.

Rock Hudson blushed and slowly sank down in his chair. Foucault put his hand on top of the actor's. "I did not mean to embarrass you," Foucault said softly. He began tracing his finger on the skin, connecting the purple dots on Rock's arm. Rock started to tremble. All of Foucault's hard features softened; he saw that he'd done the one thing he hated: using knowledge to manipulate. Rock Hudson's arm quivered.

"No one ever touches me anymore," Rock whispered. Michel traced a star on Rock's forearm. He placed his hand on Rock's hand. "I'm so scared," Rock said.

"Oh, Rock," Roy said. He put his hand on Foucault's, so there were three hands stacked together.

"I don't want to die," Rock said.

Their eyes met, focused, and left each other. There was no place to look. Foucault's gaze settled on the pores of Roy's nose. There were no pores on Rock's nose. There wasn't even any loose skin, the way there was a few years before. Rock's nose was still perfect.

"To want," said Foucault, "to be able to desire, presupposes a self who knows the limits of his own being."

"What?" Roy said. "What are you talking about?"

"I'm afraid to die too," Foucault said. "We all are."

"Our time is so short," Rock said.

"If it is," Roy said, "then why won't you SLEEP WITH ME?"

Rock's answer stuck in his throat. Foucault was of no help; once again he was thinking on an entirely different plane. Roy diddled with Rock's knuckles, still expecting some rational answer. The oscillating fan heaved in the corner. Roy looked up at Rock and then at Foucault; Rock Hudson's eyes darted to Roy's orange tank top, which encapsulated, in one garment, all that could and could not be said between these all-too-mortal men.

There was a rattle at the glass. It seemed that one of the spectators had overheard them; he nodded his head vigorously. From far away, a man moaned out loud. Another spectator had printed a sign that he was holding up to the glass. It said, "Michel, Is God Dead?" Foucault smiled and shook his head. As if on cue, another American put up his sign. It said, "What about the Shroud of Turin?"

That night, alone in bed, Rock couldn't sleep. He thought about Roy Cohn and the pathos in his voice. Rock wondered what Foucault would tell him to do. Roy did not inflame his desire. And yet, as Foucault said, we are now less controlled by repression than by stimulation. "Oh," Rock thought, "oh, oh, oh. I can't sleep. Is this what the French mean by a 'White Night'?"

The evening nurse came in to take Rock's temperature. He pretended to be asleep, and the nurse left quickly. "Yes," Rock thought. "Yes, I will. Yes. I can no longer say no. I will follow the master's words. Yes I will, yes, yes, yes." On the next day, he planned to agree (while throwing a "significant look" at Foucault), to sleep with Roy Cohn. A bedding that would rewrite history.

The last weeks of Roy, Rock and Michel were blissful. The three of them began to be inseparable. Foucault slept with Rock Hudson and Rock slept with Roy Cohn. Foucault and Roy Cohn felt no need to sleep with each other, but they became *special friends*. The nurses smiled when they saw them coming. People stopped flashing cameras in their faces. To the very end, they sat in adjoining leather armchairs, their faces radiant from the powerful goat injections streaming through their veins.

WILLIE

• MICHAEL LASSELL •

WILLIE WAS BLACK and sixteen, but he lied about his age. You
can't get laid when you're sixteen, or at least you couldn't back
in stinking 1970. Now it's all the kids do. Smoke dope. Get
laid. Things haven't changed. It's just the kids get younger,
more careful if they're smart, and they are smart. Willie was
sixteen, I was twenty-two, twenty-three, something like that.
And I was black and blue from falling downstairs the night
before at Partners, but underneath the bruises I was white.
More or less.

I'll tell you right now I talk too much and I need a lot of
attention. A shrink told me that. Sometimes I tell bad jokes. It
annoys people sometimes. Some people. I'm no saint at a
party—when I used to go to parties.

"Speaking with authority is no mean thing," I said when I
met him. First words out of my mouth when somebody finally
introduced us. I remember it like it was yesterday. Only it
wasn't yesterday. It was nearly twenty years ago. It was Berk
who introduced us, in a way. We'd been staring at each other
for an hour, Willie and me, so I finally walked over to where he
was standing with old Berkeley, and Berk said to Willie, "Talk
to Gar while I roll some joints," and off he walked without a
word to me, the rude prick. Willie said something I don't
remember—paid me some compliment, I think it was—and
out came: "Speaking with authority is no mean thing." I have
no idea what I meant by that, and it was a hell of a thing to lay
on a street kid for no reason at all. "No mean thing," I actually
said, "though it doesn't take any particular expertise." I used to
talk like that all the time, even though it makes me sick to think

about it, and it kind of nauseated me even then. I don't remember what he said next or what I said by way of reply. Sometimes when you're drunk, you don't remember everything that happens. Sometimes nothing. I remember plenty from those days, but not much good.

I remember at one point I said, "What's your name?" and he said, "Willie," and I said, "Like willy-nilly," and he said, "Oh, yeah." He didn't ask questions much, just kept answering mine, not giving away one piece of information that wasn't strictly required to be polite. And Willie was polite. He just wasn't a conversationalist, that's all. And when I run out of questions, I start talking about myself. Maybe it pisses some people off, but it's a defense, I guess. Anyway, that's what I did. Willie didn't interrupt and he seemed interested. Sexually, that is. More interested that I'd be, or than was necessary, which was his way of indicating that he was waiting for me to ask the Big Question, which he would then be happy to answer in the affirmative. "Besides," he said later, "what did I have to say? That I go to high school and had a great geometry lesson that day? I didn't know anything you'd care about." He was wrong. He could have said anything.

Even if I wasn't drawn to him like a magnet, which I was, even if I didn't have instant designs on his body, which I did, even if I wasn't more than slightly mellow, about which there was no question, I would still have been interested. That's the thing about people. They underestimate how much they have in common. They underestimate how fascinating someone else might find the smallest piece of information about them, particularly if the person in question is a sucker for eyes the size of plums. Suppose Willie *had* said, "I had a great geometry lesson." Suppose I said, "Tell me about it." Suppose he then said that he finally grasped the concept of—I don't know, what? —congruent angles, for example. Then I could drop back on my own experience with congruent angles, and then we'd have something in common. Geometry was a bitch. All those axioms and theorems. Thank God I had a good memory. I hated geometry, but I loved my teacher, until she went off and got married in the middle of the tenth grade. People were going off and leaving a lot in those days. There, you see? A whole world opens up the minute the slightest detail is revealed. I would have respected Willie if he had told me about congruent angles. And I would have felt an instant kinship with him as people that was more than just wanting to hold him in my arms. Because all he had to do was say "congruent angles" and he would have been part of my world. But people don't do that. They hide.

Anyway, Willie was big for his age. Too big for his own good, I used to tell him. He was big and black and had muscles from his neck to his calves, though most of his bulk was in the upper body from working out so hard on his chest, back, and arms with a set of weights he found that somebody was throwing out. His skin was dark. Not some medium brown color like most black people two or three hundred years out of Africa. Willie's skin was dark, dark black, the kind with blue and purple tones in it, not the reds and greens and yellows that go into brown. A person could spend a lifetime lost in the colors of black men's skins and never see them all. It was one of the first things I liked about him, that skin darker than anyone I had ever seen. It was smooth and warm over hard muscle and bone. Like a panther's skin. But that would come later.

Willie had big eyes and a broad nose, thick lips and a wide open smile (pretty much the opposite of me). But it was hard to look at him sometimes because of those shit teeth he had, all rotted away from too much macaroni and Coca-Cola instead of milk and meat. Like everybody else, he looked his best when he was smiling, except for those teeth, and he always held his lips tight when he felt a laugh coming on and then shoved a hand up in front of his face if he couldn't stifle it. Naturally, I couldn't resist trying to crack him up. It was fun, but it was sad, knowing how much pain there must have been in those teeth at his age and nobody around to do a damn thing for him. Willie liked white men and smart men, which was all right with me, because fairly white and reasonably quick on the uptake were about all I had to offer. Willie liked getting fucked too, a fact he slipped into the conversation about my army career in case I couldn't tell. And that was fine with me, because that is just my style of making myself known.

Berk, by the way, was this hippie friend who kept his long red hair perfume clean with handmade herbal shampoo he bought in a Greenwich Village health food store, to which he would go every now and again by a train they used to call the Pennsylvania Railroad. He was an assistant librarian at the college, so he wore thick, rimless glasses and had a scrawny little mustache. He was pretty dumb for a librarian, which you would have thought was pretty smart, but he was having these parties all the time so the local fags could meet each other. Berkeley, whose real name was Howard, was goofy-looking in what everybody said was an odd, kind of cute sort of way if you liked them like that. He had a huge cock that never really got hard, at least not in my experience. Anyway, that's how I met Willie.

Berk lived in a black neighborhood in those days. But that was nothing special, we all lived in one of the black neighborhoods, or else in scummy downtown. Who could afford to live anyplace else? The university was buying up all the good property for laboratories and dormitories for spoiled rich kids, and the Puerto Ricans were moving up from the harbor, where they had already displaced the Italians, who were making it big enough on the docks to finally move to the suburbs, taking all the good restaurants with them. Berk liked to be called Berkeley, but I called him Berk or Berkshire (after the mountains), and he used to come home from the library carrying a few hundred books, and there'd be this hefty black teenager cruising him all the time. So one day Berk just said, "I'm having a party tonight for some gay friends"—Berk felt that it was his political duty to use the word *gay* at least once in every sentence— "and you're welcome to join us." And the kid, who was Willie, said sure. Later, Berk told Bud that he thought he was going to get Willie in bed after the party, but Bud had the same idea for himself as soon as he saw the kid, because Bud was the most radical of all of us, by his own estimation, and Bud thought sleeping with a black teenager was politically avant-garde. Bud was an asshole. But Willie liked tall men and thin men and blond men with beards, so I lucked out. Bud had cut his off because beards were a sexist oppression of women. Gary said it was because Bud had crabs.

The others were surprised, too, that I put the make on Willie. I thought Chris Wood and Ira Rubin, who were into three-ways, were going to keel over, and Miguel was being a pain in the butt about it, but he was a pain in the butt about everything, particularly when he wasn't getting what he wanted, and he was most decidedly not getting me, at least not again. So everyone was being a dickhead. Didn't know I was into "dark meat," they said, didn't know I was a "dinge queen." Fucking assholes, all of them. No wonder there's racism all over this fucking country. Nothing pisses me off more than hearing members of one oppressed group ragging on people they feel superior to. What goddamn pointless no-dick nerve.

Anyway, the whole thing was a joke to me. I mean, I know it might sound weird to the goons in Mississippi underneath their white sheets—and I knew plenty of them in the army—but there's a lot of things about a lot of people, a lot of *groups* of people that I find more than a little objectionable, but skin color just isn't one of them. Maybe it was that book about George Washington Carver I read when I was eight years old, I don't know. Because there were zero black kids around where I grew up, or my old man would have moved, which was when it was polite to say "Negro" instead of "Colored," which is the word my old man always used when he wasn't saying "nigger."

So I met Willie at Berkeley the librarian's Halloween party and fell over an ugly rag rug Berk's sister made on a feminist commune in Vermont, because it takes a few good drinks to invite anybody home for the night, especially if the answer is likely to be yes, so I was showing off a little. After I came to, just slightly dazed from the bong on the head, Berk told everybody that his sister had to tell the other commune women that she was giving the rug to a woman or else they wouldn't let her use the loom or whatever it was. Bud thought that was right on, Gary thought it was sexist, and Chris Wood said he liked the colors. Anyway, we left, Willie and me, and everybody else was pissed off. About us or something else. I don't know.

Willie wasn't wearing a costume, thank God. In fact, nobody at this Halloween party was wearing a costume except the transvestites, but that wasn't because it was Halloween. But Willie wasn't wearing a coat either, just a turtleneck sweater. And it was cold. Real cold. The way it can be in New England when it takes a mind to it. I kept asking him if he was warm enough and should we walk faster, but he kept saying, "I'm fine," which I did not believe for a minute, because he looked like every inch of his skin must be covered with goose bumps. He kept pulling his head as far as it would go into the neck of his sweater.

"My grandmother used to live here," Willie said between his chattering brown teeth as we crossed the highway spur they stopped building right in the middle of this shit city. It was the first personal thing he ever said about himself. At least that I can remember.

"Where?" I said. "Here?"

"Yup," he said, "right here," but not like he was sad. Just cold.

What people told me was that it used to be a nice neighborhood before it got run down and became a black neighborhood and got run down some more. So they bulldozed it, except for the block where the old Jewish bakery was on Sunday mornings, and they started to build this highway that was going to bypass downtown. But they ran out of money, like they always do. So now they had this hundred burned-out acres of ruined city like Germany after World War II and a highway that came to a dead end with the medical school on the ghetto side of it and the telephone company on the university side. It was a mess.

I tried to get Willie to tell me some of this over again, just to hear him talk, but he was too cold.

"Was it a nice old house?" I asked him.

"No," he said. "Just a dump, like all the others."

We kept walking.

I lived in one room of an old house that looked like a dead Swiss chalet squeezed behind an old garage where they still took cars upstairs on a huge elevator. That was on one side. The back was all parking lots and the backs of dirty brick buildings, most of which were abandoned, but one of them had the Arthur Murray Dance Studio in it, so every Tuesday night or so you could see six or eight old people waltzing around and stepping out onto the fire escape for a smoke. A rabbi lived on the other side in an old town house that had cream-colored paint peeling off the red bricks underneath. He had the only decent patch of yard on the block.

Anyway, we got to my place and snuck past the old witch

who stood guard at the door, although nobody was asking her to, and managed to get safe inside the upper back room, which is where I lived, if you can call it that. I called it "hanging up my jeans." Willie didn't want to take his clothes off for a while. I thought he was being shy or something, and I knew he was jailbait no matter how old he said he was, but only if anyone cared about him enough to press charges, which obviously no one did, or they would have fixed his teeth. It was a real shame to be as beautiful a kid as Willie and not have anyone care if your teeth rotted out of your mouth. I mean, I hated my old man for a lot of things, but at least he kept me fed until I got out of high school. Willie lived with his mother, but he was on his own in all the ways that matter.

"You've done this before, haven't you?" I asked him. I am not interested in anyone's virginity.

"Hundreds of times," he said and took off his sweater like that proved it. If you ever want somebody out of their clothes, just accuse them of being a prude. It works every time.

I was right about his being cold. His skin was as cold as the bare wood floor under the sink. I stripped him down and ran my hands over him so there wouldn't be any mistake about what I had in mind, and he let me know that what I had in mind was fine with him. Then I made him get into bed, under all the covers I could find, including my coat. I turned the radiator up full, which sent loud knocking sounds through the old pipes. Then I stripped myself and climbed in with him.

I had to just hold him for about a half hour, he was so cold, just hold him and warm him up. Myself, I'm always warm, even though I tend to be skinny. I'm lucky about that. It's something I got from my mother, and it's something people like about me. Once somebody told me that people had healing in the warmth of their hands. I don't think I ever healed anybody of anything, but I've warmed up some hands and feet in my time, and before long Willie was warm and we were doing what came naturally. I could tell by the way I slipped into him without trouble that he'd done it before. More than once. Or else he was ready. Those sounds he was making into the one thin pillow were not pain sounds. And it was love in his eyes when he kissed me goodnight and said thanks. I was drunk, sure, but I remember thinking, "What kind of world is this when one roll in the hay with a stranger can inspire such gratitude? What kind of a situation do we have here when a kid with as much beauty as Willie had pouring out of him feels a need to thank people for just touching him?" I didn't know the answer, but I felt the same way. "Don't thank me," I told him, but not out loud, "I'm not worth it."

We fell asleep, but before I finally dozed off I could see stars through the branches of the tree in the rabbi's yard next door. The tree had an old truck tire on it that the rabbi's children swung on like a swing. The children all had names from the Old Testament, which I recognized from Sunday school, which my mother made me go to against my will. I remember thinking, "That's nice," when their mother called them inside for lunch one day. She sounded like a smart kid rattling off the answers to a Bible quiz. She was younger than her husband, who had a gray beard and worked, of course, for the university. Her hair was still dark under her pale cotton kerchiefs, and her hands always looked clean, cool, and pale when she was tending her garden, which was full of purple irises. Nothing but. Sometimes I'd watch her just sit and stare at them for hours. But it was cold now, and the irises were not in bloom.

I woke up a few hours later. It was already getting to be light in the gray kind of way it gets when there are too many clouds for a sunrise. Willie was curled up in my arms, his butt up against my crotch, and he was now warm enough that there was a layer of sweat between us. I had a hard-on, as usual, and I didn't have to shift myself around much to get back inside him. I just held myself there until we were breathing together, inhaling and exhaling, in and out, and he woke up and we fucked again before he even turned around.

Willie had the kind of eyes that said "I love you" even when what he was really saying was, "I gotta pee." So I let him use the sink, which I hated for anyone to do, but I didn't want him to have to walk down the hall to the head. It was too cold for a kid who had such a hard time getting warm.

I remember later when his skin got dry and chalky sometimes that it reminded me of the frost on the dark earth that first morning while I watched him piss in my sink. He was embarrassed, sure, and kept trying to hide that big thing of his from sight, but I just lay there smiling my face off and watching his chunky ass flex while he got the last drops of piss out and ran steaming water into the sink to kill the smell of it. That was our first morning. All Saints Day, it was, the morning after Halloween. We took a shower together down the hall while the old ladies banged on the door and I sucked Willie off. Then I lent him a jacket and took him out for a hot breakfast. I walked him to his school bus, but I didn't kiss him.

"Thanks," he said again, and I said, "I'll see you later," and I did.

Anyway, Berkeley, Bud, Chris, and Ira might have been surprised, and Miguel was still being a pain in the ass that I got to take Willie home and that I kept doing it all the time they were standing around waiting for me to get tired of the kid so they could have a shot. Only they didn't know everything. And one of the things they didn't know was how I felt about Willie and that Willie wasn't the first black man in my life. By 1970 I'd already balled every color of the rainbow—men and women—so the race thing was not the big issue they all thought it was. Miguel in particular was hard to figure, since he was always trying to get into my pants. I didn't get it, but why should I have told them everything? They didn't tell me everything I wanted to know, not even the things I asked them to tell me. For some reason, whenever I was around them, I felt like a kid begging for more food.

I don't know when our unconsciouses all got together and agreed that they were going to have authority over me, but they had it, or we all thought they did, which is pretty much the same thing. Anyway, they thought the way to keep an upper hand was not telling me things, which is exactly the same way I kept them from having more control than I wanted them to have. It's what they call a symbiosis in biology. And I learned about it in basic, not at some cocksucking Ivy League school.

Anyway, Willie was not the first.

The first black guy I'd ever known was named George. I'd seen others before, but I actually knew Georgie, at least to talk to. His father was a janitor out in the boonies, so he wound up going to our school. The first time I saw him was in the first week of junior high, at gym class. He had a locker down the row from me, and when he was peeling off his clothes I just kept wondering whether his color changed anywhere, or what. But when he stood there naked, he was the same color on the tip of his dick that he was on his nose, and that was a lesson to me. Georgie was dark, but not as dark as Willie. And he was small—small, smooth, and muscular, a gymnast, in fact, in the days when a black gymnast had about as good a shot as a black doctor on Park Avenue.

I used to watch Georgie on the high bar and on the rings and wonder what it was like to touch flesh like that, which seemed more real than my own. I had no definition in those days, and my ribs stuck out everywhere—like a broomstick with TB, my old man used to say. I'd watch Georgie sail around that gym horse switching hands, and watch Coach Hesse, his eyes twinkling with reflected fluorescent light as Georgie went through his turns, feet pointed, legs parallel, always perfect and always ready to improve, Hesse standing right under him during his dismount to make sure nothing ever happened to his prize pupil, Georgie just trusting the mean fuck like mad. And I'd watch them together and think, old Coach Hesse comes alive when Georgie's around. Old Coach Hesse thinks he's got some purpose in life when he lucks onto a kid like George. Old Coach Hesse acts more like Georgie's father than he does to his own fat kids, certainly more than my old man ever acted toward me. I don't ever remember seeing that kind of light in my old man's eyes, like he suddenly saw in me the reason to be alive he'd been waiting to see for years, like old Simeon and Anna in the temple who God said could live until they saw the Messiah. Maybe I was wrong to be looking for it. Maybe the only reason we're each alive is just to be alive. But I kept searching for some hint that my father saw in me his own immortality. I never saw it, never saw much from him but anger and boredom. But I saw it in Hesse's eyes with Georgie, and it was more than his usual horny leer when he was trying to get some tennis fruit to suck him off, which everybody knew was going on, so it probably wasn't.

I'd watch Georgie in the halls at school laughing with the other jocks and with his girlfriend, who was the only black cheerleader (her mother was a maid, the whole thing was completely degrading). And I'd watch him in class with his broad smile whether he knew the answers or not. And I'd watch him in that locker room and in that shower rubbing white foam all over that dark skin, getting his dick half hard soaping it, me getting half hard watching him until I had to turn away. And him always real intense on whatever he did, history or floor exercises, and always smiling in-between. And the only time I ever touched him was by accident, passing in and out of the shower. Our arms would glance off each other, and I'd say, "Sorry, George," and he'd smile wide off his face and say, "Hey, Gar, how're you doing?"

And that's as physical as we ever got, but I still think of Georgie as the first man I ever had sex with. Because after school when I'd be moping around the house being bored with nothing to do because I didn't feel like cooking dinner for the old man or whatever, I'd slip out of my clothes and pull my pud and think of licking the sweat off Georgie's chest and legs and of wrapping my mouth around that cute little wiener of his and of working my dick into his smooth, hard butt and kneading those cheeks with my hands. And I'd dream about me and Georgie and Coach Hesse and that smile and that twinkle in his eye.

After I got out of high school, my old man called me a fag one day for no particular reason, so I enlisted in the army to prove he was wrong. I knew all kinds of guys in the army, from all over the country, most of them poor and most of them young, like me. Most of them assholes, too.

There were these two particular black guys in basic in godforsaken Texas. Peckerman was from Indiana and must have been only part black because he had nearly blond hair and light skin with freckles, and eyes that shifted from gray to green, and how else would he get a name like Peckerman? —which is what everybody called him, Pecker-Man. He was a typist by trade, and he didn't care who knew what. He'd go walking down the barracks and some wise honky'd say, "There goes one nelly nigger," and then some black dude would say, "That ain't no nigger, that there's a faggot." And Pecker-Man would say, "You don't know shit from chocklit puddin' 'bout me till I got my dick up your ass, white bitch." Or sometimes "black cunt," whichever he thought was more appropriate.

Some guys thought he was just angling for a discharge, but nobody wanted to talk to Pecker-Man anyway, not blacks and not whites, at least until Leroy came along. Leroy was being a badass dude from D.C., and he had the cut scars to prove it. Leroy was black as the ace of spades and enlisted to beat some heavy felony rap. He'd already done grand larceny time and wanted no more part of prison. Everybody called him Big Leroy, and nobody crossed Big Leroy.

Anyway, everybody used to say that Leroy was putting it to Pecker-Man in a big way, like he got used to in jail, because they were always together, but I never saw them doing anything, and I was watching. "I fuck what I want to fuck," Big Leroy used to say to anybody who said anything to him about Pecker-Man, "and it's gonna be your mouth if I hear one more jiveass word out of it." But he told me one time that he hung around Peckerman because he couldn't stand everybody picking on the guy like he was some kind of disease. "Peckerman's a brother, man," he told me, "and I stick by my brothers till they do me wrong." I liked that "brother" stuff, you know? 'Cause there was nothing like that where I was coming from.

I don't remember much about what happened after that, except me and Leroy used to raise hell a lot, drinking our guts out whenever we got a chance to blow the camp, and one morning me and Leroy woke up in the barracks all beat up. It made us feel closer than we ever did before, but we didn't talk much after that, after we figured out neither of us remembered anything. We didn't want anybody to know we couldn't remember, and I'm not sure even we really wanted to know, either.

Then we were shipped out, even Pecker-Man. To Vietnam, of course. "Nam," the geeks back home always called it. I always called it Vietnam. We were there about a year and Peckerman and Leroy got sent out on patrol one time, which Peckerman wasn't even really trained for, but he was being punished by some chopper-jock Louie for something, and Big Leroy bought the VC ambush and went down. One guy who came back—there were only two, both of them brothers—said Pecker-Man screamed like a drunken mammy when he saw Big Leroy go down and ran into the jungle blasting his ammo away at rotten bamboo. They never found either of them, but guessed they were both dead when they found some VC kids playing with two human dicks, both of them black. They skewered the VC with their bayonets for Leroy and Peckerman. I got a lot to be sorry for. I never killed any kids, but I never stopped the others either, but that was when it was still cool to be stoned and what they called merciless. That was before. It wasn't until after that everybody got uptight about the dope and the whores and killing VC brats. As for me, I fucked any hole that stood still long enough to drop a load in it. I never expected to live long enough to get a disease. It was a bitch. Before and after.

After the war everybody was saying that I ought to be glad I was alive and I ought to do something with my life. Well, I was glad to be alive, more or less, but I figured I'd already done with my life what had to be done, what with having defended democracy on foreign soil, and I didn't have the slightest idea what the hell else I was supposed to do with it now. So I went to college courtesy of Uncle Sam, and met Willie in Collegetown, USA. Under ordinary circumstances I couldn't have gotten a job raking leaves at this place, but because this was like 1969 and I was a vet, and the vets were getting fucked over royally everywhere you looked, I couldn't get into the shit colleges I had the high school grades for, only the ones with terrific reputations, lots of money, and liberal enough politics to set up special programs for those of us who qualified as underprivileged. I didn't fit any of the major groups, but I slipped in because of my purple heart and my limp and because I told them my grandfather was full-blooded Cherokee.

So there I was at old Alma Mater, too old and too smashed up to play ball, which I never really liked anyway, learning how to talk about things I didn't understand in a way that was guaranteed to keep anybody else from understanding them, either. That's when I met Willie. Right after I dropped out. And I was just bumming around town, taking drugs and getting laid when I could, just like everybody else, in school or out. I even got it on with this Vassar dyke who was going to cure me of being a fairy for some reason, but then I got into acid, so she was the last.

I was so bored sometimes I couldn't even keep walking down the street. I'd just slow down to a halt and stand on the sidewalk until somebody or something made me move. I wasn't even going to go to Berk's fucking Halloween party, but I knew nobody would be at Partners until it was over. I'm glad I went, as it turned out.

So Willie moved in with me, and at least I had somebody to go home to and talk to and warm his feet.

I was walking down the street one night in a snowstorm, and I met this jerk Albert I knew. He was a psychiatrist at the university hospital, but he was a fruit, just like everybody else. I'd been with Willie about two months at the time. Albert was a nerdy kind of Brooklyn type, and we were chatting about this and that in the snow in front of the Mental Health Center. Albert'd been at some of Berk's parties, too. So we were talking, and one thing leads to another, and he says, "Tell me about this thing you have for black men." And I say, "I don't have 'a thing' for black men." And he says, "What about Willie?" And I say, "Willie is a person, not a thing."

So Albert lays out this theory that white guys who like black guys secretly hate themselves and so they choose sex objects as different from themselves as possible. And then he says that white guys who like fucking black guys—I don't know who was talking to him about Willie and me, but it could have been anybody—were as racist as the Ku Klux Klan, and were all into domination of oppressed people because they feel so oppressed themselves by their own self hatred. Well, I already knew what I thought about guys whose lovers looked just like them, and what I thought was that those people hated themselves so much the only "relationship" they could stand was essentially masturbatory because they couldn't begin to inflict themselves on anyone but a narcissistic surrogate, which was pretty twisted. And I told him so. Which probably pissed him off, since his own cretinous boyfriend, a notorious slut everybody's had at least twice, looked so much like him they had to sew name tags in their boxer shorts to tell themselves apart. Which I also told him.

Besides, I told him, warming up now in the cold, I had no *political* objections to being fucked myself, which he implied, I just didn't like the way it felt. And besides, I told him, it wasn't about *race*, which is something I would have thought a big deal psycho-whatever-he-was would know, but about class, which is something else I did not learn in hallowed halls of ivy but in the grunt corps, and which was one of the last things I ever said to my old man before he died (but not before he told me that VC weed turned me into a commie and that I was solely responsible for my mother's death, for which I would willingly have killed him if he wasn't doing so admirable a job himself). Sometimes I'm not sure what fight I'm fighting, which is why I seem to be fighting some things too hard, but I may also have told old Albert that I did not limit my fucking escapades to members of my own sex or to people whose skin colors differed from my own, and I probably wound up my little lecture by suggesting that it was probably a breach of professional ethics to drop two cents worth of free, unasked-for psychiatric evaluation in my lap unless he was going to offer the whole long-haul analysis on similar terms and that I could tell him more about self-hatred by reading any one of his own journals than he could tell about mine from some casual observations at a party or some third-hand cut-rate gossip. And then I told him his lover was shitty at sex and that if he had any self-esteem at all, he'd dump the twerp.

By this time my ears were nearly frozen off, since earmuffs are so goddamned dorky, and so we parted company that night on Park Street, which never did have a park on it to anyone's certain knowledge, and for once in my life I didn't feel like my brief college career was wasted, and I don't even think I wanted a drink.

I went home and asked Willie if he felt oppressed by my wanting to ball him, and he said no. And I asked him if he would feel better if he got to ball me occasionally or to have psychiatric counseling, and he said only if I wanted him to, and I told him that I was glad he was seventeen now because it made me feel like less of a child molester, and he said that if I wanted to feel like a child molester he would dress up in a diaper, as long as I didn't make him leave. Then I kissed him and helped him write a book report on *Ivanhoe*.

But times were shitty. And then they got worse.

Education was what we argued about mostly. Why it was all right for me to quit college but not for him to quit high school, and him with only one full year to go after next September.

"They just make fun of me," he'd say, "for being black and being gay and for being stupid and having shit teeth."

"So you stay in school until you're not stupid. And you get a decent job and fix your teeth, and then that's two less things to be made fun of. Then they can make fun of your skin color and the men you sleep with—and then we, we'll both know there's nothing you can do about that, so they're the assholes." I've never met anyone yet who didn't have at least one thing you could make fun of if you were the kind of asshole so low to the ground you couldn't shit unless it was on the head of somebody you brought down by kicking them in the nuts. "You're a gay black man, Willie-boy," I said, "and there's nothing to be ashamed of in that unless you choose to be. If God had wanted you white and straight, that's how you would have come down the chute."

There was a pause while he thought about it and decided if he was going to let me in or close me out.

"Calling a nigger 'boy' is politically incorrect," he said and started to grin, holding up his hand so I wouldn't have to look at his teeth. He smoked a joint and I wished I had enough money to fix his teeth. But my job running the garage elevator next door barely kept us dressed and fed. So I just kissed him, over and over again. It was all I knew how to do.

Willie stayed in school and with me in the leftover dive on High Street, which was actually the name of the street, if you can believe it. And once he told me his mother never even asked him why he wasn't staying home anymore, and that burst my bubble about how much better life would have been if my old man had died of cancer and my mother had hit the bottle from grief.

Willie had this cousin Tina, who was a drag queen, which is how everybody wound up finding out Willie was queer, because Tina had a mouth on her like a hand grenade, dangerous before it went off and ugly after. That was Tina. A cunt with a prick. I made a habit of never fucking with her, literally and otherwise. Tina used to hang around the White Castle downtown, smoking cigarettes and drinking coffee and trying to pick up the lowlife. She must have given a lot of blow jobs in her day, Miss Tina, just to pay the rent, because I can't imagine paying much for a skinny-ass transvestite hooker who didn't even shave before she went out for the night in a red wool dress she'd wash in the bathroom sink and dry in the oven. "You want a man, you don't want one in a dress," I said whenever I saw Tina coming down the street, swinging her hips from wall to curb. "You want a dress, get a real woman."

I hated Tina because she gave Willie such a hard time and was always hitting on him for the cash I'd given him for his lunch and such. I hated Tina, but I try not to be too hard on people just because I don't agree with them. My fellow students, as my teachers at the college used to call them, seemed to belong to a secret club that agreed on how to think about something, and everybody else was always wrong and took the heat for disagreeing. I always figure if I disagree with someone, I'm fifty percent responsible for the controversy even if I'm sure I'm right, which was less often than I let on to Willie at the time. He was too young to have to listen to me talking out loud about whether he was too young to be in a relationship with me and whether I was doing the right thing. He's too young to get too dependent on me, I used to think, because I'm too unreliable, but it's hard to train somebody to be independent of you when you love them, even if it *is* the right thing. At least for them.

Anyway, I saw parts of a lot of soldiers in the service who were so sure they were right they forgot there might be consequences to insisting. Just like a belligerent drunk. I should know. I'm nasty when I've been drinking. That's why I started smoking dope. "Stick to your principles," I say, "but if you get mowed down, be sure to remember you could have stepped aside." Weigh the cost. Decide and change your mind if you have to, but the VC heading south were just as right in their own minds as the U.S. infantry heading north. All that bloodshed was people being right in two different languages, drowning each other out because both sides were too fucking stupid to look in each other's eyes and figure out another way. So their side won. And we were still right, according to the daily news, and a lot of beautiful people got blown away in the process.

"Try to believe in a God who'd allow that," I'd say to Willie on those cold winter mornings when he said he wanted to go to church. Usually he just went to the bakery out in no man's land

and came back with rolls and pastries, and we'd sit and read the paper and rename the cat while we ate them, and the rabbi's children built a snowman in the yard you could tell was Jewish because they gave him a little beanie and a beard made out of the string mop.

It was on those Sunday mornings I'd be the most unsure about Willie, him just sitting there naked, not saying much, feeling more than he was letting on. I mean, a good father would encourage a kid to believe in something more than the stinking world. Not like my old man. "Life sucks, kid," he'd tell me, "and so do you." I know he was just bitter because of my mother dying and having a weird kid he didn't know what to do with. I knew it was all horseshit, but it still hurt like hell, you know? Inside? Before I got old and tough enough to turn it off.

But I wasn't Willie's father. I was his lover. But he was so young and needed to know so much that I kept thinking like a father. I wanted his teeth fixed and I wanted him to finish school and get a good job and be happy. I wanted to protect him from what was coming down and I wanted to teach him how to take care of himself for the times when I wasn't around. Sometimes on Sunday mornings I'd be hung over and full of remorse and feeling much older than I usually felt, which was older than I was, and I'd feel like I let him down. Then he'd take my throbbing head in his soft, sweet lap and massage my forehead and temples with his cool long fingers and sing along with the radio. I could feel his stomach going in and out when he breathed and hear the vibrations of his singing through his abdomen wall, and I wished that he could put into words how he was feeling and just vibrate them into my ear through his stomach like that and stop being afraid.

And that was when this Black Panther cousin of Willie's got arrested for murder and the city went berserk. The only evidence against the blood was the lunatic testimony of an old wino even Tina thought was too fucking crazy for trade. But the FBI and the CIA and the Secret Service and the National Guard and God knows who else were all over the place, and things were starting to stack up as white against black, same as everywhere else. And everybody was pissed off, and it was not a good time for a pair of black and white faggots to be walking down the street hand in hand. Whoever said Love Conquers All never had the shit kicked out of them by a dozen punks with baseball bats.

So I went to this party with Willie one night way over in the deep black part of town. Tina was there with a few of her Puerto Rican cohorts and their tattooed boyfriends. The Panthers weren't there because Huey Newton hadn't met Jean Genet yet and hadn't said it was cool for queers to be revolutionaries (you get what kind of times these were, right?). Anyway, none of the Panthers were hanging around with the pansies yet, the way they did later, because it was still uncool to be gay, much less black and gay, much less black and gay and married to a honky. So I was taking a lot of heat at this party, even though I'd known some of the people there for ages, and most of them knew Willie and me. Unfortunately, the day of this party the federal court had ruled to admit the lunatic's testimony and denied Willie's cousin bail. Now the suspect was Tina's baby brother, and she had her tits in a wringer and her ass way up on her back. And she was poking her poison tongue into the ear of this real pretty man named Randall J. Now, I had a hard-on for Randall J. for as long as I could remember, but he showed no signs of interest in me, which Miguel told me was because Randall was hip and didn't suck no white dick. It was a disappointment, sure, but one thing I learned was, there's no limit to prejudice. So when Randall J. walked into the kitchen where I was leaning against the fridge and said, "What the fuck you doin' here, no-dick white motherfucker?" I got mad. Okay, I admit I was three sheets to the wind, and so were some of the brothers who started taking up Randall J.'s persecution, and Willie was trying to keep them off me, but I was just so fucking angry that I started to cry.

It must have been the quality of the weed we'd been doing, but I just broke down altogether, which threw everybody for a loop. They had to sit me down on the bed on top of everybody's coats and just let me sob it out, which I did, harder than I cried even when my mother died and left me alone with my old man. Well, I felt like a fool blubbering on a pile of coats in a tiny bedroom off a smaller kitchen, even though some of my black friends told Randall J. off right to one of his faces, but I knew then and there that Willie and I were headed for a nosedive, because something inside me said, "Gar, you have let them see too much of the wrong thing at the wrong time," and when we got home Willie was pissed.

"Man, you can't never, you can't never cry," he steamed.

You'd have thought he had dog shit in his mouth the way he said it.

"You cry and they'll stomp all over your white ass."

Another five years of shoving down the hate and Willie'd understand that sometimes there's no controlling how anger comes spilling out. Could be murder. Could be suicide. You never knew.

"Men don't fucking cry," Willie was saying, slamming the closet door and opening it to slam it again. Which is just what my old man told me at my mother's funeral.

But I was wishing he could have cried, was wishing he could have cried green puke and barfed up every time somebody'd called him nigger or faggot or moron or shit-for-teeth and he couldn't do a thing about it. I knew he'd cry sooner or later if he lived long enough, but I knew that I scared him too bad by letting him look too deep inside too soon. And the chink I'd been making in his armor was now welded shut. And the sound of it was the sound of a cell door slamming. Him in. Me out. Sayonara. Good-bye.

So I blew it. Or life blew it. Whatever. Maybe I was wrong all the time to be with such a kid. I don't know. The older I get, the less I know.

Shortly after this party fiasco, some heavy Panther types told Tina to tell Willie to tell me to lay my dick off the brotherhood, and pretty soon after that Willie and me were a dead item. Willie'd never been in a war, but I had.

We blamed it on politics, on the Panthers, on the trial that was finally thrown out of court years later, and on the stinking shit times we were all living in. There wasn't any big scene. We just stopped being with each other all the time. Willie started staying overnight at Tina's house, and I started seeing Miguel, but he said I was fucking him so hard I must be thinking I was getting even with Randall J. So that didn't last too long either. Miguel's got a mouth that lands him in jail, and I was spending a lot of time holding my guts over a toilet bowl while Miguel screamed Spanish obscenities at the local constabulary.

The Panthers got Tina out of her dress for a while, and she was running around the streets in a safari jacket and aviator sunglasses with a .357 Magnum strapped to her bony ribs, and I knew *that* was lethal. I also knew that if the Panthers weren't letting Tina give head she'd never make it in the new order, and I wasn't surprised to hear she split for Philadelphia with a bike mechanic. Willie was carrying a gun, too, which I didn't like, but maybe he needed the protection. I saw him one day, which is how I found out about Tina, and he told me that the Panthers had talked him into quitting booze and drugs and he was studying the wisdom of Allah through the writings of Mohammed. I told him, "Good," because that's what he wanted to do. He was looking for something, and I wanted him to find it. So his escort Panther was giving him the nod to go and he said, "Well, I gotta go," and I said, "I hope you're happy," and he said, "Yeah, well." Then he threw his arms around me and hugged me (which is how I found out about the gun), and his eyes were flashing "I love you" all over the street, but his uptight soul brother was flashing a different message, so I let him drag Willie off to the revolution without so much as a good-bye kiss.

Some years later, sometime in the seventies, it must have been, after Canada anyway, I was living in a green stucco dive under the Hollywood Freeway when I med Andre, the next great love of my life. I used to go to this disco and watch the Mexican kids dance with their sisters and sometimes their sisters' husbands. This one night a pork-faced asshole who looked like he'd been drawn for a bad Saturday morning cartoon show was coming on to me, which was flattering in a way, except he was such a turd. He kept lisping and drooling through the braces on his teeth, and if I'd had more to drink I'd probably have set him back a few grand by ripping my knuckles apart on his face. But I just turned my face away and asked whoever it was standing there to dance. (I could still dance until about eleven if I didn't start drinking before nine.) Anyway, the guy turned out to be cute, cute and black, and he said sure. He turned out to be a terrific dancer, too, so we danced for two hours nonstop while the geek drooled at us from the losers' part of the stag line waiting for us to be done so he could ask me to dance, so I led Andre off the dance floor in the opposite direction.

"I live about half a block from here," Andre said, and I said, "I always wanted to visit that part of the world," and about twenty minutes later my dick was inching happily into his asshole.

In the morning I found out there were two things about Andre that surprised me: One, he had two children, two, he had never let another man fuck him before. "Why me?" I asked.

"I don't know," he said. "You just seemed right."

I liked Andre. For our second date I brought him a can of dark cherries in sweet syrup as a kind of joke present, 'cause I was his first, and he was my first virgin. He laughed right away and threw his arms around my neck, and twenty minutes later he had a dick up his ass for the second time.

I was falling in love. I could feel it. I liked him. I liked the kids. I thought, "Maybe there's hope after all." But I was wrong.

"Who's Willie?" he asked when I came to one morning.

"I don't know," I lied. "Why?"

"You kept talking about him in your sleep," he said, which I didn't think was odd, but I didn't tell him who Willie was. There'd be plenty of time for that later if everything worked out.

We used to take his kids around with us a lot. Ursula was seven and Brandon was five. We went to the zoo and Knott's Berry Farm. We went to the park and to the circus, where we sat so close to the action that the clowns handed each of them a balloon, Ursula on Andre's lap, Brandon on mine.

The thing was, their mother was white. A strung-out white junkie who just took off one day and left Andre with the kids, which was fine with him. And me, because when the four of us were together it was just like we were made for each other. He'd only gotten married to shut up his mother in the first place. After the wife split, Andre took his kids to live in Hawaii because his mother, an old Baptist battle-ax, told Andre that if she found out he was screwing men she'd go to the authorities and have the kids taken away. And she would have done it too, since he didn't have legal custody. You only had to look at the acid-green dress she wore to church to know she didn't know the meaning of the word *bluff*.

I used to love holding hands with Andre and the kids, all four of us, walking down the street. Of course it shocked hell out of people, but we didn't care. Most people need shocking, and we were a family in love. Except Andre, who wasn't in love with me. He was in love with the man who kicked them out of the house in Honolulu because the kids were getting on his nerves, and Andre was only back in L.A. to dispose of the kids in the most socially acceptable way, leaving them at his sister's place in the Simi Valley. I was a monkey wrench in this well-oiled, unspoken scheme of his, and so one fine day after I hadn't seen him for a while because that whole day we spent shopping for tropical fish drove me nuts, I knock on Andre's front door and his sister opens it.

"Hey, Gar," she says. "Uh, Andre's gone. Didn't he tell you?"

Well, no, he hadn't told me. And now he was already back in Honolulu with the German pilot who hated kids, so there wasn't much I could do about it.

"Andre doesn't like to get hit," the sister said, and I kind of remembered the last night I saw him, the night of the tropical fish.

The kids were in a bad mood that day and it was too hot and I was drinking beer to cool off. Then I yelled at Brandon when he pissed in his pants in the car, and Ursula started crying and never really stopped the whole day except to down her burger and fries, but then her paper crown broke and she started all over again. I went out by myself that night because Andre didn't want to leave the kids alone, or so he said. When I got back he was sitting there. I remember it clear as day. And I remember that something happened, and I said, "Well, what has that Nazi got that I don't have?" And I remember taking a swing at him, but I don't remember if I hit him or not. I remember he threw the can of dark cherries at me and that both kids woke up screaming. But I don't exactly remember what it was he was saying while he was throwing it.

It turned out to be the last time I saw Andre. About a year later he sent me school pictures of the two kids in Hawaiian shirts, but he didn't say where they were or what his plans were. He just thought I'd like to see the pictures. There was no return address, but the postmark looked like it said California. I headed East.

I fell in with a bunch of artists when I finally got to New York. Don't ask me how. We'd just pal around being friends and they'd be talking about this show and that show, and what gallery owner was the biggest pig, whatever. And when somebody got horny, we'd just get it on. Sometimes it would be one, sometimes another. Nobody was getting married. We were all drinking and smoking and fucking around, and they were doing paintings and sculptures and shit, and I was selling tokens in a subway booth in Queens and wondering what would be happening at the Factory later that night, as if I couldn't guess.

I was living in the Chelsea Hotel, where there was dog shit in the hall from some famous composer who'd gone off his nut after his boyfriend died, and I used to fuck this transvestite actress named Candy Darling now and again on the bathroom floor. I was living with a midget lesbian named Dora, dealing drugs a little, just to make up the rent most months. But I got busted and did some time Upstate. No big thing. No big maximum security scene. But I got fucked enough times by black men and white and brown and even one red man to shut anyone up about Willie. I never got to liking it, just putting up with it, like life. Unfortunately, I never really got back on my feet again after that and was sort of bumming around the Village trying to get by on spare change to augment my disability check thanks to some goon deciding I had chronic alcoholism as a result of Vietnam-era combat stress, which was a true hoot, but I cashed the checks just the same.

I didn't dare get caught around drugs or I'd wind up back in jail, or at least that's what the probation fruit told me at our first and only session. So I was hanging around Sheridan Square one time, trying to hit up the out-of-towners for the price of a bottle when they got off the subway, and I hear someone yell, "Gar!"

Well, I haven't used "Gar" since I left California, and I've had a few since. Lately it's been Marco for no reason I can remember except that whatever I was telling people my name was, "Marco" is what they were hearing. Anyway, I turn around and there's this real handsome black man standing there like a model out of *GQ* fucking magazine. The suit is five-hundred bucks, minimum. He's got a pocket hanky that matches his tie and another half-thou worth of attaché case and a bunch of flowers in the other. He's got on thin horn-rimmed glasses with tinted lenses and this huge smile under a broad nose. He's got the most beautiful teeth I've ever seen.

"Hey, man. It's me. Willie," he says. "Don't you remember?"

And my memory starts to chug and churn, and my head is shaking back and forth like no-no-no. Only something pleasant is rising on my spine, and I say, "Holy shit, Willie, what happened to your teeth?" And he puts down the briefcase and throws his arms around me, and he starts to cry and keeps crying and hugging and laughing until maybe I'm crying a little bit too.

"God, Willie, you look terrific," I say. "What're you doing with yourself?"

"I'm a dentist," Willie says, and I just about fall out.

"No shit," I say, like it's a question.

"No shit," Willie says. "I'm in private practice with an oral surgeon who's also gay. Our office is on Fifth Avenue, just north of Washington Square."

"You went to college," I say so proud I can hardly stand it.

"Had to," he says. "And dental school."

"You look fucking fabulous, Willie," I say, and he does. Fucking fabulous. Like an angel.

"And I owe it to you, Gar. For making me stay in school."

"Shit," I say. "You stayed because you wanted to stay if you stayed after I took off for parts unknown. You wanted an education. I knew that. You just weren't sure. I'm sorry I didn't stay in myself long enough to get a decent job."

"Things are pretty rough with you, aren't they, Gar?" I never could put one over on Willie.

"Well, I cannot tell a lie," I say, "as the namesake of Washington Square once said. Now the pigeons shit on his statue."

"I've got plenty of money, Gar, here—"

And then the little asshole goes for his wallet.

"What are you, crazy?" I say like the cabbies taught me. "I'm gonna take money from you?"

"I took money from you."

"You were just a kid."

"Well," he hesitates, now that I remind him about who is who, "how about a drink or dinner at least, just to catch up on old times?"

"Shit, Willie," I say, "I'm in a little bit of a hurry right this minute. I'll tell you what. You give me your card—you got a card, don't you? You got to have a card if you're a dentist—"

"I've got a card."

"Well," I continue, "I'll give you a call, and you can look at my teeth, or what's left of them. How's that?"

Willie grins just like old Georgie used to do in junior high, only now he doesn't put his hand in front of his face. Now he reaches into his pocket and pulls out his card, which has on it: WILMINGTON D. HAMMOND, DDS.

"I never knew it was Wilmington," I say, and he laughs. I never knew he needed glasses, either. "I'm proud of you, Willie," I manage to squeeze out. "I'm glad things worked out for you."

"Because of you. Because of everything you did," he says, just as polite as ever.

"Whatever," I say.

"You'll call me," he says. "You've got to promise, or I won't let you go."

"Don't worry, Willie," I say. "You were the best piece of ass I ever had, and I've had a few."

And he smiles again and hands me the flowers. "You take these," he says, just like he bought them for me. "You always liked them."

Purple irises, the whole bunch.

So he hugs me again and steps into the street, hailing a cab, which screeches to a halt on a dime.

"Call me," he shouts as he gets into the taxi.

"I will," I say. "Don't you worry."

Only I don't, of course. It's not good to call in situations like these. Besides, times change, and so do people. A bunch of white goons offed a black kid in Bensonhurst last week. There's been a lot of progress in a lot of years, but we're all still pigs in a jungle. "It's not race," I keep saying. "It's class." But people don't listen, not to me anyway. I'm just a madman ranting like a fool on the street and cradling myself to sleep with memories of shittier times than these, and of pretty Willie, sleeping in my arms on a cold and bitter Halloween.

I'm trying to stay off the booze for good now. Most of my friends are dead, or I've lost track of them. Some VA quack says my liver is shot and it's my only chance, which is probably bullshit scare tactics, but I got half a lung missing from the cigarettes, and they warned me about that too, so maybe they're right. It's hard to be dry and clean too, 'cause all these feelings and memories keep coming up and catching in my throat, like they'll choke me to death if I don't have a drink. Then somebody suggested that I might have a better chance if I sat down and thought about all this Willie stuff and cleared away the wreckage of my past, he called it.

What did I have to lose?

One thing's to be clear about, though. I never thought of Willie as wreckage. I wouldn't be surprised to be told that's what he thinks about me, which is why I never phoned him up, though he seemed really glad to see me. His life is fine without me, at least for now. I like to feel needed, you know?

But I felt happier than a pig in shit standing there in the dusk with two dozen hothouse irises in one hand and Willie's calling card in the other. And I stood there while the sun went down and knew that whatever anybody says about Willie, the two of us was never wrong. And I knew if anybody looked in my eye, they'd have seen what I saw when old Coach Hesse was watching Georgie on the high bar, that twinkle of something I never saw in my old man's eye, that one drop of salt water and pride in the corner of an eye that lets me know that God's in His heaven and all's right with the stinking world.

And who knows? My teeth really do need some attention. I always figured I'd be dead before they wore out. And maybe sometime I'll get myself together and give Willie a jingle, strictly for professional reasons, of course, and maybe we'll see what happens if I stay sober long enough.

I just wish thinking about all this stuff didn't make me so damn thirsty, which is another long story altogether.

MY FACE IN A MIRROR

• ALEX JEFFERS •

HE CAME OUT of the dressing room. The broad, padded shoulders of the blazer structured his torso, gave it some weight and solidity, began to resolve the contradiction of his growing four inches in as many months without gaining ten pounds. He'll be as big as his father. "You look sharp, Toby," I said, "a real clothes horse."

He fussed with the pleats of his trousers, curled his toes against the carpet. "I guess I need new shoes too," he mumbled, staring at his feet.

"Socks too, I think. And after that you can help me pick an outfit."

He grinned, and looked younger than the moment before, his own age again. "Okay." He has his father's eyes, the color of stainless steel, set at a tilt above cheeks still full and pale with youth. "Allen," he said with the same degree of gravity as when, the year before, he explained away his broken arm, "will you show me how to tie a tie?"

The tie Toby'd chosen to honor his father's first gallery show was light, handkerchief-weight silk, pale blue with alternating stripes of carmine and black. It hung around the collar of the navy blazer, as vivid as a victory flag on a coffin. I touched his shoulders, moved him to face the three-fold mirror. He was almost as tall as I. My hands spoke a phrase I couldn't read, reversed in the glass, as they turned up his shirt collar, positioned the tie. He smelled of new, expensive fabrics and his father's cologne, and the angles his chest forced on my elbows made me clumsy in lopping the silk through its half-Windsor.

He watched my hands and I watched his face as I tightened the slipknot around his throat.

After we had him all fitted out Toby decided he wanted to wear his new clothes to lunch. The salesclerk snipped off the tags and charged them to my account. "Thank you, Mr. Pasztory," she said while I signed the slip and she folded Toby's jeans and T-shirt into a bag. "Your son looks very distinguished in his new clothes."

"He's not my son," I said quickly, almost involuntarily. Then, remembering, I looked around. He was riffling through a carousel of ties, safe and sound.

Glancing up at me, she pulled off my copy of the sales slip and tore it nearly in two. "Oh." Her voice was small and she looked hurt, as though she'd offered candy to a child and been rebuffed. "I'm sorry."

"Thank you for your help." Taking the bag, I turned away, touched Toby on the neck, led him to the escalator. The hard leather soles of his new loafers clattered on marble.

I am weak, not in the physical sense, not often, not yet, but the smallest thing can throw me. In the men's department all the suits seemed to be black. The clerks were all young and very fine and abnormally solicitous. Toby rubbed up against me the way he does, touched my hand from time to time, took my measure with practiced, edgy eyes. At last, wool flannels and twills, serges and gabardines aside, he said, "This is dumb. You've got lots of suits, Allen. Dad doesn't want you to look like you just came from the office, not tonight." He held up a sharply tailored pinstripe collapsed around the wooden shoulders of its hanger, grunted, put it back. "Does he?" Toby needed a haircut; that would be our final mission, after lunch. His glasses were slipping down his nose. "Come on."

The twelve-year-old son of the man who has meant my sanity for most of the last seven years led me down aisles of fabric and shiny chrome, over travertine and industrial carpet, through zones of new age music and freakish new wave. I let him lead me, watched him move with the suppressed cunning of a soccer player, followed him wondering what he had in mind for me, for this stodgy, suit-wearing, fearful man he knew more thoroughly than he did his mother.

He led me to the shoe department, sat me down on a plush

banquette that exhaled under my weight. "Feet first," Toby said. His eyes were hard with a sort of urgent solicitude. Despite the eyes, Toby doesn't look like his father. I'd say he looks like me if there was any chance of it, but he resembles his mother. In the small-bonedness they share, the impervious pallor of their skins. The impression he gives of looking over his shoulder, a kind of skittishness that is, in his mother, profoundly disturbing but in Toby, solid as his father, reassuring: he's looking over his shoulder after me, watching to be sure I'm keeping up. He went along the display of shoes, cordovan, burgundy, tan, black, brown, and I stared at my hands. My hands knotted in my lap. I have never been big, never worn much flesh on my bones, but it seems to me, now, that my hands used to carry more weight. Large enough to play the piano, although I never have. There was no place for a piano in my parents' silent house. Toby's father gave me a ring, once, gold, a wedge of polished onyx bearing two interlaced initials in vermeil: *A & J*. If I could wear any ring I would wear that one, but it became quickly distracting, I couldn't think to speak, couldn't concentrate when I was talking to myself, became inarticulate in my native language. Jeremy understood, and he gave me a chain to hang the ring around my neck, wear the pledge against my heart—but my hand looks naked without it, and most of the time, these days, I don't care to see what my hands are saying. They are economical prophets, my hands, speaking in fingers-and-thumbs with a fine disdain for euphemism or false hope. It is only in my second language that I can lie.

"What do you think?" Toby had brought me a single tapered cowboy boot with dangerously pointed toe. It was black. I have never owned a pair of black shoes. I took it from Toby's hand. The leather of the shaft touched my hands, smooth and soft and traced with sprawls of stitching that felt, to my fingers, like scars. It had a certain undeniable weight. The vamp was black snakeskin; a tracery of silverplate ornamented the toe.

"I don't know, Toby."

"Try them on, at least."

"They're more comfortable than they look," the salesman said. He knelt before me, calm, professionally servile, took my foot between his thighs. Without asking if I knew my size (I did, I do), he removed the shoe, measured the foot, and stood again. "I'll be right back."

"Do you have another color?" I asked before he'd gone too far. He said he'd check.

"But black is just right," Toby said and took the boot back, examined it from the sole upward. An inverted circumflex, a haček, creased the skin between his heavy brows. "Black's just what I have in mind." He sat down beside me.

"Why?" I reached out for the boot, covered its toe with my hand, covered Toby's fingers. As he verges on adolescence a new kind of physicality shapes our closeness, there is a certain tension that we both, I think, acknowledge and appreciate and remain wary of. In any case we know each other's ways: we are affectionate together, this is yet a given. It was after several of his schoolmates witnessed the traditional family-hug among the three of us, Toby and me and his father, that Toby's arm was broken. "I've never worn black shoes," I said softly.

He pulled off his spectacles, balanced them by the bridge on the pad of one finger. It is a habitual gesture, one that I've come to expect his father to perform for all that Jeremy doesn't wear glasses. The haček was there again. "Time for a change." His hand turned over, under mine, the fingers slid between my fingers. "Time for a major change." He crooked his upper lip at me. The down above it might be beginning to darken.

I said, "I'll try them on."

The salesman brought back only one box. "Just black in your size, I'm afraid." He knelt down all in one long movement combining the sinuous and the brisk, opened the box at my feet. Nestled in white tissue paper, spoon-fashion like long-accustomed lovers, somehow the boots looked blacker, more black, elementally and essentially black. He handled them familiarly, as intimately as he grasped my foot and pressed the crimps out of my instep between his palms. "You have a very high arch," he said, slurring the *r*'s in an apparently calculated manner. A connoisseur of feet, he straightened out my toes, holding the fixed complicit smile of a man whose position excuses liberties, and eased my foot into the boot. It fit as snugly as a narrow glove. Simply, efficiently, he removed my other shoe, slid the second boot over my heel.

"How do they feel?" Toby asked before the salesman could.

"Fine."

"Can you stand?" asked the young man who still held my left foot in his lap, who looked up at me, engaged, amused, his head cocked nearly into his shoulder, an invitation, a sure dare.

I leaned forward. Even if I were well, even if I were single and didn't live fifty miles away across a state line. "We'll see," I said. It wasn't possible. The salesman nodded, sat back on his heels, stood up, moved out of my way. I set my feet flat on the carpet. They felt strange, encased so closely in this new skin and canted by the heels so that they splayed outward. When I stood, gingerly, it seemed that my hips swayed forward to accommodate a shift in my center of gravity and my shoulders slipped back and down a notch on the spine. I took one step forward. My ankle nearly buckled, but the second step was surer. In the boots I was as tall as the salesman, an extra three inches, it seemed, taller than Toby. Pacing around the carpeted shoe department I felt as though all my bones were realigning themselves, as if I had become a new kind of being, a skeletalized armor-plated machine. Ordinarily I walk with short, quick, straight strides that propel me on a steep trajectory; in the boots I ambled on cocked ankles and with long swinging steps, striking the heels against the floor with a jolt. I must have looked unsteady because Toby grasped my elbow. Neither his father nor Toby can speak to me in the language my parents taught me, but there are certain gestures that mean more for their very lack of articulation. "How're you doing?" Toby asked. Behind the glittering lenses of his spectacles his eyes seemed to quirk and wink.

"Fine," I said, trying to drawl. "Do I look like an old cowpoke?"

"You look like you'd be happier on a horse." His teeth glittered too. "Don't get them if you don't like them, Allen."

I walked away from him. "I didn't say I didn't like them." At the base of one of the display cases was a mirror angled to show how the new shoes looked afoot, from the front. The pointed toes of the boots turned up slightly to show the silver toe guard more clearly; the underside of the soles was still an unmarred pale grayish-tan. One trouser leg crumpled up above the scalloped cuff of the boot. I leaned down to work it over the shaft, and my face appeared in the glass at an unaccustomed angle, from an unexpected direction. I suppose my face is as familiar to me as his is to any man who shaves every day, but you expect to see it at a certain time and in a specific mirror, and if you have shaved routinely for some years the mirror serves only to clarify what hot water and shaving cream have already demonstrated and which the blade of your razor will prove: that you are alive, are there. I am as vain as the next man—which is to say I think I'm better-looking than many of the next men, but I don't check my appearance in every window I pass; I keep my hair short enough that once I've brushed it in the morning I needn't look at it again. If a lesion should develop on nose or cheek, no doubt I'll become as morbidly curious about it as I am about the four purple blots on my left ankle, but this hasn't happened yet, and the drawn gauntness, the pallid crêpeyness that surprised me may have been a reflection of the mirror's tilt and the obscure lighting.

Straightening up too fast, I overcompensated and nearly staggered. The jolt took me in knees and ankles. The back of my throat closed and tasted bile. I turned to the salesman and said I'd take the boots. After he'd removed them from my feet and replaced my old shoes, placed the boots tenderly in their box, rung them up, he gave them to me in a large paper bag and said, "You shouldn't wear them more than a couple of hours at a time for a few months, until you get used to them."

We were to meet Jeremy at one for lunch; it was just past eleven. I let Toby carry my bag as well as his. "Am I going to buy a black Stetson too?" I asked him.

Toby used his father's credit card to buy me a pair of pre-weathered black jeans, a dark blue flannel shirt, and a black suede bomber jacket. He preferred the slick leather one with coyote-fur lining, but I felt I should draw the line somewhere. Jeremy's income is less secure than mine.

"Were you taking notes when you were five?" I asked Jeremy's son. Only give me back my mustache and I could have been a refugee from 1980.

He shuffled his feet. "Is this how you dressed when I was five?" He moved his chin once, twice. "When you met Dad? I don't remember."

"If I could've afforded to. Everyone wanted to look like a Marlboro billboard back then."

He shook his head again. "I don't remember. I don't remember when I met you, Allen." His voice had a faintly edgy tone.

"I don't remember either. Didn't I watch you being born?"

Shifting his parcels to his left hand, Toby put his right arm around my hips. If I'd been wearing the boots I'm sure I would have staggered, have fallen.

BIG SKY

• NOEL RYAN •

I HAD A stare that could make you wild. I could stare the violence out of you, stare you into fists and your teeth closed tight and you would need to beat or kick at the staring.

In Montana, standing on the side of the mountain above our farm, you look far, far to the mountains on the other side of the valley, and then you see the river there, and you look down beyond where the river slinks out across a far, wider valley, and you follow that until you are utterly lost in all that space, those endless shadowy valleys and shaley-black mountains piled across mountains and sky and clouds. It was supposed to make you think of God and thrill and inspire you to religion. It did not thrill or inspire me. It frightened me, that hugeness, the long and the high and the upward and the ageless and the impossibility of breaking it into words or even thoughts.

I stared at people as if they, too, were those wordless valleys and soprano mountains I know here in Montana, as if they, too, were huge spaces with something ancient aching at them. I looked at them and between my eyes and theirs looking back or not, there was the unanswered, that immensity where words back up into themselves like a train or spiral out like hunting hawks until they are gone into the sky. People are immensities—like skies. I see it in the space between us, between our eyes and our words.

It got so that I couldn't hear words. When I was 16 or 17 is when it happened. It wasn't a physical thing, not as if the fluids in my eardrums dried up or the little hearing hairs inside died—it became so that I couldn't hear words, just the hail and thundercrack of sound, big storms of sound, downward sweeping torrents and cloudbursts of sound, noise, but sometimes unscrolling into a music. I would sit in the classroom and listen to the nuns up at the blackboard and their voices would come out like singing, but like opera singing, and I would sit and watch them with their pointers tapping a fraction or a Latin verb, but what I heard was the singing, like a Gregorian chant or the Indian praying you hear at night from the reservation. The meaning of words slipped off the edge of the sound, like spaghetti from a fork, and I would hear only the music, the sound, nothing that made a word or caused a feeling I recognized.

At first it was just in school, but soon enough after it moved all over my life. I had a job in a grocery store for a while and the old couple who owned it, friends of my mother, would give me all kinds of directions, but I couldn't make out what they were saying. Here a quack, there a quack, everywhere a quack quack. It got so they would explain one thing and I would do it and then another thing and I would do it. But you can't run a store that way so they let me go. They were the ones who told my mother that I had problems.

My mother especially I could not understand. But then she never gave me directions. She just yelled. She just called names. "You little . . ." and I would stare at her, and her words would fire into a hard brick, a weapon. Sometimes she would shake her voice over her head like a Zulu shakes his spear. My mother said she knew that look on my face, that defiance, and she would beat it out of me, that stare. She would show me. And the beating would happen.

I got good marks in school because our tests were based on what was in the books, not what the nuns said. But I had to be taken out of school anyway. And it was not because Joseph Greycloud kicked me in the head with his ice skate. It was because I talked to myself. I couldn't help it or stop it. But it wasn't for Joseph Greycloud kicking me with his ice skate. I wouldn't even notice I was yelling until the class stopped and everyone would be looking at me and I would be saying things out loud that teenage boys in Catholic schools weren't supposed to say, or even think. I shouted obscenities at the end. It was my sex hatching, I suppose. Something had to be done. The beatings didn't stop. My mom thought she could beat it all out of me because the nuns were afraid of me.

My brother Don had this friend, Eleanor, who went to Vassar. That was really something for Helena, a Helena girl at Vassar. She went off to Vassar with a load of responsibility. It was as if all of Helena were attending Vassar with her, that whatever she achieved was a collective achievement. Helena is like that. People think they have a say in your life.

Eleanor graduated from Vassar with honors. She was going on to the University of Virginia to law school. Her parents gave a big welcome-home party for her out at the golf course. They rented the clubhouse and hired caterers and strung Japanese lanterns out across the ninth fairway and along the stream and over the wooden bridge. They hired the Shenanigans, a country western band with Irish singers and a comedian. Don was Eleanor's date.

In the mail, hand-addressed, came my gold-embossed invitation, as formal as a wedding invitation. Inside the invitation was a smaller printed envelope and a card you filled out saying whether you would attend or not and how many guests would be in your party. You could bring anyone you liked. I brought my school friend Kent. I had this crush on him.

At the bottom of the invitation was printed this phrase— *"Répondez, S'il Vous Plait."* RSVP. I liked that phrase very much and I used it on everyone as if I could speak French. I had tried to teach myself the French language once. It was fun sometimes to be very haughty and say *"Noblesse Oblige."* I thought about writing a letter to my father and leaving it at the boardinghouse where he moved after he left us. In the letter I would tell him how I was doing in high school. I might send him my report card. Three A's! I would tell him I was getting so good at the piano that I could play Chopin waltzes (but not the polonaises) and some Bach. Imagine, Pop (I would write), you have a son who can play Bach on the piano! *Répondez, s'il vous plait!* Respond, if you please. The French aren't afraid to be what they are, say what they think, make demands. Respond, please. If you please.

One of the A's I got in seventh grade was in declamation class. We were to give a memorized reading from literature and tell something personal, an anecdote about ourselves. I memorized "Friends, Romans, Countrymen" from Shakespeare's *Julius Caesar*. For my personal story I told about the time my father took me up into the Continental Divide on the sheep hunt. I told about seeing the moose.

Loretta was in our declamation class. Her family came to Montana for a while and then moved on. They were poor and brown and came and went and no one really noticed them. Loretta was silent and didn't stay around long enough to have friends. In the declamation class, she stood up and recited *Old Ironsides* by Oliver Wendell Holmes. Then she told her anecdote about herself and her little sister. The family had moved to Montana from Louisiana, where Loretta's father had worked in the oil fields. But one day, in Louisiana, Loretta and her sister went out by a river to go swimming. Loretta's little sister jumped into the river first but the backwater was nested with water moccasins and they killed her. The classroom glittered with the pointed tails of serpents. Loretta told this story in a soft, two-note voice, as if she was saying something very polite to a grownup.

After that I used to stare at Loretta until she complained at me. I used to stare, wondering how a person could be normal when such terrible things had happened to them. I used to think terrible things made you tormented and theatrical, like Heathcliff or King Lear. There was nothing about Loretta to indicate she had known such horror. Sometimes I think once you know horror then that is all you are ever able to know. Nothing else is real enough.

My mother said it never happened about the window upstairs. Once she came to the mental hospital out at Warm Springs to visit me and started calling me names and I told her I didn't like her talking to me that way, that my doctor said I didn't have to let people talk to me that way. And then I said (Oh brother, had I been waiting for a long time to say it!), "and you had no right to push me out of that window that time. No right. You could have killed me!"

She went mad. Deadly. "No such thing ever happened!" she shouted. "You made that up. Some story to tell that doctor to make me look bad! Everything you say is made up! You're a filthy liar!"

She was wearing a silk bandanna and she untied it and ran it against her nose. "If you only knew what this was doing to me. I didn't drive over MacDonald Pass and then another 50 miles to sit here and be told I am a liar! You just shut up, *mister!*" I could see her throwing herself uptop her rage like a bronco-buster, a pony—she'd ride that rage until they both were still and bent and winded. "I hope you never live to know what misery you have caused me!" is what she shouted at me.

I told my mother very sarcastically that the rules of the hospital were that you couldn't shout or use bad language or get violent or they would put you into the locked ward, sometimes for a month.

No threat like that ever stopped my mother. "*I* am not a patient here!" We were sitting out at the picnic benches in the park. I saw a nurse on the porch look up, look over at us.

I stared at my mother. Her shouting silenced my mind, froze it up like gears in winter. She knew my look, but out here with the nurse watching she couldn't hit me. "You are just exactly like your father!"

The window happened. It happened. She was just too ashamed of what happened. What she did was push me out the window. When I was little. About six, I guess. It was during the time when my father still lived with us but would come home drunk all the time. He came home drunk the day she threw me out the window. I wonder where my three older brothers were that day? I wonder why I was home all alone with my mother the morning she threw me out the window?

We had no money. By the time I was 13, 14, my older brothers had found girls, married, and gone. They each moved out and went to college. My brothers studied in the sciences and each is, today, a kind of scientist—pharmaceuticals, bio-chemistry, metallurgy—working as a technician here in the Northwest.

I was alone at the farm with my mother and we had no money, just that empty farm, and when Snarge died my mother said "No more dogs. That's it." My mother worked as a secretary in a federal government office, Internal Revenue, or maybe it was the Federal Reserve. She was a GS4—a secretary. On Sundays I would ask her for 50 cents to go to a movie but she would say no, there was no money for movies when I couldn't get out and hold down my own job. I had been fired from the grocery store. There were no jobs for 13- and 14-year-olds in Helena at that time.

I would walk in town and go down by the train station to my father's boardinghouse. He was not often there but I always hoped and took the chance. I was afraid to call him up. He could say no over the phone but when I got him face to face he would give me something. He got jobs out of highway crews, so often he would be gone—off to places like Chinook or Havre or West Yellowstone. I would rap on the screen door of the boardinghouse and usually someone would be in the living room listening to the radio or playing cards. They would usually tell me that my father had gone off, but if he was there they would go upstairs and get him. He was never gruff with me. He would come out on the porch smelling like whiskey. I would ask him for 50 cents for the movies and he would give me a dollar. We never talked about anything. He didn't know who I was except that I was his youngest son. I gave him no excitement in that.

Movie musicals on Sunday afternoon. You wouldn't think something like that could mean so much to someone. In Montana movies weren't supposed to mean that much to a guy. I should have been out playing baseball, my mother said, but I couldn't do that. I went to the show like my mother went to Mass—for hope. Movies were like some future that lay ahead, a suggestion that there was more and at least something other to life. Give to airy nothing a local habitation and a name. That's Shakespeare. I knew I would rather die and go to MGM than to Jesus' heaven.

I know why she threw me out the window. I don't know why she pretended it didn't happen, but then she got hurt that day pretty bad herself. My father came home that morning drunk. He had been out all night and just ran out of places to go and be and was left with his home and his family. Home and family were hell for my father, just simply hell.

I knew he was violent when he was drunk but he never hurt

us kids, just her. "Get help!" she screamed. She had locked him out and he was at that moment downstairs breaking the kitchen door window and jiggling with the chain lock. "Go get someone!" She tried to push me out my bedroom window but I hung on. I was screaming—No! It was a long drop from that second-story window. There was nothing but a few bushes. "Get help!" She bent my fingers back from the windowsill and then hit me with her palm on my forehead and I just dropped. I landed in the bushes and rolled onto the lawn and then I took off howling down the road. There were some people, drifters who had rented a cabin down the lane from us. I ran into their cabin without knocking and the lady saw the blood on me from my nose and the man bolted toward our house and the woman kept me there with her, though I was crying and hysterical and my blood scared me. They put my mother into the hospital with a broken arm (my father had tackled her in the front yard) and my father in jail for a couple days to cool him off. My brothers and I stayed at home. My aunt Tess from Butte came and stayed with us, keeping a rifle propped near the kitchen door in case my father came back unexpectedly.

Eventually my father did move back home but he didn't stay long. There were more fights and finally he left. I was eight years old when he left for good. I think finally he gave up. I think he saw there was nothing at this place for him. Sell the junkers. Do whatever you like, he said. It was just after he left for good that my father came back out and took me on the sheep hunt and we saw the moose. I think he wanted to be friends but then he was almost 50 years older than me.

The farther into Montana you go, the farther you get from ideas. I first knew that when my father took me on the sheep hunt and we saw the moose.

In Helena, the capital of Montana, you get all the ideas up at the legislature and the church. From the mountainside near our farm you can see Helena built down there in a pocket of the mountain in what was a gold-mining gulch, Last Chance Gulch. I spent most of my time up on the mountainside the first summer I couldn't go into town. I couldn't because I did something dumb. I kissed my friend, ex-friend, Kent at Eleanor's party. There will never be an end to that. If there is an idea of me down there in Helena, well, that's where they got the idea.

You go back into the mountains and you get away from ideas. And you go up beyond that, into the actual wilderness where there aren't even any trails, just mountains and forests and the deer and bear, the moose and the mountain lion, there you find no ideas at all except those you brought with you. I can stand on the mountainside above our farm and say "I've changed." I can go down to Helena and stare at those people like I would stand in a cemetery and stare at the stone angels. Those people are their own tombs and they do not frighten me any longer. I got good help at the hospital and I see a therapist two times every week. I have to take lithium for stability, but I read and I go to school two nights a week up at the college. I am studying literature. I am changing. They are not, those people there in the town. The miracle that had happened to me is no less than if you found a way to make stones burn.

Eleanor's party took place out on the grand lawns of the golf course on an evening when hot moonlight pressed against you, a blue pressure with only one answer in it. Walking out in that night with my friend Kent was like crawling in pain across the bottom of a sea because I loved him.

We were too young to be given drinks by the white-coated bartenders. Older boys sneaked us a few. Kent and I were not at Eleanor's party to socialize. We were too young. We had conspired beforehand that we would get drunk. I saw my chance when all the guests, standing out there under a great canopy like a circus tent, turned toward Eleanor's father who was saying something proud. I stole a bottle of champagne from one of the washtubs behind the bar. Kent and I were off across the bridge and down the ninth fairway. We sat in the sand trap near the seventh green. There was that moonlight and me circling Kent like some doomed planet. We popped the bottle and drank it. We laughed, we were silly. And then we wrastled a bit and it was then I put my hand *there* and I kissed him, hard and serious. I thought that was what we both wanted. I thought that was the quotient of us—some kind of love. Kent pushed me off him and ran away. I think he ran all the way home from the golf course. I don't think he told his parents. I think for a while he didn't tell anyone.

I called him up next day but he wouldn't talk to me. I called a few more times and he would never come to the phone, always had his mother or father or sister lying for him.

Then I knew I had done something very wrong. I knew I had better stay away from town. Something in me turned dark. Sunday I would go in town to the movies. No one ever was around town on Sunday afternoon. Empty streets full of dust and beer smells. One Sunday I saw Kent at the movies with a group of boys. They didn't see me. I was sitting in the back on the side. I wanted to sit with him and his friends but the thing that had turned dark and hard inside me said no, said beware. I was 15 then.

They put my father in the Veterans' Hospital at Fort Harrison, a few miles outside of Helena. I couldn't go visit him. They had rules about children and I wasn't yet 18 and couldn't go on the wards. Who knows what you might see. My brothers went out and visited my father. They said he had had some kind of breakdown, a physical breakdown from work, a breakdown from exhaustion. I would always tell my brothers, "Say hello to Dad for me." And they would come back very depressed and evasive and I would ask if they said hello for me and they would say yes, they'd told him. That's all they would ever say. My mother walked around like some triumphant empress with her cruelty dragging at her face and contorting it. No one said anything about my father dying. His sickness didn't seem to have anything to do with dying. They were afraid to tell me he was crazy.

I like to ice-skate. I like Montana when winter comes. Winter occupies the mountains like a foreign army. You don't argue with it. It has its own rules. It has its own force.

I loved to ice-skate then. I used to skate alone. It was the only truly graceful physical thing I could do. The sailing in the wind, the white chill and the gray sky, your body feeling its joy in being a mortal thing, moving swiftly in the elements like only birds and fish can move.

The skating rink was actually a big, natural pond in the city park—and that was where Joseph Greycloud and his friends surrounded me. They caught me by the far fence and his friends stood around as if they didn't notice what was happening, shielding Joseph Greycloud. He sneered first at my girly way of skating, and then he said things like he had heard I was a queer and his friends all looked at me with dead eyes and with their jaws clamped. Joseph Greycloud did all the talking and I just stared at him. He couldn't get an answer out of me or a plea or fear. His fists closed. He knocked me flat. I had hoped at first it was just horsing around but then I was on my knees and I saw as I looked up from the ice, saw the pleasure and the vengeance in Joseph Greycloud's eyes, that this licking had been all planned out. Joseph Greycloud just said one word—"Queer!"—and shoved me back flat across the ice. Then he kicked me in the head with his ice skate. There was blood all over and they skated quickly away and left me there. I went to the warming house. One eye was closed already because the blood was filling it. Blood all over me. They took me to the hospital. I had eight stitches. I still have a slight scar, a white line. It healed very well. No one asked me what happened. At school the boys said sarcastically, "Fell down, uh? Fell down and hit your head, uh? Shouldn't be skating so fast." Everyone knew what happened. Everyone knew about Kent and me on the golf course. Everyone knew everything.

It was as if I was the only one in Helena, Montana, who knew what happened to me and there was no one on my side. I think my father would have been on my side, even if he knew the truth. But that winter he was out at the military hospital and I couldn't go see him.

No one mentioned the scar. Then or ever. Not even my brothers. It just wasn't there.

I couldn't go into the military hospital because I wasn't old enough. I went out there with my brothers and waited around in the garden while they were inside visiting. The hospital had a veranda going all the way around the second floor. The building was painted yellow, pale yellow, and the veranda had shutters like venetian blinds that hung down and opened sideways. I sat on a stone bench and my brothers wheeled my father out to the veranda. They were standing around him while he sat in his wheelchair in light-blue pajamas that looked as if they had a paisley design and a bathrobe, a white bathrobe, thick toweling it looked like. His white hair was slicked back. He had probably just been given his bath. He stretched his head and looked out and down at me, smiled and waved his hand. He turned his head and spoke with my brothers and they gathered around him and lifted him up out of the wheelchair and they opened one of the veranda blinds and held onto him and he stood there wobbly and leaning out and calling to me. How ya doin'? he called, and I told him I was doing just fine and asked him how he was doing. He said he was doing just great. And then we looked at each other smiling and waiting for one or the other to shout something. Are ya still practicin' the piano? he called and I said yes, I would play something for him when he got out. Good, Good, he said, smiling. He certainly had gotten old quickly. He seemed so fragile and trembling. We'll go see a picture show when I get back on my feet, he called, and then he let out a big, sad sigh. Okay? Sure, Dad. Okay. They settled him back down into his wheelchair and took him away from the window and the last I saw of him was his hand waving up over the window ledge. For me. Goodbye son.

I had been shouting too much. The staring had turned to shouting.

They got some of the older boys from the senior class to come to the classroom and they were real friendly to me. None of the older boys were friendly to any of us. There were three of them, plus Sister Mary Benedict. They all talked very politely to me, asking me how I was doing and had I seen this or that movie and whatnot, walking me out of the school and across the schoolgrounds and behind the church and then on to the rectory where Monsignor Wilkens had been called.

Bill, my oldest brother, got there and sat in the rectory with us. Bill drove me home to get my things. I asked if I could come live with him and his wife but he said I needed something more than that right now. He was very kind to me. My mother stayed in her room and wouldn't talk to me. She had a big argument with Bill. I heard her tell him I would do anything to cause trouble for her. I was just like my father. Late that evening Bill drove me across the mountains to the mental hospital at Warm Springs. I was there the first time for three years. I've been back twice, when things get strange on me. A few years went by and I spent six months there again and a year later about four and a half months. In between I've been able to get some schooling. The stays at Warm Springs get shorter because I'm getting better. I am changing. That is the key. Changing.

All the day of my father's funeral she was on the phone. I have never known anyone so indifferent to death as my mother. She kept calling people and asking them advice about wills and probates and community property and social security payments and military benefits. She had half the town pitying her and supplying her with information. She wanted to sell the farm right away and move to Phoenix with her sister. It wasn't until a week or so after the funeral that she found out my father had left his rights to the farm to us kids and not her. So we were co-owners and for the first time ever she got real nice to me, but I didn't then and I won't ever sell my interest in this farm. My brothers, they don't care. The property isn't worth a thing. Good for nothing, but it's part mine and she isn't going to use it to buy herself a red Impala so she can cruise around Arizona. She hates me now. Absolutely hates me. She went off to Phoenix when I had gone back into the hospital for the second time. She sent me a letter saying she wanted me to come live with her in Phoenix with my aunt. Fat chance!

I didn't sit in the first pew at my father's funeral because my brothers and their wives were there and two of them had babies so they needed the whole front row. My mother sat there centerstage looking as if she were weathering an ocean gale, her lips pulled into a tight little knot, screwed into place just like her hair. I was kneeling behind her all during the Mass. And at some moment or another she leaned her butt back on the pew and was looking for something in her purse (not a hankie, that's for sure, probably a Chiclet). She was fiddling there, turned half-around, looking deep into her purse, when I saw her whole face change. Her eyes, her mouth, changed completely. I saw the look there on her face, like someone pulled the plug down at the bottom of her heart. She got a smirk on her of the merciless, of triumph. It was the look Joseph Greycloud had on his face the day he kicked me with his ice skate. Now she could get away with anything.

I live alone here on the farm. I have cleaned the place up quite a bit. I sold Dad's junkers. They are gone and tall grass covers the field at the back of the house. My brothers have suggested that I rent a few rooms out to the college people. My brothers would like to see me prosper a bit. I will rent some rooms, I believe, though living here with strangers will be awkward at first, no less for them than for me. But then, I am also now a college person, two nights a week.

I spend time at school and I have a part-time job through the state rehab. I work at the historical library out at the state capitol. I shelve books four hours a day. I am learning to catalogue books, give them a number and a letter. I love looking through the new acquisitions, the stiff, clean volumes about western history. Frontier artists did not portray the violence. They painted the survival. I could spend a whole day just looking at the original paintings of Charlie Russell. What a sense of humor old Russell had!

I often walk the upper trails on the mountain. I am quite close to the town, yet, frequently, in the mornings and especially in the snow, I see footprints of deer, of bear, of smaller clawed creatures, the great regal stamp of the moose like something Henry the Eighth might use to seal a letter.

From the mountainside you can see far out into the valley and there, if you know where to look, you can see the cemetery. It is in a woods. There is a stone wall around it and an iron gate you pass through.

Now and then in winter I walk the five miles to the cemetery. I cannot have a driver's license because the medication I take puts me in danger of having a seizure behind the wheel. I do not go to the cemetery in summer since there are always families there laying flowers, or worse, funerals taking place. In the winter there is no risk of running into families, but I do call the funeral home and ask if there are any services that day and if there aren't then I am safe. I don't like people staring at me when I am at my father's grave.

My father had been dead for a couple of years before I went

out to visit the grave. That first visit was a bad day for me at the cemetery. I got there and walked to where I thought my father's grave was but I couldn't find his stone. I was among a thousand stones there, sticking up in the pine woods, covered with snow, and I had to walk on hundreds of graves and brush the stones off until I could read the names. Still, I couldn't find my father's grave. It was as if he was hiding from me.

After a good hour of stomping around in that snow in the graveyard and getting more and more angry and frustrated I heard my shouting. I usually heard it after it had been going on for a while. I looked around quickly but I was still the only one out there in the graveyard so no one heard me and no one would call the police. Nevertheless, I was in a rage and I sat down on the steps of one of those mausoleums and started to cry and then the whole, stone-filled load seemed to need crying for. I couldn't find my father's grave. Oh, I simply howled.

But my doctors had told me some practical things to do. *Think it through*, they said, *just get yourself quiet and think it through.* And so I just sat there and had some coffee and smoked a cigarette and calmed myself down and tried to remember my father's funeral, coming out here behind the hearse and just being there again, living through it. Not the sorrow, just the scenery. And then I knew where he was buried. I was way off. I remembered where I was standing and what I was looking at as they lowered the casket.

It only took me 10 minutes to find it. So it worked. Proof that I am changing, that I can control my life, one moment at a time, if I must. One day it will be natural to me. One day it will no longer be fear. I stood by my father's grave and talked to him about that. I don't know if he was anywhere listening. But it was a good moment there, thinking that I was talking to him, and telling him what was going on with me and that I had found him and he could be proud of me.

I would like to write a book about my father. I would have to make most of it up because I never have known much about him. I would like to write about the sheep hunt and the moose.

It was a morning, no, it was still night, 4 A.M., but even in the night in Montana at wintertime the snow glows as if some kind of supernatural light were shining there beneath it. He woke me when the sky was clear, clear and still and moonless, the stars frozen in multitude. We drove up onto the MacDonald Pass and then followed a somewhat cleared trail off and farther up into plateaus of snow. We came to the sheep ranch and there were many hunters but I was the only child. A bottle of whiskey was passed around and the men poured themselves some in their coffee cups as we stood out near the sheepfolds awaiting instructions from the sheep rancher. No one questioned my being there. My father just told me to stay close and if I got tired to follow our tracks back to the ranch. He must have trusted me a lot to say that.

It was time to round up the sheep from the surrounding mountains. What we had to do was go in a great circle, up canyons and across ridges, and bring the scattered flocks down to the ranch so they wouldn't starve and freeze. Already some had been found stranded and dead. Frozen. So we set off, my father and four or five others in our group, heading out into the mountains and ringing those copper bells and shouting. There were clumps of sheep around trees and they turned their woolen foreheads and snouts and weak black eyes at us and we sent them down the mountain and went on upwards. The wind was stiff and grainy with snow. On the higher fields we found many sheep, shooed them together and got them moving down. The trees thinned higher up; we could see a hundred miles across the landscape in every direction, the snow-covered mountains and the lonely, frozen valleys and the timber there, the white and coal-blue of the world, the heavy silver sky, seamless with the day pushing down behind it. From those deep, lonely valleys we could hear the *baaa* and the clonk of the sheep bells as the animals heard us coming. The men went into the woods. I could hear their old dented copper bells and their shouting and whistling to one another, so it wasn't likely I would get lost. I know now my father was keeping an eye out for me. We went into the woods again. And on the slopes and in the darkness of the forest, I could hear the men and the sheep moving across the snow.

My father was leading up a ridge where the trees were thick. He went around one side of some trees and I went around the other. Then I was standing against a pine tree—under its lowest branches where the brown pine needles formed a cleared, damp circle and the earth was black—and out there in a clearing was a moose. I could have touched him, this large, muscley, thick brown-coated moose standing still and listening to the movement around him. He lifted his long potato-shaped head back a little and those immense antlers reached up like ocean waves, so bony and gray and ridged, touched the tree limbs 10 feet up. The moose lowed like a cow but with a high, frightened, warning pitch to its voice. Its mate was probably nearby hidden in the trees. I crept back behind the tree but stopped because my father was standing right behind me and he put his hands very gently on my shoulders as if pressing me to stop, pressing me until I stood still in the snow, and he pulled me back against him and we stood there and respected the moose. We kept our distance and stayed silent as snow while the moose turned and passed before us and onto one of its trails, knowing we were there yet knowing we were unarmed, not hunters.

I could smell cigarettes and whiskey on my father and the close, snowmelt heat of his wool coat. I could feel the strength in his arms as he held me pressed to him and he crossed his gloved hands down across my chest and kept me safe. I laid my head back against his big winter coat and we stood in absolute silence, as if struck there in marble, watching and so close to something very rare and my father was, I suspect, as wonderstruck as me, and the moose moved through the snow and into the shadows to gather his love to himself and then lead on into the mountain fastnesses and farther up, into its safety and into its life.

THE RIDE HOME

• PETER CASHORALI •

"*OLOKUM ES EL gobernante del agua profunda,*" Pedro says. "*El hermafrodita; el que esta amarrado al fonde del mar con una cadena dorada para que el mundo arriba se mantenga estable.*" His voice is like a doll's, high and nasal, and because he takes his time with each syllable, he could almost be pouting. Mark can't understand a word he says. "*Cuando el vida esta alborotado, cuando las cosas estan revolcadas, suplicate a Olokum; cuando los eventos de tu vida te oprimen, pidele a Olokum.*" He sounds like Truman Capote, but Jorge and Ricardo, dark hair beginning to escape from Ricardo's ponytail, are both looking down at the table and frowning as they listen to him. Ricardo's smoking, and taps ashes into the remains of his dinner. "*Pero siempre acuerdate que a Olokum le gusta mucha privacida,*" Pedro admonishes, making an important point.

Frank leans across the table to Mark and says, "Would you like to go into the living room? This is going to take a while."

"Sure," Mark says, putting his napkin beside his plate and standing up. "Great meal." Jorge looks over and nods graciously, closing his eyes, though Frank did the cooking.

Frank says, "I'm glad you liked it. Your husband's been telling us what a fussy eater you are." They step down into the living room. The floor has been stripped and re-stained recently; it's very light and has the effect of making the mosaic of cracks in the walls look intentional. A pair of white pillow-couches face each other across a glass coffee table and Frank lowers himself into the nearer of the two. It puts his back to the dining room. He picks up a black stone box from the table and opens it, holds it out to Mark. "Marlboro?"

"Mm, thank you, no," Mark says, seating himself at the end of the couch. He straightens his glasses and runs a hand through his overgrown crew cut, not unhappy with the gray that's begun spreading like a change in climate. "I'm quitting. For the third time." He watches Frank set a cigarette in his mouth, thumb a Bic lighter and grimace as he brings the tiny flame to the tip of the cigarette. Mark says, "You don't speak any Spanish, either?"

"Well," Frank says, considering, "a little." He puts the Bic on the table and leans back into the white couch, blowing a mass of blue smoke up to the ceiling.

"Well, I speak a little myself. 'The pencil sharpener is in the back of the room.' I mean, do you understand it? You know, conversations?"

"Oh, I always know what Jorge is saying," Frank says, craning his head over his shoulder to glance at his lover. During dinner, Mark noticed Frank staring at Jorge; he looked like a weasel watching a chicken too powerful to bring down: predatory, hopeless, bitter and tender. When Frank turns back, he catches Mark watching him. Mark tries to cover himself with a smile. Frank returns the smile and says, "He's having a 'religious' difficulty that Pedro has to help him with. Pedro's a *santero*. But you've already met him, haven't you?"

"Yes, he read the shells for me once. He seems all right. Not, you know, inspiring, but not a fake."

"Oh, he's genuine, all right. There's no question about that."

"You're just not drawn to *Santeria?*"

"Please." Frank rolls his eyes up to the bloody whites and waves the suggestion away. Mark can see one of Jorge's religious statues over his shoulder, a Virgin holding Baby Jesus up to her cheek. They look like they're smirking at him and Frank.

Mark says, "So what's the story with Jorge? Ricardo won't tell me a thing."

"Jorge wants to be a *santero*, like Pedro. So he has to be sponsored by one of the spooks. The *orishas*," he says, tasting the word as though it's a dirty penny. "So, first one claimed him, and then this other one who's always really jealous claimed him, too. Well, he can't just say, 'No, thanks,' to the second one"—he lowers his voice—"because she's a real bitch. So, there has to be this long complicated rigamarole, where he offers himself to this *third* one, who's too big or important or something to take him up on his offer. But the third one is connected to the second one, somehow, so she gets satisfied, and then he's free to go with the first one. Oh, it's very complicated," he says, his voice a mix of spite and satisfaction.

"Jesus, you sure have it all down."

"Well, I live with it all around me," Frank says, opening his hand like a fan to indicate the statues of the Virgin Mary and saints that inhabit most of the shelf space in the living room. "It's not like I have to pay much attention to it."

"Well, yes," Mark says, wanting to show off what he knows. "I pick up weird fragments myself. That third *orisha* is called Olokum, Ruler of the Watery Abyss. She's meant to be the unconscious. Perfect, huh?"

"What is?" Frank asks, taking a wrinkled handkerchief out of his back pocket.

"That Jorge is going to resolve this unresolvable difficulty by offering himself to the Watery Abyss. You know: I throw myself on the mercy of the court?"

Frank smiles tolerantly and then gives a long ripping cough. He clears his throat into the handkerchief, wads it up and stuffs it back into his pocket. Mark shudders. Frank says, "What I don't understand is why Pedro's over here every night. I mean, everyone seems like they already know what to do."

"Well. Because they like handling the material."

"Oh, I suppose," Frank says, not interested. He takes the last deep drag on his Marlboro, holding it down, then lets it dribble slowly out of his mouth. He runs out of breath and blows the last bit out. "He thinks he's cured himself."

"Excuse me?"

"Jorge. Right after we met, he went into the hospital. Spinal meningitis. It was killing him." Mark isn't sure how to respond. Ricardo already told him that both Frank and Jorge have AIDS, that they're both stable at the moment, but neither of them has mentioned anything to him. Ricardo said he hadn't told them that Mark has been exposed, though Mark suspects he may have confided in Jorge during one of their late-night phone calls. Frank says, "So when he was in the hospital, someone introduced him to *Santeria*. And he started praying—not *praying*," he corrects himself, rolling his eyes with annoyance. "Whatever it is they do. I'm still not sure. And eleven days later, they let him out of the hospital. That was a year ago, and he hasn't been back since." His voice is flat as a tour guide's.

"Wait a minute," Mark says, incredulous but leaping for the miracle. "You're saying he cured himself of meningitis with *Santeria?*"

"Yes," Frank says, looking at him.

Mark frowns, trying to take it in. "No. I don't understand. How did he cure himself?"

"How do those people get cured on those born-again television shows?"

"Well. Faith . . . Those are faith healings. Well, no, wait, those are faith healings like wrestling programs are sporting events." Frank's lack of response to what he's saying is what's giving Mark so much trouble. He shakes his head. "No, I'm still not getting it. If Jorge cured himself with *Santeria*, why aren't you in there with them right now?"

"Because it's horseshit," Frank snarls, picking a white thread off his blue overshirt and rolling it into a ball. He drops it into the ashtray.

"You don't believe he's really cured himself," Mark ventures.

But Frank says, "Horseshit," in a lower voice, just a grumble, and Mark lets the matter drop, sure that Jorge's cure is wishful thinking.

He listens to the conversation in the next room, wishing they were speaking English. He has a few phrases of Spanish himself, but the way a parrot might have them, and even simple dialogue is beyond him. It occurs to him, as it often does, that secret spiritual knowledge could in fact be passing back and forth in the voices he's listening to, even Ricardo's. It seems likely that it would be something he'd hear plainly and not understand. He frowns and crosses his legs, shaking his foot, and tries to catch what they're talking about. Probably recipes: what to do and say and mix together and burn. He says, "Well," and puts his hands on his knees, pushes himself up briskly. "I think I'll try to join the seminar."

"Going to break through the language barrier?" Frank asks, lifting the lid off the cigarette box.

"Well, I'm going to try. I'll let you know if I find out anything interesting." He walks back to the dining room.

Jorge has his chair turned sideways to the table so he can tip it back against the wall. His head has been shaved for *Santeria*, and he caresses it as he listens to Pedro explain something to him and Ricardo. Ricardo has his elbows on the table, and his hair, straight and coarse as a horse's tail, veils his face. As Mark approaches, Ricardo straightens up and sweeps his hair back impatiently with both hands, re-securing it at the nape of his neck. It begins escaping again as soon as he takes his hands away, but for a moment, pulled back tight, it draws out the broad cheekbones that Ricardo hates and the long almond eyes and perfect eyebrows that he loves. He's frowning as he listens to Pedro, and the corners of his mouth are tucked back, which means he's dying to state his own opinion. As Mark approaches, Pedro stops talking and looks up at him blankly; Mark flashes his simpleton's smile—lips stretched back but kept closed, chin drawn down a little—to show he doesn't understand a word. Pedro narrows his eyes and goes on with his dissertation. Mark slips into the chair beside Ricardo and listens to their voices.

Pedro could be passing on the secret history of the universe, but he could just as easily be giving a recipe for flan, or the plot summary to a soap opera. What Mark finds so odd about Pedro is how little authority seems to attach itself to him. He's no one Mark would notice at the supermarket, just a small-boned Cuban who looks a little like a malnourished Boris Karloff. He doesn't even dress the part of *santero:* The jacket over the back of his chair is just denim, so old it looks like yellow-gray velvet. Not that Mark wants to see skull jewelry or owl feathers on him, but he thinks that if Pedro knows anything, it should leave its mark somehow. But the only thing that shows when Mark looks at him is that he doesn't question the importance of what he's saying.

"Olokum saca lo que esta escondido en el fondo del corazon," he says to Ricardo, and Ricardo looks down into his plate. Two butts have smoldered out at the plate's rim, and he seems to be staring at a clock face. *"Los que estan bajo sentencia de muerte o los que quieren intervenir de parte de ellos deben de suplicar a Olokum,"* Pedro says, tapping the tip of his finger on the table to drive in the following point: *"Pero siempre con mucho cuidado."*

Por que saca ella lo que esta escondido, Don Pedro?" Jorge asks, trying to score points.

"*Porque ella significa firmeza,*" Pedro says to him, then turns back to Ricardo. "*Y la firmeza no se pude sostener sobre los secretos.*" He lifts his eyebrows expectantly at Ricardo.

Ricardo doesn't meet his eye, just says, "*Si, Don Pedro,*" and Pedro's eyebrows lower.

Jorge brings his chair down with a clump and smiles at Mark, says, "So you've decided to join us."

His voice is like a drink of eggnog and Mark finds him ravishing; he has a desire to babble like an idiot in front of him and he pities Frank for being so stuck on him. He smiles back and says, "Oh, definitely." Jorge's eyes are lighter than his skin and seem to give off light rather than let it in. His forehead bulges slightly, swelling between his eyes and pushing them toward the sides of his face. It makes him look forceful but a little unconscious to Mark, like a handsome killer whale, and in fact he's wearing a T-shirt with the word *Orca* on it, beneath a print of one. "So what're you guys talking about?" Mark asks.

"We're not talking about anything," Ricardo says, on guard before Jorge can do more than lower his eyelids.

"Well, that's what I thought, pal," Mark says, nudging Ricardo's shoulder with his.

Pedro's eyes flicker at Mark; and he says to Ricardo, "*Tu amigo esta interesado o no?*"

Ricardo responds, exasperated but nudging Mark back, "*El esta interesado, lo unico es que nunca esta serio.*"

"*Entonces llevatelo de la mesa. Esta otra parte tiene que ser un secreto.*"

"That's a good idea," Jorge says eagerly. "Why don't you show him my altar to the dead?"

"*Pero, Don Pedro,*" Ricardo protests, ignoring Jorge. "*El no entiende nada. Solo conoce quince palabras en Espanol.*" Pedro takes the rim of his dinner plate between his thumb and forefinger, moves it a fraction of an inch away from him, waiting. "*Esta bien, Don Pedro,*" Ricardo sighs. He pats Mark's arm and stands up. "Have you seen Jorge's altar?"

"When we first got here," Mark says.

"Well, come and look at it some more."

"Oh. Right," Mark says, getting to his feet. Pedro waits until they step away from the table before he addresses Jorge.

Frank's reading the *Wall Street Journal* as they pass behind him. Without turning, he says, "Find out anything interesting?" Mark grunts at the back of his head and the double page of small type and lets Ricardo lead him into the hallway.

The altar is set up in a closet at the end of the hall, just past the bedroom. It's a table that completely fills the closet, spread with a white cloth and covered with glasses of water and white candles. A picture of Jorge's grandmother is prominent in an ornate frame. Ricardo says, "That's Jorge's grandmother."

"I know. He introduced me when we got here. Did I get you in trouble?"

Ricardo stoops down to move the offering to the dead closer to the altar; it's a small portion of the fettucine and veal they had for dinner. "No," he says. "Pedro's just never sure how much you understand."

"Well, pal, tell him the truth. Tell him I'm a retard who doesn't understand anything."

"I did. He doesn't want to take chances."

"Great." He watches Ricardo make a gesture to the altar or perhaps to Jorge's grandmother as though he's dipping his hand in something and putting some on his forehead. "I thought you weren't going to get real heavily involved in this."

"In what?" Ricardo asks nervously, standing up.

"This. *Santeria*. You said you were just picking out the parts you liked. Now we're over here and you're learning catechism from Pedro."

"It's not catechism, it's just things I need to know."

"Yeah, okay, but you're still serious about it. What happened?"

Ricardo watches the candles burn. "It works," he says.

"You mean Jorge? Yeah, Frank told me. I guess Jorge sacrificed chickens or something and it cured his spinal meningitis. The surgeon general's coming over tomorrow at ten to hear about it."

Ricardo turns to him, his cheeks sucked in, full lips pursed, eyes bugged open: his furious face. He stares at Mark for a couple of seconds, as though he's letting his poison ducts fill before striking. It's a face Mark makes fun of when they're joking together, but one that always makes him stop what he's doing when it's turned on him. "Lower your voice if you're going to be an idiot," Ricardo hisses. "Nobody said he cured himself. The *orishas* are containing the virus in him. They put it to sleep so it doesn't reproduce and kill him before somebody can find a cure." He thinks about it a moment and adds, "Frank doesn't know *anything* about it. Didn't you hear him coughing at dinner? It sounded like somebody tearing *wall*paper off the wall."

"I just don't think Jorge makes a convincing endorsement for anything spiritual. He's a nice guy, and he's got a nice ass, but he's a flake."

"He's keeping himself alive," Ricardo says fiercely. Pedro's voice carries from the dining room devoid of words, something simple and almost somber played on a piccolo. "The *orishas* keep him alive. He believes in them. I don't know what you're afraid of. Nobody's asking you to drink potions or anything." He waits, but Mark doesn't say anything. "You're being a donkey about this."

"You know what I'm afraid of, Ricardo," Mark says. Ricardo knows; after they both received the results of their HIV tests, he sat up with Mark all night as the shock wore off, and Mark's panic gave way to recrimination and then to rage and exhaustion, and finally they made love and fell asleep. But Mark's answer doesn't satisfy him, and he frowns, moves one of the candles on the altar so it's more in line with the others. Mark sighs and looks away. The door to the bedroom isn't closed all the way and he can see a slice of the room. The bed is buried under a mound of clothes, and beyond it, on the bureau, is a statue of Saint Lazarus and a candle burning in a purple glass. He can't make out the sores painted on Lazarus's bare chest but knows they're there from other Lazarus statues he's seen. He says, "Is that the problem with Frank and Jorge tonight? *Santeria?*"

"No." Ricardo's face lights up and his voice turns low, conspiratorial. "They're fighting because Jorge won't sleep with Frank. And he's still trashing around a lot."

"That figures," Mark says, pretending not to be interested. "Safe sex?"

"What do you think?"

"Right. Mr. Spirituality."

"*Niña,*" Jorge calls from the dining room, "*donde estas?*"

"*Aqui, mija.*"

"*Ya puedes regresar.*"

"*Mil gracias, malcreado*," Ricardo says under his breath, the twist he gives his mouth a translation for Mark's benefit, who grins appreciatively. "'*Si, mija, ya voy*," he calls.

Mark smooths Ricardo's hair. "Don't worry, pal," he says. "Pedro would much rather be talking to you."

"Really?"

"It's pretty obvious. What's he doing with Jorge, anyway?"

"Jorge got presented to him by someone. And then, well, you know. The *orishas* had saved him, so Pedro couldn't say no."

"What are you two doing in there?" Jorge's voice is like honey blown through a trumpet.

"Come on, let's go back in," Ricardo says, eager to rejoin the other conversation.

"No. You go in; it's more entertaining to sit with Frank."

"Frank's sweet," Ricardo says reproachfully, which means he's not impressed with him. They walk into the living room and Ricardo goes on to the dining room, saying something that makes Jorge laugh delightedly.

Mark sits down on the couch opposite Frank's. The *Wall Street Journal* stays up and Mark doesn't say anything, content to look around the room in silence for a while. Jorge's collection of religious statues dominates the shelf space, and though the different images of the Virgin and saints are interesting—especially a large figure of *Santa Barbara* with a chalice in her hand and a tower at her feet—Mark's seen them in other *santero* homes. He looks for some trace of Frank. Ricardo told him this was Frank's place before he met Jorge, and Mark figures most of the furniture and the stereo are his, but all the decorations seem to be Jorge. Everything is either religious or one of the constructions Jorge makes out of salvaged marble: trophy bases, dismantled lamps, candy dishes cemented into ornate white pagodas. Mark twists around in his seat. There's a white cabinet with glass doors beside the writing desk, and its shelves are jammed with some kind of pottery. He's trying to picture who opens the doors, Frank or Jorge, when the newspaper crackles.

"Are you looking at my Roseville?" Frank asks, the newspaper still held in front of him but the top half folded down, so his face shows.

"That stuff in the cabinet? That's yours?"

"I collect it," he says, closing the paper, then folding it and laying it down on the coffee table. "Would you like to see?"

"Well, yes," Mark says, a little shyly.

Frank stands up and walks over to the cabinet, opens it and squats down, his knees cracking quietly. "Why don't you come over here."

"Oh, no, is he showing off that tacky pottery again?" Jorge calls from the table. His voice has an edge of bitterness to it that Mark hasn't heard before, and he looks into the dining room. But Jorge has already turned back to the conversation, which seems to be excluding him at this point. Pedro has finished saying something to Ricardo; some course of action he should follow, perhaps, because Ricardo lowers his eyes and shakes his head: No, he doesn't want to. He bows his head and shakes it again, more slowly: He isn't able to; he won't. Pedro watches him patiently.

Frank says, "I love showing this, and I never get a chance." Mark sits down on the floor beside him. Frank hesitates over his first selection, then says, "Oh, here's a nice piece," and lifts a small vase from the bottom shelf. He hands it to Mark.

Mark takes it from him carefully, hating how fragile it is and hoping it doesn't jump out of his hands. He doesn't know anything about vases and racks his brain for something to say. It's a green vase, a very faint green, and about eight inches high, with roses in low relief wandering around it. He turns it in his hands a few times, following the roses, which are yellow with white centers, and says, "Hm. May I see another?"

"Yes, just set that one down on the floor. Well, no, right here next to the cabinet." Frank's eyes dart among his treasures a moment, and then he takes out another vase. It's squatter than the first and colored a pinkish brown like weak chocolate milk, the roses pale yellow on spikey maroon branches. He smiles at it as he passes it to Mark.

Mark holds it in both hands. The roundness is comforting, and he likes the feel of the roses against the palms of his hands; the colors are soft and very pleasant, like armchairs for the eyes. He says, "So is Roseville collectible, or is it just something you like to collect?"

"Oh, it's collectible, all right," Frank says. "I just got that at a garage sale last week. A hundred and ten dollars."

"For this?"

"For that. And it was a good price."

"For you or for the person selling it?"

Frank laughs happily, complimented. "Let me show you my favorite," he says.

"Please." Mark carefully sets the second vase down beside the first and holds out his hands to take the sugar bowl Frank's holding. As it passes between them, their eyes catch for a second, and Mark has a good look at how important this piece is to Frank. He pulls his head back involuntarily, slightly repulsed, but accepts the sugar bowl from him. He frowns down at it, baffled by what its attraction could be.

What's most puzzling to him is how the stuff could be collectible in the first place. It's the sort of thing people's grandmothers keep on end tables. He rubs one of the roses—pink roses raised on the dull yellow surface of the bowl, all of them open—with his thumb, pretending to admire it. No, not really grandmotherly; the Roseville has an age, but it's not exactly elderly. He gives the sugar bowl a turn, following the rose branches; they've been painted on with a few deft strokes, and the roses puff up from them, solid as bread. It seems hopeful more than anything, optimistic with its mild pleasant colors. He works the ball of his thumb against another rose, trying to remember what it reminds him of. Then it comes to him that it's like a prop rosebush in an old movie. Roses that grow in the front yard of a cottage in a movie where nothing terrible happens to anyone, perhaps a light comedy from the forties, after the war, and the feeling of intense and even stuffy safety comes from the fact that the front yard is actually inside a studio. "Roseville," he says, and now he holds the sugar bowl still in front of him, just looking at it, and feelings of comfort and security wash through him.

Frank sees that he's getting it now, and says softly, "Some evenings I just take it out and look at it one piece at a time until I get to that one."

"Jesus, I'll bet," Mark says. He shakes his head. "You know, I never like stuff like this. I'm really surprised." Frank grins and holds his hands out for the sugar bowl. Mark passes it back to him.

"Jorge wanted to use some of this for his dead altar. I absolutely refused."

"The dead don't need all those tacky roses," Jorge informs them from the table.

Mark didn't realize their conversation could be overheard. "I always thought the dead liked roses," he says, peering past Frank's shoulder at Jorge. Ricardo stops talking to Pedro and looks at Mark, then down at his plate, embarrassed.

"They do unless they can't get them," Frank mutters, putting the sugar bowl back into the cabinet. "Then they get snotty." He's dropped his voice to a low growl and it catches in his throat. He begins to cough and stands up, impatiently trying to force his chest clear, so that he puts a lot of voice into his coughing.

Jorge sighs and rolls his eyes, says, "Why don't you go to bed, you sound terrible." Frank continues coughing, the blood rising in his face as though it's going to break through the skin. He pulls out his handkerchief. Jorge watches it, frowning. He says, "You're just going to wind up in the hospital."

Frank clears his throat into the balled-up handkerchief, passing the mass of phlegm so delicately that he looks like he's tasting a carnation. He wipes off the corners of his mouth and puts the handkerchief back in his pants. Jorge looks away. "You just worry about your voodoo," Frank says, out of breath, "I'll take care of myself."

Jorge doesn't like "voodoo," but he raises his eyebrows as though lifting them over a puddle. "Fine, Frank," he says. "Whatever you want."

"Fuck you."

Mark sighs and tries to catch Ricardo's eye to signal him it's time to go, but Ricardo's watching Frank and Jorge. Other people's domestic traumas are usually one of Ricardo's joys; he tends to be an avid backer of both sides in private, and a silent but fiercely involved spectator during the actual fireworks. Now, though, he's not frowning in concentration, he's just watching, and he looks unhappy. Mark wonders if the fight is coming at a bad time in the conversation with Pedro, intercepting some vital bit of spiritual practice. He walks up behind Ricardo's chair, bends down to his ear and murmurs, "Time to go, huh, pal?"

Ricardo nods and stubs his cigarette out in his plate, which by now is a wasteland of ashes and butts burned to the filter. Jorge says, chidingly, "So soon."

Mark shrugs and smiles. "Work tomorrow."

"Well," Jorge says indulgently, "next time you'll come over on a Friday so you can visit for a while." He picks up a glass and puts it in his plate, wipes his fingers on a napkin. "Can I get a ride with you and your husband?" he asks Ricardo.

"I thought you weren't going out tonight," Frank whines.

"Do you think I'm going to stay here and listen to you cough your lungs out all night?" Jorge asks, precise as an elocution excercise. It hits Frank hard. Mark winces and backs up a step. Pedro stands up and slips into his denim jacket, working his shoulders back twice for a comfortable fit.

Jorge continues, reasonable and cold, "*You're* not taking care of yourself; why do you expect me to stay home and do it for you?" Pedro leans down and says something into Ricardo's ear. Ricardo's eyebrows draw together and his lips part in an expression of pain. Pedro says it again, something reasonable, and the gesture he uses while he speaks—palm up, fingers spread apart—makes whatever he's saying seem like the only thing that can be done. Jorge says with finality, "I have business to take care of." Ricardo brings up a sigh that lifts his shoulders and then lets them collapse and nods his head, not happy, and Pedro puts a hand on his back for a moment.

Frank's just taken the last straw. The blood leaps back up into his face like purple lace and he roars, "*Business?* You don't have a *job*. You're going out to the bars."

Jorge is surprised but holds his ground. He looks Frank in the eye and says, "Don't tell me what to do." The back door closes and a second later the screen door bangs lightly, but he and Frank hold each other's eye a little longer. Jorge snorts loudly and turns away.

Mark picks up his and Ricardo's coats from one of the chairs and looks at Ricardo, who looks back at him but doesn't respond. Mark doesn't see what's so engrossing about the fight; Ricardo's told him about others where they've taken cooking utensils and even tools to one another. Perhaps he's waiting for tonight to escalate, but Mark wants to escape before then. He drops the big overcoat in Ricardo's lap, then puts on his own scarf and bomber jacket.

Jorge watches him zip up, absently curling his mustache over the edge of his upper lip with his thumb. His eyes wander to the chair where Pedro was sitting and he stares at it for a moment. "Where's Don Pedro?" he asks.

Mark says, "Uh, I think he left," and pats Ricardo's shoulder to get him moving.

"He left? Without saying anything? Where did he go?" Mark shrugs, nervous, but Jorge isn't really speaking to him. Pedro's action translates itself, and as it does, Jorge's forehead darkens and bunches up between his eyebrows; it makes his eyes look even lighter, and blind as headlights. He turns them on Frank. "*Frank,*" he says, like an accusation, the judgment and the sentence in a single syllable.

Frank sneers as though he's having a facial cramp. "Take a little responsibility for your own actions," he says, each word like a piece of ice hitting a sidewalk.

Jorge slaps the table and silverware jumps in the plates. "If you're going to die, motherfucker, you do it by yourself. I don't need to go with you."

"Get out if you're going, and don't come back," Frank screams, as though his throat is turning into rags.

Jorge turns his back and says, his voice leashed but vicious, "This is my house as much as it is yours."

Ricardo has finally stood up and gotten into his big coat, though he's still not moving. Mark says, his voice pitched so it won't interrupt, "Frank. Jorge. Good night," and puts his palm in the small of Ricardo's back, escorts him to the door, which he pulls open with his other hand. He glances back as Ricardo passes in front of him and out the screen door. Frank's face is flushed yellow and purple and he's glaring at Jorge; Jorge is turning around to say something to Frank. As he turns, his face swollen with rage, his eyes pass over Mark's without connecting, and a sensation like falling runs up Mark's legs and into his stomach, as though the floor is a thin sheet of ice over a rushing river. Mark goes out, closing the two doors so that neither of them slams.

They walk quickly through the rose garden and up the driveway to the car. Mark expects Jorge to come out after them, demanding his ride, but a volley of voices erupts in the apartment. He unlocks the door for Ricardo, who gets in, reaches over and returns him the favor. Mark gets in, pumps the gas twice and starts the car. He backs down the long driveway. The blinds are down in Frank and Jorge's apartment; nothing shows through them except an even yellow light. He eases the car over the sidewalk and into the street carefully, so the muffler doesn't scrape, shifts into drive, and takes off down Argyle.

Ricardo fumbles in his purse for his cigarettes. "Do you believe them?" he asks.

"I don't believe *you*," Mark says. His voice is jittery. "You were watching them like you paid for tickets."

Ricardo laughs nervously, lighting his Benson & Hedges menthol. "I wasn't. So were you." The car is small, a Mazda, and Mark can see him without turning his head. Ricardo looks out the window to examine some teenagers hanging around the pay phones by a 7-Eleven.

"Admit it," Mark says, maneuvering in the erratic late-night traffic. "You wanted to see some blood. That's why you weren't moving." A white pickup cuts in front of him to turn into the parking lot of the Tick-Tock Coffee Shop. "Jesus Christ," he says, hitting the brakes. "Are you wearing your seat belt?"

"Yes," Ricardo says, pulling it across his chest and buckling it in. "And slow down, you fucking wacko."

"Hey, *you* don't have to worry: *I'm* at the wheel," Mark says, quoting a coke-fiend who once gave them an unforgettable ride home through the Hollywood Hills. Ricardo laughs. Mark says, "Is that how it usually is with them?"

"No. Not all the time." He sounds defensive.

Mark grins and says, "No, just whenever you've seen them together, right?"

Ricardo doesn't say anything. They cross Sunset, and the traffic evaporates; it's all concrete buildings, deserted sidewalks, empty parking lots. They see only one person: a young guy with a silver ghetto-blaster on his shoulder, his music bouncing off the wall of a studio and emphasizing the silence. Even though there's no one to see, he walks with a stylized strut. As they pass him, Ricardo says, "I asked Pedro to set up an altar for us."

"We've already got one."

Ricardo frowns. "No," he says, "that one's for the *orishas*. I asked him to set up an altar for the dead. Like Jorge has."

Mark doesn't look at him. "For me?"

"No, for me," Ricardo says, his voice clear but heavier than usual. "For my work. It would really help me."

"What would it help you do, Ricardo?" Ricardo doesn't answer, and Mark feels him retreat into privacy: not snapping shut, like a clam, but becoming more opaque, denser, like a wall of fog, so that Mark can't even tell where he is. Mark exhales through clenched teeth. "Right. I see. You want to invite 'the Dead' into our house, and your reasons don't concern me." He rolls his eyes at Ricardo like a pair of bowling balls. Ricardo's expression is one Mark hasn't seen before: He's staring at the dashboard, his lips pressed shut, but behind them his jaws are slightly distended. It makes him look like his mouth is full of something he can neither spit out or swallow. Mark says, backing off, "Oh, Christ, fine. Have him set up your altar. Just don't put it in the living room, okay?"

They turn onto Willoughby and begin the final stretch home through a sleeping neighborhood. The houses are dark on their small neat lawns and all the curbs are lined with cars. Camphor trees have sole possession of the sidewalks, the black trunks reaching up into clouds of small leaves that shift and stir restlessly in the night air. Mark drives on under the trees and lets himself settle down. He has to call his doctor sometime this week for another T-cell count, but all he wants to do tonight is get home and burrow into bed. Ricardo makes a sound in his throat and at first Mark thinks it's random. Then he realizes Ricardo is getting ready to say something. He thinks it might finally be some information about what he's doing in *Santeria*, and inclines his head toward Ricardo. The preliminary silence presses into his ears.

Ricardo says, his voice small and unhappy, "I don't know if I'm going to be able to take care of you." Mark freezes behind the wheel; for a moment the car is uncontrolled, rolling down the street on its own. "I couldn't live the way they do. It's like a punishment for something. I'm not strong enough for that." His voice is low and self-concerned and barely makes it out of his mouth; Mark has to strain to hear him. He drives on with no breath in his chest, waiting to hear how this is going to touch him. Shadows and light from the street lamps slide up the hood of the car and drop into the street behind them. Ricardo says, "I'm afraid I'm going to fail you," is silent for a moment, then says, "I don't want to see you waste away." His voice comes apart. Mark looks over at him. His profile is framed against the passing green of front yards; he's crying but his face is composed and hopeless, as though he's looking at something that doesn't move.

Mark says, "Ricardo. Ricardo," not because he knows what to say, but just to get him to look up.

"What," Ricardo says, his voice like something broken and thrown away, and he turns his face to Mark.

But now Mark's afraid to look at him. He doesn't want to see his own funeral in Ricardo's face; he's afraid that if he does he won't be able to breathe again, that he'll pull the car over under one of the camphor trees, turn it off and just let the leaves fall on him. "What," Ricardo repeats, and his voice is so flat and lifeless that Mark has to look at him. The amount of misery in Ricardo's face amazes him. It's as though he's turned back to look at Mark from the beginning of a journey into loss and solitude that will take him years to complete, a journey that terrifies him. Mark wants to save him from it. He reaches out and takes hold of Ricardo's leg, slides his hand down to just above the knee and squeezes, as though he's filled with strength and can pass it on through the palm of his hand. "It's okay, pal," he says. "It's okay. We're almost home."

PART TWO

WHY I DO IT

• FELICE PICANO •

YOU CAN SEE us anytime, me and Cal, if you ever ride the subways. I'm the guy pushing. He's in the wheelchair. It's a new one. Bought it with some of his Social Security money, some of the disability insurance. All of it Cal's. All the money. Cal has all the money.

You've probably seen us once or twice. We work different lines. Never rush hour though. Too much traffic, too many people. Cal likes the night hours, but it isn't always his choice and now it's gotten dangerous at night. So I call those shots and it's afternoons, before three and after seven when the rush hour's over.

Sure you've seen us! You'll be sitting there with your afternoon newspaper in front of you, crazy to read about the *Social Register* madam or the guy that married a hundred and seventeen women in thirty-nine states or you'll be really into that paperback—the White House held for ransom, the Zongians attacking with nerve-stuns, Lord Chester finally about to place his noble pecker into the chambermaid's brimming quim—and there we are.

I swing open the subway train doors, and we're in your car. Sudden as rain or trouble. Everyone feels it. People look down, up, away, anywhere. We're that embarrassing. But once we're inside, it's no problem really. Cal is slicker than most beggars. He sits there in his wheelchair really kinda well dressed for a bum in his hand-knitted sweater or monogram polo shirt in summer, his big arms, his hands with the little wicker basket, (just like the one the nuns all carry) and his big tousled head, blond, fresh smelling, good-looking, clear-eyed, and only the pant legs tucked under his stumps tells you anything's wrong. Right?

I'm behind him, the mousy guy pushing the wheelchair through car after car, out onto the express stations when we get there and the free transfer stations like Fulton Street or Fourteenth or the 42nd Street Shuttle, and you hardly notice me. Nobody remembers the color of my hair, or what I'm wearing, or the color of my eyes or the worn out sneakers, or anything about me. I'm behind. Pushing. Not where the action is.

That's Cal. His big hazel eyes. And the memory of the boy who used to step out of his front door and see you putting out garbage next door and he'd say, "Hey man, how about tossing this back and forth a little" and before you can make up an excuse the basketball is in your hands, chest high, or the football in your outstretched hand and you say, "Sure. Why not. For a minute." That's the kind of guy Cal is, and why I love him, you know.

So people give.

He keeps the wicker basket out there, no cards with pencils like that wizened, purple-skinned black deaf-mute, no spiel like the skinny guy who goes on and on about how he has a wife and three kids on Welfare only it ain't enough to live on to feed the babies. No spiel for Cal, and even the basket is sort of casual, like hey, what's this doing here, but since it's here, brother, sister, why not drop somethin' in. No small change please. Like the priest at St. Veronica's I got a headache today, only want to hear the rustle of bills. Cal never comes out and says it. He seldom says anything on the trains. He doesn't have to say anything. We just roll slowly through the cars, pulling a heartstring here, a memory there, a possibility there, sympathy, compassion, all the shit that goes by the name of human emotion.

Before they locked up the bathroom johns on accounta all the guys perving in front of little kids, we used to count our take in there, no matter the ammonia stink and the guys whacking off looking at anyone who came in. Now we usually wait to count it till we get home. But it don't matter. We've never been robbed. The transit cops watch out for us. Some of them drop into the basket, "Hey sport. Hard times. Things'll get better. Believe it." And Cal gives them THE SMILE. That's what I call it. THE SMILE. And everyone thinks sweet potato pie and clean diapers and Easter ham dinner and all that.

'Course I know better. I know the nights when someone's dropped a ten in the basket and after three hours we add up and there's like, say, thirty bucks there, more than enough for food and our rooms and Cal counts it and says to me "Hey Bud—" he always, only calls me Bud, though my name is Frank—"hey Bud, let's get some lubricant for our heads." And off we go.

This can be one of two types of drinking. Either a quiet four or five doubles at one of the few easy Irish shanty places still on Eighth Avenue. Watching *Taxi* reruns or whatever game is on the set, a really nice few hours with maybe some good bullshitting which Cal likes to do so much with some locals. Or it can be an all-outer. That's what I call the nights when Cal really gets wasted and I gotta grab the rest of the bills away from him and wheel him out into the night, screaming and cursing, and I gotta try to find some asshole cabbie who speaks Ukrainian or Portuguese or something who's so desperate for a fare that he's willing to take these two geeks—me and Cal looped to the eyes—back down to where we live.

Once I get Cal up the elevator and into the apartment, making sure to avoid his arms—always his arms, so strong, so long—that's when it can really get rough. I shut the door and wonder. But not for long. That's when one of two things happens. Either he really gets sad and slumps and just wheels into his room slamming the door behind him and stays there all night, all the next morning, sometimes all the following day. If I get up from the cot where I sleep watching TV on that twelve-inch screen set we picked up on the street last year and which I managed to fix up pretty good and if I go to his closed door, I can hear him in there sobbing. What I think they call dry sobbing, like that rubber thing that keeps on rising and falling inside the water tank behind your toilet. Or he's silent. He doesn't even sleep those nights.

Then there are other nights when we get home from a stink he's on and Cal is boiling over, swearing at the cabbie, at the cheapskates on the trains and the no-account heartless cockteasing cunts in the bar. That's when I have to watch out. After all these years, I never do watch out enough. Even though I know how long and how strong his arms are, and even though I know how fast he can move, even without legs, I've still never figured out how to get out of Cal's reach when he wants to get at me.

I mean I love the guy, I really do, but sometimes, when he reaches me in one of his moods it's more than a guy can take, you know what I mean? The hitting I can take easy enough. The guy's got to let it out sometime, on someone, right? And that's why I'm there. Little Bud always ready to take a beating, if I have ta. And after he's done hitting me and swearing at me, and he's tired and he makes me go get him a beer and he tells me to undress him and you know wash him, that's all right too. I know it's not normal some of the things I do for Cal when I'm washing him, but like he said, what cunt is going to put up with his stumps and all, you know what I'm saying. And by now I'm used to what he's gotta have, and it's all right, really. I'm not humiliated anymore by what he makes me do and sometimes when I'm doing it and he's feeling good, he plays with my hair, and his voice gets deep and sweet and he tells me what a good buddy I am to him, watch your teeth huh, Bud, that's better. Yeah what a good buddy I am.

Then I can put up with it, you know. 'Cause then I know it's all over, and his anger is gone, and he'll go to sleep and rest up and be his old self again next morning and we'll go out and he'll let me see the world, this fucking world, and how it just kinda brightens up when Cal's there, wheeling along with me pushing in back of him, the subway stations, the Port Authority, the peeps, the pimps, the hustlers, the junkies, the girls. And Cal there, wheeling along like the Prince of the Streets, his eyes glimmering full of it all, taking it in, and newstand guys offering us a *Daily News* for nothing, and maybe a pack of Camels or chewing gum, and hookers saying "Hey Baby, how you hanging?" and the cops stopping to smile and nod. And there's Cal taking it in, laughing, getting people to pay and to give and to be kind. And especially when Cal turns around and say's to me "Hey Bud, whatta' think? Is it a good day? Is this a good day, Bud? And before I can answer, he gives THE SMILE.

I really love the guy, you know.

LIGHTS IN THE VALLEY

• ANDREW HOLLERAN •

"PROUD OF *ME* for coming," Ned said over and over again in the taxicab taking him and Oliver from the hospital on the East Side in which they had visited Louis. "He said he was proud of *me* for coming! When *he* was the one who was sick. What did he mean?" he asked Oliver, before getting out in front of the Port Authority Terminal. "He meant he was proud of you for coming to see him, since he knows how shy you are, and how hospitals probably terrify you." But that was before my mother fell, and my father had his stroke, he thought as the bus took him to the airport that afternoon. That was many operating rooms, many Intensive Care Units, ago. That was before what Mister Lark calls The Avalanche. Now I'm a veteran of these places. Yet going to see Louis did terrify me—because Louis shouldn't be in a hospital, he thought. Louis should be at the door of a nightclub, saying: "Oh, darling, I'm so glad you got here. Come meet my new husband—before he's kidnapped by all these dragons!" It was just as well I have to take care of my parents, he thought as the plane took him back to Ohio, it was just as well they had crumbled when they did; the event had taken him out of New York, away from a nightmare his friends were stuck in. ("You got out just before the bomb dropped," said Oliver.)

News came to him from New York from Mister Lark and Oliver, following his return home: Louis had undergone radiation which wiped out the tumors on his gum; then they reappeared. He was trying another new drug. He fainted in the elevator after a series of blood tests. He had diarrhea. He took a nap each afternoon. He had a Buddy. In Ohio, Ned took a walk each night in a cemetery near his sister's house from which he could see, on the opposite hill, the blaze of a shopping mall; on winter nights, the only light in the darkness—and when he glanced through the dark bare sycamores at the bright hill to the east, he knew Louis lay beyond that blaze of light, in the darkness to the east, over the dark hills of Pennsylvania, across New Jersey, the Hudson River, on the island of Manhattan, sick. And he would walk round and round the oval among the gravestones in that deserted cemetery, trying, in the cold wind, beneath the crystalline stars, the occasional lights of a passing jet, to understand what had happened. But neither he, nor anyone else he knew, could.

News reached even Ohio eventually of what was going on— entered the big white frame houses in the old farming town, in which his family had always lived, through the transistors of the television set. One evening his sister turned to him, after a segment of "The NBC Nightly News," and said: "Why *are* gay men so promiscuous?" And he—snug in the den of the family home in Hamilton—looked at her blankly and could not think of a thing to say. He started to say: Because they cannot form functional unions, with children, and families. Because they cannot seem to even form liaisons that endure very long. Because they are greedy, like all human beings. Wouldn't you have all the sex you wanted, if you could? Because sex is the most transcendent, marvelous experience, the greatest adventure a person can have on earth. Because they are dogs, and go sniffing each night in public parks. Because they are human. Because, because. Then she took out another cigarette, and he said: "Why do you smoke?" A car turned at the end of the street, and they went back to viewing the news of a world that always seemed to him so far, far away when he was at home in that house in that garden in that town.

He belonged to a family that regarded long distance calls as self-indulgent as psychoanalysis: Not all the advertisements of the telephone company could erode that. He was glad of it now. He did not want to be that close at the moment. He wanted time. A space in which to breathe—an hour, a morning, a day of silence, on which absolutely nothing happened; like the air pocket a person trapped in a car sinking into a lake uses. Air pockets; that's all he wanted—pockets of nothingness, silence, inaction. Moments when the phone did not ring. That allowed him to write letters. He liked to write letters; he liked to receive them; each morning he went down to the mailbox with a sense of exhilaration, wondering what he would find. Occasionally a sales catalog containing photographs of male models Louis had followed around Manhattan—had constructed small shrines to in his apartment—connected him to his other self. But, more important, the postal service—like the house, the yard, the hedge—moved the world back a step; kept it at arm's length, or at least the time it took letters to cross the space between Cincinnati and New York. Letters kept bad news at least two days away; gave one a breathing space. The telephone attacked; shattered the silence that seemed, after New York, some work of art, something he would stop in the middle of the uneventful day and listen to, look around at, contemplate. He began to loathe the ring of a telephone; a telephone that, in New York, he approached with the anticipation he now felt walking to the mailbox; a telephone that, in New York, had always been an invitation, a tale of some sexual adventure the night before, a manifestation of Life. Now the telephone announced Doom. There were three in the house. One he considered the most dangerous, because through it he had received the news of his father's stroke, his mother's fall, his two friends' deaths. He regarded it now the way prehistoric man viewed a rock or tree invested with spirits. If it rang he got up and walked to another part of the house and used one that had not been contaminated with bad news. As it was, he answered any telephone in such a muffled, guarded tone, people always asked: "I'm sorry. Were you sleeping?" He wanted to reply: *Yes, sleeping. Wake me when it's over.* Life had assaulted on so many fronts he now only wanted discrete, limited, concrete absolutions: an hour of perfect silence, a morning without the telephone's ring. He lived now—as do primitive societies— from day to day.

One winter night he sat by his mother's bed at the rehabilitation center overlooking a dark valley sprinkled with isolated lights—a valley Washington had led troops into during the French and Indian War—reading aloud to her from a book she had found in the library, called *How Not to Worry*. His mother, her body incapacitated, helpless, bedridden, poured all her energy into paranoid fantasies; and across her face, her alarmed eyes, her furrowed brow, her drawn-back mouth, he would see, in a single hour, activity so strenuous, so physical, it was like a soccer match played over the features on her face in which she was all the players. It left him exhausted just to watch. He wanted her to stop worrying. He wanted himself to stop worrying. So he got this book and read aloud to her. The author said we should contain worry the way we prevent water from spreading from one compartment to another in a damaged ship. Seal it off. Analyze the problem. Ask how it can harm you. Answer the question: "What is the worst thing that can happen?" He wanted to laugh as he sat there beside the bed of this paralyzed woman. The worst thing that can happen, he thought, is that you will have to live in bed unable to move the rest of your life, or one day you will take off your shoe and discover a purplish growth on the skin of your foot. Then loss of weight, a tuberculosis associated with birds, herpes of the brain. That is the worst that can happen. He sat there reading to his mother: "Don't let the thing causing you to worry spoil more hours than it has to. Keep it apart, in a chamber of its own. I once knew a young man so worried he began losing sleep." Meanwhile his mother's roommate (a young woman stricken with multiple sclerosis whose plans to marry were now postponed) prepared herself for a nightly visit from her fiancé. She was cheerful and composed while her fiancé visited, and then, the moment he was out the door and down the hall, put her face in her hands and burst into tears. He read aloud from the book while she turned over on her side and sobbed. Outside the lights twinkled in the valley. He wanted one thing: to survive his mother and father. He wanted to see them out. Then he could go. Out of shame or love, he was not sure. He did not finish *How Not to Worry*, or the murder mystery, or the biography of Katharine Hepburn. He and his mother lost interest partway through each one of them; there were things in life far beneath the printed word, or at least the organized shape of a book. He read letters instead, and wrote them, and allowed the time it took for them to cross the Appalachians to act as a sort of buffer.

And when he took his walk at night down to the cemetery he looked at the glowing windows of the houses he passed—the children playing hockey on the frozen puddles of a driveway in the glare of floodlights—and marveled: No one in this town has to worry about AIDS. They were as miraculous as a colony of people on the moon. He enjoyed being among them on these icy winter nights. He knew he had not escaped; but then that was what he assumed he felt subconsciously. Evil was a location, a telephone, a place. Even the season was geography. If I can just get to spring, he told himself, if I can just see leaves on the trees again and swim in the lake. That's all I want. He felt as helpless in stemming the plague, however, as he did caring for his parents; his parents he knew constituted a holding action, a losing battle, a war he would not win, a wall that was crumbling no matter how he patched it, an inevitable claim he was coming face to face with for the first time and attempting merely to postpone. The other was beyond the scope of reality as he had known it thus far. But both were the same fact: Death. "Freud said no one believes in his own death," he wrote Mister Lark, "but it is even worse than that. We've simply forgotten things come to an end. No one quite realizes that: Everything has to be turned in. Like a library book. A rented canoe. A person you make love with, who then dresses and goes home. God is an Indian-giver. It's a hard lesson for children of all ages to accept." (And Mister Lark wrote back: "My dear boy, life without death would be *unbearable!*") "We were such a lucky generation," he wrote. "No wars, since Vietnam, no floods, no disease, no malnutrition, poverty. Our great worry, dental plaque. All that was required of us: that we floss before bedtime. No wonder all this is such a shock."

He wondered as he walked around the cemetery on those cold nights why it really was such a shock, despite their lack of preparation for it; whether they should have been able to foresee it; whether he could, as a homosexual man, have lived his life any differently these past fifteen years. Such speculation seemed suited to those dark nights in the cemetery, when he could let his mind wander exactly where it wanted to. He knew it was useless. But then everything seemed to conspire to lead him to thoughts like these. One morning the neighbor came over with a Living Will he asked Ned to witness; the neighbor's wife had just died after several weeks in the hospital so horrifying, her husband wanted to make sure it could not happen to him. He told Ned you could purchase a blank will at a local stationer's for only fifty cents. Ned drove downtown and got one; but when it lay on the desk in front of him, he realized he had no one he should leave his things to. He was still in some elemental way unattached to this world; that was what it meant to be a bachelor.

He was a bachelor—that's all—in the eyes of the community he now found himself living in. There was a greenhouse down the road from his sister's house; every morning he saw a man walking down the street to work in it, not long after the big yellow buses, bearing children had gone past on their way to school—a man his sister saw go by one day and said: "He's gay. He lives with his family. But his boyfriend is Carol Fanshaw's hairdresser. I've been trying to get them to take me to a jazz club downtown John won't let me go to."

"Why not?"

"It's in a black neighborhood."

For a moment, he viewed himself as he might have been, had he not moved to New York: a man, tall, thin, balding, walking down Hartley Lane on his way to work in a greenhouse in the bottom of the ravine on a frosty winter morning, a man married women could go to black jazz clubs with downtown, where their husbands wouldn't go. He liked greenhouses, he liked frosty winter mornings, but he could not imagine the women in houses he walked past saying: "He lives with his family, but his boyfriend is that man who runs the garage down in the ravine." That's why he had gone to New York. He had wanted life to be more passionate than that. So he had gone to Manhattan; and found, entering rooms filled with other men, a prestige he could not have any other way. In this town, he was only that most peculiar of things: an unmarried son. A middle-aged bachelor walking to work on a late November morning. In New York he had been something else. But each time he returned to Ohio at Christmas, he'd known that the value he had in New York—in the eyes of his friends, lovers, the people who turned to look at him when he walked into the Spike or up the steps of the Sandpiper—could not be conveyed, did not translate, was worthless, like a foreign currency once you cross the border. Even his friendships with Louis, Oliver, Mister Lark all seemed strange and insubstantial from the viewpoint of

Ohio; like people one sees in the light of day after spending hours with them in the red gloom of a nightclub. What had they amounted to, anyway?

In the morning he would awake, slide off the bed onto his knees and say morning prayers for Louis (and John, and Michael, and Peter—the list kept getting longer as the months went by). He did not think his prayers could help them, and yet if he did not pray for them, he felt he was remiss; so each morning he tried to direct at the end of his prayers some form of—what? he wondered. Good wishes? Love?—their way, and asked God to give them courage; as if the throne of heaven really could be stormed, as the nuns said, with constant prayer rising from the hearts of people all over the world. Or as if there were vibrations, invisible energies that could be transmitted mentally. The others were easy to name, but Louis always gave him pause. He thought Louis symbolic of something, but what he was not sure. Louis did not write letters—or rather, he had stopped, since becoming ill—and this silence made him even more immense. At times Louis seemed to him, from a distance of time and place, merely a prince of Fun. As harmless, as genial, as Santa Claus, the Easter Bunny. In this light his illness seemed even more sadistic, malicious. At other times he thought of Louis as a bawd, a pimp; some eastern deity with seven heads and nine arms, enormous, bronze, with a green patina. The prince of Debauch. That was America, no doubt: In this country, the Prince of Debauch *was* Santa Claus. Or rather: deciding which Louis was did not matter. Like a lover about to leave a companion who discovers he is ill, he found it inexcusable to waffle in his opinion of Louis, and his own past, now. Whatever he was, Louis was in a bad place, and needed help. And he was not there. So he prayed for him. Or rather, he thought of him, since he was too skeptical to suppose that saying, "Please God, make Louis better," would have any effect whatsoever. There was a woodpecker in the yard that fall that perched on the TV antenna and tapped away at the metal as if there were insects hidden in it. He liked to watch it beating its head against the metal with the rigid, manic movements of a bird in a cartoon. One morning he was kneeling saying his prayers, asking God to give Louis courage, when his mind stalled and the sound of the woodpecker tapping its beak against the antenna on the roof came to him, and he thought: My prayers have as much chance of reaching God, of helping Louis, as that woodpecker has of finding a bug in the antenna.

For a while he carried this cynical analogy around with him as a badge of intellectual toughness, until a neighbor told him the woodpecker beat the antenna not because it supposed insects could be found in it, but because it wanted to sharpen its beak—a fact that reduced him once more to humility. Humility seemed the only safe thing now. He didn't believe God would help when he got down on his knees each morning, and he didn't believe the government would—because homosexuals were still a disposable, superfluous population, a kind of embarrassment, if not irrelevance—and he didn't believe intellectuals could help, and he didn't believe plays or novels could help, and he didn't even believe the great American panacea, Money, could. He thought someone in a laboratory somewhere he couldn't see might, but that was pure chance. An apple had to fall on someone's head; the rest was just the spectacle of human cruelty. He knew what Oliver, Mister Lark, others were doing for Louis. He believed in giving comfort; and even if there were moments when the thought of his other friends falling ill so terrified him, he refused to concede the possibility—he sometimes thought they were all going to contract it sooner or later, that it was like the Spanish influenza after World War One: a germ as easily got as a cold. That November in New York, Mister Lark marched to the Hudson River one night carrying candles and a single rose, in memory of the dead; tossed the candles, the flowers, into the river; and though he described it as a long-overdue expression of the charity that had been left out of homosexual life before now, it seemed to Ned vaguely sinister and oppressive. The Hudson River was not the Ganges, he thought. (Or was that, too, just a matter of time?) Life seemed now encroached upon by everything he loathed, all values reversed, the wheel of fortune completely turned. Instead of praying he wondered who would be alive last, like the winner of a Tontine, to look back at the others and pity them.

After prayers he dressed, went downstairs, had breakfast and drove to the nursing home, in which his father was confined after suffering a stroke. Like a bee carrying pollen from flower to flower, he carried a message from his father—no matter what he, concerned now only with his own death, the only exit he could imagine from the nursing home, did not say—to his mother, in the rehabilitation center, twenty miles away on another hilltop. One day he found the lobby of the nursing home filled with patients, assembled in wheelchairs, and a man who had been invited to play the trumpet for them. The young man hitched up a machine that allowed him to accompany songs from which Frank Sinatra's voice had been removed. The trumpeter had large hands with prominent veins, dark eyes and a thick black mustache. Behind him a glass wall revealed a bleached golden lawn, a tiny ravine in which a stream ran, a line of higher hills along the valley, and on the top right corner of one of them, a cloud, caught by the treetops of the woods up there. The cloud and the trumpet player merged in his mind: First he thought of hiking up that hillside to the cloud, caught in the treetops, the air sparkling and moist. Then he thought of introducing himself to the trumpet player and driving with him westward across the country: days spent setting up the music equipment, playing in nursing homes, sweaty nights in hot motels. Or they would begin a new life here together, in one of the white frame houses in the ravine. Instead the young man played his final song, disassembled the machine and speakers, packed his golden trumpet in its case, while the patients—too ill to applaud, the ones in the front row sagging facedown over their restraining straps—watched. A deer came up to the window, then turned away and went back across the lawn to the woods, and an hour later Ned found himself seated at the wheel of his car in a traffic jam caused by commuters from the city, staring through the windshield at that stationary wisp of a cloud high above the gas station, furniture stores, supermarkets clogging both sides of the road. The cloud seemed to beckon him, like the dark, appalled eyes of the trumpet player, and he vowed to go up into the hills some afternoon and walk. But he did not. He remained down in the valley shuttling back and forth between nursing home, rehabilitation center, and his sister's house.

The roads were often icy. Some hills he would go down in neutral they were so steep; like hang gliding. When he got home late, the telephone would ring and he would pick it up to hear the voice of Mister Lark saying: "Ah-dear-boy-forgive-me-for-calling-you-but-it-was-impossible-to-reach-you-earlier, how is your mother and father, too, hmmmmmm?" in one continuous silken murmur. And, having solicited that information, he would go on to give Ned some gossip from New York about a book, a play, a dinner, a march, or meeting so-and-so on the street. "I no longer answer the phone myself," he said. "I have Robert Folkezijn answer, and ask whoever is calling the topic. I have him ask: 'Is it sex, death, or gossip?' The deaths go on, dear boy. Spruill says he wouldn't care if he got it, but I wonder. You know, it's like that money we lent to Mexico and Brazil. We were having all that sex, and Shitibank was lending Mexico all that money. I know. *I* proofread the loan agreements at Sherman and Sterling! The whole society went overboard, let's face it. But then as Franklin said: 'I have thought of a remedy for everything but prosperity.' Empires always attract flies, and viruses." Mister Lark's voice soothed him—and save for the one disadvantage (that once on the phone, Mister Lark was there to stay for at least an hour), his were the calls Ned enjoyed. "And how is Cincinnati?" Mister Lark would ask, as if it too were a relative. He had once, years ago, taken a bus fourteen hours from New York to that city to hear a Bulgarian chamber music group play the Trout Quintet, when he was young and viewed Art with more romantic eyes; now he would not go five blocks to the YMHA to hear the same piece unless it was free.

Talking to Mister Lark on the phone was like having tea with a favorite aunt: There was the illusion that the world was a place in which certain things were done, and not done—the most important issue who was chosen to sing Turandot that year at the Met—and everything essentially sane. In fact the world seemed so insane to Ned at this point, he was unable to sleep through a single night without waking up often in darkness. Sleep—like the old T-shirt he wore to bed—came apart during the night, and he found himself sitting up in the dark room, listening to the distant wash of car tires on the wet pavement, or the tap of a branch against the window, trying to remember what Mister Lark had told him about Zinka Milanoff; and when he got up and went into the bathroom to pee, he felt he was face to face with some essential vacuum at the center of existence—as if only at three in the morning, in a suburban house, standing above a toilet, did one approach the nature of

God. "The Avalanche," Mister Lark called it. "When parents start to die, when mortality loosens the great snowmass, and everyone goes tumbling down at once."

"How is Louis?" Ned would ask Mister Lark, and the answer was always: "Fine. Busy as ever. I watched him last night at Studio running around to all these women, whispering in their ears, and making them smile, and I finally asked him what he *said* to everyone, and do you know what his answer was? 'I flatter them.' Simple, *n'est-ce pas?* You can never go wrong flattering people," said Mister Lark. "That is of course because we are all basically chimpanzees."

(Though he made exceptions; once he telephoned and got Ned's sister instead, and each time afterward he called Ned, he asked, "How is your dear sister? We spoke only a moment, but she seemed to me—well, so good.")

She was good. She was his unquestioning support during this nightmare. She accepted him there without any questions. He envied the world she had created through her own managerial efforts. ("Relax?" she said to him one day when he remarked that sometimes he imagined married life as a sort of resting place, a temple in which one could finally find peace. "You don't get married to relax!") Her house in this green neighborhood, between a cemetery and a golf course, threaded daily by the big yellow buses, the sacred cocoons bearing the sole industrial product of the place (children), was a refuge; an arrangement so quiet, and sane, the mailman's arrival was the chief event. Life was a series of reprieves, he began to think. He wished to live now as antiseptically as a nurse in rubber gloves. He wanted to prune the dead limbs off the apple trees in the backyard, while starlings clustered on the red berries of the holly bush, and the winter sun turned the frozen lawns on the opposite hillside a soft gold. He wanted to live.

"Please, please, can I go to the mall? Just this once! Please!" his niece wailed to her mother in the kitchen on those autumn afternoons, the way he had once wailed to Louis: "Please, *please*, see if I can come to the Island this weekend." His sister worried about the renovation of her kitchen. His nephew had no one to play with. Past life came back. And present beauty. The doorbell would ring once a week, and he would open it to find, beside the gray stone wall, backed by the delicate branches of a juniper through whose dark branches the fading dusk sent a golden light that aureoled his head, a prince in search of the Holy Grail—the paperboy asking for a dollar thirty cents. Then the bus would stop at the corner and deposit the sacred cargo, and as he watched, through the kitchen window, the children would form into little groups that told their popularity, or lack of it, their moods, animated or forlorn, their feelings, happy or dejected, returning home. He was the delight of divorced women—friends of his sister's who came over, and told him, on the paddle-tennis court, of the fear the other wives felt toward them, the inevitability of being deserted by younger boyfriends, the delicacy of going on dates with divorced men their age; because Ned, outside marriage, too, understood. There was one other unmarried man in the neighborhood, a dentist who lived behind his sister, but he never once saw the man. Sometimes he would awaken in the morning, look out the window and see the yard crew the dentist employed instead: three Hispanic men who pulled up in a truck, got out, cleared the lawn of dead leaves and broken branches with rapid, nervous strokes, piled the leaves in the back of the truck, and then drove off. They looked like the men he'd had sex with in his neighborhood park in New York. Here they were as approachable as the frost that silvered the backyards when he looked out the window of his room—or the truck they pulled up in, and then vanished with, like bank robbers; or the dentist who lived there but was never once seen; or the young men with splotchy red cheeks and hair still curling at the neck from a shower, carrying gym bags as they walked beside the road up a wooded ravine on the way to the nursing home.

At the other end of day, he was the only one at home when his brother-in-law's father came by to have dinner. His sister felt the family should have dinner together—he had forgotten this custom, of assembling everyone to eat not because they wanted to but because the principle was important; a principle, he had also forgotten, more honored in the breach than the observance. At most once a week the family was reduced to the odd discomfort of making small talk over the dinner table as if they were complete strangers. But most evenings, individual schedules prevented them from sitting down together. And on Fridays, when his sister's father-in-law, a widowed man of eighty who kept busy going around all day to meetings of the Lions Club, his church, raffles, fund-raisers, the bakery to get

day-old bread and pastries, would appear at the back door with
several bags of breakfast rolls, they were the only two there.
Everyone else was: working downtown, sleeping over at a
friend's house, playing paddle tennis. His sister would phone to
say she was late, the dinner on the stove, go ahead. Ned would
sit down in the breakfast nook with the father-in-law, the
distant hills twinkling with lights of innumerable shopping
centers and neighborhoods like theirs, as the snow began to
flutter down. After inquiring about everyone's health, they
would eat together in silence, until the old man raised his
handsome head and said to Ned: "Got a girlfriend yet?" "Not
yet," Ned would say, and resume lifting the spoon of soup to
his lips. The old man had a girlfriend: a woman of eighty-two
he occasionally brought to the house, all dressed up for a
church bingo game. Then—moments later—the widower would
raise his head and say: "You know, I haven't eaten tuna in two
years." "Well," said Ned. "Isn't that something?" And he lowered his eyes, thinking that without sex, life was a blank.
Without sex, or rather without a history, prospect, or possession of marriage, one was a ghost.

He was afraid to even have sex, however—he lived in Cincinnati among a race who had not heard the news from the capital,
who did not even know enough to mistrust him, yet he mis-
trusted himself. He confined his appreciation of men to
looking—at the handsome sergeant seated at a desk in the Army
Recruiting Center in the local mall, sitting in the stillness of a
midweek morning waiting for someone to walk in and justify
his existence; the muscle-builders opening a gym downstairs;
the clerk in the deserted bookstore; the traveling businessman
who used the pool he visited at a nearby Holiday Inn, the only
indoor pool in the area heated in winter, where, at eleven in the
morning on a snowy Tuesday he would find some pale IBM
representative with enormous nipples doing sit-ups before the
clouded windows. The young men who packed his groceries in
the supermarket, the clerk demonstrating Christmas lights to
him at Sears, the silhouette walking toward him against a
golden sky as he waited to pull out of the Sears parking lot onto
the busy, slushy highway—made him realize that no matter
what had happened, no matter how senseless homosexual desire
seemed to be, his desire was as elemental and profound, he
wrote Mister Lark, "as the mere *outline* of a man walking

toward me on a highway at dusk. Not even a person! A silhouette!" "Whatever you do," Mister Lark wrote back, "don't pick up hitchhikers."

His own body he refused to look at even in the shower, or toweling himself dry afterward in the tiny bathroom while the windows clouded up. The skin that covered it suddenly seemed to him as vast as Russia: an endless expanse on which the handwriting on the wall might appear. He realized it was possible that one evening he would take off his shoes—that casual, domestic moment—and see a dark purplish spot on the instep; or that he would go to the dentist and learn there was a sore in his mouth—like Louis; or wake up one morning on soaked sheets; or suddenly develop diarrhea. (Louis's last letter: "It's three a.m., I'm sitting on the john with Montezuma's revenge.") Everyone was healthy before he got sick. So he stopped looking at himself in the shower; he divorced himself from his body. It came down to the body, after all: the body he had so carefully, enthusiastically cultivated in the city—trudging back and forth between his apartment and the gymnasium, like some voice student training her instrument; like the woman who lived in the building behind him in Manhattan, practicing scales on summer evenings across the clotheslines hung with laundry, while he did sit-ups and dips between the kitchen chairs. One evening in the parking lot of the rehabilitation center he met the physical therapist by accident, who said, after talking about his mother and her future: "She needs someone to do for her. She needs another body." That was it. If she wanted to rub her eye, his hand had to. If she wanted to turn in bed, his arms were the only means. It was a question of the body, after all—the machine everyone took for granted: what one did with this house the soul had been temporarily furnished: What to do with the body during that relatively brief span of time when one had one.

If You Trust In Anyone But Jesus, You're A Fool said one of the portable signs outside a Baptist church on the road between the rehabilitation center and the freeway he drove to help his mother with his body. "Why did you trust people?" his sister asked one evening, driving past it. "In what sense?" he said. "In the sense that they could give you something," she said. "You mean VD? But all that was cured with penicillin," he said. "I mean AIDS," she said. "No one knew about AIDS," he said.

"Getting AIDS is like being told you were exposed to asbestos in the high school you went to, learning years later it can cause cancer. It's retroactive. Nobody knew at the time." It was all bad luck; an accident.

When he got to the center he walked down a long, gleaming hall in which young men who had injured their spines lay on portable frames, stomach-down to allow bedsores to heal. They silently watched him walk down the corridor. One had fallen out of a tree in which he lost consciousness waiting for deer to appear; one had dived on the Fourth of July into the shallow end of the new pool he had just installed to celebrate a business success; one had driven his car into a telephone pole after stopping for a few beers following a football practice. Paralyzed weight lifters and hunters and professional linebackers, they lined the corridor now on their Stryker frames watching him with their silent eyes walk by. Accidents. On those icy nights on that hilltop overlooking the dark valley with its twinkling lights, he sat beside parents whose sons had crashed cars, whose daughters would never walk, whose own parents had broken their necks getting up one night to go to the bathroom, and he thought: Like Louis in New York. All accidents. Like the men who learned years later they had been exposed to Agent Orange, the teenager who loses control of his father's car and cripples two friends in the front seat for life, the queens returning to their families to die of a virus originating in Africa. Louis is a casualty, an accident, of the unpredictable, the unforeseen, the unimaginable, a mutating virus—Life is change. He read *The National Enquirer* now.

His eye went to the stories in the *Cincinnati Press* each day, which told of accidents, robberies, disasters. He imagined, wandering through the huge department stores in the mall, that there was an invisible store even more gigantic in which various tragedies were on sale: One could go to any of the many departments on different floors, but you could not leave the store without choosing one of them. Moments after his arrival at the rehabilitation center, a nurse's aide would wheel his mother out to him—her arms and legs in splints, her face bright red and slathered with Vaseline, exhausted by her physical therapy like an athlete after a long afternoon on some cold playing field. Together they would go down to a room filled with tropical plants and, while the wind whirled the snow around in miniature tornados on the field outside, read the letters of sympathy she had received. People always rose to the occasion. But like prayers for Louis nothing could really help. Nothing could give her back those millimeters of jellied cells through which, all her life, electrical impulses had passed unimpeded from the brain to the remotest muscles of her arms and legs. He left the rehabilitation center after dark, circling the hilltop from which he could see the lights twinkling in the valley below, then descending into the forests that obliterated them, conscious of a place he had never known before: the Palace of Accident. His own car hit a patch of ice exiting the freeway one December night, spun round a few moments, came to a stop inches from a deep ravine, but he was not even alarmed; the spinning seemed to occur in a dream; since Louis's illness, his parents' accidents, nothing surprised him anymore. Or rather, everything seemed arbitrary.

Yet he felt grateful for these other accidents right now: they provided an escape, a relief, from his own. Driving between the nursing home in which his father lay, losing circulation in his legs, so depressed he turned his face to the wall now when addressed, and the rehabilitation center in which his mother patiently attempted to move her hand across a piece of playwood, one-sixteenth of an inch at a time, it was important to him to keep *their* romance alive, *something* intact, in a world in which everything else had disintegrated. Though he had come out here the moment he learned of his mother's fall, it looked as if he were running away from Louis—failing him. He felt as if he, and the world, were split up, all of a sudden, and scattered not only between New York and Cincinnati, but the various hills of this town. And on those evenings of great depression, or, conversely, desire engendered by a few words with the computer salesman in the locker room at the Holiday Inn following his swim, he would get in the car and drive downtown. "Everybody's got a hungry heart!" the radio sang that winter, and he thought: You bet. Driving down through the red taillights of the other cars, down the freeway into the city, it seemed to him everything—his family's travails, Louis's illness, the sprawl of shopping malls, the computer salesman's chest, the icicles dripping down the side of a cliff above the highway in the light of the moon—would all, all of them, be distilled, like attar of rose, into the pale white body of the man he hoped to meet at the baths. But when he arrived, he found, in the lounge, one tired businessman in a towel, snoring on a banquette, while the images of "Family Feud" flashed across his plump white stomach. And he went downstairs and sat in an alcove by the steam room, waiting for someone to walk in: content, to merely be there, in the temple where he somehow belonged: hiding.

One night while he was sitting beside the vending machine watching the sandwiches revolve, an unemployed biologist working part-time as a school janitor came in—a kind, stocky fellow who stuttered and lived at home with his parents in a town twenty minutes from Ned's. They met again at a dirty bookstore in the edge of an enormous parking lot attached to a shopping mall—and then in the parking lot itself, late on a Sunday afternoon when the stores were closed. When he telephoned him at home to arrange a meeting, his mother answered, and then the biologist came on, stuttering, with gaps so long between syllables, Ned sat there finding peace in the stillness between consonants, half-listening for wind chimes, thinking: Plague or no plague, I suspect I would eventually have been sitting at this telephone somewhere down the road, waiting for this man to complete the word "together." He was forty. He could not say for sure how the life he had been leading—much less the society in which he had lived—would have evolved, but he sensed he would have eventually grown too old, or tired of it, and come back here looking for peace and innocence. The janitor agreed to meet him in the enormous dark and empty parking lot that stretched beside a freeway called the Miracle Mile on the blazing hill Ned saw from the cemetery. Ned had never had sex in a car. The janitor had never gone to New York. And that summed up the difference. The glove compartment of the janitor's decrepit Pontiac was stuffed with pornographic magazines, bottles of amyl nitrite, lubricant and cockrings; and when they had sex the first time in the car, Ned had to stop to wait for the janitor to stutter: "Would you please bite my nipples harder?" It became clear the janitor was at the other end of a journey Ned was completing, and he was not surprised when the janitor moved to New York after Thanksgiving.

Mister Lark came out in the other direction a week before

Christmas—on his way to get an heirloom, a sea chest from an aunt in Peoria, Illinois, who was moving into a retirement home. They embraced on the station platform, Mister Lark crushing Ned against his ubiquitous three-piece suit, and murmuring over and over again in a priestly monotone: "Dear boy, dear boy, how good to see you again at last." The impression that they were meeting in some British war movie only deepened when, beyond the shoulder he was looking over, Ned saw a pale, gaunt, shrunken young man get off the train, followed by a porter carrying his bag, which a middle-aged woman, the youth's mother, Ned assumed, bent to pick up after kissing him on the cheek. He stared at the young man, whose illness he recognized instantly, as if he were a soldier returning from some far-off, horrible war. The young man stared back at him, his eyes outraged. He looked furious. They stared at each other—across the awful chasm that separates the sick from the well—and then the mother picked up the suitcase and began dragging it across the platform, as she said: "I haven't carried anything this heavy since I was pregnant with *you!*" And they went off nearly at the same pace, he shuffling like an invalided soldier, she dragging the valise.

Mister Lark turned back to Ned and said: "It just gets worse, dear boy. It's like living in the Blitz. You never know when the next bomb is going to go off."

"How's Louis?" Ned said.

"Fine," said Mister Lark, "except he's blind. He lies at home all afternoon now listening to Mozart. Imagine discovering Mozart, so late in life. But then Louis was a creature of the discotheques. And you?" he said. "He asks about you—how you are holding up?"

"Okay," said Ned.

"You know, I worry about what you're getting into," he said, sitting down on a bench not far from the train. "I know you feel you have a duty to your parents, but you must realize this condition of your mother's could go on for years and years. What will you do then? I don't think she would want you to give up your own life for hers."

"Oh, she does," said Ned. "Anyway, I have no life. To give up. Or rather, what else should I do with the life I have?"

The conductor on the platform began to call "All aboard!"

They stood up. "You won't stay overnight?" said Ned. "I can't," said Mister Lark. "My aunt is moving Wednesday. Though please give my best to your sister—I spoke to her only a moment, but it was enough to feel her essential goodness. Dear boy, I don't want you to think this is the end of everything. Louis was, as you know, planning to go around the world before this happened. On the *QE2!* This is no reason to stop living!" he said as he stepped into the train. "Keep writing! I read your letters to him. I'll call you if anything happens!" he said as the train began to move. He waved. Ned waved back. And the train went around the corner, and Ned saw a man turn toward him down the platform who looked exactly like the trumpeter. That's all there is now, he thought as he and the man walked toward each other to the stairs: Helping other people, and sex. But the man didn't look at him; and there seemed to be lacking that intensity, that medium conducive to desire, that characterized the space between two people in New York. ("They look at you," Mister Lark told him a month after he'd moved to Manhattan, when he was still perplexed by the frank gaze of strangers on the street, "because they want to see what you are. It's not always sexual.") But at least it was a look. Out here, those little houses on the hillside contained most people's emotions. Out here no one looked. Out here you just passed each other in cars. He got into his. Seeing Mister Lark for twenty minutes had produced a letdown, he realized as he turned the ignition key, rather than joy; a confirmation that he was alone now, and everyone he cared for scattered irrevocably. He drove home calmly, listening to an all-talk radio program argue school integration ("There are only two topics in American life," Mister Lark said, "Negroes and cholesterol") and when he found himself at the spot where his car had spun on the patch of ice, he pulled off the road onto the gravel ledge that had saved his life, put down the window, and sat there watching night fall across the hills and ravines. Life is organization, he thought. Things cohere, then disintegrate, then cohere again—in little clumps called Childhood, Family, Youth, Friends. Now I am in a period of disintegration, he thought, and everyone I love is scattered and I am all alone. He sat there for an hour looking at the twinkling lights until he got cold.

SKINNED ALIVE

• EDMUND WHITE •

I FIRST SAW him at a reading in Paris. An American writer, whom everyone had supposed dead, had come to France to launch a new translation of his classic book, originally published twenty-five years earlier. The young man in the audience who caught my eye had short red-blond hair and broad shoulders (bodyguard broad, commando broad) and an unsmiling gravity. When he spoke English, he was very serious; when he spoke French, he looked amused.

He was seated on the other side of the semicircle surrounding the author, who was slowly, sweetly, suicidally disappointing the young members of his audience. They had all come expecting to meet Satan, for hadn't he summed up his pages a brutish vision of gang rape in burned-out lots, of drug betrayals and teenage murders? But what they faced now was a reformed drunk given to optimism, offering us brief recipes for recovery and serenity—not at all what the spiky-haired audience had had in mind. I was charmed by the writer's hearty laugh and pleased that he'd been able to trade in his large bacchanalian genius for a bit of happiness. But his new writings were painful to listen to and my eyes wandered restlessly over the book shelves. I was searching out interesting new titles, saluting familiar ones, reproaching a few.

And then I had the young man to look at. He had on black trousers full in the calf and narrow in the thighs, his compact waist cinched in by a thick black belt and a gold buckle. His torso was concealed by an extremely ample, long-sleeved black shirt, but despite its fullness I could still see the broad, powerful chest, the massive shoulders and biceps—the body of a professional killer. His neck was thick, like cambered marble.

My French friend Hélène nudged me and whispered, "There's one for you." Maybe she said that later, during the discussion period after the young man had asked a question that revealed his complete familiarity with the text. He had a tenor voice he'd worked to lower or perhaps he was just shy—one, in any event, that made me think of those low notes a cellist draws out of his instrument by slowly sawing the bow back and forth while fingering a tremolo with the other hand.

From his accent I couldn't be certain he was American; he might be German, a nationality that seemed to accommodate his contradictions better—young but dignified, athletic but intellectual. There was nothing about him of the brash American college kid, the joker who has been encouraged to express all his opinions, including those that have just popped into his head. The young man respected the author's classic novel so much that he made me want to take it more seriously. I liked the way he referred to specific scenes as though they were literary sites known to everyone. This grave young man was probably right, the scandalous books always turn out to be the good ones.

Yes. Hélène must have nudged me after his question, because she's attracted to men only if they're intelligent. If they're literary, all the better, since, when she's not reading, she's talking about books. I'll phone her toward noon and she'll say, "I'm in China," or, "Today, it's the Palais Royale," or, "Another unhappy American childhood," depending on whether the book is a guide, a memoir or a novel. She worries about me and wants me to find someone, preferably a Parisian, so I won't get any funny ideas about moving back to New York. She and I always speak in English. If I trick her into continuing in French after an evening with friends, she'll suddenly catch herself and say indignantly, "But why in earth are we speaking French!" She claims to be bilingual, but she speaks French to her cats. People dream in the language they use on their cats.

She is too discreet, even with me, her closest friend, to solicit any details about my intimate life. Once, when she could sense Jean-Loup was making me unhappy, I said to her, "But you know I do have two other . . . people I see from time to time," and she smiled, patted my hand and said, "Good. Very good. I'm delighted." Another time she shocked me. I asked her what I should say to a jealous lover, and she replied, "The answer to the question, 'Are you faithful, *chéri?*' is always 'Yes.' " She made vague efforts to meet and even charm the different men who passed through my life (her Japanese clothes, low voice and blue-tinted glasses impressed them all). But I could tell she disapproved of most of them. "It's Saturday," she would say. "Jean-Loup must be rounding you up for your afternoon shopping spree. " If ever I said anything against him, she would dramatically bite her lip, look me in the eye and nod.

But I liked to please Jean-Loup. And if I bought him his clothes every Saturday, he would let me take them off again, piece by piece, to expose his boyish body, a body as lean-hipped and priapic as those Cretan youths painted on the walls of Minos's palace. On one hip, the color of wedding-gown satin, he had a mole, which the French more accurately call a *grain de beauté.*

Since Jean-Loup came from a solid middle-class family but had climbed a social rung, he had the most rigid code of etiquette, and I owe him the slight improvements I've made in my impressionistic American table manners, learned thirty years ago among boarding-school savages. Whereas Americans are taught to keep their unused hand in their laps at table, the French are so filthy-minded they assume hidden hands are the devil's workshop. Whereas Americans clear each plate as soon as it's finished, the French wait for everyone to complete their meal. That's the sort of thing he taught me. To light a match after one has smelled up a toilet. To greet the most bizarre story with the comment, "But that's perfectly normal." To be careful to serve oneself from the cheese tray no more than once ("Cheese is the only course a guest has the right to refuse," he told me, "and the only dish that should never be passed twice").

Also not to ask so many questions or volunteer so many answers. After a two-hour train ride he'd ask me if I had had enough time to confide to the stranger at my side all the details of my unhappy American childhood. Like most Frenchmen who have affairs with Americans, he was attracted to my "niceness" and "simplicity" (ambiguous compliments at best), but had set out to reform those very qualities, which became weaknesses once I was granted the high status of honorary Frenchman. "Not Frenchman," he would say. "You'll never be French. But you are a Parisian. No one can deny that." Then to flatter me he would add, "*Plus parisien tu meurs*," though just then I felt I'd die if I were less, not more Parisian.

But if Jean-Loup was always "correct" in the salon, he was "vicious" and "perverse" (high compliments in French) in the boudoir. The problem was that he didn't like to see me very often. He loved me but wasn't in love with me, that depressing (and all too translatable) distinction ("*Je t'aime mais je ne suis pas amoureux*"). He was always on the train to Bordeaux, where his parents lived and where he'd been admitted to several châteaus, including some familiar even to me because they were on wine labels. He'd come back with stories of weekend country parties at which the boys got drunk and tore off the girls' designer dresses and then everyone went riding bareback at dawn. He had a set of phrases for describing these routs ("*On s'éclatait;*" "*On se marrait;*" "*On était fou, mais vraiment fou et on a bien rigolé*"), which all meant they had behaved disreputably with the right people within decorous limits. After all they were all in their own "milieu." He slept with a few of the girls and was looking to marry one who would be intelligent, not ugly, distinguished, a good sport and a slut in bed. He was all those things, so he was only looking for his counterpart. He even asked me to help him. "You go everywhere, you meet everyone," he said, "you've fixed up so many of your friends, find me someone like Brigitte but better groomed, a good slut who likes men. Of course, even if I married that would never affect our relationship." Recently he'd decided that he would inform his bride-to-be that he was homosexual; he just knew she'd be worldly about it.

With friends Jean-Loup was jolly and impertinent, quick to trot out his "horrors," as he called them, things that would make the girls scream and the boys blush. Twice he showed his penis at mixed dinner parties. Even so, his "horrors" were, while shocking, kindhearted and astute. He never asked about money or class, questions that might really embarrass a French man. He would sooner ask about blow-jobs than job prospects, cock-size than the size of a raise. In our funny makeshift circle—which I had cobbled together to amuse him and which fell apart when he left me—the girls were witty, uncomplicated and heterosexual, and the boys handsome and homo. We were resolutely silly and made enormous occasions out of each other's birthdays and saint's days. Our serious, intimate conversations took place only between two people, usually over the phone.

I neglected friends my own age. I never spoke English or talked about books except with Hélène. A friend from New York said, after staying with me for a week, that I was living in a fool's paradise, a gilded playpen filled with enchanting, radiant nymphs and satyrs who offered me "no challenge." He disapproved of the way I was willing to take just crumbs from Jean-Loup.

Brioche crumbs, I thought.

I didn't know how to explain that now that so many of my old friends in New York had died—my best friend, and also my editor, a real friend as well—I preferred my playpen, where I could be twenty-five again but French this time. When reminded of my real age and nationality, I then *played* at being older and American. Youth and age seemed equally theatrical. Maybe the unreality was the effect of living in another language, of worrying about how many slices of *chèvre* one could take and of buying pretty clothes for a bisexual Bordelais. At about this time a punk interviewed me on television and asked, "You are known as a homosexual, a writer and an American. When did you first realize you were an American?"

"When I moved to France," I said.

That Jean-Loup was elusive could not be held against him. He warned me from the first he was in full flight. What I didn't grasp was that he was running toward someone even he couldn't name yet. Despite his lucid way of making distinctions about other people ("She's not a liar but a mythomaniac; her lying serves no purpose") he was indecisive about everything in his own future: Would he marry or become completely gay? Would he stay in business or develop his talent, drawing adult comic strips? Would he remain in Paris or continue shuttling between it and Bordeaux? I teased him, calling him, "Monsieur Charnière" ("Mister Hinge").

Where he could be decisive was in bed. He had precise highly colored fantasies, which I deduced from his paces and those he put me through. He never talked about his desires until the last few times we had sex, just before the end of our "story" as the French call an affair; his new talkativeness I took as a sign that he'd lost interest in me or at least respect for me, and I was right. Earlier he had never talked about his desire, but hurled it against me: he needed me here not there, like this not that. I felt desired for the first time in years.

My friends, especially Hélène, but even the other children in the playpen, assumed Jean-Loup was genteelly fleecing me with my worldly, cheerful complicity, but I knew I had too little money to warrant such a speculation. He'd even told me that if it was money he was after he could find a man far richer than me. In fact I knew I excited him. That's why I had to find him a distinguished slut for a wife. I had corrupted him, he told me, by habituating him to sex that was "hard," which the French pronounced "ard" as in *ardent* and, out of a certain deference, never elide with the preceding word.

He didn't mind if I talked during sex, telling him who he was, where we were and why I had to do all this to him. I was used to sex raps from the drug-taking 1970s. Now, of course, there were no drugs and I had to find French words for my obsessions, and when I sometimes made a mistake in gender or verb form Jean-Loup would wince. He wouldn't mention it later; he didn't want to talk anything over later. Only once, after he'd done something very strange to me, he asked, laughing as he emerged from the shower, "Are you the crazy one or am I? I think we're both crazy." He seemed very pleased.

For the first year we'd struggled to be "lovers" officially, but he devoted more of his energy to warding me off than embracing me. He had a rule that he could never stay on after a dinner at my place; he would always leave with the other members of the playpen. To stay behind would look too domestic, he thought, too queer, too *pédé*. After a year of such partial intimacy I got fed up. More likely I became frightened that Jean-Loup, who was growing increasingly remote, would suddenly drop me. I broke up with him over dinner in a restaurant. He seemed relieved and said, "I would never have dared to take the first step." He was shaken for two or three days, then recovered nicely. As he put it, he "supported celibacy" quite effortlessly. It felt natural to him, it was his natural condition.

I went to New York for a week. By chance he went there after I returned. When we saw each other again in Paris we were as awkward as adolescents. His allergies were acting up; American food had made him put on two kilos; a New York barber had thrown his meaty ears into high relief. "It's terrible," Jean-Loup said, "I wanted my independence, but now that I have it . . . Undress me." I did so, triumphant while registering his admission that he was the one after all who had wanted to be free.

After that we saw each other seldom but when we did it was always passionate. The more people we told that we were no longer lovers, the more violent our desire for each other became. I found his heavy balls, which he liked me to hold in my mouth while I looked up at him. I found the mole on his smooth haunch. Because of his allergies he couldn't tolerate colognes or deodorants; I was left with his natural kid-brother smell. We had long passed through the stage of smoking marijuana together or using sex toys or dressing each other up in bits of finery. Other couples I knew became kinkier and kinkier over the years if they continued having sex or else resigned themselves to the most routine, suburban relief. We were devouring each other with a desire that was ever purer and sharper. Of course such a desire is seldom linked to love. It can be powerful when solicited but quickly forgotten when absent, since it may never have played a part in one's dreams of the future.

Perhaps the threat of ending things altogether, which we'd just averted, had made us keener. More likely, Jean-Loup, now that he thought he'd become less homosexual by shedding a male lover, me, felt freer to indulge drives that had become more urgent precisely because they were less well defined. Or perhaps I'm exaggerating my importance in his eyes; as he once said, he didn't like to wank his head over things like that ("*Je ne me branle pas trop la tête*").

I was in love with him and, during sex, thought of that love, but I tried to conceal it from him.

I tried to expect nothing, see him when I saw him, pursue other men, as though I were strictly alone in the world. For the first time when he asked me if I had other lovers I said I did and even discussed them with him. He said he was relieved, explaining that my adventures exonerated him from feeling responsible for me and my happiness. He was a lousy lover, he said, famous for being elusive; even his girlfriends complained about his slipperiness. That elusiveness, I would discover, was his protest against his own passivity, his longing to be owned.

Things changed day by day between us. He said he wasn't searching for other sexual partners; he preferred to wait until he fell in love, revealing that he didn't see us becoming lovers again. Nor was he in such a hurry to find a distinguished and sympathetic slut for a wife. When I asked him about his marital plans, he said that he was still looking forward to settling down with a wife and children someday but that now he recognized that when he thought of rough sex, of *la baise harde*, he thought of men. And again he flatteringly blamed me for having corrupted him even while he admitted he was looking for someone else, another man, to love.

Once in a very great while he referred to me playfully as his "husband," despite his revulsion against camp. I think he was trying to come up with a way that would let our friendship continue while giving each of us permission to pursue other people. Once he somberly spoke of me as his *patron* but I winced and he quickly withdrew the description. I wouldn't have minded playing his father, but that never occurred to him.

I'm afraid I'm making him sound too cold. He also had a sweet kid-brother charm, especially around women. All those former debutantes from Bordeaux living in Paris felt free to ask him to run an errand or install a bookcase, which he did with unreflecting devotion. He was careful (far more careful than any American would have been) to distinguish between a pal and a friend, but the true friends exercised an almost limitless power over him. Jean-Loup was quite proud of his capacity for friendship. When he would say that he was a rotten lover— elusive, unsure of his direction—he'd also assure me that he'd always remain my faithful friend, and I believed him. I knew that he was, in fact, waiting for our passion to wear itself out so that a more decent friendship could declare itself.

He wasn't a friend during sex or just afterward, he'd always shower, dress and leave as quickly as possible. Once, when he glanced back at the rubble we had made of the bedroom, he said all that evidence of our bestiality disgusted him. Nor was he specially kind to me around our playmates. To them, paradoxically, he enjoyed demonstrating how thoroughly he was at home in my apartment. He was the little lord of the manor. Yet he'd compliment me on how well I "received" people and assure me I could always open a restaurant in New York someday if my career as a writer petered out. He didn't take my writing too seriously. It had shocked him the few times he'd dipped into it. He preferred the lucidity and humanism of Milan Kundera, his favorite writer. In fact none of our playmates read me, and their indifference pleased me. It left me alone with my wet sand.

He took a reserved interest in my health. He was relieved that my blood tests every six months suggested the virus was still dormant. He was pleased I no longer smoked or drank (though like most French people he didn't consider champagne alcoholic). During one of our sex games he poured half a bottle of red Sancerre down my throat; the etiquette of the situation forbade my refusal, but it was the only time I had tasted alcohol in nearly ten years. We were convinced that the sort of sex we practiced might be demented but was surely safe; in fact we had made it demented since it had to stay safe.

He was negative. While he waited for his results, he said that if they turned out positive his greatest regret would be that he wouldn't be able to father children. A future without a family seemed unbearable. As long as his boy's body with its beautifully shaped man's penis remained unmarked, without a sign of its past or a curse over its future, he was happy to lend himself to our games.

Sometimes his laugh was like a shout—boyish, the sound, but the significance, knowing Parisian. He laughed to show that he hadn't been taken in or that he had caught the wicked allusion. When I was in the kitchen preparing the next course, I'd smile if I heard his whoop. I liked it that he was my husband, so at home, so sociable, so lighthearted, but our marriage was just a poor invention of my own fancy.

It reassured me that his sexuality was profoundly, not modishly, violent. He told me that when he had been a child, just seven or eight, he had built a little town out of cardboard and plywood, painted every shutter and peopled every house, and then set the whole construction afire and watched the conflagration with a bone-hard, inch-long erection. Is that why just touching me made him hard now (bone-hard, foot-long)? Could he see I was ablaze with ardor for him (ardor with a silent *h*)?

The violence showed up again in the comic strips he was always drawing. He had invented a sort of Frankenstein monster in good French clothes, a creature disturbed by his own half-human sentiments in a world otherwise populated by robots. When I related his comics to the history of art, he'd smile a gay, humiliated smile, the premonitory form of his whooping, disabused Parisian laugh. He was ashamed I made so much of his talent, though his talent was real enough.

He didn't know what to do with his life. He was living as ambitious, healthy young men live who have long vistas of time before them: despairingly. I, who had already outlived my friends and had fulfilled some of my hopes but few of my desires (desire won't stay satisfied), lived each day with joy and anguish. Jean-Loup expected his life to be perfect: there was apparently going to be so much of it.

Have I mentioned that Jean-Loup had such high arches that walking hurt him? He had one of his feet broken, lowered and screwed shut in metal vices that were removed six months later. His main reason for the operation was to escape the bank for a few weeks. His clinic room was soon snowed under with comic strip adventures. After that he walked with a bit of a Chaplinesque limp when he was tired.

I often wondered what his life was like with the other young Bordelais counts and countesses at Saint Jean-de-Luz every August. I was excluded from that world—the chance of my being introduced to his childhood friends had never even once entered his head—which made me feel like a *demi-mondaine* listening avidly to her titled young lover's accounts of his exploits in the great world. Although I presented Jean-Loup to my literary friends in London, he had few opinions about them beyond his admiration for the men's clothes and the women's beauty and apparent intelligence. "It was all so fast and brilliant," he said, "I scarcely understood a word." He blamed me for not helping him with his English, though he hated the sounds I made when I spoke my native language. "You don't have an accent in French—oh, you have your little accent, but it's nothing, very charming. But in American you sound like a duck, it's frightful!"

I suppose my English friends thought it was a sentimental autumn-and-spring affair. One friend, who lent us her London house for a few days, said, "Don't let the char see you and Jean-Loup nude." I thought the warning seemed bizarre until I understood it as an acknowledgment of our potential for sensual mischief. Perhaps she was particularly alive to sensual possibilities, since she was so proud of her own handsome, young husband.

After I returned to Paris, I spent my days alone reading and writing, and in fair weather I'd eat a sandwich on the quay. That January the Seine overflowed and flooded the highway on the Right Bank. Seagulls flew upstream and wheeled above the turbulent river, crying, as though mistaking Notre Dame for Mont-St. Michel. The floodlights trained on the church's façade projected ghostly shadows of the two square towers up into the foggy night sky, as though spirits were doing axonometric drawings of a cathedral I had always thought of as malign. The gargoyles were supposed to ward off evil, but to me they looked like dogs straining to leap away from the devil comfortably lodged within.

I went to Australia and New Zealand for five weeks. I wrote Jean-Loup many letters, in French, believing that the French language tolerated love better than English, but when I returned to Paris Jean-Loup complained of my style. He found it "*mièvre*," "wimpy" or "wet."

He said I should write about his ass one day, but in a style that was neither pornographic nor wimpy. He wanted me to describe his ass as Francis Ponge describes soap: an objective, exhaustive, whimsical catalog of its properties.

I wanted someone else, but I distrusted that impulse, because it seemed, if I looked back, I could see that I had never been happy in love and that with Jean-Loup I was happier than usual. As he pointed out, we were still having sex after two years, and he ascribed the intensity to the very infrequency that I deplored. Even so, I thought there was something all wrong, fundamentally wrong, with me: I set up a lover as a god, then burned with rage when he proved mortal. I lay awake, next to one lover after another, in a rage, dreaming of someone who'd appreciate me, give me the simple affection I imagined I wanted.

When I broke off with Jean-Loup over dinner he said, "You deserve someone better, someone who will love you completely." Yet the few times I had been loved "completely" I felt suffocated. Nor could I imagine a less aristocratic lover, one who'd sit beside me on the couch, hand in hand, and discuss the loft bed, the "mezzanine," we should buy with the cunning little chair and matching desk underneath.

But when I was alone night after night, I resented Jean-Loup's independence. He said I deserved something better, and I knew I merited less but needed more.

It was then I saw the redhead at the reading. Although I stared holes through him, he never looked at me once. It occurred to me that he might not be homosexual, except that his grave military bearing was something only homosexuals could (or would bother to) contrive if they weren't actually soldiers. His whole look and manner were studied. Let's say he was the sort of homosexual other homosexuals recognize but that heterosexuals never suspect.

The next day I asked the owner of the bookstore if she knew the redhead. "He comes into the shop every so often," she said, with a quick laugh to acknowledge the character of my curiosity, "but I don't know his name. He bought one of your books. Perhaps he'll come to your reading next week."

I told her to be sure to get his name if he returned. "You were a diplomat once," I reminded her. She promised but when I phoned a few days later she said he hadn't been in. Then on the night of my reading I saw him sitting in the same chair as before and I went up to him with absolute confidence and said, "I'm so glad you came tonight. I saw you at the last reading, and my *copine* and I thought you looked so interesting we wished we knew you." He looked so blank that I was afraid he hadn't understood and I almost started again in French. I introduced myself and shook his hand. He went white and said, "I'm sorry for not standing up," and then stood up and shook my hand, and I was afraid he'd address me as "sir."

Now that I could look at his hair closely I noticed that it was blond, if shavings of gold are blond, only on the closely cropped sides but that it was red on top—the reverse of the sun-bleached strawberry blond. He gave me his phone number, and I thought this was someone I could spend the rest of my life with, however brief that might be. His name was Paul.

I phoned him the next day to invite him to dinner, and he said that he had a rather strange schedule, since he worked four nights a week for a disco.

"What do you do?" I asked.

"I'm the physiognomist. The person who recognizes the regulars and the celebrities. I have to know what Brigitte Bardot looks like *now*. I decide who comes in, who stays out, who pays, who doesn't. We have a house rule to let all models in free." He told me people called him Cerberus.

"But how do you recognize everyone?"

"I've been on the door since the club opened seven years ago. So I have ten thousand faces stored in my memory." He laughed. "That's why I could never move back to America. I'd never find a job that paid so well for just twenty hours' work a week. And in America I couldn't do the same job, since I don't know any faces there."

We arranged an evening and he arrived dressed in clothes by one of the designers he knew from the club. Not even my reactionary father, however, would have considered him a pop-injay. He did nothing that would risk his considerable dignity. He had white tulips in his surprisingly small, elegant hand.

All evening we talked literature, and, as two good Americans, we also exchanged confidences. Sometimes his shyness brought all the laughter and words to a queasy halt, and it made me think of that becalmed moment when a sailboat comes around and the mainsail luffs before it catches the wind again. I watched the silence play over his features.

He was from a small town in Georgia. His older brother and he had each achieved highest score in the state-wide scholastic aptitude test. They had not pulled down good grades, however;

they read Plato and *Naked Lunch*, staged *No Exit* and brawls with the boys in the next town, experimented with hallucinogens and conceptual art. Paul's brother made an "art work" out of his plans to assassinate President Ford and was arrested by the FBI.

"I just received the invitation to my tenth high-school reunion," Paul said.

"I'll go with you," I said. "I'll go as your spouse."

He looked at me and breathed a laugh, save it was voiced just at the end, the moving bow finally touching the bass string and waking sound in it.

Paul's older brother had started a rock band, gone off to New York, where he died of AIDS—another musician punished. He had been one of the first heterosexual male victims—dead already in 1981. He contracted the disease from a shared needle. Their mother, a Scottish immigrant, preferred to think he had been infected by another man. Love seemed a nobler cause of death than drugs.

"Then I came to Paris," Paul said. He sighed and looked out of my open window at the roofs of the Ile St. Louis. Like other brilliant young men and women he suspended every solid in a solution of irony, but even he had certain articles of faith, and the first was Paris. He liked French manners, French clothes, French food, French education. He said things like, "France still maintains cultural hegemony over the whole world," and pronounced "hegemony" as "*hégémonie*." He had done all his studies as an adult in France and French. He asked me what the name of *Platon's Le Banquet* was in English (*The Symposium*, for some reason). He had a lively, but somewhat vain, sense of what made him interesting, which struck me only because he seemed so worthy of respect that any attempt to serve himself up appeared irrelevant.

He was wearing a white shirt and dark tie and military shoes and a beautiful dark jacket that was cut to his Herculean chest and shoulders. He had clear eyes, pale blue eyes. The white tulips he brought were waxen and pulsing like lit candles, and his skin, that rich hairless skin, was tawny-colored. His manners were formal and French, a nice Georgia boy but Europeanized, someone who'd let me lazily finish my sentences in French ("*quand même*," we'd say "*rien à voir avec . . .*"). His teeth were so chalky white that the red wine stained them a faint blue.

His face was at once open and unreadable, as imposing as the globe. He nodded slowly as he thought over what I said, so slowly that I doubted the truth or seriousness of what I was saying. He hesitated and his gaze was noncommittal, making me wonder if he was pondering his own response or simply panicking. I wouldn't have thought of him panicking except he mentioned it. He said he was always on the edge of panic (the sort of thing Americans say to each other with big grins). Points of sweat danced on the bridge of his nose, and I thought I saw in his eye something frightened, even unpleasant and unreachable. I kept thinking we were too much alike, as though at any moment our American heartiness and our French *politesse* would break down and we'd look at each other with the sour familiarity of brothers. Did he sense it, too? Is that why our formality was so important to him? I was sure he hadn't liked himself in America.

Speaking French so long had made me simplify my thoughts—whether expressed in French or English—and I was pleased I could say now what I felt, since the intelligence I was imputing to him would never have tolerated my old vagueness. Whereas Jean-Loup had insisted I use the right fork, I felt Paul would insist on the correct emotion.

Sometimes before he spoke Paul made a faint humming sound—perhaps only voiced shyness—but it gave the impression of the slightest deference. It made me think of a student half-raising his hand to talk to a seminar too small and egalitarian to require the teacher's recognition to speak. But I also found myself imagining that his thought was so varied, occurring on so many levels at once that the hum was a strictly mechanical downshift into the compromise (and invention) of speech. After a while the hum disappeared, and I fancied he felt more at ease with me, although the danger is always to read too much into what handsome men say and do. Although he was twenty years younger, he seemed much older than me.

"Would you like to go to Morocco with me?" I asked him suddenly. "For a week? A magazine will pay our fares. It's the south of Morocco. It should be amusing. I don't know it at all, but I think it's better to go somewhere brand new—" ("with a lover" were the words I suppressed).

"Sure."

He said he hadn't traveled anywhere in Europe or Africa except for two trips to Italy.

Although I knew things can't be rushed, that intimacy follows its own sequence, I found myself saying, "We should be lovers—you have everything, beauty and intelligence." Then I added: "And we get on so well." My reasoning was absurd: his beauty and intelligence were precisely what made him unavailable.

I scarcely wanted him to reply. As long as he didn't I could nurse my illusions. "That would depend," he said, "on our being compatible sexually, don't you think?" Then he asked, with his unblinking gravity, "What's your sexuality like?" For the first time I could hear a faint Georgia accent in the way the syllables of *sexuality* got stretched out.

"It depends on the person," I said, stalling. Then, finding my answer lamentable, I pushed all my chips forward on one number: "I like pain."

"So do I," he said. "And my penis has never—no man has ever touched it."

He had had only three lovers and they had all been heterosexuals or fancied they were. In any event they had had his sort of *pudeur* about using endearments to another man. He had a lover now, Thierry, someone he met two years before at the club. The first time they saw each other, Paul had been tanked up on booze, smack and steroids, a murderous cocktail, and they had a fistfight which had dissolved into a night of violent passion.

Every moment must have been haloed in his memory, for he remembered key phrases Thierry had used. For the last two years they had eaten every meal together. Thierry dressed him in the evening before Paul left for work and corrected his French and table manners. These interventions were often nasty, sometimes violent. "What language are you speaking now?" he would demand if Paul made the slightest error. When Paul asked for a little tenderness in bed, Thierry would say, "Oh-ho, like Mama and Papa now, is it?" and then leave the room. Paul fought back—he broke his hand once because he hit Thierry so hard. "Of course *he'd* say that it was all my fault," Paul said, "that all he wants is peace, blue skies." He smiled. "Thierry is a businessman, very dignified. He has never owned a piece of leather in his life. I despise leather. It robs violence of all the"—his smile now radiant, the mainsail creaking as it comes around—"the *sacramental*." He laughed, shaking, and made a strange chortle that I didn't really understand. It came out of a sensibility I hadn't glimpsed in him before.

Paul longed for us to reach the desert; he had never seen it before.

We started out at Agadir and took a taxi to the mud-walled town of Taroudannt. There we hired a car and drove to Ouarzazate, which had been spoiled by organized tourism: it had become Anywhere Sunny. Then we drove south to Zagora. It was just twenty kilometers beyond Zagora, people said, that the desert started. I warned Paul the desert could be disappointing: "You're never alone. There's always someone spying on you from over the next dune. And it rains. I saw the rain pour over Syria."

Paul loved maps. Sometimes I could see in him the solitary Georgia genius in love with his best friend's father, the sheriff, a kid lurking around home in the hot, shuttered afternoons, daydreaming over the globe that his head so resembled, his mind racing on homemade LSD. He knew how to refold maps, but when they were open he would press his palms over their creases as though opening his own eyes wider and wider.

I did all the driving, through adobe cities built along narrow, palm-lined roads. In every town boys wanted to be our guides, sell us trinkets or carpets or their own bodies. They hissed at us at night from the shadows of town walls: lean and finely muscled adolescents hissing to attract our attention, their brown hands massaging a lump beneath the flowing blue acrylic *jellabias* mass-produced in China. To pass them up with a smile was a new experience for me. I had Paul beside me, this noble pacing lion. I remembered a Paris friend calling me just before we left for Morocco, saying he had written a letter to a friend, "telling him I'd seen you walking down the boulevard St. Germain beside the young Hercules with hair the color of copper." In

Morocco there was no one big enough, powerful enough or cruel enough to interest Paul.

Perhaps it was due to the clear, memorable way Paul had defined his sexual nature, but during our cold nights together I lay in his great arms and never once felt excited, just an immense feeling of peace and gratitude. Our predicament, we felt, was like a Greek myth. "Two people love each other," I said, "but the gods have cursed them by giving them the identical passions." I was being presumptuous, sneaking in the phrase, "Two people love each other," because it wasn't at all clear that he loved me.

One night we went to the movies and saw an Italian adventure film starring American weight lifters and dubbed in French, a story set in a back-lot castle with a perfunctory princess in hot pants. There was an evil prince whose handsome face melted to reveal the devil's underneath. His victim ("All heroes are masochists," Paul declared) was an awkward bodybuilder not yet comfortable in his newly acquired bulk, who had challenged the evil prince's supremacy and now must be flayed alive. Paul clapped and chortled and, during the tense scenes, physically braced himself. This was the Paul who had explained what Derrida had said of Heidegger's interpretation of Trakl's last poems, who claimed that literature could be studied only through rhetoric, grammar and genre, and who considered Ronsard a greater poet than Shakespeare (because of Ronsard's combination of passion and logic, satyr and god, in place of the mere conversational fluency which Paul regarded as the flaw and genius of English): this was the same Paul who booed and cheered as the villain smote the hero before a respectful audience thick with smoke and the flickers of flashlights. It was a movie in which big men were hurting each other.

Jean-Loup would have snorted, his worst prejudices about Americans confirmed, for as we traveled, drawing closer and closer to the desert, we confided more and more in each other. As we drove through the "valley of a thousand casbahs," Paul told me about threats to his life. "When someone at the club pulls a gun on me, and it's happened three times, I say, I'm sorry but guns are not permitted on the premises, and it works, they go away, but mine is a suicidal response." Paul was someone on whom nothing was wasted: nevertheless sometimes he was not always alive to all possibilities, at least not instantly. I told him I was positive, but he didn't react. Behind the extremely dark sunglasses, there was this presence, breathing and thinking but not reacting.

Our hotel, the Hesperides, had been built into the sun-baked mud ramparts in the ruins of the pasha's palace. We stared into an octagonal, palm-shaped pool glistening with black rocks that then slid and clicked—ah, tortoises! There couldn't have been more than five guests, and the porters, bored and curious, tripped over themselves serving us. We slept in each other's arms night after night and I stroked his great body as though he were a prize animal, *la belle bête*. My own sense of who I was in this story was highly unstable. I flickered back and forth, wanting to be the blond warrior's fleshy, harem-pale concubine or then the bearded pasha himself, feeding drugged sherbets to the beautiful Circassian slave I had bought. I thought seriously that I wouldn't mind buying and owning another human being—if it were Paul.

The next day we picked up some hitchhikers who, when we reached their destination, asked us in for mint tea, which we sipped barefoot in a richly carpeted room. A baby and a chicken watched us through the doorway from the sun-white courtyard. Every one of our encounters seemed to end with a carpet, usually one we were supposed to buy. In a village called Wodz, I remember both of us smiling as we observed how long and devious the path to the carpet could become: there was first a tourist excursion through miles of casbah, nearly abandoned except for an old veiled woman poking a fire in a now roofless harem; then we took a stroll through an irrigated palm plantation, where a woman leading a donkey took off her turban, a blue bath-towel, and filled it with dates which she gave us, with a golden grin; and finally we paid a "surprise visit" on the guide's "brother," the carpet merchant who happened to have just returned from the desert with exotic Tuareg rugs whose prices, to emphasize their exoticism, he pretended to translate from Tuareg dollars into dirham.

We laughed, bargained, bought, happy anytime our shoulders touched or eyes met. We told everyone we were Danes, since this was the one language even the most resourceful carpet merchants didn't know ("But wait, I have a cousin in the next village who once lived in Copenhagen").

Later, when I returned to Paris, I would discover that Jean-Loup had left me for Régis, one of the richest men in France. For the first time in his life he was in love, he would say. He would be wearing Régis's wedding ring, my Jean-Loup who had refused to stay behind at my apartment after the other guests had left lest he appear too *pédé*. People would suspect him of being interested in the limousine, the town house, the château, but Jean-Loup would insist it was all love.

When he told me, on my return, that he would never sleep with me again—that he had found the man with whom he wanted to spend the rest of his life—my response surprised him. "*Ça tombe bien*," I said ("That suits the situation perfectly").

Jean-Loup blurted out: "But you're supposed to be furious."

It wasn't that he wanted me to fight to get him back, though he might have enjoyed it, but that his vanity demanded that I protest: my own vanity made me concede him with a smile. Feverishly I filled him in on my recent passion for Paul and the strategies I had devised for unloading him, Jean-Loup. It's true I had tried to fix him up a week earlier with a well-heeled, handsome young American.

Jean-Loup's eyes widened. "I had no idea," he said, "that things had gone so far." Perhaps in revenge he told me how he had met Régis. It seems that, while I was away, a dear mutual friend had fixed them up.

I was suddenly furious and couldn't drop the subject. I railed and railed against the dear mutual friend: "When I think he ate my food, drank my drink, all the while plotting to marry you off to a millionaire in order to advance his own miserable little interests . . ."

"Let me remind you that Régis's money means nothing to me. No, what I like is his good humor, his sincerity, his discretion. It was hard for me to be known as your lover—your homosexuality is too evident. Régis is very discreet."

"What rubbish," I would say a few days later when Jean-Loup repeated the remark about Régis's discretion. "He's famous for surrounding himself with aunties who talk lace prices the livelong day."

"Ah," Jean-Loup replied, reassured, "you've been filled in, I see" ("*Tu t'es renseigné*").

All sparkling and droll, except a terrible sickness, like an infection caused by the prick of a diamond brooch, had set in. When I realized that I would never be able to abandon myself again to Jean-Loup's perverse needs, when I thought that Régis was enjoying the marriage with him I'd reconciled myself never to know, when I saw the serenity with which Jean-Loup now "assumed" his homosexuality, I felt myself sinking, but genuinely sinking, as though I really were falling, and my face had a permanently hot blush. I described this feeling of falling and heat to Paul. "That's jealousy," he said. "You're jealous." That must be it, I thought, I who had never been jealous before. If I had behaved so generously with earlier loves lost it was because I had never before been consumed by sensuality this feverish.

Jealousy, yes, it was jealousy, and never before had I so wanted to hurt someone I loved, and that humiliated me further. A member of the playpen dined at Régis's *hôtel particulier*. "They hold hands all the time," she said. "I was agreeably surprised by Régis, a charming man. The house is more a museum than a . . . house. Jean-Loup kept calling the butler for more champagne, and we almost burst out laughing. It was like a dream."

Every detail fed my rancor—Régis's charm, wealth, looks ("Not handsome but attractive").

Everything.

Paul had a photographic memory, and, during the hours spent together in the car in Morocco, he recited page after page of Racine or Ronsard or Sir Philip Sidney. He also continued the story of his life. I wanted to know every detail—the bloody scenes on the steps of the disco, the recourse to dangerous drugs, so despised by the clenched-jaw cocaine set. I wanted to hear that he credited his lover with saving him from being a junkie, a drunk and a thug. "He was the one who got me back into school."

"A master, I see," I thought. "*School* master."

"Now I study *Cicéron* and prepare my *maîtrise*, but then I was just an animal, a disoriented bull—I'd even gotten into beating up fags down by the Seine at dawn when I was really drunk."

He gave me a story he had written. It was Hellenistic in tone, precious and edgy, flirting with the diffuse lushness of a pre-Raphaelite prose, rich but bleached, like a tapestry left out in the sun. I suppose he must have had in mind Mallarmé's *The Prelude to the Afternoon of a Faun*, but Paul's story was more touching, less cold, more comprehensible. That such a story could never be published in the minimalist, plain-speaking 1980s seemed never to have occurred to him. Could it be that housed in such a massive body he had no need for indirect proofs of power and accomplishment? Or was he so sure of his taste that recognition scarcely interested him at all?

The story is slow to name its characters, but begins with a woman who turns out to be Athena. She's discovering the flute and how to get music out of it, but her sisters, seeing her puffing away, laugh at the face she's making. Athena throws the flute down and in a rage places a curse on it: "Whoever would make use of it next must die." Her humiliation would cost a life.

The next user is a cheerful satyr named Marsyas. He cleverly learns how to imitate people with his tunes: "Prancing along behind them he could do their walk, fast or slow, lurching or clipped, just as he could render their tics or trace their contours: a low swell for a belly, shrill fifing for fluttering hands, held high notes for the adagio of soft speech. At first no one understood. But once they caught on they slapped their thighs: his songs were sketches."

Apollo is furious, since he's the god of music and his own art is pure and abstract. He challenged Marsyas to a musical duel:

Marsyas cringed before them like a dog when it walks through a ghost, bares its teeth and pulls back its ears. Anguished, he had slept in the hot breath of his flock; his animals had pressed up against him, holding him between their woolly flanks, as though to warm him. The ribbon his jolly and jiggling woman had tied around one horn flapped listlessly against his low, hairy brow, like a royal banner flown by a worker's barge.

To the gods, as young as the morning, Marsyas seemed a twilit creature; he smelled of leaf mold and wolf-lair. His glance was as serious as a deer's when it emerges from the forest at dusk to drink at the calm pool collecting below a steaming cataract.

And to Marsyas his rival was cold and regular as cambered marble.

Since Marsyas knew to play only what was in front of him, he "rendered" Apollo—not the god's thoughts but the faults he wedged into the air around him. The sisters watched the goat-man breathe into the reeds, saw him draw and lose breath, saw his eyes bulge, brown and brilliant as honey, and that made them laugh. What they heard, however, was color that copied sacred lines, for Marsyas could imitate a god as easily as a bawd. The only trick was to have his model there, in front of him.

If Marsyas gave them the god's form, the god himself revealed the contents of his mind. His broad hand swept up the lyre, and immediately the air was tuned and the planets tempered. Everything sympathetic trembled in response to a song that took no one into account, that moved without moving, that polished crystal with its breath alone, clouding then cleansing every transparency without touching it. Marsyas shuddered when he came to and realized that the god's hand was now motionless but that the music continued to devolve, creaking like a finger turning and tracing the fragile rim of the spheres.

The satyr was astonished that the goddesses didn't decide instantly in their brother's favor but shrugged and smiled and said they found each contestant appealing in different ways. The sun brightened a fraction with Apollo's anger, but then the god suggested they each play their music backwards. The universe shuddered as it stopped and reversed its rotations; the sun started to descend toward dawn as Apollo unstrung the planets. Cocks re-crowed and bats re-awakened, the frightened shepherd guided his flock back down the hill as the dew fell again.

Even the muses were frightened. It was night and stormy when Marsyas began to play. He had improvised his music strophe by strophe as a portrait; now he couldn't remember it all. The descending figures, so languishing when played correctly the first time, made him queasy when he inverted them. Nor could he see his subject.

The muses decided in the god's favor. Apollo told Marsyas he'd be flayed alive. There was no tenderness but great solicitude in the way the god tied the rope around the satyr's withers, cast the slack over a high branch of a pine and then hoisted his kill high, upside down, inverted as the winning melody. Marsyas saw that he'd won the god's full attention by becoming his victim.

The blood ran to Marsyas's head, then spurted over his chest as Apollo sliced into his belly, neatly peeled back the flesh and fat and hair. The light shone in rays from Apollo's sapphire eyes and locked with Marsyas's eyes, which were wavering, losing grip—he could feel his eyes lose grip, just as a child falling asleep will finally relax its hold on its father's finger. A little dog beside his head was lapping up the fresh blood. Now the god knelt to continue his task. Marsyas could hear the quick sharp breaths, for killing him was hard work. The god's white skin glowed and the satyr believed he was inspiring the very breath Apollo expired.

As I read his story I stupidly wondered which character Paul was—the Apollo he so resembled and whose abstract ideal of art appeared to be his own, or the satyr who embodies the vital principle of mimesis and who, after all, submitted to the god's cruel, concentrated attention. The usual motive for the story, Apollo's jealousy, was left out altogether, as though pique were an emotion Paul didn't know (certainly he hadn't shown any in eight days on the road). His story was dedicated to me, and for a moment I wondered if it were also addressed to me—as a reproach for having abandoned the Apollonian abstractness of my first two novels or, on the contrary, as an endorsement for undertaking my later satires and sketches? It was unsettling dealing with this young man so brilliant and handsome, so violent and so reflective.

At night Paul let me into his bed and held me in his arms, just as he sometimes rested his hand on my leg as I drove the car. He told me that, although Thierry often petted him, Paul was never allowed to stroke him. "We've never once kissed each other on the lips."

We talked skittishly about the curse the gods had put on us. I pathetically attempted to persuade Paul he was really a sadist. "Your invariable rage after sex with your lover," I declared, melodramatically, "your indignation, your disgusting excursions into fag-bashing, your primitive, literalist belief that only the biggest man with the biggest penis has the right to dominate all the others, whereas the sole glory of sadism is its strictly cerebral capacity for imposing new values, your obvious attraction to my fundamentally docile nature"—and at that point my charlatanism would make me burst out laughing, even as I glanced sideways to see how I was doing.

In fact masochism sickened him. It reminded him of his own longing to recapture Thierry's love. "He left me," he would say. "When calls come in he turns the sound off on the answering machine and he never replays his messages when I'm around. His pockets bulge with condoms. He spends every weekend with purely fictive 'German businessmen' in Normandy; he pretends he's going to visit a factory in Nice, but he's back in Paris four hours later; he stood me up for the Mister Bodybuilding contest at the Parc de Vincennes then was seen there with a famous Brazilian model . . . He says I should see a psychiatrist, and you know how loony someone French must think you are to suggest that."

When a thoughtful silence had reestablished itself in the car I added, "That's why you want to reach the desert. Only its vast sterility can calm your violent soul."

"If you could be in my head," he said, not smiling, "you'd see I'm in a constant panic."

To be companionable I said, "Me too."

Paul quickly contradicted me: "But you're the calmest person I know."

Then I understood that was how he wanted me to be— masterful, confident, smiling, sure. Even if he would someday dominate, even hurt me, as I wished, he would never give me permission to suffer in any way except heroically.

I drove a few miles in silence through the lunar valley, mountains on both sides, not yet the desert but a coarse-grained prelude to it—dry, gently rolling, the boulders the color of eggplants. "You're right, except so many of the people I've known have died. The way we talk, you and me, about books and life and love. I used to talk this way with my best friend, but that was in America and now he is dead." That night, in Paul's arms, I said, "It's sacrilegious to say it, especially for an atheist, but I feel God sent you not to replace my friend, since he's irreplaceable, but . . ."

A carpet salesman assured us the desert was about to begin. We had been following a river through the valley, and at last it had run dry, and the date palms had vanished, and the mountains knelt like camels just before setting out on a long journey. In Zagora we saw the famous sign, "Timbuctoo: 54 days." In a village we stopped to visit the seventeenth-century library of a saint, Abu Abdallah Mohammed Bennacer, a small room of varnished wood cases beside a walled-in herbal garden. The old guide in his white robes opened for us—his hands were wood-hard—some of the illustrated volumes, including a Koran written on gazelle skin. Paul's red hair and massive body made him rarer than a gazelle in this dusty village. That night a village boy asked me if I had a "gazelle" back in Paris, and I figured out he meant a girlfriend and nodded because that was the most efficient way to stanch a carpet-tending spiel.

Paul continued with his stories. The one about the French woman he had loved and married off to the paratrooper, who had already become his lover. The one about the Los Angeles sadist he ridiculed and who then committed suicide. About his second date with Thierry, when he'd been gagged and chained upside down in a dungeon after being stuffed with acid, then made to face a huge poster of the dead L.A. lover. The one about the paratrooper scaling the mountain at the French-Italian border while cops in circling helicopters ordered him to descend immediately—"and applauded in spite of themselves when he reached the top bare-handed," Paul exulted, "without a rope or pick or anything to scale the sheer rock face but balls and brawn."

We're too alike, I thought again, despairing, to love each other, and Paul is different only in his attraction to cartoon images of male violence and aggression. Unlike him, I couldn't submit to a psychopath; what I want is Paul, with all his tenderness and quizzical, hesitating intelligence, his delicacy, to hit me. To be hurt by an enraged bull on steroids doesn't excite me. What I want is to belong to this grave, divided, philosophical man.

It occurred to me that if I thought only now, at this moment in my life, of belonging to someone, it was because my hold on life itself was endangered. Did I want him to tattoo his initials on a body I might soon have to give up? Did I want to become his slave just before I embraced that lasting solitude?

The beginning of the desert was a dune that had drifted through the pass between two mountains and had started to fill up the scrubland. A camel with bald spots on its elbows and starlet eyelashes was tethered to a dark felt tent in which a dirty man was sprawling, half-asleep. Another man, beaming and freshly shaved, bustled out of a cement bunker. With a flourish he invited us in for a glass of mint tea. His house turned out to be a major carpet showroom, buzzing with air-conditioning and neon lamps. "English?"

"No. Danish."

That was the last night of our holiday. The hotel served us a feast of sugared pigeon pie and mutton couscous, and Paul had a lot to drink. We sat in the dark beside the pool, which was lit from within like a philosopher's stone. He told me he thought of me as "gay" in the Nietzschean, not the West Hollywood, sense, but since I insisted that I needed him, he would love me and protect me and spend his life with me. Later in bed he pounded me in the face with his fists, shouting at me in a stuttering, broken explosion of French and English, the alternately choked and released patois of scalding indignation.

If the great pleasure of the poor, or so they say, is making love, then the great suffering of the rich is loving in vain. The troubadours, who speak for their rich masters, are constantly reminding us that only men of refinement recognize the nobility of hopeless love; the vulgar crowd jeers at them for wasting their time. Only the idle and free can afford the luxury (the anguish) of making an absence into the very rose heart of their lives. Only they have the extravagance of time to languish, shed tears, exalt their pain into poetry. For others time is too regulated; every day repeats itself.

I wasn't rich, but I was free and idle enough to ornament my liberty with the melancholy pleasure of having lost a Bordeaux

boy with a claret-red mouth. All the while I'd been with
Jean-Loup I'd admitted how ill-suited we were and I sought or
dreamed of seeking someone else either tepidly or hotly, depending on the intensity of my dissatisfaction.

Now that Jean-Loup had left me for Régis, I could glorify
their love and despise them and hate myself while sifting through
my old memories to show myself that Jean-Loup had been
slowly, if unconsciously, preparing this decampment for a long
time.

When I am being wicked I tell people, "Our little Jean-Loup
has landed in clover. His worries are over. He's handed in his
resignation at the bank. He'll soon be installed in the château
for the summer and he can fill the moat with his *bandes dessinées*.
The only pity is that Jean-Loup is apparently at Régis's mercy
and Régis is cunning. He holds all the cards. If he tires of
Jean-Loup, the poor boy will be dismissed without a centime,
for that wedding ring doesn't represent a claim, only a—"

But at this point bored, shocked friends laugh, hiss, "Jealous,
jealous, this way lies madness." Jealousy may be new to me but
not to them. My condition is as banal as it is baneful.

And then I realize that the opposite is probably true: that
Jean-Loup had always dealt with me openly, even at the end,
and had never resorted to subterfuge. As soon as he knew of his
deep innocent love for Régis he told me. I am the one who
attributes scheming to him.

He always wanted me to describe his ass, so I'll conclude
with an attempt not to sound too wet.

I should admit right off that by all ocular evidence there was
nothing extraordinary about it. It wasn't a soccer player's muscled bum or a swimmer's sun-molded twin *charlottes*. It was a
kid brother's ass, a perfunctory transition between spine and
legs, a simple cushion for a small body. Its color was the
low-wattage white of a winter half-moon. It served as the
neutral support (as an anonymous glove supports a puppet's
bobbing, expressive head) for his big, grown-up penis, always
so ready to poke up through his flies and take center-stage. But
let's not hastily turn him around to reveal "Régis's Daily Magic
Baguette," as I now call it. No, let's keep his back to us, even
though he's deliciously braced his knees to compensate for the

sudden new weight he's cantilevered in his excitement, a heavy divining rod that makes his buttocks tense. Concave, each cheek looks glossy, like costly white satin that, having been stuffed in a drawer, has just been smoothed, though it is still crazed with fine, whiter, silkier lines. If he spreads his cheeks—which feel cool, firm and plump—for the kneeling admirer, he reveals an anus that makes one think of a Leica lens, shut now but with many possible f-stops. An expensive aperture, but also a closed morning glory bud. There's that *grain de beauté* on his hip, the single drop of espresso on the wedding gown. And there are the few silky hairs in the crack of his ass, wet now for some reason and plastered down at odd angles as though his fur had been greedily licked in all directions at once. If he spreads his legs and thinks about nothing—his fitting with the tailor, the castle drawbridge, the debs whose calls he can no longer return—his erection may melt and you might see it drooping lazily into view, just beyond his loosely bagged testicles. He told me that his mother would never let him sleep in his *slip* when he was growing up. She was afraid underpants might stunt his virile growth. These Bordeaux women know to let a young wine breathe.

ABOUT THE AUTHORS

GEORGE STAMBOLIAN is professor of French and Inter-disciplinary Studies at Wellesley College, a trustee of the recently established Ferro-Grumley Foundation, and a member of the Advisory Board of the Lesbian and Gay Studies Center at Yale University. His most recent books are *Homosexualities and French Literature* (with Elaine Marks), *Male Fantasies/Gay Realities: Interviews with Ten Men*, *Men on Men: Best New Gay Fiction*, and *Men on Men 2*. He has written and lectured extensively on gay life and fiction, and likes living best in Amagansett, Long Island.

BRUCE BENDERSON is the author of a recently published collection of stories *Pretending to Say No*, which includes "A Happy Automaton." Another of his stories was selected for the anthology, *Between C & D*, and a third, "The United Nations of Times Square," was published as a separate book. His stories have been twice nominated for the Pushcart Prize. He has translated the work of Philippe Sollers and has completed two screenplays. He continues to write stories and has begun a novel about Miami Beach, where he lives when not in New York City.

CHRISTOPHER BRAM was raised in Norfolk, Virginia, and lives in New York City. He is the author of three novels, *Surprising Myself*, *Hold Tight*, and *In Memory of Angel Clare*, and has written two screenplays, including a film adaptation of David Leavitt's *The Lost Language of Cranes*. His was the title story of *Aphrodisiac: Fiction from Christopher Street*, and his book and movie reviews have appeared in *Newsday, Lambda Book Report, Christopher Street, The New York Native,* and *Premiere.* He is currently working on a novel that will develop the characters in "Meeting Imelda Marcos."

PETER CASHORALI's poetry has appeared in *Five Fingers Review, Mirage, Santa Monica Review,* and the anthology, *Poetry Loves Poetry.* Born in Walpole, Massachusetts, he lives in Los Angeles, where he is completing a collection of short stories. "The Ride Home" is his first published fiction.

BERNARD COOPER is a graduate of the California Institute of the Arts and teaches literature at the Otis/Parsons Institute of Art and Design in Los Angeles. His fiction and nonfiction have appeared in *Harper's, Grand Street, The Georgia Review, Shenandoah,* and *The Fiction Network,* and his essay "Beacons Burning Down" was chosen for *The Best American Essays of 1988.* A collection of his creative nonfiction, *Maps to Anywhere,* was published earlier this year. He is currently writing a novel.

PHILIP GAMBONE graduated from Harvard University, was a fellow at the MacDowell Colony, and teaches writing at the Harvard Extension School. His many short stories have appeared in such periodicals as *The New England Review and Bread Loaf Quarterly, Wisconsin Review, Greensboro Review, Chattahoochee Review, Kansas Quarterly,* and *Tribe.* A collection of his stories, *The Language We Use Up Here,* will be published next year. He is also a regular contributor to *The Advocate, The Lambda Rising Book Report,* and *Bay Windows.* He lives in Dorchester, Massachusetts, where he is writing a novel.

ROBERT HAULE was born in Detroit and lives in San Francisco, where he has studied writing with Aaron Shurin. His stories and poetry have appeared in *Vector* and *The San Francisco Sentinel.* He is currently writing a series of poems about anger.

WILLIAM HAYWOOD HENDERSON comes from Dubois, Wyoming, and currently holds a Wallace Stegner Fellowship in creative writing at Stanford University. One of his short stories appeared in *The Crescent Review.* He is now working on a novel,

Native, an excerpt from which will be published in the forth-coming *Faber Book of Gay Short Fiction* edited by Edmund White.

ANDREW HOLLERAN is the author of two novels, *Dancer from the Dance* and *Nights in Aruba*, and a collection of essays, *Ground Zero*. His "New York Notebook" column in *Christopher Street* received a Gay Press Association Award, and his stories and articles have also appeared in *New York*, *The New York Native*, and *Wigwag*. Born in Aruba, N.A., he attended Harvard and the University of Iowa's Writers' Workshop, and is a trustee of the Ferro-Grumley Foundation. He divides his time between New York City and Florida, where he is writing a novel.

ALEX JEFFERS lives in Providence, Rhode Island, where he is a student in creative writing at Brown University. His poetry and fiction have appeared under different pen names in *New Dimensions*, *Antenna*, *Mandate*, and *North American Review*. He is currently completing two novels, one of which, *Safe As Houses*, will develop the characters in "My Face in a Mirror."

JOE KEENAN has studied at New York University's Musical Theatre Program and has just completed the book and lyrics for a new musical called *The Times*. His first novel, *Blue Heaven*, was published in 1988, and he is currently working on a second Philip and Gilbert novel, tentatively titled *Puttin' on the Ritz*. Born in Cambridge, Massachusetts, he lives in New York City.

MICHAEL LASSELL was born in Manhattan and lives in Los Angeles, where he is the Managing Editor of *L.A. Style* magazine. He is the author of a volume of poetry, *Poems for Lost and Un-Lost Boys*, and received an Amelia Chapbook Award. His poetry has also appeared in *Gay and Lesbian Poetry in Our Time*, *Poets for Life*, and in several periodicals, including *The James White Review*, *Fag Rag*, *Central Park*, *Edge*, and *Zyzzyva*. He is an active journalist and critic, and his fiction has been published in *The Pacific Review*, *No Apologies*, *Frontiers*, and *Torso*. He has just completed a second collection of poetry, *A Rendezvous with Death: Poems from the Plague Years*, and has begun a novel.

CRAIG LEE is the co-author of *Hardcore California* and for several years was the Music Editor of *L.A. Weekly*. His writings have appeared in *The Advocate*, *The Los Angeles Times*, *L.A. Style*, and *Slash*. He is currently working on a television documentary on metaphysical and paranormal phenomena and on a sociological study of Thai "bar boys." He lives in Los Angeles and Thailand. This is his first published story.

PAUL MONETTE has written four novels, *Taking Care of Mrs. Carroll*, *The Gold Diggers*, *The Long Shot*, and *Afterlife*, two volumes of poetry, *No Witnesses* and *Love Alone*, which received a Words Project for AIDS Award, and a memoir, *Borrowed Time*, which received two Lambda Literary awards. He has also written several novelizations and has been the recipient of two Ingram-Merrill awards. He lives in Los Angeles, where he is completing a novel, *Halfway Home*, that will develop his story in this collection.

MARTIN PALMER lives in Anchorage, Alaska, where he is a practicing physician and an instructor of English. His poetry has appeared in *The New York Quarterly*, *The Alaska Quarterly Review*, and *Gay Sunshine*. He is working on a collection of stories and a collection of poetry.

FELICE PICANO is a co-publisher of the Gay Presses of New York and lives in New York City. He is the author of eight novels, *Smart As the Devil*, *Eyes*, *the Mesmerist*, *The Lure*, *An Asian Minor*, *Late in the Season*, *House of Cards*, and *To the Seventh Power*, two books of poetry, *The Deformity Lover* and *Window Elegies*, a collection of stories, *Slashed to Ribbons in Defense of Love*, and two volumes of memoirs, *Ambidextrous* and *Men Who Loved Me*. He edited an anthology of gay fiction, *A True Likeness*, and his writings have appeared widely, including poems in the recently published *Poets for Life*. He has just finished a science fiction novel, *Dryland's End*.

NOEL RYAN's stories have appeared in *The Village Voice*, the two *Christopher Street* anthologies, *Aphrodisiac* and *First Love*, *Last Love*, and in *The Manifest Reader*, which awarded him a First Prize for fiction. Born in Butte, Montana, he lives in San Francisco, where he is working on a novel, *Genevieve the Aunt*.

MATIAS VIEGENER was born in Buenos Aires and lives in Los Angeles, where he is completing a doctorate at UCLA and teaching writing at the California Institute of the Arts. His fiction has appeared in several periodicals, including *Mirage*, *The Jacaranda Review*, *Dear World*, and *Against Nature*, and he has worked on a variety of performance pieces in California. He has begun a novel that will continue the story presented in "Twilight of the Gods."

EDMUND WHITE has moved from Paris to Providence, where he is Professor of English at Brown University. He is the author of five novels, *Forgetting Elena*, *Nocturnes for the King of Naples*, *A Boy's Own Story*, *Caracole*, and *The Beautiful Room Is Empty*, which received a Lambda Literary Award. He has also written two works of nonfiction, *The Joy of Gay Sex* and *States of Desire*. His stories, reviews, and essays have appeared in such publications as *The New York Times Book Review*, *The Times Literary Supplement*, *Vogue*, *Granta*, and *Christopher Street*. He is the recipient of a Guggenheim Fellowship, an Ingram-Merrill Award, an Award for Literature from the American Academy of Arts and Letters, and the first Bill Whitehead Award. He is completing a biography of Jean Genet.

BIL WRIGHT is a member of Other Countries, a black gay men's collective based in New York City. He has presented performance pieces at Yale University, the Martin Luther King Center in Atlanta, and the Westbeth Artists Center in New York. He is working on a collection of stories about family relations called *Orchids and Cornrows*. "When Marquita Gets Home" is his first published fiction.

PUBLICATIONS OF INTEREST

Fiction on gay subjects has appeared in several mainstream periodicals in recent years. The following is a selective list of journals and magazines that *regularly* publish gay fiction. Contributors should inform themselves of the editorial policy of each publication before submitting manuscripts.

ADVOCATE MEN. P.O. Box 4371, Los Angeles, CA 90078

AMETHYST: A JOURNAL FOR LESBIANS AND GAY MEN. Southeastern Arts, Media and Education Project, Inc., P.O. Box 54719, Atlanta, GA 30308

BGM (black gay men). The Blacklight Press, P.O. Box 9391, Washington, D.C. 20013.

BLACK/OUT. National Coalition of Black Gays, P.O. Box 2490, Washington, DC 20013

CHRISTOPHER STREET. P.O. Box 1475, Church Street Station, New York, NY 10008

THE EVERGREEN CHRONICLES: A JOURNAL OF GAY AND LESBIAN WRITERS. P.O. Box 6260, Minnehaha Station, Minneapolis, MN 55406

FAG RAG. P.O. Box 331, Kenmore Station, Boston, MA 02215

THE JAMES WHITE REVIEW: A GAY MEN'S LITER-

ARY QUARTERLY. P.O. Box 3356, Traffic Station, Minneapolis, MN 55403

MANDATE. Mavety Media Group, 462 Broadway, 4th floor, New York, NY 10013

MIRAGE. 1987 California Street #202, San Francisco, CA 94109

OTHER COUNTRIES (black gay men). P.O. Box 21176, Midtown Station, New York, NY 10129

OUT/LOOK: NATIONAL LESBIAN AND GAY QUARTERLEY. P.O. Box 146430, San Francisco, CA 94114-6430

THE PYRAMID PERIODICAL FOR GAY PEOPLE OF COLOR. P.O. Box 1111, Canal Street Station, New York, NY 10013

RFD: A COUNTRY JOURNAL FOR GAY MEN EVERYWHERE. Route 1, Box 127E, Bakersville, NC 28705

TORSO. Mavety Media Group, 462 Broadway, 4th floor, New York, NY 10013

TRIBE: AN AMERICAN GAY JOURNAL. Columbia Publishing Co., Inc., 234 East 25th Street, Baltimore, MD 21218